RHODA BROUGHTON

(1840–1920) was born near Denbigh, North Wales;
granddaughter of a wealthy Queen's Counsel for Dublin
and an English baronet, she had a privileged childhood.
Her family home, Broughton Hall in Staffordshire, was
the inspiration for many of her novels. She was the third
of four children and was educated largely by her clergyman father. Orphaned and homeless in her early twen-
ties, Rhoda Broughton wrote her first two novels, *Not
Wisely but too Well* and *Cometh Up as a Flower*. Originally
published in the *Dublin University Magazine*, owned by
her uncle Sheridan Le Fanu, they were published in
book form in 1867, establishing her as a witty and
daring 'sensation' novelist: a reputation confirmed with
the publication of *Red as a Rose is She* (1870) and
Goodbye, Sweetheart! (1872).

Rhoda Broughton made her home with her elder sister,
first in North Wales, then in Oxford and later in Rich-
mond, moving in with a cousin in Headington Hill, near
Oxford, when her sister died. Her friends included
Matthew Arnold and, for a time, Mark Pattison, later to
be satirised in *Belinda* (1883). She would also winter in
Chelsea where she had a distinguished and devoted
following, including Anne Thackeray Ritchie and
Henry James. Rhoda Broughton wrote novels at the
rate of about one every two years. Following the failure
of *Alas!* (1890), she abandoned the three-volume form,
and wrote a series of satirical novels, including *A
Beginner* (1894), *Dear Faustina* (1897), *Foes in Law*
(1899) and *A Waif's Progress* (1905). A brilliant convers-
ationalist, witty, informed and audacious, Rhoda
Broughton was herself amused by her reputation: 'I
began my life as Zola,' she once said. 'I finish it as Miss
Yonge.'

BELINDA

RHODA BROUGHTON

With a New Introduction by
TAMIE WATTERS

Published by VIRAGO PRESS Limited 1984
41 William IV Street, London WC2N 4DB

First published in Great Britain in 3 volumes by
Richard Bentley and Son 1883
First published in 1 volume by Richard Bentley and Son 1887
Virago edition offset from Richard Bentley and Son 1887 edition

Introduction copyright © Tamie Watters 1984

British Library in Cataloguing Publication Data

Broughton, Rhoda
Belinda. —(Virago modern classic)
I. Title
823'.8 [F] PR4174.B56
ISBN 0-86068-505-5

Printed in Finland by Werner Söderström Oy,
a member of Finnprint

INTRODUCTION

Rhoda Broughton never married. Yet beneath her brusque manner and laughing wit lay a passionate heart, given to fierce loving and hating. *Belinda* (1883), which restored her waning popularity as Queen of the Circulating Library, is as revealing of the woman as of the talents of the novelist. Beneath the surface of this glittering dark comedy, passion rages not only in the lovesick Belinda entrapped in a January–May marriage, but also in the author's merciless portrait of the skinflint January, a caricature of an eminent Victorian who betrayed her friendship. Though he headed an Oxford college, she boldly wrote her novel while living in Holywell Street, at the heart of male-dominated Oxford.

The audacity was of the kind that spurred the young Rhoda—thrust out into the world in 1863 upon the death of her adored father, squire and parson of Broughton Hall in Staffordshire—to produce *Not Wisely but too Well* and *Cometh Up as a Flower*, novels of such an original stamp that they set a whole new trend in fiction. Both were serialised in *The Dublin University Magazine*, owned by her uncle—the novelist Sheridan Le Fanu—before their joint debut (with some modifications and in reverse order) in England in 1867.

Rich in autobiography, they feature pert-tongued girls of ancient families undergoing decline and cruel displacement by moneyed industrialists. The heroines are as unconventional in their candour as they are in their rapturous response to the 'lean-flanked' guardsmen who own their loyal hearts. Though George Lawrence's *Guy Livingston* (1857) supplied *Not Wisely* with its 'royally made' and worldly hero Dare Stamer, both novels had a disarming freshness. Motherless, like Rhoda at twenty, the heroines enjoy a freedom in their assignations and love-making, not normally granted to Victorian maidens, and suffer horribly when thwarted in their love. That Rhoda Broughton wrote in the wake of some such affair seems a natural conclusion in view of the recurring theme in five of her first six novels. But she also said as much in *A Fool in Her Folly*, her confessional novel in press at her death in 1920. Despite Michael Sadleir's exploration in 'Rhoda Broughton's Secret: Melodrama of the Breaking Heart', (TLS 30 Nov. 1940), we still do not know *who* set her afire.

Cometh Up, brought out anonymously by Bentley, was almost sunk by abusive criticism and outraged morality. Nell, a tousled-haired tomboy—who tells with pathos and humour her own story of falling 'neck and crop' in love with Dick M'Gregor—was said to mask a male author, 'ignorant of all that women either are or ought to be', and one who credited them with only two phases of existence, 'the delight of being kissed by a man they like, and the misery of being kissed by one they don't like' (*Athenaeum*, April 1867). Mrs Oliphant, bundling the author into the 'Sensation School' with those tale-spinners of shocking incident, Miss Braddon and Ouida, protested that the wholesome heroine of the past has been replaced by one who 'now waits for flesh and muscles . . . and a host of other physical attractions, which she indicates to the world with a charming frankness' (*Blackwoods*, Sept. 1867). Rhoda Broughton's graphic depiction of love-making, with heroine as eager participant, had taken the novel a step beyond the passion of *Jane Eyre*. Charmed by the naturalness and manner of telling, *The Times* pronounced *Cometh Up* 'strikingly clever and original', thus helping to boost sales almost rivalling those of *East Lynne* (1861) and *Lady Audley's Secret* (1862).

The novel's plot, hinging on letters as in *Belinda*, is weak. Rhoda Broughton's strength lay elsewhere—in situation, characterisation (notably women), dialogue, and witty narration. Her colloquial style, having the earthy tang of her native Cheshire and Staffordshire, yielded itself to piquant observations and graphic imagery in which nature seems to be in a constant state of amours. The larding of the first novels with quotes was a practice she returned to in *Belinda*, perhaps to show Oxford *her* learning. Aided by modern and classical languages learnt from her father she had romped through his vast library and was said to have Shakespeare by heart.

Though she pretended not to mind the critics, the imputations of vulgarity and immorality greeting the more daring *Not Wisely* scarred her. In *Red as a Rose is She* (1870), she attacked ludicrous Victorian propriety which was shocked at the mention of 'legs' and yet exhibited colossal nudes in dining rooms under the titles 'Jupiter and Leda' or 'Venus Sleeping surprised by Satyrs'. She set the opening of the novel in North Wales, where she lived with a married sister, and took the opportunity to lash out at Welsh piety, where 'Spite is permissible on the Sabbath, though hot potatoes and novels are not.' This novel, which Gladstone was observed to be reading in his club, so established the writer that she declared her authorship with *Goodbye, Sweetheart!* in 1872. James Joyce's naming of *Red as a Rose* along with the *Arabian Nights* as the sailor Murphy's favourite reading in *Ulysses* is analogous to the arctic explorers of the Sir George Nares 1872–1873 expedition who named a mount 'Rhoda' in tribute to her stories which entertained them in lonely hours.

Part of growing up for a girl of the 1870s and 1880s was a surreptitious reading of Rhoda Broughton beneath the bedclothes. The novels were a celebration of egocentric youth and constituted a mild form of sex education. They also revealed the claustrophobia ('a woman's soul is such a small room') created by a society in which marriage seemed to be a woman's only vocation.

By the mid-seventies, Rhoda Broughton, whom George Bentley described as a 'wilful beauty' with 'the clear, clean, warm complexion of strong passion' and Augustus Hare as 'a good looking, very smart, young lady', was a familiar sight in the great houses of London during her sojourns in town. Her originality and wit, even more marked in her person than in her books, opened doors and won her enduring friendships with such great men as Matthew Arnold, Henry James, the Earl of Lytton (poet and Viceroy of India), and the renowned soldier, Garnet Wolseley.

Her reception was not so happy in Oxford where she and her widowed sister, Mrs Newcome, settled in 1878 upon the recommendation of Matthew Arnold, who assured them of a warm welcome from the university town. The aura of Bond Street, that the elegantly-gowned Rhoda brought into Holywell, aroused as much suspicion as her reputation as a racey popular novelist. A self-appointed guardian of university morals mounted a campaign to ostracise the sisters, insisting upon confusing Miss Broughton with Miss Braddon whom she was sure had as unsavoury a past as her own Lady Audley. Mrs Oliphant, residing in Oxford in 1879, observed, 'Miss Broughton . . . has . . . much fluttered the dovecotes.'

The shunned Rhoda acquired the first of her famous dogs and set about writing _Second Thoughts_ for the amusement of her dying friend Adelaide Sartoris, sister to Fanny Kemble. She also found herself taken up by the Pattisons—the Rector of Lincoln College found her amusing and more knowledgeable about German literature than any woman in Oxford; his gifted and attractive wife relished her talk and became fast friends with the sympathetic Ellinor Newcome. By November 1879 Rhoda was writing to George Bentley of 'her old friend Mark Pattison—one of the acutest intellects here'. For Rhoda Broughton, friendship was the salt of life, and according to the novelist Mary Cholmondeley, 'She would have rent the skin from her own body if she could have succoured one of those she loved.'

Appearing in May 1880, _Second Thoughts_—in which she had eliminated 'violent passions' and 'broad expressions'—won critical acclaim for its improved style, as well as for its hilarious send-up of the aesthetes (antedating _Patience_) and its _Pride and Prejudice_ love story, but it did not sell. So she sat down to write the story which she had contemplated earlier but had rejected as too _risqué_, ' . . . since the public like it hot and strong I am not the person to disoblige them'. She was obviously referring to _Belinda_, in which the star-crossed lovers, upright products of Victorian society, are propelled by love into desperate acts. Belinda Churchill, whose passion translates itself into 'a chill set face', is a close cousin to the ardent early heroines from ingenuous Nell to the feminist Lenore in _Goodbye, Sweetheart!_ All suffer from thwarted love and show the author's unsurpassed knowledge of a woman's heart.

But _Belinda_ is in a class by itself; not because the Professor slouching along on his great flat feet threatens to upstage the lovers, but because of the art and maturity she brings to the old theme. The effect of the brilliant opening chapters, which recreate for us the attractions and May beauty of Dresden, a mecca for Victorians, is that of a lyrical poem, showing forth youth and love in their glory and fragility. As the English holidaymakers pass their days in sightseeing the pear tree outside the Churchills' lodgings significantly blossoms and then drops its petals. It does not really matter that David Rivers, just out of Oxbridge, is a matchstick hero; he epitomises youth. The large fragrant nosegay that he hurls like Cupid's arrow at Belinda on May Day contrasts with Professor Forth's wilted violets. The urgency that Rivers break through his own shyness and the defences put up by Belinda's 'stiff-necked virgin pride' to seal in words and open betrothal what they feel in their hearts, is in keeping with the book's theme. 'There are days on which Heaven opens to us all, but to most of us the next day it shuts again.'

The novel wittily reveals how events, other people and our own temperaments conspire against us. The meddlesome Miss Watson, barging in like a rhinoceros and clinging like a gnat at inappropriate moments, might be a character from an absurdist comedy. Actually, Rhoda who excelled at observation, not invention, took her from life, her model bitterly protesting to Bentley.

Belinda suffers from an affliction that makes her psychologically more interesting, if less endearing than the impulsive early heroines. 'How is it that her heart is so burning hot and her words so icy cold?' Here we have a self-portrait of the caustic Miss Broughton from whom the faint-hearted fled. In fact, the Churchill sisters present the two faces of Rhoda Broughton. Edmund Yates thought that Sarah Churchill, with her 'audacity' and 'piquant observation', resembled the novelist more than any other character in her fiction. (Interestingly, Garnet Wolseley—who probably aroused more passion in Rhoda by his attentions than he realised—chided her in a letter from Cairo for a cold note and urged her to write again, 'and if you do perhaps the icicle would thaw a little discovering the heart which I know is there but which it is not only difficult to touch but to discover so deeply is it hidden away under an assumed exterior'.) The characterisation of Belinda may well be a key to the author's 'buried life' which went underground after a searing adolescent romance.

Belinda may ask what she can do to help herself 'tied down by her nature', but it is what she does do in the agony of hurt pride and desperation that gives us our story, with its grim as

well as comical elements. Her action is so multi-layered in
motivation that it is hard to understand Sadleir's contention
that 'the central episode—Belinda's marriage to Professor
Forth—is not truly accounted for' (*Things Past*, 1944). She
badly needs an escape route from her grudging grandmother
and her own torment, and though she never pretends to the
high-flown aspirations of Dorothea in marrying Casaubon in
Middlemarch, she has the wan hope that the pursuit of knowledge, with Forth as a guide, will bring its distractions. The
famous Hobbema painting in the National Gallery—scene of
Forth's proposal—gives us the real clue to her acceptance.
Belinda, misled by Miss Watson's gossip, sees Rivers in the
male figure disappearing up the poplar-lined road and perversely throws her life away. The death wish is never far from
Rhoda's frustrated lovers. In *Not Wisely* (*D.U.M.* version) the
already-married Dare shoots himself and the heroine.

The wry commentary wards off sentimentality, but the
enormity of Belinda's situation, bound to a niggardly old
pedant, cries out for sympathy, and we become implicated in
her feelings as every emotional nuance is registered. It is
significantly another May, the second since Dresden, when
Belinda begins to behave like a Maenad. The pastoral beauty
of Oxbridge (Oxford)—to which Rhoda had obviously lost her
heart—provides as heady an atmosphere as Dresden for
young love. Choice love poetry and erotic imagery add to the
tension.

Forth's incongruity among scenes of youth and beauty
make him the comic centrepiece of the book. This is so from
his entry, at the May Day festivities, where we pick out his
'slovenly middle-aged' figure in clerical black among the
strapping German soldiers, as he moons absently along, hands
clasped behind him and hat tipped back on his head. Swipes
are taken at the scholar who has no facility in the spoken
language though in 'correspondence with half the savants of
Germany' and whose esoteric research, 'The Fragments of
Menander', has been read by 'not less than three people'; but
he comes in for the worst trouncing on the score of meanness.
The paltry bunch of violets foreshadows the man who hides
the bacon in the cupboard lest his servants steal it and who
wishes his household drudge and secretary dead when she can
no longer perform her services.

Rhoda Broughton's wit runs the gamut from sunny good humour rippling round the pug Slutty, who reserves a special bark 'for tramps and Miss Watson', and round Sarah, attach- ing and dispatching suitors, to black comedy directed at Forth's senile mother, incarcerated in an upstairs room like the mummy in the cupboard of Strindberg's *Ghost Sonata*. Quips abound at the expense of the Germans who muzzle their dogs, at the expense of *trade* and of Oxford. The develop- ment in North Oxford to house dons, only recently allowed to marry, is derided as 'an ugly, irrelevant, healthy suburb that would not disgrace a cotton city of today'. The women there are so 'shockingly *fagoté*' that Belinda needs no trousseau. On Slutty, transported to these new environs, 'an academic life . . . has begun to tell. She could not well look stouter or less intellectual if she were one of the old Fellows of St Bridget's [Magdalen College]'. So Rhoda, never one to leave the battlefield, paid off her debt to the town that snubbed her.

The book's humour and ringing lines from Carlyle's *Sartor Resartus*, which turn the tide for Belinda and reveal the author's own Victorian probity, did not blind Bentley to its pessimism and underlying sensuality; Rivers, running his lips over the palm of Belinda's hand excites more *frisson* than much of today's explicit sex. Thinking *Belinda* too dark, he ran it reluctantly in *Temple Bar* where her novels were usually serialised. Sales boomed! Though the three-volume edition had such a slow start that Rhoda concluded she had gone out of fashion because 'The world resists being amused without being improved, too, and I never laid any claim to improv- ing', Mudie's Library soon had to order fifty more copies to meet the demand. Rhoda thought the critics 'civiller' to *Belinda* than any previous book of hers.

Mark Pattison inevitably recognised himself in Forth as his niece read *Belinda* to him in April 1883. His outward circum- stances were so similar: the disparity in years between himself and his wife, his habit of surrounding himself with young women (which led Pater to describe him 'as romping with great girls in the gooseberry bushes'), and the relative obscur- ity and meagreness of his writings for one who shunned undergraduates and administrative duties in order to devote himself to scholarship. Rhoda had also caught his tastes and manner—the harsh nasal voice, the relentless precision of speech, the mania for high tea and early hours, the horror of open windows and cut flowers. Worse, she seemed to know he was the kind of man who made his wife, forced to winter in the South of France for health, account for the very cost of her ribbons. With great bravado Pattison called at 27 Holywell and announced himself as Professor Forth, but in his heart he knew that Rhoda had evened an old score.

The breakdown in their friendship stemmed from his attachment to Meta Bradley, who recognised herself in the Girton girl who warmed Forth's coat and helped him on with his galoshes. Tongues began to wag in the winter of 1880–1881 when Meta turned a visit to the Rectory into a two-and-a-half month siege, and her alarmed uncle, G. G. Bradley, Master of University College, began to cut the Rector. Like others, Rhoda found it offensive that Meta ruled over Pattison's table and brazenly flirted with him. So she chided her old friend about letting a presumptuous girl take him over. Little did she know that he had committed himself to Meta the previous summer and that his dearest hope was to dupe others into the belief that his relationship with Meta was paternal. 'I believe it could be done, and with Mrs Grundy's full consent . . . you the indispensable daughter, and staff of my old age! That view once accepted we may do what we like.' Pattison left no doubt of what he liked. When Meta departed the Rectory, he wrote, 'Dear God! I must have you back again . . . with infinite possibilities of kissing.'

When his hopes were dashed by an anonymous letter revealing a knowledge of his affair with Meta, he jumped to the conclusion that Rhoda had written it and aired his suspicion. Mrs Pattison learning of this in Draguignan, France, wrote to a friend of her anger 'at its having been supposed that Miss Broughton would have anything to do with such a disgusting act,' for she knew of 'no *woman* who has a higher sense of honour.' Pattison, however, nursing his delusion, sent a female spy into the Holywell household who let slip his suspicions and brought down Rhoda's wrath upon him. We can be pretty sure that the caricature began to take form on that fateful day, 11 March 1881. Rhoda might have felt that she was also settling accounts for his wife, who confessed to a friend that her husband's pettiness and tendency to place an evil construction on the most innocent behaviour had provoked a passionate resentment in her and 'poisoned so many years of my young life and drove me to desperation and the verge of utmost folly'. (Belinda's very feelings.)

Emelia Francis Strong had at twenty-one married the nearly fifty-year-old Pattison with Dorothea Brooke's mystical aspirations, but the marriage broke down in 1875 when she begged out of further sexual relations. By the end of the decade she had formed an attachment to the Liberal politician Sir Charles Dilke, whom she married after Pattison's death. Her likeness to Belinda is mainly circumstantial, for she was an accomplished woman who wrote on French art, championed suffrage and technical education for women, and formed a literary salon that included Browning and Prince Leopold.

Pattison appears never to have apologised to Rhoda though her innocence was beyond dispute, (T. Watters, 'Oxford Provocation', *Encounter*, April 1971). A year after *Belinda*'s publication, he succumbed to cancer, his beloved books covering the bedclothes. Rhoda had been more prophetic than she knew in her novel's final scene. Though Jowett dropped her from his guest list for her attack on a Head of House, *Belinda* did not seriously undermine her growing popularity in Oxford. The devoted sisters had created such a warm ambience in their Holywell home and won such a reputation for generous hospitality and witty, informed talk, that their invitations and company were much sought after. When the ambassadress to Vienna, Lady Paget, visited Oxford in 1884, she found one or two of the men and Miss Broughton the exception to the prevailing 'stiffness and narrowness' and 'want of facility, grace, and elevation in the forms of daily life . . . Miss Broughton is . . . brusque and direct . . . Her room was filled with dogs, birds, and flowers, and were [*sic*] much more human than any of the other rooms I went into in Oxford.' Ethel Arnold observed that in the years 1883–1884, 'the Oxford tide began to turn', and that Rhoda in Holywell soon became the focal point of 'all that was socially most "worth-while", both in the undergraduate world and in the world of Don-dom'.

It was Ethel Arnold's sister Mrs Humphry Ward who used Pattison as the model for the alien scholar, Squire Wendover, in *Robert Elsmere* (1888). Critics have spilt much ink in com-

paring Rhoda Broughton's Professor of Estrucan with other
fictional characters based on Pattison. Besides Squire Wendover, there is Otho Lawrence in W. H. Mallock's *New Repub-
lic* (1876) and Casaubon in George Eliot's *Middlemarch* (1872),
though here the identity is hotly debated. Unlike the others
with their more philosophic approach to the scholar in society,
Rhoda took an Austenesque look at the man himself and his
treatment of others. Perhaps for this reason, Charles Grant
Robertson, a Fellow of All Souls, declared, 'Professor Forth
. . . a far truer portrait of Mark Pattison than the portrait of
him in *Robert Elsmere*' (*The Times*, 9 Dec. 1940).

If it were not for the identification with Pattison, Forth
could be seen as one of Rhoda Broughton's humorous mon-
sters, mountains of egoism in their disregard for others, and
descendants of Mr Collins and Catherine de Burgh. A forerunner can be detected in the aesthete Francis Chaloner in
Second Thoughts, who upon learning of the heroine's fortune
proposes that they 'burn like a pure and gem-like flame on
one altar', while the best of those to come is the septugenarian
in *Mamma* (1908), who has reduced her family to servants
competing for her favours.

Belinda was a cathartic experience for Rhoda Broughton. In
its successor, *Dr Cupid*, humanity and good humour abound.
The novels are a history of her struggle to control her excesses
of style, her country-gentry prejudices, and her emotions. She
prayed that the spirit of Jane Austen would fall upon her.
Some of it did, for her contemporaries began to dub her the
Victorian Jane Austen as she turned to terse satiric novels in
the 1890s.

But *Belinda* stands out as her boldest and perhaps cleverest
novel. For her early novels—and *Belinda* as eighth in a canon
of twenty-five is early—she has been hailed as the forerunner
of the sex novelists. Perhaps *Belinda* with its satirical commentary on Oxbridge and its exposé of domestic malaise and
extra-marital frolics behind the staid facade of academia
might equally be considered the forerunner of the university
novel, made familiar to us in recent years by David Lodge's
Changing Places and Malcolm Bradbury's *The History Man*.

Tamie Watters,
Mapledurham Village, Oxfordshire, 1983

The writer is grateful for the use of manuscript material in the following collections: Bentley Papers in the British Library and University of Illinois, Urbana; Pattison Papers, Bodleian Library, Oxford University; and Delves-Broughton Collection, Cheshire Record Office. Quotes from Lady Paget and Ethel Arnold are respectively from *Embassies of other Days* (1923) and 'Rhoda Broughton as I Knew Her', *Fortnightly Review*, August 1920.

PERIOD I.

‘ Mignonne, allons voir si la rose
Qui ce matin avait disclose
Sa robe de pourpre au soleil
A point perdu ceste vesprée,
Les plis de sa robe pourprée
Et son teint au vostre pareil.
Las ! voyez comme en peu d'espace,
Mignonne, elle a dessus la place !
Las ! Las ! ses beautez laissé cheoir !
O vrayment marastre Nature
Puis qu'une telle fleur ne dure
Que du matin jusques au soir !
Donc si vous me croyez, Mignonne,
Tandis que vostre âge fleuronne
En sa plus verte nouveauté,
Cueillez, cueillez vostre jeunesse,
Comme à ceste fleur, la vieillesse
Fera ternir vostre beauté.’

BELINDA.

CHAPTER I.

'Along the crisped shades and bowers
Revels the spruce and jocund Spring.'

Not less lustily than elsewhere is the spruce and jocund
Spring revelling in the Grosse Garten at Dresden on this
May Day. And though there is still in her very frolic a
disposition to pinch sharply, a certain tartness in her green
smile, yet many glad subjects have come forth to do homage
to her new Queendom. Yes, many; for to-day the Dres-
deners—as I am told is their custom on each fresh May
Day—have issued out on foot and in carriage to welcome
the year's new sovereign. They are holding a sort of
flower-feast; everybody is throwing bouquets to everybody
else. Above their heads the trees are breaking into little
leaf; upon the side-paths throng the foot-passengers; along
the drives the carriages gaily roll. Here is a very smart
turn-out. Surely this must be the King and the Queen?
Not at all! It is only Graf von S. reclining with a self-
satisfied air alone in a barouche, richly filled with choice
nosegays, and drawn by four chestnut horses, with a crimson
velvet postillion jigging up and down in front, and a crimson
velvet outrider trotting bravely behind. An Englishman
would feel a fool in such a position, but far indeed from a

like frame of mind is that of this splendid and happy German.

Well, here come the King and Queen really now, with their mouse-coloured liveries; come, bowing and smiling with as much affability as if they were real big royalties; no one troubling himself to get out of their way; not a police-man to be seen; no open space imperatively cleared, as when the Princess of Wales comes trotting serenely down the drive. Here are soldiers in plenty; but soldiers think-ing for the most part neither of war nor beer; soldiers with their martial hands full of innocent daffodillies and fresh sweet Nancies. Gardereiters in their light blue uniforms and flat blue caps, pricking hither and thither on their sleek horses, carrying bouquets of roses, azaleas, deutzias, hyacinths, and seeking here and there with grave gray eyes for the happy fair ones for whom they are destined.

Two bands are clashing merrily out; a great booming thump on the big drum makes the horses start and fidget. Now, for a change, comes a real English turn-out. One need not look twice to decide its nationality. The square sitting, bolt-upright servants in their quiet liveries; the plain but shining harness; the great glossy-coated bays stepping together like one horse—who can doubt con-cerning them? Now more English in hired carriages; but do not judge us by these, O kind Saxons; these are not our best! And yet it is in one of these very hired carriages that are sitting a pair of young women, of whom their England has no need to be ashamed, and who are not at all ashamed of themselves. Not that the present is their happiest moment, for the expression of one face is cross, and of the other anxious.

'Shall we go home, Belinda?' asks the cross one morosely.

'Why, we have only just come!' objects Belinda.

A Russian carriage passes; a coachman with a hat like a beefeater and a long cloth frock pulled in with gathers at the waist. Then more Germans, with bunches of narcissus at their horses' ears and in their servants' breasts. Now a Gardereiter perched on the box of a coach, driving six-in-hand, and with a confiding lady in a pink bonnet beside him tranquilly enjoying her position, nor any wise disturbed by the hopeless muddle into which her hero has got his innumerable reins. Another blue Gardereiter flings her a bouquet, but it is ill-aimed, falls upon the road, and the wheels pass over it. This sight is too much for the fortitude of Belinda's sister.

'I must take some desperate step to attract attention,' she says crossly, yet with a vein of humour streaking her ill-temper; 'what do you recommend? Shall I be frightened at the big drum, and give a loud shriek, or will you?'

'Certainly not I!'

'I cannot think what has happened to them! They must be wrong in their heads. Are you aware that not one of them has thrown us a single bouquet?'

'Why should they?' answers Belinda; 'we know none of them.'

'Even though they do not know us, they might toss us a handful of flowers,' says Sarah grumblingly. 'I am sure we look wistful enough, and that requires no great amount of acquaintance!'

'I should think it extremely impertinent if they did!' replies Belinda loftily.

The other pouts.

'For my part, then, I wish that they would begin to be impertinent at once!'

But for such insolence the Saxon army appears to have no sort of bent. In silence the neglected girls drive on. And the sun shines, and the east wind blows, and the big drum booms, and the great brass instruments blare, and still they trot round the bit of dull water, up the straight drives, past the Museum of Antiquities. A rain of spring nosegays falls around them, but not one is aimed at their humble landau; not one drops, even by accident, into their empty laps.

Here come the King and Queen again; the mouse-coloured and silver outriders; the suave and middle-aged pair of little royalties. The gloom on Sarah's face deepens, and even in Belinda's eyes the anxious, seeking look has grown intensified. If they know no one in this gay foreign throng, whom is she seeking?

'After all,' she presently says, 'you knew, Sarah, when you were so anxious to come, that we should meet no acquaintance here except Professor Forth, and——'

'Well, and why is not he here, pray?' cries Sarah, with a burst of genuine ill-humour that seems sensibly to ease her. 'Did not I order him to be punctual to the moment? Even he would be better than nothing!'

Belinda smiles ironically.

'That is an enthusiastic form of encomium upon the man that you are going to marry!'

But Sarah does not heed. Her eyes are directed to the side-walk, where the brisk foot-passengers pass and re-pass.

'There he is!' she cries in a disgusted voice; 'certainly there is no mistaking him! Did you ever see such a gait in your life? Look at him slouching along on his great flat feet!'

Belinda looks as directed; and sure enough, amid the strapping soldiers erect and tall, detects without difficulty a slovenly middle-aged figure, clerical, if you judge by its coat; scholarly, if you decide by its spectacles. With his hands behind him, and his hat set somewhat on the back of his head, he is mooning absently along.

'Is it possible?' cries Sarah, half-rising from her seat, and in a tone that is almost awful from its ire. 'Yes; it is monstrous; it is unbelievable! but it is nevertheless true that he has not brought me a bouquet after all!'

'Yes, he has,' replies Belinda quietly, 'only it is so small that it requires a keen sight to perceive it.'

As they speak, the object of their observation becomes aware of their vicinity, and turning his moony scholar's gaze towards them, awkwardly aims at them a tiny bunch of not particularly fresh violets. It falls into his betrothed's lap, but not long does it remain there. With an angry gesture, and before Belinda can stop her, she has tossed it out into the road; and the Gardereiter, with his six black horses, and his confiding companion, who are just in the act of again passing, drive over it, and grind it into the dust. Thanks, however, to his near-sight the donor is saved from witnessing this humbling spectacle.

'I am afraid that my aim was not good,' he says innocently, as the carriage draws up at the side-walk, exploring, as he speaks, the interior through his spectacles in search of his missing posy. 'I fear that the nosegay I directed towards you must have fallen short, and never reached you.'

'Oh yes, it did,' replies Sarah, with a sort of ferocious playfulness; 'but, as it was too large for me to carry, I put it outside.'

'How late you are!' cries Belinda hastily, trying by a rapid change of subject, and a sweet, good-natured smile, to erase the traces of this suave speech. 'After playing us so false, you cannot expect to find us in a very good humour.'

'I was delayed by an accident,' replies the lover irritably. 'I found the east wind so very much keener than I was aware of'—shivering a little, and buttoning his coat more tightly over his narrow chest—'that, as I am extremely susceptible to cold, I was compelled to return to my lodgings for a second overcoat.　Sarah knows'—with a rather resentful glance at his *fiancée*—'that I am extremely susceptible to cold.'

But Sarah heeds him no more than she does the east wind of which he complains.

'Ah!　Bravo!' she is crying joyfully, as another bouquet —a real one this time—large as a Cheshire cheese, fragrant as a hot-house, choice and costly as should be young Love's tribute, comes flying into the carriage.

She has stretched out both hands to grasp it; no doubt as to its destination troubling her triumph, although to a looker-on it would have seemed as if it were aimed more at the other sister, at Belinda, who has also half-stretched out her hands, but has quickly withdrawn them, and turned with patient attention, though with something of a blank look on her face, to the Professor's fretful sarcasms on the absurdity of an *al fresco* entertainment in such weather.　But though he misses nothing in her civil listening, though her head is turned towards him, and quite averted from her sister, yet her ears miss no one syllable of that sister's exuberant thanks.

'Come near, that I may bless you!' she hears her cry coquettishly.　'You see I have not a hand to give you; but you must blame yourself for that.　What a giant it is! How fresh!　How good!'—evidently smelling it.　'It has quite put me into good-humour again with this odious entertainment.　I assure you I never was so flouted in my life. What boors they are!　How different it would have been if they had been Frenchmen!' etc. etc.

Perhaps it is that her volubility leaves no space for answers from the person she addresses.　Certain it is that he is strangely silent.　Is it not odd to accept gratitude so bounteous with so entire a dumbness?　In pondering on this problem, Belinda presently loses the thread of the Professor's plaints; awakes from her musing to find him first gazing at her with surprised offence, then gone; then succeeded in his station at the carriage-door by some one; some one else who has no spectacles, who does not stoop nor cower before the east wind; some one young, in short —word of splendid compass! He is young: not with the conventional youth loosely assigned by society to any unmarried male under eighty, but really young; some one who three-and-twenty years ago did not exist.

Who that was not young and callow would be staring at her with all his eyes, and saying aggrievedly under his breath:

'Why did you not catch it? You knew I meant it for you!'

She looks back at him: a happy, red smile warming the face that men have often blamed as chill and high.

'I did my best!'

'What are you two gabbling about?' cries Sarah restlessly, cutting ruthlessly short a sentence of her betrothed's. 'Are you saying anything about me? Ah! I see you both look guilty!'

Neither undeceives her.

A quarter of an hour later the two girls are bowling homewards to their grandmamma and their apartment in the Lüttichau Strasse, leaving behind them the King, the Queen, the Graf von S. in his barouche, and the brave soldiers, both blue and green. Belinda has bent her delicate head, and is laying her cheek most tenderly against the blossoms in her sister's lap.

'Let me beg of you not to mumble them,' cries Sarah politely, interposing a prohibitory hand. 'You always seem to have an idea that flowers ought to be eaten.' Then, seeing a quite unaccountable flash of indignation in her sister's eyes, adds generously: 'If they were not all wired, as I see they are, I would spare you an orchid or two.'

'Would you indeed!' replies Belinda ironically. But further than this her magnanimous silence does not give way.

CHAPTER II.

A NIGHT has passed since the Professor's damaged violets
bit the dust. It is now morning, and at the window of her
bedroom in the Lüttichau Strasse, with the sash flung high
(to the deep astonishment of the German Dienstmädchen,
to whom the smell of an unaired room, further flavoured
with departed sausages and old beer, is as dear as to the rest of
her nation), Belinda sits, the sun warming her hair, and the
tart air freshening her face. She is looking fixedly out on
the pear-tree in the garden-scrap below—the pear-tree that
a week ago was pinchedly struggling into flower, that has
been daily whitening ever since, and now seems to stagger
under its burden of blossom-snow. Yet I doubt whether
she sees it.

'Is it possible?' she is saying to herself, almost with
awe—the awe that a great joy gives—'is it possible?'

A slight noise makes her turn her head and see the tall
white door open to admit her sister.

'Are you alone?' says the latter, cautiously peeping.

'Of course I am alone,' replies Belinda crossly. 'Am
I in the habit of receiving in my bedroom?'

This not particularly gracious answer is, however, quite
enough for Sarah, who forthwith enters, and steps friskily
across the sunshiny parquet, looking as clean as a cherry, as
pink and white as a May-bush.

'The moment is apparently not a propitious one,' she says, laughing, and drawing a chair close up to her sister's knees; 'but as my need is sore, I am afraid I cannot afford to wait for a better. I have come, my Belinda, to ask a favour of you.'

'Then you may go away again at once,' replies Belinda with surly decision, 'for I tell you, once for all, I will not grant it!'

'What! refuse even before you hear what it is?' cries the other, lifting those brows which nature, slightly abetted, perhaps, by a pair of tweezers, has drawn in the thinnest straight line across her wrinkleless forehead.

'Do you think I do not recognise that well-known formula?' asks Belinda severely. 'I am sure that I have heard it often enough. It means that you expect me to tell Professor Forth that you have every intention of jilting him!'

'You word it coarsely,' replies Sarah composedly; 'but I have heard worse guesses.'

'Then I absolutely and flatly refuse the office!' rejoins Belinda firmly. 'WHY you engaged yourself to him in the first instance——'

'WHY indeed?' interrupts the other, casting up both eyes and hands to heaven. 'You may well ask!'

'And yet,' pursues Belinda, regarding her sister with an air of stern wonder, 'when you wrote to announce your engagement to me, you said that you did not know what you had done to deserve such happiness!'

'I did not—I did not!' cries Sarah, reddening for once with genuine shame, and putting her fingers before her face. 'Do not say it; it is not true! It was not about him; it was one of the others!'

'*One of the others!*' echoes Belinda, scornfully curling up her fine nose. 'How pleasant and dignified to be bandied about! ONE OF THE OTHERS!'

'It may not be dignified,' replies Sarah impudently, though under the lash of her sister's words even her throat has crimsoned, 'but it is not so very unpleasant!'

'You know,' continues Belinda sternly, 'that I took a solemn oath to wash my hands of your affairs last time, when I had that painful scene with poor young Manners, and he walked round the room on his knees after me, clutching my skirts and sobbing!'

'He always sobbed!' interjects Sarah hard-heartedly. 'I have seen him cry like a pump!'

'I have already told six men that you had only been making fools of them,' continues the elder sister, contemptuously passing by her junior's lame attempt at palliation.

'Six! Come now, gently.'

'I repeat, six! In fact, I think I am rather understating it ; and I *will not* tell a seventh!'

'A seventh ! ! !'

'If you imply that I am exaggerating, I am quite willing to count. First'—checking off on her long white fingers, beginning with the thumb—'first, young Manners !'

'We have had him once already !'

'Second'—travelling on to the forefinger—'Colonel Greene. Poor fellow ! he sobbed too !'

'More shame for him !'—brazenly.

'Third, the young clergyman whom you picked up at the sea-side, and whose name I never can remember.'

'No more can I !' cries Sarah, with animation. 'How strange! Pooh! What was it again? Did it begin with a B?'

'Fourth,' continues Belinda relentlessly, arriving at her third finger—'fourth, old Lord Blucher, who was so deaf that I could not get him to understand what I meant.'

But Sarah's light mind is still on the track of her lover's lost initial.

'I am almost sure that it began with an L!' she says thoughtfully.

'Fifth'—extending her little finger—'Mr. Brabazon.'

'You counted him before!'

'I did not!'

'I think you did.'

'I am sure I did not; but, to make certain, we will begin all over again. First'—returning to her thumb— 'poor young Manners——'

'Stop!' cries Sarah loudly, putting her fingers in her ears, and abandoning the search for the young clergyman's name. 'I will grant that there were six, sixteen, sixty— anything to put an end to that intolerable arithmetic of yours!'

Belinda is preparing to begin on her other hand, but at this concession she lets them both drop in her lap, and ceases counting. There is a silence. Sarah's roving eyes are despondently fastened on the white earthenware stove, and Belinda's large grave gaze is straying through the window, taking in at once the poetry of the blooming pear-tree and the prose of the Bohemian railway, and the ugly straight stuccoed houses beyond it.

'What could have been your inducement in this case,' she says presently, turning with a judicial air to the offender, 'I am quite at a loss to conjecture; it certaintly could have been neither pleasure nor profit!'

'It certainly could not,' answers Sarah, sighing profoundly and wagging her head from side to side; 'anyone who saw him would exonerate me from the suspicion of either motive!'

'Such a conquest could not have even gratified your vanity!' pursues Belinda relentlessly.

'Yes, but it did!' replies Sarah, abandoning her dispirited pose, and speaking with an animation which shows that she does not altogether relish this wholesale depreciation of her latest victim; '*you* may not think much of him, but I can assure you that he is considered a great luminary at Oxbridge. At the house where I met him they could not make enough of him; it seems he has written a book upon the Digamma!'

'And what is the Digamma?' asks Belinda curtly, totally unmoved by this evidence of erudition.

'You do not know what the Digamma is?' cries Sarah, lifting her eyebrows, and speaking with an air of pompous astonishment. 'Well, then,' breaking into a laugh, and even demeaning herself so far as to be guilty of the faintest possible shadow of a wink, 'to tell you a secret, no more do I!'

'You cannot live upon the Digamma, I suppose!' says Belinda grimly, not much infected by her sister's mirth.

'I should be very sorry to try!' still laughing.

'Then I am quite as much in the dark as ever!' rejoins the other, inexorably grave.

'Well, it was not *only* the Digamma, of course,' says Sarah, frowning in reluctant retrospect; 'though, as far as I could make out, that appeared to be his *cheval de battaille;* but he was looked upon as a genius generally. You should have seen how they all sat at his feet—such feet!—and hung on his words. There was one girl—she was at Girton —who waited on him hand and foot; she always warmed his great-coat for him, and helped him on with his goloshes!'

'Well?'

'Well, you know,' impatiently, as if stating something too obvious to be contradicted, 'one would not have been human if one could have stood calmly by, and looked on. I rushed into the fray. I too warmed his great-coat and put on his goloshes. Ugh! what a size they were! I could have lived roomily and commodiously in one of them!'

'Well?'

' *Well*, indeed! I do not call it at all well! I call it very ill!'

'There I have the good fortune thoroughly to agree with you.'

'Well, as I was saying,' resuming the thread of her narrative with a heavy sigh, 'I rushed into the fray. I was successful, dreadfully successful! You know the sequel, as they say in books.'

'I do not know the sequel,' replies Belinda sternly; 'all I know is that I will have neither part nor lot in it!'

'No? and yet,' fawningly, 'it would come so much better from you.'

'Better or worse, it will not come from me.'

'When *you* break it to them,' sidling up with a cajoling air, 'it does not hurt them nearly so much! I declare I think they almost like it!'

No answer. A silence cut into only by the uncouth shriek of a departing engine.

'Why at least did you drag him here?' asks Belinda presently, still opposing a front of granite to her sister's blandishments.

'I am afraid I cannot quite defend it,' replies Sarah, in a small voice, and again hanging her head; 'but, to tell the truth—which indeed I always try to do—times were slack! There was nobody else much just then, and I thought I could at least make him fetch and carry!' Then, with an acute change of key and access of emotion : 'I was grossly deceived ; he is too disobliging to fetch, and too much afraid of over-fatiguing himself to carry!'

Another pause. A quick wind-whiff tosses through the window a little storm of pear-petals, and throws them on Belinda's lap.

'Now if the cases were reversed,' says Sarah, kneeling down at her senior's elbow, and folding her hands with an extremely insinuating gesture of supplication, 'if *you* were in difficulties——'

'I never am in difficulties.'

'I do not see much to brag of in that, for my part!' springing to her feet again.

'No more do I,' replies Belinda drily. 'I am never in difficulties, as you call them, because I never have any temptation to be; perhaps if I had I might; but as you are well aware,' stifling a sigh, 'I have not, and never had, any charm for men!'

'It is very odd, is not it?' says Sarah, not attempting to combat this assertion, but looking at her sister with an expression of compassionate curiosity. 'I cannot think why it is. I have often wondered what the reason could be; sometimes I think it is your nose!'

'My nose?' repeats Belinda hastily, involuntarily glancing round in search of a mirror, and putting up her hand to her face; 'what is the matter with my nose?'

'There is nothing the matter with it,' rejoins Sarah, still speculatively gauging her sister's attractions; 'perhaps it would be better for you if there were; it is only too good! I cannot fancy any man venturing to love such a nose; it looks too high and mighty to inspire anything short of veneration!'

'It is not so *very* high either!' cries Belinda hurriedly, drawing from her pocket a very fine handkerchief, and applying a corner of it in careful measurement to her traduced feature. 'There!' marking off a small portion with her thumb; 'only that much.'

'It is not a case of measurement,' says Sarah gravely; 'I have seen noses several hands higher that were not nearly so alarming. It is a case of feeling; somehow yours makes them feel small. Take my word for it,' with a shrewd look, 'the one thing that they never can either forgive or forget is to be made to feel small.'

Belinda laughs, a little bitterly.

'It is clear, then, that nothing short of amputation could make me attractive, and I am afraid even that might fail; but I do not know why we digressed to me at all.'

'I had a little plan,' says Sarah, her airy gaiety giving sudden place again to gloom at the returning thought of her own sorrows; 'but you have frightened it away.'

'What is it?' very shortly.

'Well, you know,' instantly resuming her wheedling air and her coaxing posture at her sister's knees, 'that we are going to drive to Moritzburg to-day, you and I. Of course Professor Forth,' with a slight grimace, 'will be on duty there to meet us; equally of course, young Rivers, who seems to have contracted a not altogether reprehensible habit of dogging our steps, will be there too.'

'Well?' averting her head a little.

'Well, I thought—but you are not a pleasant person to unfold one's little schemes to—I thought that for once you might be obliging, and pair off casually with my dear, and take an opportunity of softly breathing to him that nobody —I least of all—will try to stop him if he effects a graceful retreat to Oxbridge and the Digamma!'

'And meanwhile you?' in a rather low and suppressed voice, and with face still turned away.

'And meanwhile I,' replies Sarah, jovially, 'killing two birds with one stone—keeping the coast clear, that is to say, and marking my gratitude for that haystack of gardenias—shall be straying hand-in-hand through the vernal woods with——'

But that sentence is destined never to be ended.

Belinda has risen from her seat with a gesture so sudden and violent as almost to destroy the equilibrium of the girl so caressingly propped against her, and has thrust head and neck out of the window, as if, even in this fresh room, she gasped for air.

It is a moment before she speaks; and even then her voice sounds odd.

'I have already told you that I utterly decline to be mixed up in your entanglements. I forbid you to mention the subject to me again.'

'Whew-w-w-w!' says Sarah by and by, in a low key, when she has recovered the breath reft from her by stupefaction at her sister's procedure, enough to speak at all; remaining seated meanwhile in stunned isolation on her lonely stool. 'Forbid! What an ugly word! After all,' speculatively, 'I am not much surprised that men are frightened at you. I am frightened at you myself sometimes; and so no wonder that they shake in their shoes, and dare not call their harmless souls their own.'

'How many times are you going to tell me that?' cries Belinda, veering round in sudden passion. 'Do you think that it can be very pleasant to hear that I can never inspire anything but alarm and aversion? I am as well aware of it as you can be; but I am a little tired of hearing it.'

'And you might inspire such different feelings,' says Sarah, in a tone of the purest artistic regret; 'it *is* a pity to see advantages which would have made me famous if I had had them, absolutely thrown away upon you! I suppose,' with a sigh, 'that it is the old story of the people with large appetites and nothing to eat, and the people with plenty to eat and no appetites.'

CHAPTER III.

' For mirth of May, with skippis and with hoppis,
The birdis sang upon the tender croppis,
With curiose notes, as Venus' chapell clerkis.
The roses yong, new spreding of their knoppis,
Were powdered brycht with hevinly beriall droppis,
Throu' bemes rede birnyng as ruby sperkis,
The skyes rang for schouting of the larkis.'

AWAY they go to Moritzburg, when the noon sun is warm
and high; away they go, handsome, gay, and chaperonless.
There is no reason why their grandmother, who is a perfectly
able-bodied old lady, should not escort them; but as she is
sixty-five years of age, has no expectation of meeting a lover,
and is quite indifferent to spring tints and German Schlosses,
she wisely chooses to stay at home.

'If you cannot behave like young gentlewomen without
having me always at your heels, why, all I can say, my
dears, is that I am sorry for you,' is the formula with which
she mostly salves her own conscience and dismisses them.

The result is perhaps not worse than that of more pre-
tentious exhortations; for the girls, having a sense of being
on parole, do behave like young gentlewomen: at least
Belinda always does, and Sarah very often.

They get into their carriage in a quick and cautious
manner; casting, meanwhile, apprehensive glances towards
a house a good deal lower down the street, and which they
will be obliged to pass.

'Sarah,' says Belinda impressively, unconsciously speaking half under her breath, 'if you hear a window open, mind you do not look that way. She is quite capable of bawling at us from the balcony; and if she finds out where we are going to, she is certain to insist on coming too.'

'If she gets into this carriage to-day,' replies Sarah firmly, 'it will be over my dead body!' and away they go.

With lowered parasols and held breath, they pass the dreaded house—pass it in safety. Not a sound issues from its silent casements. Away they go, across the Elbe, over the many-arched bridge, where the people, more leisurely than in our breathless London, are standing to watch the rafts floating down the river, and guided between the piles; through the Neustadt, where the Strong August for ever prances in bronze; past the Leipzig Railway Station, under the Acacia alley, leaving on their right the great, new, dreary barracks, backed by the pine-wood; along, along, between the young birches that, silver-trunked, baby-leaved, stand on each side of the way; off a-pleasuring into the country.

They do not talk much—at least to each other. To herself, Belinda is saying over and over the same one thing continuously: 'He will not be there! I do not at all expect him.' She says it superstitiously, in the trembling hope that if she can cajole the envious gods into believing that she does not count upon it, they may let her have her wish. 'He will not be there!' But her racing pulse and her flushing cheeks say differently; differently too say the wedded birds and the springing grasses and the opening buds. They say all together:

'He will be there! He will—he will!'

But perhaps, besides him, there may be some one else, not quite so eagerly desired.

They are not far beyond the town, and are jogging tranquilly along in the sunshine, when Belinda is roused with a start from her love-musings by an agitated series of ejaculations from Sarah.

'Belinda! She is there! On your side. Quick! Hold down your parasol! Perhaps she may not see us.'

Swift as lightning Belinda has obeyed. Totally irrespective of the sun's position, her *en-tout-cas* stoops till it shields—imperviously, one would think—the inmates of the carriage from all passers-by on that side.

But there are eyes, hard, horny, and inquisitive, to which an *en-tout-cas*—nay, a stone wall, if need be—is as glass. The coachman checks his horses; and Sarah, leaning angrily out to bid him drive quicker, perceives that he has no alternative, if he would not drive over a burly, middle-aged figure gesticulating with raised arms and waved umbrella in mid-road, and crying: 'Halt, Kutscher!' with all the power of a strong pair of lungs.

'It is no use!' says the girl, sinking back in disgusted resignation on the cushions. 'It never is any use!'

The next moment the lady to whom she alludes is presenting a hot, red face, a grizzled fringe of hair, and a large-patterned black and white plaid gown at the carriage door.

'I was afraid you might not see me!' she says, shaking hands warmly. 'How are you? Where are you going to? I thought I must just stop you for a minute, to ask where you are going to? To Moritzburg? How pleasant! I wish I were going to Moritzburg too!' Then, as no invitation follows this very broad hint: 'I dare say, now, as you seem to have plenty of room, you would not mind giving me a lift.'

'It would be delightful!' says Belinda, with suspicious precipitancy; 'but I am afraid——'

'I do not in the least mind sitting back, if that is what you are going to say. It is all one to me how I sit. If you had travelled as much as I, it would be all one to you!'

'If Belinda had travelled as much as you,' says Sarah
sarcastically, 'I am sure that her one hope and prayer would
be to be allowed to stay at home for the rest of her life.
Well,' with a would-be-valedictory wave of the hand, 'it is
too unlucky; but as we have unfortunately promised to
meet some people——'

'Some people! What people?' repeats the other inquisitively. 'Any one I know, I wonder? Professor Forth,
of course, for one,' with a meaning smile. 'I saw him
setting off this morning somewhere. I knew that it must be
an excursion of some kind, because he had two overcoats;
but I could not make out where. I asked at his lodgings,
but the Dienstmädchen did not know. And Rivers—young
Rivers?—are you going to meet him too? *A propos* what
Rivers is he? I want to find out what Rivers he is; I know
so many Rivers.'

'I will ask him at once,' says Sarah gravely. 'I will say
to him, "What Rivers are you?" *Au revoir.* Drive on,
Kutscher.'

'Where are you going to-morrow? What are you going
to do to-morrow? Will you come to Wesenstein? I want
you all to come to Wesenstein! With a little packing we
might all get into one carriage. What do you say to a long
day at Wesenstein? or, better still, Tharandt? What do
you say to a long day at Tharandt?'

But the carriage has rolled inexorably away; and the
latter part of these propositions is addressed to the empty air.

'A form of thanksgiving to be used on land!' says Sarah,
drawing a long breath, and blowing a kiss in ironical adieu
to the lessening figure of their baffled friend.

They are nearing their goal now. Along the straight
avenue of young horse-chestnuts and limes they trot; the
wind-swept flat plain on either hand, and the long vista of
tree-shaded road, ended by the Schloss.

They are driving up to the Gasthof Au Bon Marché.
Belinda shuts her eyes. If he is here, he will be to be seen
at once, or not at all. If he is not here, she will be ignorant
of it for yet one moment more. She shuts her eyes; but
in an instant Sarah's sarcastic ejaculation, obviously called
forth by the first sight of her betrothed, 'My king! my king!'
makes her open them again; open them to see that she has
succeeded in tricking the gods; that he is here; and that,
judging by his looks, he too has been shutting his eyes and
dreading.

'How do you do?' says Sarah gaily, giving him her hand.
'I have a message for you from Miss Watson; she wants to
know what Rivers you are! I was so afraid of forgetting
that I thought I had better deliver it at once. Think it
over, I advise you, against you meet her next. Bah! he
does not hear a word I say!'

A quarter of an hour later they are all seated on deal
chairs at a deal table under a primitive shed that does duty
as an arbour, waited on by a civil, homely Dienstmädchen
in a blue bib, and eating beefsteaks. At least two of them
are. Two of them are past eating. For them the beefsteak
cuts juicily; for them the schnitzel swims greasily; for them
the excellent light lager-bier foams in lidded mugs—in vain.
It is indeed dubious whether any one except Sarah enjoys
the luncheon *quâ* luncheon. The Professor is doubtful as
to the digestibility of the schnitzel, and more than doubtful
as to the prudence of lunching out of doors in a high wind
on the 2d of May. He had indeed gone so far as to have
luncheon laid in the little beer-and-smoke-stained inn parlour;
but his betrothed has explained to him so kindly yet firmly
that if he lunches indoors he will lunch alone, that he has
sullenly submitted, merely putting on ostentatiously, one
atop of another, the two overcoats which, as Miss Watson
faithfully reported, he had providently brought with him.

And yet, though the wind is high, it is not spiteful. It rocks playfully the tall oleanders in pots, and swings the little wooden boxes hung in the trees to oblige the birds, who find them a quite satisfactory substitute for nests, judging, at least, by the easy cheerfulness with which the short-tailed, wise-faced starlings go in and out of the tiny apertures.

Whether or not it has pleased or been digestible, luncheon is now ended, and Professor Forth is surveying the bill through his spectacles.

'Six marks, sixty pfennigs!' he says, proclaiming the total in a tone which announces how very far from content he is with it; 'one mark, sixty-five pfennigs a head! A very high charge, I should say; undoubtedly prices in Germany have doubled since the war! *Viermal Bifstek!*' reading aloud the items—'as it turned out, *zweimal* would have been ample. *Zweimal Kartoffeln——*'

He breaks off suddenly, for Sarah has twitched the paper out of his hand.

'In mercy spare us!' she cries. 'What can be more dreadful than the recapitulation of the items of the food one has just swallowed? It is like beginning luncheon all over again, to which, with my present feelings, death would be preferable.'

By and by they set off to visit the Schloss—the four-towered Schloss, with its round red domes, and all its little pinnacles and dormer windows—falling, as they go, into two couples, though this is not accomplished without a slight manœuvring on the part of one.

'In Heaven's name stop a moment to admire this pump!' says Rivers, in an eager whisper to Belinda. 'Nothing to admire in it?—of course there is not! I never saw an uglier pump in my life, but it will give them a good start!'

'Are you so sure that they are anxious to get a good start?' asks Belinda with a significant look ahead at Sarah, who, continually throwing back restless glances over her shoulder, lagging, stopping on every possible pretext, if she cherishes a desire for a *tête-à-tête*, certainly disguises it admirably.

'I am not at all sure,' replies the young man, with a dry laugh. 'What I am sure of is that I wish it.'

'Do you think that her back looks as if she were being tolerably civil to him?' pursues Belinda, talking on quickly and nervously; 'one can gather so much from a person's back. I am afraid that the way in which she is jerking her head about does not augur very well for him. Was not she rude to him at luncheon? he must have heard her whisper to me that he was an old skinflint.'

'Perhaps they are all right when they are alone,' replies Rivers sanguinely.

Belinda shakes her head.

'I doubt it!'

They have reached the Schloss and its broad slabbed terrace. Belinda is leaning on the old stone balustrade, low and weather-worn, that runs round it. Her eyes are fixed on the carved stone figures, weather-worn too, that stand out against the pallid fair sky in their old-world quaintness; the fat Cupids with abnormal Dachshunds; the ancient vases, rough with stone lilies and roses; the fat Cupids again.

Belinda looks at the Cupids, and Rivers looks at her; looks at her as a wholesome minded and bodied boy of twenty-two does look at his first love. To him nothing now exists save that opaque white cheek; that small disdainful nose, on which Sarah hangs all its owner's mischances; that lovely stature that makes other women look squat and bunchy. To him all creation that is not Belinda —sun, moon, stars, Schloss, Professor, bifsteks—is an irrelevant and impertinent accident.

'He might not in house, field, or garden stir,
But her full shape would all his seeing fill.'

'After all,' he says, with a trembling in his vigorous,
fresh voice, 'I do not think that I should much mind how
like a dog the woman I loved treated me in company, if
she were—if she were—as I would have her when we were
alone!'

'Would not you?' replies Belinda, suddenly changing
colour at the application that she herself makes of this
speech; and then, in fevered consciousness of her own
untimely flush, she adds with a callous, cold laugh: 'I think
I should agree with the poet:

'"Perhaps it was right to dissemble your love,
But why need you kick me downstairs?"'

The poor boy looks terribly thrown back; and indeed
what ardent young lover would not, at such a turn given to
a tender speech? And yet in her heart she had felt as
tender as he, though no human being could have guessed
it. Both now lean their elbows on the balustrade, and
look down on the garden grass, and the stiff fir-trees cut
into prim yew-shapes; so that unless you look at them very
closely you would swear that they were yews. And beyond
the grass and the firs comes the ruffled blue water, which
like a broad moat girds the Schloss around. The water is
running to-day into little waves and ridges; and trees just
greening are verdantly bordering its brim. In the garden,
beneath the fir-trees a pair of figures are seen soberly pacing.

'There they are!' cries Belinda, pointing to them, and
thankful for a safe subject with which to break the strained
silence; 'is it possible that she has taken his arm? No; I
thought it could not be! I wonder what progress she has
made towards telling him that she does not mean to marry
him.'

'Is that what she is telling him?' says Rivers, roused to

interest by fellow-feeling, and craning his neck to look;
'unhappy old devil!'

Belinda nods.

'I think so; that is what she meant to tell him; and, if
I do not mistake, his haggling over the luncheon gave him
his *coup de grâce.*'

CHAPTER IV.

'In every well-conditioned stripling, as I conjecture, there already blooms a certain prospective Paradise, cheered by some fairest Eve.'

PRESENTLY they move, and passing down the slabbed incline, and across the water into the King's garden, tread very slowly the fine gravel of the broad walk, as sentinels on either hand of which stand heaven-high firs, that yet have been clipped out of all fir semblance, and, like their brothers round the Schloss, wear the likeness of yews, cut into such tall narrow sugar-loafs that their forest kin would disown them. Silently they step along. Perhaps the utter repose, the absence of progress and hurry, the sober stillness of all around, tells sleepily upon their young spirits. Perhaps to them speech is not so easy as it was a month ago. It is Belinda who resumes the conversation.

'I suppose that it will devolve upon me after all?' she says with a sigh.

'That what will devolve upon you?' asks Rivers dreamily.

He has forgotten all about Professor Forth, and is lost in a sea of speculation as to whether ever woman in this world before had such a short upper lip.

'To tell Professor Forth that I do not think he will be my brother-in-law,' she answers, smiling.

'You think that Miss Churchill will shirk it?' absently.

The Professor is still a mist-figure to him. It is her chin now. Was there ever such a ravishing round chin?

' I think so ; she generally does.'

' *Generally !* ' awaked for a moment from his trance by shocked surprise. ' Does it often happen?'

' It was a slip of the tongue,' she answers, laughing; 'it has happened once or twice before.'

' And you?'

The bold wind has loosened a very small strand of her hair, and is blowing it against her cheek. How many years of his life—ten? fifteen? twenty?—would he give to be allowed to replace it behind her ear.

' And I? Oh, I dry the victims' eyes, and tell them that there is as good fish in the sea as ever came out of it.'

' And yours?' that little lock is still frolicking distractingly; ought he to tell her of it? ' Who dries your victims' eyes?'

' They have not any eyes to dry,' she answers precipitately. ' I do not mean that they are blind, but that there are no such people; they do not exist.'

' You mean, I suppose,' he says, reddening, 'that I had no business to ask about them?'

' I mean what I say, neither more nor less: they do not exist!'

Her tone is cold and trenchant, as of one who would check a displeasing topic. In point of fact it is intense shyness—the shyness of hearing herself talked about, and talked about by him—that makes it so; but to a listener it has all the effect of a freezing haughtiness, repressing impudent intrusion. She hears it herself with bitterness.

' Is it any wonder that no one has ever loved me?' she says internally.

It is clear that he hears it too.

' You are offended,' he cries miserably. ' I wish to

heaven that I had never come to-day! Everything has gone
wrong! You let Professor Forth help you out of the
carriage! you let him hand you the potatoes——'

She smiles involuntarily.

'On the contrary : he recommended me not to take any ;
he said they were rancid!'

'You let him pick up your pocket-handkerchief!'

Again she smiles more broadly.

'He certainly did not avail himself of the permission.
I think that his knees are scarcely supple enough for him to
be very anxious to pick up even Sarah's.'

As she speaks she puts up her hand and carelessly pushes
back her wandering lovelocks ; but one little tendril still
escapes and frisks in the breeze.

He thrusts his hands hard down into his pockets to resist
the intense though monstrous temptation to aid her in its
recapture.

'If you knew,' he says hurriedly, 'what I felt when you
drove up to the Gasthof to-day ; in what an agony of dread
lest you should think me presumptuous for having forced
myself into your party—lest you should murder me with one
of those terrible frozen looks of yours——'

'One of those terrible frozen looks of mine?' repeats she
with a puzzled air. 'It is very odd! I wonder how I do
them?'

'You may think me as great an ass as you please,' pursues
he rapidly—'and, indeed, you would not be human if you
did not—but I give you my word of honour, for the first
moment I dared not look. I shut my eyes!'

At that she smiles subtilely.

'How, in Heaven's name, have you managed to make
me so much afraid of you?' continues the lad, with gathering agitation. 'You are never rude ; you are not sarcastic ;
nothing makes you angry ; you speak most softly ; and
yet——'

'And yet,' she says, finishing his sentence for him with a rather bitter smile, 'and yet you shake in your shoes before me! I know you all do. Ever since I grew up—nay, before; I think that at fourteen I began to inspire dread—I have always been hearing how frightened people are of me. It is so pleasant! No doubt you had been told it before you came to know me, had not you?'

In the eagerness of that query she has stopped and faced him, the colour hurrying up to her cheeks, and her eyes fastened in imperative asking on his.

He does not answer for a moment. He is dizzily marvelling whether blood of so wondrous a tint had ever flooded lily cheek before. She repeats her question with emphasis:

'Had not you?'

'I—I—*had* heard that you snubbed people!'

'Have you found it true?' she says, in a low and rather anxious voice. 'Have I—have I—' hesitating, 'snubbed you?'

To this question she has honestly expected a reply in the negative, and is proportionately startled by the virile energy of the affirmative that instead follows. 'That you have—times out of mind!'

'Have I?' she says, in a key of genuine bewilderment. 'How? when? where? What is it that I do?'

He does not answer.

'Is it,' she goes on diffidently, Sarah's dictum as to the one unforgivable sin committible by women against men flashing across her mind, sinister and appropriate—'is it that I make you feel small?'

'Small! Yes,' assents he, with pungent emphasis; 'I should think you did! invisibly, imperceptibly small. But that is not the worst. I was prepared for that. I had heard it was your way!'

She laughs grimly. 'What a pleasant way!'

'There are days on which—I do not know how you do
it—you make me feel as aloof from you as if——'

'As if what?'

'As if I were down here, and you were——'

'And I were what?' with an accent of sincere and
puzzled curiosity.

'And you were—and you were—one of the heavenly
host up there!' ends the young man, baldly and stammering.   But love is no brightener of the wits.

'One of the heavenly host?' repeats she, justly infuriate
at this stale comparison.   'An angel, in short!   Must I
always be an angel, or a goddess?   If anyone knew how
sick I am of being a goddess!   I declare I should be
thankful to be called a *Fury*, or even a *Ghoul*, for a change!'

So saying, she turns her shoulder peevishly to him; and
leaving the garden, begins to walk quickly along the road
by the water, as if to make up for her late loitering.   He
keeps pace with her, dumb in snubbed contrition, stupefied
by love and, unhappily for himself, fully conscious of it;
burningly aware of the hopeless flatness of his last simile,
and rendered by his situation quite incapable of redeeming
it by any brighter sally.

Presently they leave the water and all its rioting wavelets,
and pace through the fir-wood towards the little Schloss—
the big one's quaint baby-brother.

Beneath the fir-trees the blue hepaticas flower plentiful
and late, and the young stitchworts open their fresh eyes to
the spring.   Regardless of ten-groschen penalties, Belinda
leaves the road, and stoops to pick the little blossoms.

Docilely following her motions, he stoops and picks too.
He picks to more purpose than she, indeed; for when,
by and by, they straighten themselves again and compare
results, his is by far the largest nosegay.

'Will you take them?' he says, timidly proffering them,

for her tart speech has robbed him of his last barleycorn of courage ; 'or shall I—shall I—carry them for you?'

What would not he carry for her? A newspaper parcel down St. James' Street; a bulging carpet-bag through Rotten Row !

'Thank you, I will carry them myself,' she answers, stretching out her pretty, bare hand for them. 'They shall make up to me,' smiling, 'for the gardenias of which I was deprived by—an accident. Do you know that I was not allowed even to smell them? Did not I bear my loss like a Trojan?' Then, hesitating a little, she steps a pace or so nearer to him, and, half shyly holding out her own little bunch, 'Exchange is no robbery,' she says with a soft look. 'Will you,' gently mocking his frightened tone, 'will you take them ? or shall I—shall I—carry them for you?'

He makes her no answer; he is quite unable. The tears have sprung to his eyes. He is very young, has never loved before ; and it seems to him that at that fair hand holding out its little blue bunch Heaven opens to him.

There are days on which Heaven opens to us all, but to most of us next day it shuts again.

Above them the pines lay their dark heads stilly together against the fair sky, that looks austere, yet not unkind. Here the loud wind is kept at bay, and whispers scarcely more noisily than they themselves are doing in their safe retreat.

With what halting words of lame ecstasy he would have thanked her will never now be known. Dumbly he has received her gift, refraining, by what iron constraint put upon himself, from any least detention of those cool, pale fingers that just unintentionally touch his, and then innocently withdraw. The labouring syllables that are struggling to his lips are for ever driven thence by the sound of a high-pitched young voice calling clearly through the still wood :

'Where are you? What has become of you? We have been searching high and low for you. Have you been searching high and low for *us?* Ah! evidently you have!' laughing ironically. 'Well, now you have had the good fortune to find us!'

Ere the end of this sentence, Sarah has frisked up to them, and, for the time, Heaven's door shuts in their faces, and Earth's dull portals reopen for them.

'Are you aware that there is a fine of ten groschen for leaving the road?' calls out the Professor from the distance, but nobody heeds him.

'Are you picking flowers?' asks Sarah demurely. 'How nice! Pick me some.' Then, turning to Rivers, she adds maliciously: 'I am not greedy; I shall be quite content with that miserable little bunch that you are clutching so tightly. Give it me!'

But at that he finds his tongue again.

'Not if you were to go down on your knees to me for it!' he cries tragically, lifting his right hand and holding his poor little prize high above her restless, small head.

'Not if I were to go down on my knees?' repeats she in accents of the deepest incredulity. 'Come, that is *trop fort!* It is worth putting to the test.'

As she speaks, she sinks at once upon her knees on the crushed herbage, and, joining her hands as in prayer, looks up at him, and says, in a small, childish voice, whose alluring properties she has tested on many a hard-fought field, '*Please!*'

She might as well have knelt to and allured one of the solemn straight pines. He does not even avert his eyes from her, as though, if he saw her, he must yield. He looks her full in the face, and says doggedly:

'Not if you knelt there till the Day of Judgment!'

'What are you about, Sarah?' comes the Professor's

voice again, from the road, where the ten-groschen penalty still keeps him. 'Are not you aware that although the grass may appear dry on the surface, the ground still contains a great deal of latent moisture!'

But a second time he speaks to the wind.

'Not if I knelt here till the Day of Judgment?' repeats Sarah, still hardly believing her own ears; then, wisely taking the only course left open to her, with as good a grace as may be: 'If that is the case, of course I will get up again at once!'

So saying she rises, apparently not at all put out of countenance, and flicks the bits of grass from the knees that had bent in vain.

'Do not you wish to see the King's boars fed? I understood you to say that you wished to see the King's boars fed!' shouts the Professor, striking in snappishly the third time, the contumely with which his remarks have been treated beginning to tell very perceptibly upon his tone.

'The King's boars?' repeats Sarah, *sotto voce*, descending to a degrading pun, and accompanying it with a wink that is worthy of it. 'Do you think the King has room for one more in his menagerie? if so, I might be permitted to offer him mine! Yes,' raising her voice, and beginning to trip back towards her betrothed, 'of course we are coming!'

She has not gone two steps, however, before she bethinks herself; and, turning back, tucks her arm determinately under her sister's.

'Belinda,' she says resolutely, 'you have not seen the Little Schloss! you have not seen the lighthouse! you have not seen the pheasantries! you shall see the boars!'

So saying she sweeps her off hurriedly ahead; and Rivers, cursing fearfully, is compelled to follow with the Professor, with whom he has about as much in common as a non-reading, hard-rowing, footballing, cricketing undergraduate mostly has with an exceptionally stiff-backed and donnish Don.

Nor is the Professor, whose contempt for undergraduates in general is not to be equalled save by his aversion, very much better pleased with the arrangement.

However, it does not last long. A few minutes of brisk walking brings them to the clear space in midwood—the sandy spot railed round with palings where his Majesty of Saxony's pigs have their daily rations dealt out to them.

There the girls sit down on the wooden bench provided for the accommodation of admiring spectators. Many dark forms have already arrived, and are rooting and grubbing hither and thither. They have immensely long noses, long dark hair, large dark ears; hind-quarters that run away like hyænas, and a general air of absurdity and unpiglike pigness. Amongst them are several fierce-looking old gentlemen with their ugly lips lifted over formidable tusks, shaggy as bears, and with their long gray hair wet and shiny, as if they had been rolling in some muddy place. Every moment there is an arrival; a fresh pig, two fresh pigs emerging from the wood and trotting hastily, with ears anxiously erect, to the rendezvous, afraid of having arrived too late.

About the whole family, when united, there is a general unamiability; a spiteful biting and nipping at each other; a squeaking and angrily grunting; a wrathful pursuit and hasty flight. The little piglets, tawny-coloured and striped like tiny tigers, toddle sweetly about in their artless baby-hood.

Irresistibly attracted by the childlike graces of one of these latter, yet smaller, more striped, weirder than its brethren, Sarah has run after it, and is now scampering in pursuit round the arena.

The Professor, relieved at having found a sandy spot, is standing, stork-like, at a little distance off, poised on one leg, and cautiously seeking for traces of moisture on the sole of the other boot.

Once more Rivers and Belinda are alone.

'I will be the death of her!' says the boy, with an angry smile, shaking his fist in the direction of the sportive Sarah.

But apparently the latter's ears are nearly as long as those of the objects of her chase.

'Whom will you be the death of?' she cries, desisting suddenly. 'The mischief is in the pig! I cannot catch it; and I am sure I do not know what I should have done with it if I had: Well,' having by this time come up to them again, 'of whom will you be the death?'

'Of you,' replies the young fellow stoutly, though in his heart he is a little scared at the unexpected distance to which his threat has carried. 'Yes, of you,' looking full at her with his straightforward, handsome, angry eyes; 'at least, if I am not the death of you, as I should like to be, I will be even with you some fine day—see if I am not!'

She looks back at him, coolly pondering, but does not answer. A flash of almost compassionate astonishment is darting across her mind that any man in the possession of sight, health, and vigour—any man, more especially at the most inflammable of all ages, can look at her with the unsimulated indifference, slightly coloured with dislike, that this Rivers is doing! At once he rises in her esteem. Turning away, she walks thoughtfully back to the pigs.

*   *   *   *   *

By and by, as through the long, light evening the girls bowl smoothly homewards, before the shy white stars look out, Sarah suddenly breaks the silence that, for several quiet miles, has lain upon both.

'Belinda!' she says abruptly, 'by all laws, human and

divine, that bouquet was yours! The gardenias are now the colour of old leather, and smell rather nastily than otherwise; but, such as they are, they are yours!'

And even on these terms, poor Belinda is glad and thankful to have her nosegay again!

CHAPTER V.

'He knew whose gentle hand was at the latch
  Before the door had given her to his eyes;
  And from her chamber window he would catch
  Her beauty farther than the falcon spies.
  And constant as her vespers would he watch,
  Because her face was turned to the same skies;
  And with sick longing all the night outwear
  To hear her morning step upon the stair.'

UPON the fair town of Dresden a new morning has opened —opened in sunshine, joy, and lusty growth. For one blossom-bunch that swung fragilely on the pear-tree yesterday, there are twenty to-day. The slow small leaves are beginning to break less timorously from their outgrown sheaths.

I do not suppose that Belinda can have grown in the night; but about her, too, this morning there is a look of expansion and spring: as if she also were uncurling her leaves and disclosing her shy buds to her sun.

The two girls are sitting together in the pretty be-hyacinthed, be-china'd, Anglicised salon that looks to the street. The morning sun does not shine on that side of the house, and it makes the room dark; but so it is, that all the blinds are drawn to the bottom; nor does either, as would seem natural, make any attempt to pull them up again.

'So you never did it after all, yesterday?' Belinda is saying in a tone of disapproving surprise.

Sarah shakes her head.

'No; love's chain still binds us!' she answers, making a face.

'You will do it to-day?'

'No!'

'To-morrow?'

'I think not.'

'The day after?'

'It is improbable.'

'If you are waiting,' says Belinda, stopping in mid-row of the stocking she is knitting to look severely at her sister, and speaking with an extremely clear and decided accent, 'for me to do it for you, you will wait, as I told you yesterday, a very long time.'

'I am aware of it,' replies Sarah calmly. 'Since I realised that you are engaged in a little pursuit of your own, I have abandoned the idea.'

'Pursuit!' cries Belinda, with a shocked start, and crimsoning. 'You are the first person who ever dared to say that I pursued any one!'

'You would have been much pleasanter if you had,' rejoins Sarah coolly. 'Well, do not let us quarrel over a word! I did not say what part you took in the pursuit— whether you were the hunter or the hare!'

But Belinda has stooped her angry, blonde head over her stocking, and is speechlessly knitting her resentment into it.

'After all,' says Sarah, discourteously jerking the slumbering pug off the sofa, and throwing herself down on it, 'it is very unselfish of me. Nobody gives me the credit for any virtues, but in point of fact it is almost entirely in your interest that I am acting!' She pauses for a moment, expecting to be asked for an explanation, but Belinda deigns no syllable. 'Supposing that I did give my Solomon the sack —by the bye, what a neat alliteration! Swinburne might have made it,' continues Sarah, yawning—'what would become of me during all those rural excursions that I see stretching ahead of us in long perspective? We could not let you and young Rivers set off upon them *tête-à-tête!* we really could not! It would pass even Granny's and my latitude! I search the horizon in vain for a sail!—I mean for any one else to pair off with! My life would be spent in trying to look the other way, and in intercepting fond glances that were not meant for me!'

'And so,' says Belinda, lifting a head whose cheeks still blaze, and speaking in a withering voice, 'and so he is to wriggle on the hook a little longer? How much longer, pray?'

'How much longer?' repeats Sarah, with a malicious look; 'why, you can answer that better than I! As long as young Rivers wriggles on yours!'

Belinda winces.

Who—high-strung and palpitating in young love's first ecstasy—would not wince at such a phrase?

'Come, now,' says Sarah, sliding off the sofa again, assuming her cajoling voice, and sitting down on the parquet at her sister's feet, tell me a little about him! I have confided to you so many touching traits about my beloved, and if you are good I will tell you plenty more; but confidence should be reciprocal: what is he doing here? Why has he come to Dresden?'

'He is learning German,' replies Belinda reluctantly.

'H'm! I wonder how much he has learnt?' with a dry laugh.

> ' "His only books were woman's looks,
>   And folly what they taught him!" '

Belinda's sole response to this pleasantry is to push her chair back very decidedly, and isolate her sister on the floor.

'What does he do when he is at home?' continues Sarah, taking no notice of this evidence of displeasure, and obstinately pursuing her catechism.

'He has just left Oxbridge,' rather sulkily.

'Where, no doubt, he took several Double Firsts!' with an ironical smile.

'He rowed stroke in the University Eight last year,' very precipitately, and reddening under this fleer.

'Is he his own father, or has he a father?'

'He has a father.'

'And what is the father—what does the father do?'

'I believe—he is in business,' grudgingly.

'In business?' with raised eyebrows, and an accent of surprise and dissatisfaction. 'Well,' more cheerfully, 'there is business and business! Have you any idea what sort of business it is?'

'Not the slightest,' very curtly.

'It is a liberal age,' says Sarah philosophically, 'but one must draw the line somewhere. I draw the line at artificial manure! Come, now, have you any reason for supposing that it is artificial manure?'

Belinda laughs a little, but most unwillingly.

'I dare say it is. I never asked.'

'Do you remember,' says Sarah, 'the little Frenchman, covered with orders—Legions of Honour and Saint Esprits by the gross—that we met at the ball at Cannes, who told me that he was "*dans le commerce*," and when I inquired what branch, and suggested that perhaps he was "*dans les vins?*" answered grandiosely, "*Non, mademoiselle; je suis dans les bougies!*"'

A pause.

The pug has arisen from the cold parquet, and, with her tail still half-mast high in the enervation of slumber, has stepped delicately on to Sarah, and cast herself with a deep, slow sigh upon her warm lap.

'Your friend does not *look* as if he were *"dans les bougies,"*' says Sarah presently, with an air of thoughtful generosity; 'still less *dans le*—— I declare I do not know what is the French for artificial manure! How Granny has neglected our educations!'

But Belinda is not attending. Belinda's head is raised, and upon her face has come a look of blissful listening. Her fine ear has detected a footfall in the anteroom outside —a footfall that not even Slutty, the pug, has yet suspected; a step that she has discriminated from that of the flat foot Gustel.

'It is you, is it?' says Sarah, in a not particularly exhilarated voice, scrambling to her feet as Rivers, ushered in by an infant English page who divides the cares of the *ménage* with Gustel, enters.

She gives him two contemptuous fingers.

Of what use to give more to a man who holds them as if they were a bundle of sticks. She might have given him ten, or twenty, or none, for all he knows. His eyes have strayed away over her, to him, totally irrelevant head, and have fastened on his mistress, asking eagerly if this can indeed be she, alive and real, whom all night long he has pursued through his radiant dreams.

'Perhaps you can help us,' says Sarah, with an innocent look 'We have just been wondering what the French for artificial manure is?'

He does not hear. Belinda's hand in his is making summer in his veins, and his happy eyes are drowned in hers as happy. But Belinda hears.

'Sarah is speaking to you!' she says, low and hurriedly.

He turns round reluctantly with a start.

'I beg your pardon! I—I—did not quite catch what you were saying.'

'I was only asking you if you knew the French for artificial manure?' she answers demurely.

'For artificial manure!' repeats he, astounded. 'Of course I do not! Why should I? Why do you want to know what is the French for artificial manure? Is it a riddle?'

'Even for his explanation he has turned again to Belinda, as inevitably as the sunflower to the sun.

'We were only talking of—of—agriculture; were not we, Belinda?' replies the other, smiling malevolently at her sister's obvious, and to Rivers incomprehensible, discomfiture.

That his Egeria could look foolish, as she is indisputably doing, would never, indeed, occur to him; but nothing short of total blindness could prevent his seeing the sudden cascade of scarlet which has poured over her. For one instant, indeed, the blest idea has darted across his mind that this lovely flag may be hung out for him; but his humility—for real love is ever most humble—at once dismisses the scarcely formed thought as too good to be true.

Perhaps it is his scrutiny, silent and intense, that embarrasses her. Of course he ought to say something. On a morning visit one must say something.

'Why are you sitting in the dark?' he asks, glancing at the carefully drawn-down blinds. 'The sun is not on this side of the house, and there is no glare anywhere to-day.'

'It is very gloomy, is not it?' replies Belinda, who is slowly recovering her countenance; 'and we are so fond of light and air, too. But it cannot be helped; we are obliged to have them down because of Miss Watson.'

'Because of Miss Watson? I do not understand.'

'She lives on the other side of the street, a little farther down, and she has lately set up a spy-glass or telescope of some kind in her window, with which she rakes us fore and aft. She told us triumphantly on Tuesday that she could see everything we did. I believe that she can tell by the movement of our lips what we are saying.'

'If I thought so,' said Sarah viciously, 'what things I would say about her!'

'It will end in our being forced to leave the apartment,' says Belinda with a shrug. 'A friend of ours was. She has now taken one that looks upon a blank wall as being her only real security.'

'Miss Watson combines all the worst qualities of the gnat and the rhinoceros,' says Sarah gravely ; 'but I think her most offensive trait—though, indeed, among so many it is invidious to give the preference to any one —is her continual persecution of us to go on expeditions with her.'

'Then I am afraid that you will look upon me as a second Miss Watson,' says Rivers bluntly, and colouring, as he delivers himself with untold difficulty of his simple errand ; 'for that is exactly what I came here this morning to do!'

'*Another* expedition?' cries Sarah, in a tone of anything but gratification. 'Why, it seems as if we had not been back five minutes from the last!'

'It would evidently be an empty civility to ask whether you enjoyed it!' says Rivers, with a rather mortified laugh. 'And you?'—the sunflower turning again greedily to its sun.

'I was not bored,' answers Belinda in a constrained voice. 'I enjoy expeditions! I like Moritzburg.'

This is all that she has to say about the hours that had

made him sick with desire in anticipation, stammering with bliss in fruition, drunk with joy in retrospect!

He looks at her with an intense wistfulness that is almost incredulity; but she gives him back no glance. How can she, knowing, as she does by long experience, that Sarah has eyes in the back of her head? Sarah, who is ostensibly, and as he in the innocence of his heart believes really, entirely absorbed in making Slutty miserable, by affecting to suppose that she looks faint and holding smelling-salts to her outraged nose.

'I thought,' he says in a chapfallen voice, 'that it would not be a bad day for Wesenstein; or, if you liked that better, Tharandt.'

'You really must be related to Miss Watson!' cries Sarah, bursting out laughing. 'Wesenstein! Tharandt! Those are her two *chevaux de bataille*. If we do not go to Wesenstein we must go to Tharandt; and if we do not go to Tharandt we must go to Wesenstein! Good heavens!' suddenly stopping in mid-laugh; 'Unberufen! I hear her on the stairs! Hers is the only voice that one can hear through the double doors.'

'She has come to make us go to Wesenstein with her!' says Belinda in a low key of consternation.

'It is the finger of Providence!' cries Sarah, resuming her merriment. 'Mr. Rivers, you want to go to Wesenstein. *She* wants to go to Wesenstein! Why should not you go together? I will arrange it for you!'

'If you do,' says the young man, stepping threateningly towards her, and speaking in a tone of the most genuine alarm and exasperation, 'I'll——'

'You will be the death of me!' interrupts Sarah pertly, finishing his sentence for him. 'I know. So you said yesterday. I wish you would invent a new threat.'

For a moment they all listen silently.

'I believe it was a false alarm,' says Belinda, drawing a long breath.

'No, it was not!' rejoins Sarah, shaking her head. 'There is no mistaking that bison's voice. She is only stopping on the stairs to ask Tommy what wages he has, and whether Granny gives him enough to eat!'

CHAPTER VI.

It is too true. While the words are yet in Sarah's mouth, the door opens and admits the red face, the grizzled fringe, and the black and white plaid gown that they have all been apprehensively expecting.

'Any admittance?' cries the burly voice, as the owner enters without awaiting an answer to her question. 'All alive and well?'

'We are all alive,' replies Sarah gloomily, giving a hand ten degrees limper even than that one which she had vouch-safed to Rivers. 'As to being well——'

'Why are you all sitting in the dark? Why are all your blinds down?' interrupts the other breathlessly, unable any longer to contain the curiosity with which she has been bursting all the way up the long stone stairs.

There is a moment of stupefied silence, as the conviction flashes coldly on all their minds that they have over-reached themselves.

'I happened to look up as I was passing,' continues Miss Watson inquisitively, 'and saw that the blinds were all drawn down. I thought that of course I had better inquire the reason at once; but I could not get any satisfactory answer out of your page-boy—Tommy he tells me his name is. I had a little talk with him on the stairs coming up; he does not seem a very intelligent boy—Tommy—does he?'

'We had him cheaper by getting him out of an idiot asylum,' replies Sarah gravely; and Rivers, moonstruck as he is, explodes.

'Grandmamma quite well?'

'Do you think that she is dead, and that that is why we have the blinds down?' says Sarah ironically. 'Thanks, she is quite well, but she is not up yet. You see it is a little early!'

At this side-stroke Rivers winces. Does not it apply equally to him? But upon the object at whom it is aimed it is absolutely wasted.

'No bad news from England, eh?'

'Thanks, no!'

'I was afraid'—her eyes wandering inquisitively round —'by seeing the blinds down, that you might have heard of the loss of a relation. No? Well, then, why *are* they all down?'

There is a moment's silence. What question can be easier, and yet more difficult, to answer? At last:

'There is no reason why they should not be pulled up now?' says Sarah drily. 'Mr. Rivers, up with the blinds!'

Mr. Rivers obeys. The houses on the other side of the street again come into sight, and the gloom flies.

'I am so glad of this opportunity to make your acquaintance, Mr. Rivers!' says Miss Watson, following him to the window, and cordially extending her large hand. 'As soon as I heard your name I longed to ask you what Rivers you are? I know so many Rivers. I am sure that I must know all your people! What Rivers are you?'

The young man has turned, the blind-cord still in his hand, towards her. His face has grown nearly as red as hers, albeit the red is of a different quality.

'That is a rather posing question, is not it?' he says, with a confused laugh, the Englishman's difficulty in discussing himself being, in his case, intensified a hundredfold by the consciousness that Belinda is eagerly listening; 'how can I describe myself?'

'"All the rivers run into the sea, but the sea is not full!"' says Sarah flippantly; and Rivers looks vexed.

There is not one among us, however wise and good and humble, who does not detest a joke upon his own name.

'I know Lord Rivers,' continues Miss Watson, fixing him with her inexorable eye. 'At least I may really say that I virtually know him; we were at the same hotel at Cairo for two nights together; and though we never exactly met, as he did not dine at the *table d'hôte*, yet there is a sort of freemasonry in being at the same hotel! How *is* Lord Rivers? is he quite well? Is there any chance of his coming here?'

'I have not the slightest idea,' replies Rivers bluntly. 'He is not the most distant connection of mine!'

'Ah! then'—with a look of enlightenment—'you are one of the *other* Rivers; one of the Stukeley Rivers—Sir Edward Rivers' family. Now do tell me, which of the brothers are you? I am always so puzzled amongst them! Are you Humphrey? or Randulphus? or a younger one still?'

'I am neither Humphrey, nor Randulphus, nor a younger one still!' answers Rivers sulkily, his usually amiable and always beautiful boy's face beginning to look rather dangerous under this continued baiting. 'I am not related to Sir Edward Rivers, and I never heard of Stukeley!'

'Then I declare that I am quite at a loss!' says she, baffled.

But as her eye shows no sign of releasing him, as she is evidently bent upon extracting from him a response of some kind, he has to make what shift he can to answer her.

'I am sure I do not know what Rivers we are!' he says, in a shy, fierce voice, looking out of the window as if with some vague idea of escape by it. 'There are a good many of us, and we live in Yorkshire; and my father is in business!'

As the back of his head is turned to the room; and as, unlike Sarah, he has no eyes in it, perhaps she is justified in putting up one hand as a speaking-trumpet to her lips, and noiselessly mouthing through it for her sister's benefit the syllables, 'Ar—ti—fi—ci—al ma—nure!' At all events, this is what she does.

* * * * *

'She is really gone!' says Sarah, turning away from the window half an hour later, after a cautious reconnoitre, and drawing a long breath. 'Mercifully, the Greenes were passing, and she fell upon them from behind, so that they could not escape her. Generally she has a way of pretending to have forgotten her umbrella, and coming back to hear what one is saying of her.'

'I wonder she has not been cured of that before now,' says Belinda gravely, 'as she never can have heard any good.'

'It is the triumph of hope over experience!' rejoins Sarah. 'Well,' with a gay look at Rivers, 'at least it is a comfort to think that she has at last found out conclusively what Rivers you are!'

'Or, rather, what Rivers I am not,' replies he drily; 'it is not quite the same thing.'

'To be neither Humphrey nor Randulphus!' says Belinda, with a happy, shy, rallying smile; 'how sad!'

'I wonder, now, what your Christian name really is?' says Sarah. 'Come out, Slutty; she is gone! Slutty always crawls under this bureau when Miss Watson calls; she hates her so! I have tried to teach her to bite her leg,

but she will not go so far as that.   Yes now, what *is* your
Christian name?'

'What should you think?' he asks joyously, his heart
leaping wildly at that small coy smile which his dear lady
has just spared him.   'What do I look like?'

'You might be *Arthur,*' replies Sarah, sitting down with
Slutty in her lap, and looking him over well and thoroughly;
'there is no reason why you should not be *Reginald;* and I
have heard of more unlikely things than your being *Guy!*'

'Wrong! grossly wrong!' replies he, enduring her
scrutiny with the most perfect *sang froid,* and, indeed,
giving her back her cool hardy look.   'I never heard a
worse shot!   And *you*—what do you think?' his tone
growing suddenly reverent, and his bold eyes veiled and shy.

'You shall give me only one guess!' she answers merrily.
'I say—*David!*'

'*David!*' repeats Sarah scornfully.   'How likely!   Try
Goliath at once!'

But Rivers, in an ecstasy of pleasure at his love's intuition,
is crying out:

'How did you know?   How did you find out?   I never
told you!'

'Was not it a good guess?' she says with a demure smile.
'No; it was not a guess!   I read it—you know you sat
before us last Sunday—in the fly-leaf of your Prayer-book in
church!'

She blushes faintly as a China rose at this admission of
how her thoughts and eyes had stolen away from praise and
supplication to spell out his name.

'*David!*' repeats Sarah, in an extremely dubious voice.
'H'm!'

'It is a family name among us,' he adds in explanation;
'among my mother's people, that is.'

There is a moment's silence.   For the first and only time

in her life Sarah wishes for Miss Watson back again, to ascertain, as she undoubtedly would by direct inquiry, who and what his mother's people are. But as she herself does not feel quite equal to the task, the fact remains wrapped in as much mystery as does the nature of his father's commercial operations.

'Well, I suppose,' says the young man, sighing heavily, and gently and reluctantly setting down Slutty (Slutty loves him; he has mastered the exact spot in her back which demands delicate and perennial scratching. She has forsaken Sarah to jump up on his lap, though she has in general but a poor opinion of men's laps, as cold and hollow pretences)—'I suppose I must be going. I am afraid that you have already had too much of me!'

He pauses, with a wistful look towards Belinda's bent and shining head, but neither girl contradicts him : the one because she so cordially agrees with him ; the other because she so passionately dissents. He moves unwillingly to the door, but there halts again. 'And—and Wesenstein?' he says desperately.

'What about it?' cries Sarah peevishly. 'Did not you hear us calling all our gods to witness to Miss Watson that we were so broken with fatigue since Moritzburg that we could scarcely lift a finger?'

'I heard *you*,' he answers bluntly, laying a significant stress upon the pronoun.

'Now I warn you,' says she, holding up her forefinger threateningly at him, 'that if you mention Wesenstein again, I shall stop my ears.'

'There are other places besides Wesenstien,' returns he pertinaciously; something about Belinda—not anything she has said certainly, for she has said nothing—but possibly the unnatural fury with which she is knitting, encouraging him to persevere.

'Of course!' very snappishly; 'Tharandt!'

'No, not Tharandt; there are other places beside Thar-andt. Loch Mühle, for instance; have you ever seen Loch Mühle?'

'Never!' very crossly; 'and I humbly hope that I never shall. Why should we go anywhere?' pursues she, burying her ill-humoured face in the sofa-cushion. 'Leave me, leave me to repose. I have not the faintest wish to go anywhere.'

'And you never do anything but what you wish yourself?' asks Rivers snubbingly, eyeing with extreme disfavour her petulant prettiness. To him she does not appear in the least pretty.

'Never, if I can help it!' replies she, raising her head, surprised and languidly titillated by his tone, which is not what she had expected in him. 'Do you?'

He laughs drily.

'Never, if I can help it; but in a large family one cannot help it.'

'In a large family,' repeats she. 'You are one of a large family?'

'It depends upon what you call large; there are six of us.'

'Five too many,' rejoins she promptly. 'And where do you come—third—fourth.'

'I come first.'

'Are you taking a leaf out of Miss Watson's book?' asks Belinda severely, joining in the dialogue for the first time.

'I think I am,' replies the other composedly.

'Well, then, we will make a bargain: I will ask you no more questions if you will promise to invite me to go no more expeditions; there!'

So saying, she re-buries her head in the pillows; and as she totally declines to raise it again, and as neither does Belinda add another syllable, he is at length obliged to with-draw defeated.

For a moment after he has disappeared, Belinda still knits violently, her forehead puckered, a warm pink wave ebbing and flowing in her cheeks, and a sharp brush between love and pride going on in her heart. For the first time in her life pride goes to the wall. She tosses down her stocking and springs to the door.

'Mr. Rivers!' she calls tremblingly; 'Mr. Rivers!'

He must have walked very slowly, for he has only just reached the double doors of egress.

'Yes,' he answers pantingly; 'yes?'

'It is nothing,' she says, faltering into deep shyness again, and quivering under the fervid expectancy of his look. 'I only wanted to tell you that—that it is not my fault; that, for my part, I should have liked to go to Loch Mühle.'

'Then why, in Heaven's name, could not you say so sooner?' asks Sarah, whose long ears have again served her faithfully, pouncing out upon them. 'I am sorry that his name is *David*,' she says reflectively, a little later, when he has gone, jubilant now, to arrange the excursion. 'I am afraid it looks ill; the poor people are so fond of Scripture names.'

*   *   *   *   *

A high sun, hot and benign; a west wind, sweet with last night's rain; myriads and myriads of blossomed fruit-trees; villages that seem built of and buried in snow; enormous bunches of pear-blossoms, that look as if the boughs must break under their weight; the ways all white with arches of cherry-bloom; the horses trotting over a carpet of strewn cherry-petals, as at some high wedding pomp; and a seat opposite Belinda, who has allowed him to open her parasol for her. Is it any wonder that Rivers has forgotten that it is near three o'clock, and that, at an hour at which most people are full, he and his company are still fasting? But *they* have not forgotten. For the last

mile and a half he has been pelted by an ever sharper
shower of anxious and peevish questions as to whether the
Kutscher knows the road; as to whether they have still a
mile, two miles, half a mile to go; as to whether he is sure
that there is a Gasthof; as to whether, lastly and desperately
this, he is certain that there is such a place as Lohmen (it
is at Lohmen that they are to lunch) at all.

'I suppose,' says the Professor finally, putting on his
spectacles in order to look full and murderously at him
through them (he does not often look at undergraduates, he
dislikes them too much), 'I suppose that you are aware
that the whole responsibility of the excursion rests with you ?'

'Yes, I am aware,' replies Rivers inattentively and
dreamily.

She has just deigned to accept a little switch from him—
a flowered cherry-bough, blossomed to the end of each
brown twig—and is daintily waving away the audacious
summer flies with it.

The Professor has five distinct good reasons for being
cross, and for most people one suffices. Firstly, he did not
want to come at all ; secondly, he has the threatenings of a
snuffly cold, contracted in the long Moritzburg grass and
among the Moritzburg pigs, and probably to be sensibly
worsened by the present pleasure-trip; thirdly, he hates sitting
with his back to the horses—a thing which his votaries indeed
seldom suffer him to do—but in this case there has been no
suggestion of offering him a front seat; fourthly, his digestion has been for so many years his master, that it now
allows him with impunity no least derangement of his meal-
times ; fifthly and lastly, Sarah has three times flagrantly
pretended not to hear him when he addressed her, and has
once crabbedly asked him to let her have a little more
room. For Sarah is, if possible, still crosser than he.

The low, trivial words that the sweet wind carries not to

her, but alongside of her ; the ardent iron-gray eyes that she is always accidentally meeting, and that instantly lose their ardour the moment they encounter hers; the dust, for, despite last night's rain, there is dust ; the sense of physical emptiness, that no tickled vanity, no warmed passions redeem, have wrought her by the time they at length alight at the door of a simple but not untempting-looking Gasthof to such a pitch of ill-humour as makes her betrothed's mild fractiousness pale beside it.

'How cross they are !' says Rivers, having for the first time realised this long sufficiently patent fact, and looking after them with sunny wonder, as the Professor hastens into the inn to order luncheon, eagerly followed by Sarah.

'And how greedy !' adds Belinda.

And having thus calmly characterised their companions' vices, they stray away together down the little garden-path, where the bloody warriors and the cat-faced pansies merrily grow in the sandy border, and forget them. They have not, however, been long left to watch the happy butterflies hover, and the young flowers blow, before a captious voice over-takes and recalls them.

'I thought,' cries the Professor from the open Gasthof door, and in a voice whose exasperation is sensibly sharpened even since it was last heard in querulous inquiry five minutes ago—'I thought, Mr. Rivers, that you gave us to understand that there was a *good* hotel to be found here ?'

'And is not there ?' answers the young man absently.

He has just thieved a sweetbriar spray, young and vernal, and is making it fit for his love's tender hand by carefully nipping off all its thorns.

'I think,' pursues the voice, 'that an inn can hardly be qualified as good when there is not a single vegetable to be procured—not even a potato !'

'Of course it cannot,' replies Rivers serenely. 'Look !'

pointing joyously out to his companions a poised butterfly opening and shutting its freaky wings on a dark pansy face; 'does not he look jolly? He is the first tortoiseshell I have seen this spring.'

'And where,' continues the voice, in an intenser key of resentment, 'there is absolutely nothing of any kind to be obtained except veal.'

'Except veal!' repeats Rivers, rousing himself with an effort into a simulation of interest; 'you do not say so! Well, but,' lapsing into unavoidable radiance again, 'does it matter much? German veal is always so good. I hope,' looking sunnily round, 'that no one dislikes veal!'

There is a sulky silence, broken only by Belinda's murmuring that she loves it, and by the Professor's remarking that all white meats are more or less indigestible. Whether they like it or not, however, further inquiry only serves to confirm the fact that they must either resign themselves to a luncheon of kalbfleisch and bread (calf-flesh being the one universally procurable flesh in Germany) or not lunch at all. Nor, when this is settled, does the calf-flesh seem in any hurry to appear. By and by, indeed, a leisurely Blowsabella of a serving-maid lays a coarse clean cloth and some knives and forks in what she calls the bavillon, a homely arbour at the garden end; and thither the Professor at once repairs, and seating himself at his place before the empty table, lays his watch before him, and seems to derive a bitter solace from counting the numerous moments as they pass, and announcing them by five at a time aloud to Rivers. But Rivers does not hear.

'Do not let us go near them,' he says in a cajoling, low voice to Belinda, wiling her away again into the sun and the flowers; 'in their present frame of mind it is not safe.'

'Well, you know it is not the first of April, and you *have* made fools of us!' she answers, a little drily.

'Are you starving?' he cries, roused into sudden, tardy compunction.

The Professor's and Sarah's pangs had left him cold as a stone, merciless as Herod.

'Famished!' replies she; but she says it with such a charming smile of absolute well-being, making mirthful her grave lips, that his misgivings fly. For all they care, the kalbfleisch may be an hour, two hours, three in coming!

It has been smoking for a couple of minutes, indeed, on the table, and the Professor and Sarah have been seen greedily to help themselves before they think it worth while to draw nigh. When at length they do:

'It is uneatable!' says the Professor, laying down his knife and fork with a shocking calmness, and regarding Rivers, as he approaches in his infuriating, senseless radiance, with a glassy look of vengeful despair.

'Impossible!' cries the young man, hastily helping himself, and boldly taking a good mouthful. 'Pah!' changing countenance; 'but it is, though! What filth!'

Nor is this expression, albeit strong, at all too strong to qualify the *plat* now set before these hungry persons. In the first place it is but too clear that the kalb has originally died a natural death, and has afterwards, perhaps in order to disguise this slight accident, undergone every possible variation of baking, boiling, roasting, stewing, frying, seething! But, after all, it is not disguised.

There is a blank, sulphurous silence. They all look at Rivers.

'I thought,' says the Professor, in a cutting, small voice, 'that you gave us to understand——'

'What does it matter what he gave us to understand?' cries Sarah, in a fury, rudely interrupting him. 'The more fools we to believe him! It would be more to the purpose if you or he or anybody would give us to understand how we are to get back to Dresden alive !'

Another murderous silence, broken this time by Belinda diffidently syllabling the word 'eggs.'

'Eggs, of course,' cries Rivers, snatching at the happy suggestion, and darting a look of enamoured gratitude at her who has made it. 'How stupid not to think of them before ! nothing in the world better than a fresh egg, nor more nutritious !'

This last clause is a poor little sop thrown to the Professor's ireful maw. In a moment he has fled swift as any scudding rabbit to the house, and in two seconds more is back again, beaming.

'Of course they can have eggs—any number; and in three minutes at the outside they will be cooked.'

But the three minutes pass, and three more, and three more again.

'I wish,' says Sarah, addressing herself in a tone of the most intense and poignant crossness to the young man, 'that you would kindly sit somewhere where I could not see you ; I think I could bear it better if you did. You look so idiotically cheerful !'

Even as she speaks, the Dienstmädchen comes into sight, sauntering deliberately down the path ; having by her want of sympathy with their sufferings clearly amply dined herself, and with a plate upon which many eggs are drunkenly rolling about together in her hand.

At this simple sight the Professor smiles faintly, and even Sarah's sulky brow grows smooth. But, alas ! too soon do they exult ! It takes but one glance to show that no new-laid eggs are these, milky and warm, over which the triumphant hens have but just ceased chuckling. Elderly, nay, veteran eggs are these, as their dirty, mottled hue but too plainly testifies. The only wonder is how a single family can have become possessed of so many addled eggs at once.

'You had better take care how you open it !' says Rivers, laughing nervously, and with an ill-timed attempt at a joke, as the Professor cautiously cracks one, his fellows looking breathlessly on ; 'it will probably go off with a bang !'

Nobody smiles.

CHAPTER VII.

'I HAVE cut my own throat,' says Rivers ruefully, taking six addled eggs out of his pocket, in which he has carried them off, to prevent their being imposed as fresh upon any more unsuspecting travellers.

It is somewhat later in the day. They have shaken the dust of Lohmen off their feet; have tramped, faint and silent, along a charming road whose wayside flowers they do not see, and through a long straggling village whose high-pitched roofs and general picturesqueness they execrate, to Loch Mühle, whither, with premature confidence in the Lohmen Gasthof's powers of entertainment, they had sent on the carriage. They have passed down a gentle incline, and found at the foot the mill-house, sitting by the brisk mill-stream. The Frau Müllerin has brought them out excellent milk, coffee, cakes, and eggs, unimpeachably, splendidly fresh, and they have eaten them at a snowy-draped deal table, to the sound of the whizzing mill and the dripping water and the carolling birds. Here by the riverlet sits the floury mill, and past it the quick stream runs, and over a small weir, a few yards higher up, the noisy bright water pours. Ostensibly to look at the weir, but in reality only urged by that rage for being *tête-à-tête* which possesses such happy fools as they, even if it be only to say to one another, 'How much dust!' or 'How many flies!'

Belinda and Rivers have left their companions, and now stand side by side at the river's edge.

'They might have got over the veal!' says Rivers, pensively regarding the eggs in his hand, previous to hurling them with vindictive force, one after the other, across the stream.

'Never!' interpolates Belinda, with emphasis.

'But it was these that gave them the *coup de grâce!*' adds the young man, wrathfully aiming the last one at an opposite rock, against which it breaks with a dull, addled thud. 'I suppose they will never make an excursion with us again?'

'Never!' repeats Belinda, with still more energy. 'I am sure that I would not, if I were they.'

'Then next time,' says Rivers hurriedly, and looking away, 'we shall have to go by ourselves.'

It is the most audacious and leading speech he has ever made her; and whether it be his own audacity or the picture his words have conjured up, his voice trembles. What a picture! A whole long summer-day!—she and he together, and alone! A day when he need never take his eyes off her; when he would ask leave to lie at her feet, and might pull her flowers and soft grasses, and could count her eyelashes and each breath she sweetly drew; and perhaps, at the very end of the day, if he were very good, and she in a very gentle mood—he has to own that she is not always gentle—she might give him one of her long white hands to kiss—once, just once! In his imagination he is already feeling its cool satin beneath his lips, when her reply comes and at once knocks down his cardhouse.

'How likely!' she says curtly, also turning her head, but in the opposite direction to that which he has turned his.

'You would not like it, of course?' he says chapfallenly, and yet with a sort of slight interrogation in his tone.

She would not like it! To herself she almost laughs.

Is it possible that he does not guess that the reason why she has turned away her face is that she dares not let him see the stir and tumult that his mere suggestion has made there. But he would be very much keener-sighted, and a much greater coxcomb than he is, if he could draw this conclusion from her harsh and snubbing words.

'I never waste time,' she says chillingly, 'in speculating as to whether I should like or dislike what is absolutely out of the question.'

There is a slight silence. Rivers feels as if a large pail of half-frozen water had been thrown over him, and were now trickling down the nape of his neck. Belinda is still hearing, with passionate vexation, the sound of her own ungracious voice. Why is it that she never can hit the *juste milieu* of cool and friendly civility? How is it that her heart is so burning hot, and her words so icy cold? Her eyes, averse from meeting the reproach of his, look across to where, on the other side of the racing beck, the rocks rise straight up, and out of their clefts slight little fir-trees grow, grasping the stony soil with their shallow roots, and dainty green birches wave, and just-new creasy ferns droop and sprout, and hang their small spring ensigns.

'What an iceberg you are!' says the young man at last, in a low tone of irrepressible mortification.

'An iceberg?' she repeats, lifting one hand to her face, and with her forefinger and thumb gently pinching her own trembling under-lip. 'Yes; so I have often been told. I think,' after a slight pause, 'that I am a little tired of being told it.'

'Are you tired of *being* it?' says Rivers, sinking his voice still more, though there is no one but the brook to overhear him, and it is much too occupied with its own sweet chatter to attend to him, and giving her a piercing look as he speaks.

For all answer she leaves him at once, and walks with such speed as if a mad bull were behind her, back to the other pair of sweethearts. He follows her, despair at his heart—the light lover's despair, that is to say, that a frown engenders and a smile kills; thinking, heart-sickly, that he will now have to redeem his own rash forward step by half a dozen tiresome retrograde ones.

But fortune deals more kindly with him than he had expected of her. The Professor and Sarah are both asleep. Coffee is generally supposed to be a wakeful potion; but in their case, mixed in nice proportions with fatigue, ill-humour, and boredom, it has had a precisely contrary effect. The Professor's head has dropped forward on his chest—always a trying position to any one beyond rosy childhood; the veins on his forehead have started forward, the blood has run into his long nose, and his under-lip protrudes. It is clearly an unintended nap, which has overtaken him accidentally, in defiance of his rules, and contrary to his sanitary principles. Sarah's, on the other hand, is the slumber, deliberately undertaken, of a person who sees in sleep the most endurable mode of getting over an irksome period of time. Her feet, carefully covered by a shawl, repose on a chair in front of her; a light ulster, rolled up so as to form a little bolster, nicks comfortably into the nape of her neck; her head is so much thrown back as to afford an excellent opportunity for cutting her charming white throat.

A smile breaks over Belinda's face.

'It would be a pity to disturb them,' she says, whispering.

'A thousand pities!' assents he eagerly. 'Would not it be better,' speaking with a timorousness born of his late rebuff, 'for us to go out of earshot?'

She looks first at the mill, then relentingly at him.

'Should you think that there was a nice path beyond?' she asks demurely.

So through the noisy white mill they go, nodding friendlily to the powdery miller as they pass. Along the river path they saunter, rocks above their glad heads—rocks, not frowning nor grand, nor by any means very big and beetling, but with finest grass and yellow wallflowers nestled in their rifts, and making mimic gardens of their little ridges and crannies.

On their other hand the small river frolicking, and on its farther side rocks again, grass again, sun and flowers again : drooping birches and straight pines. At every step that carries them farther from the mill Rivers' spirits rise.

'I hope,' he says, chuckling over the recollection—'I hope, for his own sake, that Professor Forth will awake first. If Miss Churchill sees him as we have just done I would not give much for his chance !'

'And I would not give much for it, whichever wakes first !' answers Belinda ominously.

By and by, though they are not at all tired, they sit down. After all, it is not so very unlike his vision—the vision that she had so disdainfully pooh-poohed. Nor when she speaks does she, as he half feared that she would, break the illusion, for her voice is gentle, almost apologetic.

'I should like to explain something to you, if you will attend to me.'

If he will attend to her ! Could he ever dare to think that any utterance of his idol's might be nonsense, it would be now. *If he will attend to her !* He who, if at dinner she asks him to pass the salt, listens with such entranced reverence as if it were to the Spheres together singing.

'Do I usually not attend when you speak ?' he asks, with timid irony.

He has rested his elbow on a little plat of soft turf upon the rock, and his head on his right hand, which brings him fully an inch and a half nearer her (in itself no despicable gain), and is feasting with leisurely rapture—there must be no discomfort of posture to mar such high enjoyment—on each slow turn of her head, on its thick white throat; and without any fear of Sarah's gimlet eyes derisively perforating him.

'I know,' continues Belinda, who is not leaning on either elbow, but is sitting very upright and looking shy—'I am conscious that I have taken things you have said to me— little harmless, unmeaning, civil things,' with a hasty blush of fear lest she should be supposed to have attached too much importance to them—'very awkwardly! very surlily!'

'Have you?' he answers ruefully. 'I do not think you have taken them at all! I think you have thrown them back in my face!'

'I know,' she answers penitently; 'that is what I wanted to explain to you. In point of fact,' no longer blushing, but looking at him directly with her honest eyes, 'I am not used to them!'

'Not used to civil speeches?' repeats he, in an accent of the most profound astonishment; he who when in her company is in a continual state of biting his own tongue out to prevent it from breaking into extravagant laudations; and who cannot but believe that all other created things are labouring under the same difficulty with himself!

She shakes her head.

'No; I am not. I suppose,' looking reflectively at the flower-lipped brook, 'that is an unusual case; I think it must be owing to my forbidding manner?'

'Then why, in Heaven's name, have you a forbidding manner?' asks he, in a sort of involuntary passion of wonder.

Even he cannot altogether deny the fact; and yet it seems so coarsely inconsistent with everything else about her. A forbidding manner with that throat, and those ears, and that nape to her neck! Her hair is dressed rather high in the French fashion, and she often turns her back upon him, so that he has a good view of it.

'Why have I a short nose?' replies she, with a good-humoured shrug; 'you might just as well ask me that! It is a misfortune with which I was born.'

But as he makes no light rejoinder—poor fellow! he is beyond it, up to his neck in the hopeless dulness of a serious passion—only enveloping her with the smothered flame of his silent looks, she grows shy and grave again.

'It *is* a *bonâ-fide* misfortune,' she says, slightly shaking her head; 'I have no wish to be forbidding. I think in my heart I am quite as anxious to please as any one else can be. I will even own,' with a brief, nervous smile, 'that I should like whenever I entered a room to hear a buzz of admiration run round it! No, no!' suddenly changing her tone and stretching out both hands forbiddingly towards him; 'do not try to say that I might now; if you do, I shall go back to the mill at once!'

'It would hardly be worth while,' replies he drily; 'you might put up with my clumsy compliments this once—by the bye, as it happens, I was not thinking of paying you one then—since it is, as you say, the last time!'

She has reddened painfully at the idea of having sought to avert a flattery which, after all, was not coming; but she tries to carry it off lightly.

'Perhaps it may not be the last,' she says cheerfully; 'we have always one resource left; we can ask Miss Watson to chaperon us. I never knew her refuse to go anywhere, at any time, with anybody, and she never has any previous engagement.'

He laughs, but adds quickly with reflective seriousness:

'She would be better than nothing.'

'She would be able, too,' says Belinda, idly rolling her open parasol to and fro along the narrow path in front of her, and smiling rather consciously at her own thoughts—'she would be able, too, to repair any omission she may have made in the catechism she put you through the other day. She might ask you a few more home questions as to your ancestors and your social standing, etc.'

'I am sure she is very welcome,' answers the boy straightforwardly; 'the only thing that I am afraid of, for her sake, is that she has already pumped me nearly dry! I think I have told her everything. What did I tell her—that I have just left Oxbridge?'

Belinda shakes her head.

'No, you did not tell her that; because if you had she would certainly have asked you at once if you had not been ploughed, or if you were quite sure that you had not been expelled!'

'That we live in Yorkshire?' continues he, aiding memory by lifting a hand to his forehead; 'that there are six of us? and that my father is an ironmaster?'

'An ironmaster!' repeats Belinda, suddenly discontinuing her idle fidgeting with her sunshade, and looking up with great animation. 'No; you certainly did not tell her that; an ironmaster, is he?'

There is such obvious surprise and pleasure in her tone that Rivers looks at her with some astonishment.

'Yes,' he answers, 'an ironmaster. Why, what did you think he was?'

But this is a question to which it is of course quite impossible that she can truly respond. How can she unfold to him Sarah's degrading supposition, nor her own relief at learning to what an eminently respectable branch of commerce his family belongs? An ironmaster, indeed! Why, it is the stuff of which merchant princes are made! So she only answers, with something of a stammer:

'Oh, I—I—of course I did not know! I had no idea!'

'It is to be hoped, for her own sake,' says Rivers, raising himself from his elbow, and looking proud and eager, 'that she will not get me upon the subject of my father, for it is a theme upon which I am apt to be long-winded.'

'Is it?' she answers, interested, while in her heart she is calculating how soon she can produce to Sarah this triumphant refutation of her suspicions. Probably not before they reach home.

'I know that one cuts but a poor figure swaggering about one's own belongings,' continues the young man, his love-sick air for the moment gone, and with courage and spirit in his eyes; 'but if ever a man deserved to be looked up to, my father does!'

'Does he?' now very much interested.

'If ever a man made a plucky uphill fight of it, it was he! Her heart feels a slight qualm. *Uphill!* it is clear, then, that he rose from the ranks. 'To begin with, he started in life without a penny!' The qualm grows sicker. He is going to tell her that his admirable father swept out the warehouse! Well, recovering herself, very creditable of him if he did, and Sarah need never know. 'My grandfather had got through most of his money racing,' pursues Rivers innocently. Her spirits run up like quicksilver. Though there is undoubtedly greater moral culpability in squandering your children's heritage in horse-racing than in earning them an honest livelihood with a besom, yet, such is the force of habit and association, Belinda is relieved that her lover's grandfather apparently did the one and left undone the other. 'And so father had nothing in the world but his younger son's share of my grandmother's fortune to look to; but he gave that up at once to the others, and faced the world without a stiver! You may think whether he had to put his shoulder to the wheel! For years he worked like a—like a navvy.

Poor dear old boy! when I think of what his youth was, and what mine is!'

He breaks off in genuine emotion, eyes kindling and hot colour rising. And Belinda, lovingly thinking how well such generous enthusiasm becomes him, keeps a sympathetic silence.

'And now,' continues Rivers, sighing—'now that we hoped he had got into smooth water, and might take breath and enjoy his life a little, comes this depression in iron; but,' his diffidence rushing back in floods upon him at the thought of how he has been teasing with his egotism his dear Lady Disdain, 'I do not know why I should bother you with all this!'

'I do not know why you should not,' she answers softly.

If only she could always speak in that tone! At seeing her thus gentle, approachable, humane, all his splendid hopes seem suddenly set within his reach. Would not he be a poltroon who deserved to lose them for ever if he did not now stretch out a hand to grasp them?

'I hope,' he says, not daring to look fully at her, and covertly, unknown to her, touching an out-lying ribbon of her gown to give himself courage—'I hope,' trembling exceedingly, 'that some day you will know my father.'

'Do you?' she answers curtly.

Instantly she has frozen up again. Her heart is beating even faster than his. Eager as he may be to make her known to whatever is nearest and dearest to him on earth; he cannot be more eager than she is to be made known; but her repellent voice and her chill face—in reality the outcome of a fierce shyness which she can no more master than she can control the course of her blood—give him to infer that in his last speech he has outstepped the bounds set him by her.

For a moment he keeps a hot, humiliated silence. Then, reflecting that he is but a dastard who can be beaten back from his heart's desire by one rebuff; taking comfort, too, from what she had lately told him as to her own shortcomings in manner, he plucks up courage for one more effort.

'I should like,' he says—but he has involuntarily moved half a pace further away from her, and in his tone there is less heartiness and more misgiving than before—'I should like you, of course, to know all my people.'

'Should you?' she answers drily; the very effort to steady it, the potency of the emotion which dominates her, making her voice hard and surly; and with a discouraging stiff laugh: 'I am afraid it is not very likely!'

There is a dead silence. For to-day there is no more fear of his transgressing her limits. He sits looking blankly at the brook. If, in the crises of foolish men's and women's lives there were but a go-between to interpret! But there never is!

For full five minutes the river loudly runs, and the finches piercingly sing, without any human noise to break in upon their concert. At last Belinda, who has been snatching re-morseful glances at the severe melancholy of her sweetheart's profile, hazards a timid propitiation.

'Have you many sisters?' she asks conciliatingly.

'Two,' he answers shortly, looking straight before him; 'but,' with a spurious smile, 'I have inflicted enough of my family upon you for one day.'

She is too much wounded to make any rejoinder, and the conversation, which before had flown as glibly as the stream or as the lark's roulades, drops into silence again. At their feet the rock-shadows couch. The sun's rays, no longer vertical, blaze obliquely upon the water and upon the sunlike dandelion flowers.

'It must be late,' says Belinda reluctantly, her eyes turning from the hurrying sparkles of the beck to consult his face; 'had we better be going back?'

She had hoped for an earnest protest from him, a supplication for yet a few moments more of their bright solitude. But none such comes! He makes no sort of objection; but, on the contrary, rises at once, and stands ready to attend her; and silently they return to the mill.

CHAPTER VIII.

‘ A whole long month of May in this sad plight
  Made their cheeks paler by the break of June.
‘ To-morrow will I bow to my delight,
  To-morrow will I ask my lady’s boon !’
‘ O may I never see another night,
  Lorenzo, if thy lips breathe not love’s tune.’
So spake they to their pillows ; but, alas !
  Honeyless days and nights did he let pass.’

‘WHAT a mercy it is to be alone for a change !’ says Sarah ;
‘is not it ? You do not assent with the warmth I should
have expected, eh ? And what a much richer and rarer
mercy it is that we are not to be driven a-pleasuring twenty
hot miles at a stretch, and carouse on rotten eggs at the
end !’

It is near noon, and the sisters are walking in the Grosse
Garten, that green and ample pleasure-ground, with its tall
trees and its intersecting drives, of the Dresden burghers.
Against a peevish sky the Museum of Antiquities lifts its
greenish roof; in its pool, with the little swan-house in the
middle, there is beginning to come a vernal glow from the
reflections of the young-leaved horse-chestnuts standing
round ; in the flower-beds the pansies and cinerarias bloom
purple and yellow.

Belinda’s only answer to her sister’s self-gratulations is to
stoop and console Slutty, who has returned in some disorder

from a slight excursion, having been coarsely hustled away by the shabby surly Polizei, who guard and pompously warn off profane dogs from the meagre blossoms.

'The beauty of these straight drives,' continues Sarah, thoughtfully eyeing one of the long vistas of trees that gradually lessens away to nothing, 'is that you never can be taken by surprise in them; nobody can pounce out upon you from round a corner; it is merely a question of long sight. Now, if I saw my admirer in the distance, I should simply whip behind one of these friendly trees,' looking up at an oak that, still wintrily brown, rises from the tenderly greening undergrowth. 'What would you do if you saw yours?'

'I do not know which you mean,' answers Belinda, with an awkward attempt at gaiety, for this morning she is not gay; 'I have so many!'

'No, you have not,' replies Sarah calmly; 'but you have one. How long you will keep him is another question. Judging by the crushed and flattened condition to which you had reduced him last evening, I should say probably not long.'

'At all events,' cries Belinda, whom this chance cut has stung more deeply than it was intended—'at all events, I had not reduced him to the condition of foaming rage to which you had brought Professor Forth. He said,' laughing unwillingly, 'that if he had not known that you were sincerely attached to him, he should have had difficulty in overlooking your conduct!'

'Do you think he will jilt me?' cries Sarah in a delighted voice, and with a radiant smile. 'No,' shaking her head; 'no such luck. My conduct was not good,' with a candid air; 'but it had its palliations—he fell asleep!'

'So did you.'

'But did I look like him?' drily. 'Anyhow, with my good resolutions, it was a case of "look in his face, and you forget them all."'

A pause. A solitary rider is cantering along the drive. A blue Gardereiter is practising his four-in-hand team of chestnuts in a sort of phaeton, up and down, up and down. The girls have reached a spot where there is a little quiet peep among the trees; a plot of lush green grass, vividly green, backed by sedate high firs, across which a few young birches are throwing their infinitely delicate leafage, and stretching their shining white stems.

'It seems he has a mother,' says Sarah presently, her eyes following the diminishing Gardereiter and his team.

'*Has! had*, you mean!'

'*Has.* I am afraid I let him see that I thought it a remarkable instance of longevity.' She stops to laugh, and then goes on, letting fall each little sentence with deliberate serenity. 'She lives with him; she is in her dotage; she never stops asking questions; and it seems that the chiefest of his wife's married joys is to consist in answering them.'

'Was it at that stage of his confidences that you cried out, "*Ceci est insupportable!*" and took to your heels and left him?' asks Belinda drily.

'It must have been somewhere about then,' answers Sarah modestly. 'He did not recognise the quotation, and he was displeased at the sentiment. However,' with a shrug, 'I will not do it again, for your sake, and in your interests; and if he does not fall asleep, and shoot out his under lip, I think I shall be able to hold out until we go. This is the fourth,' reflectively checking off the numbers on her fingers; 'one, two, three, four, five—in less than five weeks we shall be in London.'

'In less than five weeks!' repeats Belinda, stopping short and paling, while an expression of something very like terror looks out of the pupils of her dismayed eyes.

'In less than five weeks!' assents Sarah, nodding. 'I heard granny telling Gustel that she would not need her services after the first of June, and courteously adding how glad she would be to be rid of her. Pooh !' laying her hand on her sister's shoulder, and giving her a shrewd, good-natured glance, 'do not look so woe-begone ; it is only a case of hurrying the pace a little.'

Belinda's answer is a gesture of disgust. She walks quickly on.

'It is coarsely worded, I admit,' continues the other, briskly following, and keeping up with her ; 'but believe me, the advice is sound.'

And so it may be ; but as it is addressed to a person who is utterly incapable of making use of it, it is, like most other advice, wasted. To hurry the pace a little ! For days and days afterwards the vile phrase recurs to her, dinning in her ears. As often—and that is not seldom—as the terror which had seized her in the Grosse Garten returns, so often does the brutal consolation with which her sister had tried to allay it. And as the priceless days slip by—slip away out of the fingers stretched forth in such a fever to detain them —it takes in her ears a horrible inflection of irony. Over and over and over again it keeps saying itself to her, as she lies awake at night, hour after hour—she can lie awake with the best of them now—hearing the engines screech and the trains thunder along the Böhmischer Bahn ; watching the now withering blossoms drop from the pear-tree in the keen moonlight, and reckoning over to herself, until her brain grows dull and tardy sleep releases her, the small and diminishing hoard of precious hours during which there will be any object in living. For that what makes the essence of these days may not pass, may last on through a long transfigured lifetime, is a hope too glorious for her to dare lift her wet and dazzled eyes to its face. And meanwhile the days themselves are passing! Oh, how they are passing! To hurry the pace ! How *can* she hurry the pace ? she asks herself desperately, in the watches of the night, unconsciously accepting the detestable phrase. What can she, being she, do? How can she, tied down by her nature, by her stiff-necked virgin pride, by the very force of her dumb, pent passion, put out a finger to help herself? As easily can she make the gray irises of her eyes coal-black. Is it her fault that all strong emotion with her translates itself into a cold, hard voice, and a chill set face? With other women it translates itself into dimples and pink blushes and lowered eyes. Ah! but do they feel as she does? Sarah, for instance. When do men ever leave Sarah's company with the down-faced, baffled, white look with which Rivers has more than once quitted hers? Preening themselves rather; with sleeked feathers and cosseted vanity.

'I am not of the stuff of which the women that men love are made!' she says, thinking with an envious humility of her sister's graces, and staring blankly at the stove, beginning to glimmer white in the dawn. But for such a radical fault of nature and constitution what remedy can there be? Tamely to copy her sister's airy charms and light coquetries?

'It would be the donkey playing the lap-dog!' she cries bitterly.

And yet, despite all their mischances, and their agues, and their desperations, what superb days these are! Few? Yes, perhaps. But when one reflects how much acute happiness may be packed into five minutes, and how many five minutes there are in a month, these two may be accounted to have been largely dowered, seeing that to many a one, not held to be specially spited by fortune, it is not given in all his or her lifetime to attain to one such day. Days when round each corner lurks a splendid possibility; days when each ring at the bell may mean that Heaven has opened. Very often it means nothing of the kind; it means Miss Watson, or Gustel, or a parcel, but it *may.*

In later life you may be as fortunate as you please; a laurel garland round your head, a colossal balance at Coutts', a chaste, fond wife and paragon children, but Heaven can no longer pounce upon you from round the street corner.

> 'Parting, they seemed to tread upon the air,
>   Twin roses by the zephyr blown apart,
>   Only to meet again more close, and share
>   The inward fragrance of each other's heart.'

Yes, superb days! though on one or two of them the east wind blew piercingly, sweeping across the wide plain; and on another one or two the rain slid down from the heavy clouds, and blurred the windows.

But if it blurred the windows, did it not thereby make the task of Miss Watson's spyglass a more difficult one? and could the wind reach them in the little pine-wood behind the bleak Barracks, where they walked safe and warm on strewn fir-needles, and listened to its harmless scolding far above their happy heads.

How often they meet! how perpetually, how always! In the Alt Market, buying jonquils of the ugly German Fraus, as they sit under their great cotton umbrellas, queening it over their carrots and radishes; with the old houses, all different heights and shapes, russet-red roofed, endlessly dormer-windowed, standing round; at Plauen under the cool cherry orchards; at Meissen, in the hot Fabrik; in the Neu-Stadt, in the Alt-Stadt—everywhere. If, in after years, they revisit the bright city, what spot in all its precincts will be empty and innocent of associations to them?

Superb days! But they are going. Racing-pace they gallop by. How will it be when they are gone?

As the time passes, she grows ever less and less in a condition to face this problem. By and by she refuses to face it at all. When it comes it comes; but till then let her not be defrauded of her birthright. Let her, too, like

the Mayflies and the Painted Ladies, have her span of careless, giddy bliss.

Whenever the conversation turns upon their departure,
their journey, their arrival in London, upon anything that
lies beyond the horizon of the now and the here, if it be
possible, she leaves the room; if it be not possible, she
feverishly seeks to divert the talk into other channels.

But if she can fight thought off pretty well in the day,
the variegated, distracting, kaleidoscope day, it indemnifies
itself at night. At night there it is, and nothing but it; no
flickering leaves, or scudding clouds, or passers-by; nothing
but it: an image drawn on night's plain black canvas with
a hard, cutting clearness, as of an acid biting into steel; so
that she must look at it.

As for her, at this time she would be thankful that there
were no night at all. She does not need its refreshment.
Without it her every power seems strung up to the highest
pitch of efficiency, and she dreads, oh, how she dreads its
solitude and silence! In the daytime, however unconven-
tionally early or improbably late may be the hour, there is
always a possibility, nay, a likelihood, of seeing his strapping
figure and his burning eyes following the infant stolidity of
the page, Tommy, into the salon. But in the night this is
impossible. The night, therefore, is time absolutely wasted;
now, too, when there is so little time left to waste. Of what
use is it but for lying broad awake in, counting up how
many hours the different moments, half-hours, of their meetings make? To her, just so much of life is worth reckoning
as life at all; the rest is unimportant padding.

And he? As to him the pavement of the quiet Lüttichau
Strasse before her door is worn hollow by his footsteps; his
eyes devour her; his tongue stutters in lame speech to her,
and altogether omits to answer when addressed by any one
else. He has abandoned all other occupations in life but

that of dogging her. But he has not asked her to be his wife.

To how much more purpose would be that one short practical question than all his resultless, love-sick manœuvres; than all the enormous nosegays with which her room is over-filled and over-scented—for she cannot bear to throw away even the dead ones.

Perhaps this thought crosses her mind now and again. It certainly does Sarah's. It not only crosses it, but finds not unfrequently egress through her lips.

And meanwhile May is three-parts over. The 24th of that month is reached, and, indeed, is almost ended; for dinner is past, and the girls and their grandmother are loitering over their light and leisurely dessert.

Their grandmother is an old lady with a bright eye— strangely bright, considering that it has wept, or been supposed to weep, for a good-natured husband, five promising sons, and three dutiful daughters—with a skin that it is still no penance and that, if tradition lies not, it was once considered a high treat to kiss, and with a cap whose secret will die with her.

'Granny's religious principles are slack,' Sarah is wont to say; 'her morality is hazy, and in moments of excitement I have even known her let fly an oath; but, on the other hand, she is thoroughly clean, and she always laughs at my jokes; so that, taking her all round, I could better spare a better woman. One knows that if she were called upon for any of the sublimer virtues of life, she would be found wanting. But, after all, the sublimer virtues are the thousand-pound notes that one seldom needs to change, and granny has plenty of the sixpences.'

At the present moment her attention is absorbed in the effort, aided by a cracknel, to induce her new pug Punch to give three cheers for the Queen, with the thorough mastery

over which elegant accomplishment he has arrived credited.
On the present occasion, however, this talent seems inclined
to hang fire, for, though in general a remarkably free barker,
he is now, relatively to his sovereign, either disloyally silent
or irrationally incoherent. He will give ten cheers, or one
and a half, or five muffled ones and a sneeze, but he will
not give three.

'Granny,' says Sarah, desisting from a vain effort to make
Slutty cheer too, an endeavour which the latter frustrates by
instantly rolling over on her back, and remaining in that
position until all attempt at education is suspended—
'granny, do you know that we are going to have a long and
happy day at that everlasting Wesenstein to-morrow?'

'By all means, my dear; so as you do not ask me to go
with you.'

'I believe,' says Sarah, regarding her grandmother with
an air of cool dispassionate speculation, 'that if we were to
tell you that we were going to Greenwich Fair, or the Argyle
Rooms, you would say "By all means, my dears!" Only
that I am not at all so sure that in that case you would
add, "So as you do not expect me to go with you"!'

The old lady laughs pleasantly, as if her granddaughter
had paid her a compliment.

'Are you going to take your sweethearts with you?' asks
she gaily; 'your popinjays? No, Punch! three *cheers!*
Nobody asked you to sneeze for the Queen!'

'Our popinjays?' cries Sarah, delighted. 'Not mine,
thank God! By the bye, granny, as I have no further use
for him, I am thinking of arranging a marriage between you
and him. Your ages are suitable; and, though you have
slightly the advantage in externals, he is greatly your
superior in intellect,'

'God bless my soul! No, thank you, child!' replies Mrs.
Churchill with energy; 'I prefer Belinda's.'

'So do we all!' says Sarah, with a dry look.

At this last speech, Belinda, who has been growing ever hotter and more restless since the word 'Wesenstein' was mentioned, suddenly leaves her seat under the pretext of comforting Slutty. Slutty hates Punch and his tricks, and the *kudos* that attends them, and has now squeezed herself under a piece of furniture to which, in general, only Miss Watson's voice has power to banish her, and from beneath which there is now nothing visible of her but a small spiteful face, full of mortification and ire. As she firmly resists all Belinda's blandishing inducements to her to come forth, though the agitated beat of her tail upon the floor proves that she is not wholly unmoved by them, the young girl desists, and passes into the neighbouring salon, where, as there is no one to comment on her actions, she at once walks rapidly to the window, and looks eagerly down the dull and empty street. Not for long, however. Ere many moments have passed, a hand is laid on her shoulder; a rallying voice sounds in her ear:

'Come! he cannot be in sight yet! He will surely have the good feeling to let us swallow our coffee in peace.'

Belinda gives a great start, and angrily shakes off her sister's touch.

'I cannot think how it concerns you,' she says testily, in intense vexation at having been surprised on the watch; 'he does not trouble *you* much!'

'That is the rub,' replies Sarah calmly. 'If he did, my nose would probably be flattened against the pane as well as yours. But seriously, I should not mind how often he came—not much, at least—not more,' in candid parenthesis, 'than I always hate seeing other people made love to, if it seemed to lead to anything; but, as I live, I cannot see that you are a step further advanced than you were when I spoke to you in the Grosse Garten three weeks ago. Come now, are you ?'

For a moment Belinda is silent. Perhaps she has put that question to her own heart before now, and been as unable as now to give a satisfactory answer to it.

Instead of replying, 'What a mercy it would be !' she says irritably, bringing her hands sharply together in a wrathful clasp, 'If you could be persuaded to mind your own business, and leave me to be happy in my own way !'

'Happy in your own way !' repeats Sarah, with a shrewd look. 'Yes; and when he has taken his twelve German lessons and gone home to his papa, the ironmonger—ironmaster—what is he ?—how happy you will be in your own way then, eh ?'

The other's hands unclasp, her arms drop limply to her sides; a sudden cold pallor chases the fierce vermilion from her cheeks.

'I suppose,' she says slowly, 'that there is a sort of coarse and brutal common sense in what you say; but I wonder,' her voice breaking a little, 'that it does not occur to even you, that since I am I, and not you——'

'Granny and I both agree,' interrupts Sarah, 'that it is the most tedious courtship we ever assisted at. Granny's *idée fixe* is that it should be arranged by the first, so that he may travel with us and look after the luggage : for my own part, I rather doubt if even after the twelve lessons he will be able to take our tickets and order our baths ; at least,' breaking into a laugh, 'I know that my Schatz was not, though he is in correspondence with half the savants of Germany.'

Belinda has turned again to the window, but, that her motives may be beyond suspicion, she is ostentatiously gazing in the opposite direction to that whence Rivers will come. An occasional writhing, shivering movement of her shoulders alone betrays what suffering her sister's ruthless and irrepressible rummaging in her holy of holies is causing her.

'We do not blame him,' continues Sarah, with a candid air; 'in fairness, I must say that we do not blame him. He is always trying to pour out his poor little tale like water out of a jug; and you, for reasons best known to yourself, are always corking it back again. Mark my words,' emphasising the sentence with three pats on Slutty's chest —Slutty lying, as usual, reversed and Cleopatra-like upon her lap—'you will do it once too often!'

'What shall I do once too often?' cries poor Belinda in an agonised voice, wheeling suddenly round at bay. 'What *do* I do? If you could only explain that to me! I believe,' beginning to falter, 'that you mean well; I would—would try to take any hints you could give me.'

'I have always told you that your high and mighty airs would be the death of you,' rejoins Sarah, not perceptibly conciliated by her sister's humility. 'If you could make them up into a parcel and toss them into the Elbe, and perhaps throw in your high nose too, you would be a better and a happier woman.'

'But I cannot!' very regretfully.

'I confess,' says Sarah, after a pause, her eyes speculatively fixed on the two smart shoes extended before her— shoes whose unnatural altitude of heel, arch of instep, and crowding of lacerated toes proclaim them of the highest fashion—'I confess that I am a little disappointed that the news of our approaching departure did not bring him to the point. I should have thought that when that fact transpired, not even you could have iced him into silence.'

'He does not yet know that we are going,' replies Belinda murmuringly. 'I have not told him.'

'Have not you?' cries Sarah, joyfully leaping up and

beginning to frolic about on one toe. 'Courage! Then our best card is still unplayed!' Suddenly ceasing her frisking, approaching her sister, and speaking with great eagerness: 'You must tell him to-morrow, at Wesenstein. Choose a good place; well in the wood if possible, out of eye and ear and Watson shot. Be a little depressed, and make him ask you what is the matter with you. If you could let fall a tear or two? No? Ah!' with a gesture of impatience, 'I am sure you will spoil the whole situation! Dear me!' with an accent of sincere regret, 'what a charm‐ ing thing I could have made of it!'

'I will tell him,' replies Belinda meekly, yet wincing.

'If it is not brought to a crisis at Wesenstein,' pursues Sarah brutally, 'I warn you that I shall ask him his inten‐ tions. I have been trying to spirit up granny to do it, but you know how she always shirks every duty. It would have come better from her, but since she will not, I must. I shall tell him that you are wasting away! I wonder,' with an amused look at her sister's firm-fleshed, healthful beauty, 'whether he will be idiot enough to believe it?'

CHAPTER IX.

'But for the general award of Love,
The little sweet doth kill much bitterness.'

MISS WATSON has at length had her will. The party to
Wesenstein is hers; not, indeed, as to the defraying of its
expenses, about which she shows no ill-bred *empressement*,
but in the inviting of the guests, arranging for their trans-
port, etc. And as this arranging includes the right to bounce
not only into the sitting-rooms, which is a latitude she always
allows herself, but into the most secret chambers of the
invited guests, they begin to look with some eagerness
towards the end of this period of license. It is true that
Miss Watson meets with a good many refusals. The older-
established among the English residents into whose private
affairs her nose has been thrust throughout the winter
months, the details of whose butchers' bills, servants' wages,
discreditable members of their family, she has mastered
with grisly accuracy, combine in one deep and unanimous
'No.' Not less emphatic is Professor Forth in his negative,
based on the plea of ill-health. Nor do the very direct
questions addressed to him as to the nature and locale of
his ailments—whether he has anything wrong inside him?
—nor the confident assurance that it is all fancy, and that
what he needs is to have his liver well shaken up, by any
means avail to change his decision. But with all these deduc-

tions there is still left a considerable residuum of new-comers, who are at the stage—a very brief and early one—of thinking Miss Watson an agreeable woman who has seen a great deal of the world, a stage on which they will hereafter look back with indignant incredulity; of girls greedy for pleasure, and not fastidious as to the source whence it flows; and of handsome, solid, German soldiers, ready to follow wherever battle, beer, or maidens lead. To these is, of course, added Rivers—Rivers who hitherto has fled through back doors, has squeezed himself through attic windows, has bolted round corners, and run like a leveret whenever his long-sighted eyes have caught the farthest glimpse of a black-and-white plaid gown! For the last week this same Rivers has grovelled at the feet of the black plaid, has told her as nearly as he can conjecture the amount of his father's annual commercial gains, his sisters' probable portions, and whatever else—there is a good deal else—she may please to ask him. For does it not rest with her whether, during all the distance that parts Dresden from Wesenstein, he shall sit in glory and bliss in the same carriage with his mistress, opposite to her, so that her lightest movement may be felt thrilling all through him, eye drowned in eye, for ten or twelve delirious miles? or, parted from her, pine and rage in separation, with some senseless, smirking doll-face for *vis-à-vis*, and only now and again catch distant frenzying glimpses of his lady, exposed to the coarse homage of insolent hussar or fire-eating Uhlan?

He has attained his object, or he thinks so. The morning has broken in settled summer fairness. He has slept no wink all night. He has not broken his fast. He is first at the rendezvous. It is in the Lüttichau Strasse. For how long he kicks his heels in that gloomy thoroughfare he never knows. He would tell you that many hours passed before—several other unimportant ciphers having in the meanwhile packed themselves into various vehicles and set off—she at length comes stepping down the echoing stone stairs in her lofty, leisurely grace, clad in one of those lawny, lacy summer gowns, whose apparently inexpensive simplicity men innocently admire, and over the bills for which fathers and husbands wag their heads aghast. It is, in fact, her best gown, far too good for such an excursion, and its fellow is being thriftily saved by Sarah for future worthier London occasions. But to Belinda no occasion could ever seem worthier. She has taken her seat, and his one impulse is to spring in after her. It is only just in time that he saves himself from this fatal error.

Seeing that her companion, another young English girl, has preceded her, it follows that unless the Uhlan who is to make a fourth precedes him, the result will be that he, the Uhlan, and not Rivers, will sit knee to knee with Belinda through the long drive. As this idea strikes him, he takes his foot off the step again as if it had been made of hot iron, and hastily retreating, eagerly motions the other forward. But the innocent soldier, attributing this movement solely to politeness, and in that determined not to be outdone, smilingly waves him on, to which Rivers responds by a more desperate backing. But as in any contest of bows and ceremonies and formal civilities an Englishman must always go to the wall, the dispute ends in the worsting of the person to whom alone it is of any consequence to succeed, who sees himself hopelessly excluded from the post which he had watched and fasted to obtain; and who, pale, empty, and miserable, hurls himself into his corner over against the blooming miss, who has seen, understood, and resented his frantic efforts to avoid her.

They are off; out of the town now; stretching steadily away across the flat country, that is now nothing but one gigantic nosegay. Every look they give rests on new flowers. Every mouthful of air they draw in is the breath of lilacs.

The cherry-snow is indeed gone, melted away as quickly as its cold prototype in thaw. But its crowding successors, the flushed apple-blooms, the horse-chestnuts tardily breaking into pale spires, forbid them to remember or deplore it. What mood could be high or sweet enough to match the perfumed summer morning? Certainly not Rivers'. He has exchanged the stunned silence in which he passed the two first miles for a wild garrulity. He talks *à tort et à travers.* He says foolish things, the sound of which surprises even himself. He insists on buttoning his miss' glove : a task which—certainly from no pleasure in the employment— his trembling fingers are long in accomplishing. In fact, to be exact, he never accomplishes it at all. For the glove being too small, and the hand plump, he succeeds at last in giving the latter such a painful nipping pinch, in the effort to effect a union between starting button and distant button-hole —not by any means 'a lover's pinch that hurts and is desired' —that its owner angrily withdraws it.

From his garrulity he sinks back into a feverish dumbness, as apparently causeless as his former loquacity. How can his cruel cold lady look so calm and sunshiny under the hideous misadventure that has parted them? How dare she listen, with that sweet, high smile of hers, to her *vis-à-vis's* clumsy Teuton compliments? And what does he mean by crowding her so? Surely he could give her a little more room! And is she deaf, pray, that he must approach his ugly face so close to hers in conversation? Would not it be well to give him a hint that these are not the manners to which English gentlewomen are used? Happily his madness falls a little short of the execution of this wise project. And meanwhile the unconscious Uhlan, *sémillant,* pleased with himself, with his position, with his plain clothes

—rare luxury in which the stiff-buckramed German soldier is permitted to indulge in expeditions of this nature—airs his imperfect English, and slips from it continually back into his guttural mother-tongue, whither Rivers, despite the twelve lessons, cannot follow him, nor ascertain what amorous atrocities he may be committing in it. He is almost past deriving satisfaction from the perception of how ill-cut the plain clothes are, and of how much less comely poor Herr von——looks in them than he did yesterday in his showy uniform.

And Belinda? At first her disappointment, though decently hidden, had gone nigh to equalling his; but by and by the reflection that, once at Wesenstein—two short hours off—nothing but his own will can keep him from her side, makes her resign herself peaceably and civilly to the inevitable. Women know how to bide their time better than men do. They would pass but ill and discreditably through life if they did not. By and by, being but human and female, she yields herself to the influences around her; the soft and sugared air, the joy-drunk larks, the juicy grass fields thronged with bold dandelions and faint ladies'-smocks. What lady could ever be sweet or fine enough to deserve such a smock?

Past the rape-fields they go—rape so gloriously yellow that it looks like sown sunlight; past the pious-looking little German villages—high red roofs gathered at the church's knees; through the pleasant *freundlich* country, where everything is waxing in lusty length. And yet she is glad when Wesenstein is reached. Perhaps she would feel more emotion at arriving than she does, did she know the rational and humane intention nourished by Rivers, and which has kept him comparatively calm for the last three miles, to knock down the Uhlan upon the first sign of an intention on his part to help Miss Churchill from the carriage.

But, happily for the peace of the assemblage, the unconscious offender, attributing to insular brutality Rivers' unceremonious shouldering of him from the carriage-door, yields gracefully a privilege that he has no particular care to keep, and leaves to the other undisputed possession of Belinda's three fingers. They are the last of the party to arrive, and so have the advantage of finding preliminaries over, and luncheon spread and tempting under the trained linden trees.

Above the lilac-smothered cottages, and the cheerful Gasthof, beetles up the old white Schloss out of the solid rock on which it is built.

Between the Gasthof and the garden, where their white table-cloth promisingly glimmers, runs a little river, quickened and discoloured by last night's rain. It is spanned by a homely wooden bridge ; and on this wooden bridge Sarah is standing, employed in dropping bits of stick—little lilac sprays, anything floatable that comes handy—into the earth-reddened stream on one side, and then rushing headlong over to the other to see them come sailing and whirling through. In this mature pastime she is being helped by two large hussars and a Gardereiter. She is in the best of spirits, and has already told them all about the Professor, and how delighted she is to be rid of him.

The rest of the party are dispersed in summer sauntering about the bowery village, all but Miss Watson, who, following that God-given instinct which prompts the mole to delve, the beetle to scavenger, and the swallow to fly, is ravaging everywhere, red-faced and ruthless, making, marring, meddling. She has had a happy and instructive drive with some quite new-comers, and has succeeded, to their dismay and her own satisfaction, in extracting from them that they have a sister in a lunatic asylum. So that it is in high good-humour and content that—the complement of guests being now full—they all sit down to their homely feast.

It is true, that no sooner are they seated—seated as their own choice or as the lurking inclination of any two for each other prompts—than their hostess bustles officiously round to dislodge them.

'Three men together here, and two ladies there! Come —come! this will never do; we must manage better than this! Mr. Rivers, I must beg you to fly to the rescue: come and part these two ladies!'

In what spirit this request is received may be gathered from the fact that Rivers has at last attained to the one object and goal of all his hot vigils and fasting-days. His wooden chair is drawn up as closely as the legs of both will permit to Belinda's, and on her other hand he has successfully arranged an ugly ravenous fledgeling boy, of whom not even he can be jealous.

Though such is the quality of Miss Watson's voice, that nothing short of an utterly broken drum could prevent its finding entrance into any ear, he adopts the desperate feint of not having heard, not even when she repeats her order in a sensibly louder key.

'Had not you better try some one else?' says Sarah drily, coming to the rescue; 'it is odd, but he does not seem to hear!'

'I cannot have spoken loud enough,' rejoins the other with unconscious irony. '*Mr. Rivers!*'

'You will have to put up with Herr von Breidenbach!' says Sarah, this third appeal having met with the fate of its predecessors, glancing up at her spare hussar, who—no lady having more than two sides, and his brother soldiers having been too quick for him—is hanging lingeringly over her chair-back, reluctant altogether to abandon her even for beer and Schinken, and having just overtaken her last joke and begun to roar at it. Under these circumstances, neither is he particularly keen about obeying Miss Watson's command. However, a wily look from his maiden, promissory of far better things after luncheon, sends him off fairly contented, and the storm is averted.

'It is sad for a young man, being so deaf, is not it?' says Sarah, with her innocent air.

'Is it in his family?' asks Miss Watson eagerly. 'It is in some families, you know. In some families every member is deaf from childhood. All the Champneys of Nether-Stoney are deaf. I must ask him whether it is in his family!'

And this little squall—after all only the threat, not the reality of one—is the sole break in the golden halcyon sunshine of what Rivers, though he ate next to nothing—and that next to nothing may have been horse, or hippopotamus, for all he knew to the contrary—now looks back upon as the most regal banquet of his life.

What banqueting-hall, indeed, painted with goddesses and fair sea-women, could equal the low linden-roof above their heads? What hall-hangings could come nigh the soft little red vine-leaves, and the tiny tendrils just beginning to twist their airy fingers round the wooden trellis? What chamber-music could surpass that of the full brook and the larks?

By and by, it is true, both are drowned in the noise of the ever-waxing talk and laughter. They are almost all young; they are out on a spree; they have been hungry and now are full; is it any wonder that it needs but a very little jest to set them all off in clamorous mirth?

There is presently a Babel of tongues. The end of Miss Watson's story of how she sent in her card, and finally forced her way in, to the Great Llama of Thibet—a tale which strangers regard as a bad and glaring lie, but which her acquaintances feel to be not only probable, but true—is lost in the general din.

Sarah is in her glory. She has been nibbling marrons glacés, and teaching her soldiers to play bob-cherry with some fine forced fruit contributed by Rivers, regardless of the famine price he paid for them, to tempt his lady's palate.

Rewarded by the *succès fou* of this accomplishment, she proceeds to exhibit several others, not included in the curriculum of an ordinary education; the most admired among which is that one—not so widely known as its simple ingenuity deserves—of crossing the fore and middle fingers, and slowly passing them down the bridge of the nose, thereby discovering a chasm of great depth, apparently parting the nose into two. Before long there is not a soul at the table whose fingers are not travelling eagerly down his or her nose, some to verify the discovery as new, some to enjoy it as old. Hussars, Gardereiters, Uhlans, combine to cry ' Famos !' 'Kolossal !' And when at length chairs are pushed back, and the cherries and the revel are together ended, Sarah finds her court swelled by the admirers of almost all the other girls, unable to resist the attractions of a maiden who, to such *Veilchen Augen* and such a figure, adds talents of so varied and unusual an order.

They are so occupied in thronging round her, and she is so obliging in promising to teach them, one and all, many more tricks by and by, that Miss Watson's bawling command that they are now all to go over the Schloss passes for some time unregarded.

In time, however, she collects them, the unwilling as well as the willing — the former greatly preponderate — and sweeping them off out of the sunshine and the merry summer air, gives them into the charge of a surly, high-flavoured, and grasping-minded Verwalter, who leads them through an endless enfilade of bare rooms, cold and dank even on this warmly-honeyed May-day, and fleeces them at the end.

CHAPTER X.

'He tells her something
That makes her blood look out.'

MISS WATSON'S tyranny, however, one pair succeeds in evading. By a cautious and judicious loitering until the tail of the plaid gown has been seen safely to whisk round the corner they find themselves free, absolutely at their own disposition, for as long as the Verwalter's windy narrative may last, and with all the Schloss garden for their own—all its sunshine, all its shelter, all its old world grace.

Sun-petted, defended from each one of Heaven's rough winds, it lies at the Schloss foot. Around it rise the woody hills, the humble low hills of a flat country, but now with their humility made proud, with their insignificance rendered significant, by the inexpressible magnificence of spring.

Into the very core of Belinda's and Rivers' happy hearts has the spring spirit passed. Too happy for common speech, they sit on a time-worn stone bench, with their young and radiant eyes pasturing on the sweet, still prospect; the high and ancient Schloss, clock-towered and red-roofed, soaring out of the plenteous new leafage; and seen down a vista of thick and venerable hedges, so accurately and squarely clipped that not a leaf projects from the verdurous primness, an old stone Flora, with her lap full of garden flowers. On the prospect, I say, their eyes pasture; but from it they continually turn to each other's faces, as being yet lovelier and more joyful.

'Try to be a little depressed!' Crossing her secure bliss, Sarah's worldly-wise precept flashes, only to be contemptuously dismissed. What needs she any mean ruse to gain him?

For the moment, doubt and fear have vanished from her heart, cast out and slain by an exultant certainty of joy. How dare she, looking in his face, have any mean and unworthy misgivings as to his being wholly hers, body and soul, through all time, and through whatever may follow time? How could she, even if she wished it, feign to be low-spirited? she, in comparison with whose high and passionate content even the larks are melancholy and the river dull? What need have they for coarse and clumsy words? But, after all, words, though coarse and clumsy, are the coin in which human creatures must pay each other, and failing in which, they are often bankrupt for life.

It is doubtful whether Sarah would give much approval to a conversation—if such it can be called—of so highly unpractical a cast—a conversation made up of hot sighs, and torrid looks, and broken syllables of ecstasy; but in which there is not the most distant allusion to either priest or altar.

It is broken in upon before it has reached a more articulate stage by the voices of the Schloss seers, who, their task happily accomplished, every cold room and bad daub faithfully seen, are now let loose, like schoolboys at noon, upon the silent garden.

> 'Like to a moving vintage down they came,
>   Crown'd with green leaves, and faces all on flame;
>   All madly dancing through the pleasant valley,
>   To scare thee, melancholy.'

In a moment there is not a trim walk or finely-gravelled alley that is not alive and noisy with jokes and merriment. They intercept the view of the Flora. They steal the cowslips and little white saxifrage that grow on the sternly prohibited grass. It is impossible to escape their laughter and their eyes. They are everywhere. More universally pervasive than any one else, more turbulent, more wildly hilarious are Sarah and her little court. But yet there is a method in her madness, as her sister has soon occasion to discover; for, protected by the noise of voices round her, she presently draws Belinda aside, to whisper in the hardest, soberest, common-sense voice, 'Has he spoken?'

Belinda, thus suddenly dragged down from the empyrean, shrinks wincingly away without answering; but in vain. 'Has he?' repeats the other resolutely, taking hold of her wrist in detention; and as a faint unwilling headshake confirms the suspicion she already nourishes, 'More shame for him!' she says quickly; 'try the wood.'

There is no time for more. Next moment she is off—a frolicking madcap—with her hussars. If Rivers had overheard her—for one dreadful moment the thought flashes across Belinda, 'Is it possible?'—he could hardly have worded his next sentence differently.

'What a bedlam they have made of this!' he says, casting an irritated glance round on the Bacchic crew; 'shall we try the wood?'

Five minutes ago she would have assented gladly, not less thankful than he to escape from the empty din; but now the consciousness of the coarse and business-like intent with which, did she comply, she would be seeking those innocent shades, makes her answer with almost all her old coldness:

'I think we do very well here!'

He does not press his request; only that look of blank disappointment that she knows, comes like a creeping, chilly fog across his passionate fair face. He, too, is precipitated from the heights. They walk stupidly along, side by side, for a space. Afterwards they reflect, in bitter looking back, that they must have wasted quite a quarter of an hour of their one high holiday. Not more than a quarter, however. By the end of that time they have twice met Miss Watson, and been closely questioned by her as to what they were talking about. Once, indeed, the better to investigate this, she has joined them for several paces, and would probably have remained with them, had not the sight of another *tête-à-tête* that looked even more absorbing than theirs, ravished her away to disturb it.

No sooner is her broad back averted, than 'You were right,' says Belinda, turning to the young man with a humorous yet trembling smile, 'the wood is best.'

'Then, for God's sake, come there at once, or she will be after us!' he cries, with a hot and tragic eagerness ludicrously disproportioned to the occasion that has called it forth.

She does not now need to be twice bidden, and away they speed, casting apprehensive glances over their shoulders, glances that see black plaid gowns in every harmless bush, until the safe covert of the wood is reached.

That is not long. It is only a few paces off, just beyond the garden. And yet, near and accessible as it is, none of the revellers have as yet divined it. It has, indeed, a too-much-frequented air, of which the well-beaten pathway tells ; but, for the time, it is silent and safe.

She has sat down, a little quick-breathed from her run— they have even descended to running—on the pathside grass, and he has flung all his supple long length at her feet.

'So we are alone again,' he says, drawing a heavy sighing breath. 'My life is now one long manœuvre to be alone with you ; and how seldom I succeed !'

She laughs nervously. With whom but himself does it

lie to command her company while life lasts? She has no longer the heavenly confident certainty that blessed her in the garden. She has changed it for a hot and doubting unrest; for an avoiding, and yet at the same time for a contradictory craving to meet and answer those madly asking eyes. Why is it that the eyes alone ask?

'Perhaps it is as well for you,' she says, with a tremulous brusqueness.

'What do you mean?' he asks, speaking hardly above a whisper; already the dread that he has advanced too far, and that for the hundredth time she is going to freeze him back again, beginning to stay the beating of his leaping heart.

'I mean,' she says, forming the words with immense difficulty, and in a tone that to herself sounds dry and forbidding, 'that perhaps you would not find the charm of *tête-à-têtes* with me increase in the same proportion as their frequency.'

'Will you try me?' He cannot speak above a whisper now. How is it likely that he should, when his burning heart has sprung up into his throat and is choking him? Has not he thrown the die, upon which his universe turns?

But to her his four words have an ambiguous sound that may mean all or nothing. How, then, can she answer them?

There is a silence. So hushed and sleeping are all the winds that not even any one of the young leaves above their heads rubs, slightly rustling, against another. If those leaves, or the flowers on which they lean, or the birds of heaven could but have been interpreters between him and her! She has taken off her gloves, the better to pull the fresh grasses near her, and her right hand now lies palm upwards on her knee. Upon it his eyes, sinking for a moment from her face, have greedily fixed themselves.

What could not those five slight fingers give him, if they would?

'Why are you looking at my hand?' she asks, laughing unsteadily. 'Can you tell me whether I have a good line of life? do I live long? am I happy? do I'—'marry,' she is going to say, but she stops herself—'is there any great misfortune or dangerous illness in store for me?' She is talking rapidly and *à bâtons rompus,* feeling that she must find words of some kind, no matter what, to fill up that too pregnant silence; feeling that the cool-breathed wood is stifling, and that if she pause for one moment her tears will have way and for ever disgrace her.

For all answer, his heart-hunger mastering him, the poor boy fastens on the hand of which she speaks. There is a singing in his ears and a fog before his eyes; but he has it. In his own shaking fingers he holds that sacred palm, that never before, save in meaningless comings and goings, has he touched. In all its satin warmth and smoothness, it lies in his. Will he ever let man or devil rob him of it? He would tell you 'No.' So the supreme moment has come, and she recognises it.

'Do you see that I am to take a long journey?' she says, stooping her quivering face over their two locked hands.

What more propitious moment could even Sarah choose in which to tell him of their departure? But she does not think of Sarah.

For a moment he seems not to take in the meaning of her words. Is there room in all his seeing, hearing, understanding, for aught but the one surpassing fact that his lady has deigned at last to lay her hand in his, and that her starry eyes, soft, merciful, passionate, are, through a splendid curtain of tears, bent on his own.

After a while, 'Are you going away?' he says mistily. Even yet words come but strangely to him, and his head swims.

'Yes,' she answers, she, too, scarce knowing what she speaks; 'the cherry-blossoms are gone, and the lilacs will soon go, and so must we!' Often beforehand has she rehearsed the scene in which she is to tell him of her going. Imagination has tricked it out in various shapes and colours, but the reality is unlike them all.

He expresses neither regret nor surprise—he expresses nothing. He only lifts the long lily hand that he holds, and laying its palm against his burning mouth, softly passes his lips to and fro over the little fair lines in which her history is written.

Where is his timidity now? It was only her displeasure that had ever made him afraid; and even he can see that there is no displeasure here. She is pale, indeed, but it is with the pallor of conquering passion; and very still, but it is the stillness of one who, looking up in awful joy, sees the dawn of a superb new world breaking upon her.

'Are you sorry?' she says, with a half-sob. 'You do not tell me whether you are sorry.'

He is no longer lying at her feet. He is kneeling in his beautiful glad manhood at her knee.

'*Sorry!*' he repeats, with a sort of ecstatic scorn. 'Why should I be sorry? It is only you who can ever make me sorry again!'

So it has come. For a moment she closes her eyes, as one faint with a bliss whose keenness makes it cross the borderland and become pain, and so is gathered into his strenuous embrace.

For one second she lies on his heart. For one second the breath of her sweet sighs stirs his hair. Their faces are nearing each other slowly, in the luxury of a passionate delay, to make yet more poignant the pleasure of their supreme meeting at last, when—

'Mr. Rivers! Mr. Rivers!'

What horrid sound is this that is breaking into and murdering the divine quiet of the wood? that is breaking into and murdering their diviner union? That sound once silenced, the wood will return to its stillness; but when to them will that moment ever return? When will that begun embrace be ended?

For one instant they remain paralysed and uncomprehending in each other's arms; then, as the voice comes again, the unmistakable brazen voice, from which in less crucial moments they have so often fled in panic aversion, comes nearer and louder, in obviously quick approach to them, they spring apart, and stand dazed and panting in wild-eyed consternation that the cruel work-a-day world has so early thrust itself again upon them, and that their heavenly trance is broken.

Belinda is the first to recover the full use of her senses.

'It is *she!*' says the girl, breathing quick and short, and putting up her trembling hands to her bonnet and hair to ensure that all is neat and tight and unbetraying. 'We might have known that she would have hunted us down!'

He does not answer. Perhaps his intoxication was deeper than hers, and that he has more ado thus suddenly to shake it off. Perhaps the rage of that lost kiss—of his arms emptied of, as soon as filled with, his heart's desire—makes sight and hearing still thick.

'Mr. Rivers! Miss Churchill! Mr. Rivers!'

How loud the voice is now! It must be only just round the next corner; and a heavy foot is audible, accompanying it.

'We had better go and meet her,' says Belinda desperately; and they go.

'So here you are!' cries Miss Watson cheerfully, coming

into view, evidently *en nage* from the speed of her chase.
'What a hunt I have had for you! Did not you hear me
calling? I called quite loud. Where have you been
hiding?'

'Do you want us?' asks Belinda, modulating her
trembling voice with excessive care; and, after all her
pains, wondering whether it sounds as extraordinary to her
interlocutor as it does to herself.

'I have been collecting everybody,' cries the other,
fanning herself. 'I think,' smiling, 'that I have collected
everybody now. I want us all to keep together.'

'Why should we herd together in a drove? Are we
Cook's tourists?' asks Rivers, speaking for the first time,
and in a tone of dogged brutality, looking murderously at
her. In his face is clearly expressed the sentiment of
Balaam: 'I would I had a sword in my hand, for then
would I slay thee!'

'I always keep my parties together!' replies Miss
Watson, still smiling. 'It is so much more sociable! It
spoils a party to break it up. When I was in the Holy
Land, we went a picnic to Bethabara, twenty-five of us on
donkeys, and we all kept together. If we all keep together
there will be no difficulty about collecting at starting.'

'We are not going yet?' cries the young man, for a
moment forgetting himself, and betrayed into a tone of
passionate apprehension.

'Well, not immediately, of course. There will be plenty
of time to explore this wood a little, if you feel inclined.
Whose wood is it? The King's, eh? Not much in the
way of timber; but then there never is much in the way of
timber in a German wood. Where does this path lead to
—have you any idea? What do you say to following this
path a little, to see where it leads to?'

They have fallen into a stupid silence. That paralysis

of the will which overtakes all upon whom Miss Watson bestows her company, has seized them with a numbing force proportioned to their frenzied inward revolt. She drives them before her, unresisting, through the wood.

* * * * *

'Well?' says Sarah, in a tone of the keenest and most urgent interrogation. It is night, and they are home again. The long twilight still lies on the city, but the hour is latish. The two girls have been deposited at their house in the Lüttichau Strasse, and are climbing the cold stone stairs to their apartment. 'Well?'

Belinda's answer is to quicken her pace and race up the remaining steps.

'Two can play at that game,' says Sarah, springing after her, active as a cat, and facing her again on the landing. 'Well?'

But before she has extracted any more answer than before, Tommy has opened the door of the *étage* and admitted them.

'Well, granny,' cries Sarah, marching briskly into the salon, blinking a little from the sudden light, taking the old lady's smooth face in both hands, and giving it a sounding kiss, 'here we are! We have had a very happy day, and I am engaged, more or less, to three people. By the bye, they are all going to call to-morrow.'

'I am delighted to hear it, I am sure, my dear, if it amuses you,' replies Mrs. Churchill, placidly rearranging the dainty tulles and laces that her granddaughter's embrace had ruffled; 'but I think I have heard something like it once or twice before.'

'And Belinda is not engaged at all!' continues Sarah indignantly, looking eagerly towards her sister to see whether this direct statement does not call forth any disclaimer. But none comes.

'You do not say so?' rejoins Mrs. Churchill, in a tone of civil but tepid interest, stifling a slight yawn. She does not care much about Belinda, who does not amuse her, while the 'Daudet,' from whose pages her grandchildren's entrance has roused her, does.

'Is it possible,' says Sarah, advancing with a threatening gesture to her sister—'do you dare to look me in the face and tell me that you have not brought him up to the point after all?'

Still silence, and a look towards the door suggestive of meditated evasion by it. But this move the other anticipates by placing herself between Belinda and all means of exit.

'Did you take him to the wood?'

'Yes.'

'Did you tell him we were going?'

'Yes.'

'*And nothing came of it?*' cries Sarah in a tone of such profound and unfeigned stupefaction that Belinda, though certainly at this moment not mirthfully minded, breaks into a laugh. 'Bless my soul, what stuff can you both be made of? Granny, what stuff can they be made of?'

But granny has gone back, true as the needle to the Pole, to her novel, and declines to take any further part beyond a slight shrug in her granddaughter's affairs.

'Well, you know our agreement,' continues Sarah, beginning to walk up and down in a fervid excitement, that contrasts with the elder woman's phlegm; 'you know our agreement: to-morrow—you may think I am joking, but I assure you that I never was more in earnest in my life —to-morrow I ask him his intentions.'

A charming flickering smile breaks like moonlight on water over Belinda's face.

' I give you leave !' she says in a voice that, though low and tremulous, is distinct.

Then, vanquishing all her junior's efforts to detain her, pushing indeed impetuously past her, she flies to her own room and double-locks herself in; nor do all Sarah's plaintive pipings through the key-hole and angry rattlings of the lock avail to dislodge her.

CHAPTER XI.

'The flower that smiles to-day,
　　To-morrow dies;
All that we wish to stay
　　Tempts, and then flies.
What is this world's delight?
Lightning that mocks the night,
　　Brief even as bright.'

HAD Miss Watson's eye been glued to her spy-glass, as for six or eight out of the twenty-four hours it invariably is, and as, strange to say, it is now about four o'clock, in the ensuing afternoon she would have seen Belinda Churchill setting off for a walk alone. Humanly speaking, not thirty seconds would have elapsed before that lady would have been across the street and down it to ask why alone? why not with her sister? and why not with the dogs? The dogs ask the the same question. A Dresden walk indeed, with their poor little snouts embedded in muzzles, is not by any means the same thing as an English one—free to dogs and men as English air; but such as it is, it is better than nothing. With a muzzle one can still scamper, and even give muti-lated sniffs here and there. The prospect of a walk is the one thing that restores to its pristine hyacinthine curl Slutty's tail, which ever since the arrival of Punch has limply drooped in envy and dejection; and as for Punch, there is no number of times that he would not bark for the

Queen, for Mr. Gladstone, for the devil if required, in order to attain it. To-day they both meet with an abstracted yet peremptory refusal.

'I am going to the Grosse Garten, Sarah,' says Belinda, giving this piece of information in a not very assured voice, and apparently grateful to the numberless buttons of her gloves for giving her an excuse for bending her head over them.

'Are you?' answers the other carelessly; then, as something in her sister's manner reveals to her how pregnant with import is the walk of which she speaks, adds in quite another tone, and with an accent of the liveliest sympathy: 'My blessing go with you. How I wish I could be behind a tree to hear how he does it! But, after all,' with a shrug, 'in these cases there is never much variety; they all say pretty much the same thing; they have no imagination.'

As Belinda reaches the door it is opened by Tommy, for whom Sarah has just rung.

'Now, Tommy,' says she, addressing the boy with an extremely admonitory air, 'if three German gentlemen come to call this afternoon, mind that you do not admit them all at once. If a second comes before the first is gone, you must tell him that I am engaged, and that he must call again later. Do you understand?—one at a time.'

She is still impressing upon the page's ductile mind the all-importance of letting in her admirers singly, when Belinda passes out of hearing.

Along the street she goes. One side of it is in burning sunshine, the other in deep shadow. It seems to her an emblem of the difference between her life before and after yesterday. Why did not she bring the dogs? So royally rich in happiness herself, why should not she toss what crumbs she can to any such of God's poor creatures as ask her?

The memory of Slutty's eyes imploringly bulging, and of Punch's disappointed bark as he trotted tamely away to his cushion, returns to her with a sort of remorse. She is glad when she has passed through the town and reached the Grosse Garten; glad to see the long, broad, green drives quietly stretching away; glad to have left the city noises behind her. And yet even they have sounded melodiously to her to-day. There is perhaps only one sound in the whole world that would not now echo agreeably on her ear —viz., Miss Watson's voice; and even toward Miss Watson how faint and lessening is her ill-will. It is true that she continued to bestow her company upon them yesterday for the remainder of the afternoon; it is true that by her tyrranic overruling they were sent home in different vehicles; but could even she prevent their one moment snatched at parting, with time for but a sentence in it—and that sentence *such* a prayer to her to meet him here to-day? After to-day she will give Miss Watson leave to thrust herself and her importunities between them if she can. As she makes this reflection she smiles. I think she walks along smiling.

The Grosse Garten is not much frequented; but now and then she passes a couple of loiterers, a single man or woman, a nurse and child. She pities them all from the bottom of her heart: not one of them is going to a tryst with Rivers. She has reached the rendezvous now, a bench beside the Teich; the dull and stagnant pool where the swans are royally riding in the sunshine. He is not here, he has not come yet. She is the first at the tryst. A slight pang of disappointment shoots across her; but in a moment is stilled again. Probably in her eagerness she has walked more quickly than is usual with her. Probably she has taken less time than she calculated for. She looks at her watch. It still wants five minutes to the appointed hour. She sits down on the bench to wait, and her eyes fall on the pool. How crowded with green reflections it is; how different from the weak and pinched leafage of three weeks ago, when she and Sarah last sat here! It has gathered all the horse-chestnuts into its bosom; fans and bloom-spikes, you can see them all again as plainly as, sometimes more plainly than in the reality; wherever, that is to say, the swans' webs' oaring has not broken up the mirror into bright shivers. The remembrance of her last walk here with Sarah brings back also the remembrance of their talk; of Sarah's advice to her to hurry the pace. The recollection brings a smile of happiness, and of pride too, over her face. She has used no manœuvres, she has descended to no tricky coquetries; and yet could even Sarah have won him more wholly than she?

It must be half-past four now. Again she takes out her watch. Yes, it is now five minutes over the half-hour; but then probably her watch is fast. It always gains. Reassured afresh, she patiently resumes her waiting. The bench on which she is sitting is almost exactly opposite the spot where on the first of May he had thrown her his intercepted nosegay. At the thought she smiles again; and this time it must be broadly, for a stranger passing by looks hard and inquiringly at her, as though imagining that her smile was a recognition of and greeting to himself.

In a second she is grave again. This place is too public; when he comes they will seek one of the more private paths. When he comes? But he is not come yet! Why does not he come?

She turns her head anxiously in the direction whence she expects him to appear, a creeping disquietude beginning, despite herself, to invade her heart. Is it possible that she can have mistaken his directions? Is it possible that, as she is waiting expectantly for him here, so may he be waiting expectantly for her in some other corner of the large pleasure gardens? But she dismisses the idea. Did not his few words drop, distinct and clear as articulate words could do, into her ear? Has not she been saying them over to herself ever since? There is nothing for it but patience.

Again she fixes her eyes, not so untroubled as at first, upon the Teich, the swan-house, the swans. To the latter a child is throwing bread; a homely burgher couple have stopped to applaud. In the fostering sunshine the horse-chestnut leaves seem to grow momently larger and greener as she looks. Why does not he come? A sense of hurt maiden dignity, of hot and cruel shame at being thus made to appear so far the more eager of the two, at being kept thus long and unworthily waiting at her first love-rendezvous, has come to complicate and intensify her anxiety. In all the mental pictures that through her disturbed and tossing night she has drawn of this meeting, the one contingency that has never crossed her mind as most distantly possible, is that he should be a defaulter from it; he, whose mad over-eagerness to fulfil any engagement in which she is to have a part, has over and over again kept him raging up and down the Lüttichau Strasse for hours and hours in rain and shine, in fervid waiting, until the time has come when he may decently make his appearance. And to-day he is already half an hour late! It is impossible—incredible! And yet if any untoward accident had occurred to prevent him, surely he would have written! Perhaps even now there is a note awaiting her at home. Goaded by this thought, she takes two feverish steps in the direction of a return; then, arrested by the reflection that he may arrive in her absence and find her gone, she stops in painful irresolution. To sit still and look at the swans any longer is at all events impossible.

She walks—but with how different a tread to that with

which she had at first approached the spot!—she walks a little away; not so far as to lose the bench, to which her hopes still cling, from sight, but far enough to get a good view down the great main drive. With her trembling hand lifted to shield her eyes, she strains her gaze eagerly down it. Oh, if she could but catch the most distant glimpse of him! Under the trees spreads in glory the dazzling strong spring grass, with its brightness toned down here and there by the shadows of the dark tree-trunks, that in their afternoon quiet lie stilly on it. There is nothing!

With a sort of sob in her throat that shocks herself, she is turning away, when, at the very other end of the avenue, she becomes aware of a man's figure that has suddenly come within eye-range. It is so distant that it is no taller than a pin; but surely it has something of his walk and gait.

Catching at this new hope, she advances quickly to meet the figure. Yes; it certainly has a look of him. Well, she will not upbraid him. No hurt self-love nor petty sulks shall be permitted to mar the heavenly harmony of the first outpouring of their hearts into each other. She will not even ask him why he is late. No doubt he has some good reason, which in his own time he will tell her. But, alas! she may keep her high resolves for another occasion. She will not need them now. It requires no very near approach to the stranger to reveal that he is not Rivers; that he is not even, when you come close to him, in the very least like him.

It is such a bitter disappointment that she turns into a side alley to hide her tears; but quickly drying them again, hastily returns to the meeting-place, in the panic fear that he may have appeared there from some unexpected point of the compass. But he is not there; and as she ascertains this, with a blank heart-sinking, the city clocks strike the half-hour. It is half-past five! For a whole hour she has been dancing attendance on his pleasure; waiting here, ridiculous and befooled.

With a movement of strong indignation she begins to walk swiftly homewards; but before she has gone five yards, her purpose slacks. She cannot yet bear to face the fact that this is what her day's splendid and apparently so sure promises are to end in—this humiliated, baulked, back-coming! She will give him five minutes more. Possibly, not *very* improbably even, he may have mistaken the appointed hour, and have thought that it was half-past five instead of half-past four. In that case he would be scarcely at all late, even now.

A little recovered by this new flicker of hope, she sits down. Yes; she will give him five minutes more, and during all these five she will not look round once, or send her eyes in search of him. Perhaps that will bring her luck. But it does not. The five minutes are gone, and he is not here. She gives him ten more, and then five again. Twice she repeats her little feverish excursion to the head of the main avenue; these times she is not even deluded by the will-of-the-wisp of a possible resemblance in any of the few saunterers that occupy it, to him whom she, with a now so evident hopelessness, seeks.

It is only the clocks striking six that at length makes her really and desperately turn homewards. Each one of their tranquil strokes seems to her the beat of a cruel hammer on her heart. But putting out of the question the bootlessness of any further delay, self-respect, at length aroused, forbids her to add any more moments to the humiliating and miserable hour and a half she has already spent.

'If I had had any proper pride, I should have gone home an hour ago,' she says to herself in bitterest dejection, as she passes along. She holds her head, usually carried a little loftily, well down. It seems to her as if everybody who meets her must read in her face her deep discomfiture, and the fool's errand on which she has been. She quickens her pace to get away from them; to be safe out of the streets so full of gaudy light, where at any time she may meet an acquaintance—worse still, one of their yesterday's party; worst of all, Miss Watson.

As she nears the Lüttichau Strasse her distress lightens a little; the hope of finding there a note, a message, some solving of this most inhuman riddle, buoys up her steps and gives life again to her looks. It cannot be but that there must be some clearing up of this wretched *contretemps.* It will have, as she says to herself, to be a very bright clearing up indeed, to indemnify her for the sufferings of the afternoon—that very afternoon whose anticipated joys she had pitied every chance passer-by that she met, for not being about to share.

'Well,' cries Sarah, standing in the open salon door, and looking expectantly beyond her sister's figure for another, 'Where is he? what have you done with him? I want to fall on his neck and kiss him. I have long,' laughing, 'been wishing for an excuse to do it, and now I have an excellent one.'

Belinda had not meant to have entered the salon. She had hoped to have slunk unperceived to her room; for has not Tommy, in answer to her fevered questions, philosophically assured her that there has been neither note nor message left for her in her absence?

'Do not,' she says hoarsely; 'do not laugh. I cannot bear it. He was not there; he never came.'

'Never came!' echoes Sarah in a tone of bottomless wonder, her pretty eyes and mouth opening with a stare and a gape. 'Then,' gradually recovering the power of speech, 'then where have you been, may I ask—what have you been doing all this time?'

'I have been waiting for him,' answers Belinda, try-ing to speak steadily, though at that humiliating confes-sion such a tide of crimson rushes over her poor proud face as one would think must leave all the rest of her body bloodless.

'But it is monstrous!' cries the other in a tone of the wildest excitement; 'ça n'a pas de nom; there is some mistake. He is a man, he is a gentleman; of course he has written—he has sent?'

Belinda shakes her head.

'No; I asked Tommy.'

'*Tommy!*' repeats Sarah in a tone of the most con-temptuous indignation. '*Tommy*, indeed! That boy is ripening for the tread-mill or the gallows, or both, as fast as he can. You will hardly believe that after what I said to him—you heard me—he showed them all up at once.'

Then, ringing the bell violently, 'Tommy,' she says very sharply, 'how dare you say that there is not a note for Miss Churchill? Of course there is a note. Go this moment to look for it, and do not come back without it!'

Paying no attention whatever to his asseverations, she waves him from the room; and then follow a few moments of painful waiting. At the end of them Tommy returns with, sure enough, a missive of some kind on a salver.

'I told you how it would be!' exclaims Sarah, triumph-antly pouncing upon it and the unlucky child at once. 'How dare you tell such a story, you naughty boy? Do you know where liars go to?'

And he may pour into her unheeding ear his faltering attempt to lay the blame on Gustel, who answers the bell when he is out; she does not hear a word he says. In a fury of impatient anxiety, she is stooping over Belinda's shoulder : Belinda, whose shaking fingers can scarcely tear the envelope asunder.

A thin blue paper falls out. It is the bill from a Porzellan Handlung for a couple of Meissen figures purchased there a week ago. In an uncontrollable spasm of misery she throws it on the floor and bursts into tears.

CHAPTER XII.

'STILL at dinner, are they? I shall not detain them a moment; I am sure they will admit me; they always admit me. No, I will not wait in the salon; I will join them in the dining-room.'

Such are the sentences uttered by Miss Watson's voice, and plainly audible through the door on that same evening, as addressed to Tommy, who is opposing his puny infant strength to the forcible breaking in upon his mistresses at their dessert by the before-mentioned lady. With what result may readily be guessed.

'Have you heard about young Rivers?' cries she, thrusting the boy aside and bursting in upon them.

They are sitting, as they have sat upon so many happier evenings, the one old woman and the two young ones, in their pretty *soigné* evening dresses. For the last three quarters of an hour Belinda has been struggling to solve the problem how to swallow. It is dreadful to eat, but it is still more dreadful to have your lack of appetite noticed and wondered at. Grapes are perhaps less difficult than most other things for an unwilling palate to deal with; and she has taken a few Muscats, and is holding a small bunch between her hot and listless fingers at the time of Miss Watson's bouncing entrance. Instantly they fall with a slight patter upon her plate.

'What about him?' asks Sarah eagerly, jumping up and running towards the intruder, while Mrs. Churchill drops the little red Alpine strawberry she is in the act of lifting to her lips, and says in an amazed voice :

'Dear me, Miss Watson! how you startle one!'

'You have not heard, then?' says the other loudly, in a voice of relief. 'I am the first to tell you?'

'Yes, yes; of course. What is there to tell?' As she speaks, Sarah places herself adroitly between their visitor and her view of Belinda, and mentally thanks her gods for the failing light and the unkindled gas.

'I was at the station this evening,' begins the other, only too happy to embark upon her tale; 'indeed, I have come almost straight thence.' She is in rather dishevelled morning dress. 'I went to see the Rays off. You know how much we have been together; they would never have forgiven me if I had not!'

Despite her anxious suspense, Sarah cannot avoid a sardonic smile. It is the open secret of the whole English colony that the Ray family has been compelled, by Watson assiduities, regretfully and at great personal inconvenience, to curtail their stay in the Saxon capital.

'I took their tickets for them,' pursues the unconscious narrator—'I never mind trouble—indeed, I insisted upon it. To tell truth, I was a little glad of the opportunity to find out where they were going to book to, about which they had made rather a foolish mystery, when, just as I was counting my change, whom should I see coming up to the ticket-office but young Rivers!'

'Well?' Even Sarah is a little breathless.

'"And what brings you here, pray!" I said. "Are you come, too, to see the Rays off?" He did not hear me. I was prepared for that; you know you explained to me that he was a little deaf. By the way, that deafness should be seen to at once, and so I shall tell him, if I ever meet him again.'

If she ever meets him again! Belinda is leaning forward in an attitude of the acutest strained listening ; her heart is beating against the edge of the table with loud, hard blows.

'He evidently could not have heard me,' pursues Miss Watson fluently ; 'nor seen me either, for the matter of that, as he turned sharp round and walked off in the other direction. Of course, as soon as the Rays could spare me, I went after him and overtook him.'

'Of course !' murmurs Sarah under her breath.

'I put my hand on his arm. "Come, now, where are you off to !" just like that. He shook my hand off—you know he never had any manners—that is why I think he must be related to the Stukeley Rivers ; they are proverbially rude, as a family. "What do you want ?" he said, just as if he had not heard my question. "I want to know where you are off to ?" I said. "Where *are* you off to ?" He hesitated for a moment, and then seeing, I suppose, that I was not to be trifled with, that I was determined to have an answer of some kind, he turned his head quite away, and said so low that I could hardly hear him, "I am going back to England to-night." Then he was away like a shot, and what with the confusion of the train coming in, and seeing that the Rays had all their parcels right in the carriage—of course at the last moment one was missing—I never caught another glimpse of him.'

She stops, out of breath, her narrative ended ; nor, for a moment, does any one of her three auditors comment upon it.

Belinda has sunk back in her chair, and round her the room is spinning. Sarah, Miss Watson, granny, the dogs, all are whirling. Mrs. Churchill is the first to speak.

'I suppose,' she says, in a voice still somewhat ruffled by Miss Watson's inroad, and picking up the sugar-sifter in her delicate old fingers, 'that he was tired of Dresden. There is nothing very wonderful in that. Punch, take your hands off the table this instant.'

'But it is so sudden!' cries Miss Watson, in a loud aggrieved tone, as if Rivers' departure were a personal injury. 'Why did not he tell us? He never told me; did he ever tell you he was going?' Nobody takes the trouble to answer. 'I am sure that yesterday, at Wesenstein, nobody would have said that he had such an idea in his head, would they now?' turning directly to Belinda.

By a great exertion of the powers of the mind over their weaker brothers of the body, Belinda has forced the room and the people to stand steady and still again. By a like exertion she frames a sentence, which, though short, is not conspicuously tremulous.

'No; I think not.'

'Probably he was telegraphed for home,' says Sarah, coming hastily to her sister's rescue, and trying to divert from her the brunt of Miss Watson's eyes and speech. 'Probably he had bad news!'

'I should not wonder,' answers Miss Watson, looking down on the floor for a moment in inquisitive reflection. 'I should not at all wonder. He looked like a man who had had bad news. In point of fact, he looked shockingly ill. I never saw a man so changed in so short a time. I am so annoyed with myself,' in a tone of the sincerest vexation, 'for not having asked him point-blank!'

'I should have thought that you might have spared yourself that reproach,' says Sarah; adding, as she casts an oblique glance in the friendly dusk towards Belinda, to see how she is holding up, 'Most likely one of his relations is dead.'

'I hope it is not even worse than that,' answers the other, in a voice of mysterious curiosity. 'I hope that none of his sisters have got into a disagreeable scrape. You know that,

in the world, the Rivers women have the character of being
un peu leste.'

It is not till every possible conjecture has been exhausted,
till the few facts known have been worn bare and shiny by
turning and handling that Miss Watson at length withdraws.
She would not have gone then, had not the idea suddenly
presented itself, that, if she make haste, she will be able
before bedtime to force herself and her news upon three or
four more households.

No sooner is the outer door safely shut upon her, than—

'Tommy is incorrigible!' says Mrs. Churchill, in a tone
of irritation. 'The number of times that I have impressed
upon him not to admit that woman on any pretext whatever,
while we are at dinner!'

'Pooh, granny! what nonsense you talk!' replies Sarah,
disrespectfully. 'When that great galleon bears down upon
him, what can a poor little skiff like Tommy do? Of course
she will come to breakfast and luncheon and dinner, and we
may think ourselves very lucky if she does not insist on
thrusting herself upon us in our baths.' As she speaks, she
puts her hand under her sister's heavy hanging, limp arm,
and draws her away towards the salon. 'If you will be so
slow, granny,' she says, with a parting laugh, 'we must leave
you to carouse alone. I believe you enjoy yourself more
when you have no witnesses of your gourmandise.'

But arrived in the salon, she no longer laughs. Belinda has
thrown herself flaccidly into a chair. The curtains are un-
drawn, and through them her eyes stare out upon the street—
the street where, through the deepening gloom, the lit lamps,
but now such insignificant yellow specks, are beginning to
gain importance and use—the street so continually worn by
his eager footsteps, where she has so often heard them, up
and down, up and down, waiting, watching, for hours, if it be
past all seemliness and moderation for him to venture a visit,

on the bare chance of her throwing him out one parting
smile. All through dinner she has been dreading the evening
—dreading its suspense, the bell that will ring now and again,
the intervals that will elapse, and then the blank silence,
nothing resulting, showing that it was not he who rang.
Well, suspense is over and gone now; but she would be glad
to have it back again, seeing that it has taken hope with it.

'Well,' she says after a pause, looking up wearily at her
sister, who stands beside her with her fair arms folded and
her white brows bent in an attitude of serious reflection
very unnatural to her; 'well, what do you say now? Who
was right now?'

'I,' replies Sarah. 'I am more convinced than ever
that he left a note or message for you, and that it has mis-
carried.'

Belinda's shoulders lift themselves slightly in an unbelieving shrug.

'Notes do not miscarry.'

'He left it with the servants to send,' pursues Sarah
decidedly, 'and they—you know what German servants are
—put it into the post or into the fire, to save themselves
trouble.'

Belinda offers no contradiction, but neither does any ray
of hope brighten her dull face at this hypothesis.

'Are you quite sure,' asks Sarah, looking penetratingly
in her elder's face, so as to glean her answer from it rather
than from her words, 'are you quite sure that you did not
snub him yesterday at Wesenstein? I know that you very
often do it without intending it; that you can no more help
it than you can help drawing breath; but are you sure that
you did not?'

'Snubbed him! good heavens, no!'

She has writhed herself half over, and is thrusting her
poor face into the cushioned back of the chair, as if she

wished that she could for ever bury it there, while the blood seems to be rushing in hot shamed tinglings all over her body, as her sister's words call up before her in all the vividness of new life that scene in the wood, in which snubbing bore so small a part.

'Then it is perfectly obvious,' replies Sarah collectedly, and with cool common sense, 'as I told that hornet just now, that he has had bad news and been telegraphed for home. I hope,' with an accent of wakened anxiety, 'that it is not the iron that has gone wrong.'

'I hope it is not anything about his father,' says Belinda, startled by this suggestion out of her own hot and miserable retrospect; 'he would never get over it.'

'Pooh!' says Sarah; 'sons do not die of their fathers' deaths; and in fact, as far as we are concerned, it would simplify matters a good deal; he would be his own father then.'

For a few moments there is a silence, cut into only by the sound of Punch's snores, regular and long drawn out, through the door. It is Belinda who, contrary to what one would have expected, breaks it.

'You were always telling me,' she says with a hard smile, that yet looks as if it needed only one touch to make it dissolve into bitter tears—'you were always telling me that I was so cold to him; you were always advising and urging me to be less cold; perhaps,' with a sort of gasp, 'perhaps I have obeyed you too well; perhaps—perhaps he thinks so.'

'Do you mean,' cries Sarah, with a derisive laugh whose offensive quality is, however, lessened by the soothing gesture of a kind arm thrown at the same moment round her afflicted elder's neck, 'do you mean to say that you suspect him of having taken to his heels because you gave him two civil words and one look that was not a scowl?

If such is the case, he is a valuable admirer, and the more express trains he gets into the better.'

But Belinda is too much cast down to make any rejoinder.

'You will pardon my saying so,' continues Sarah in a counterfeit apology that is contradicted by the lurking mirth in her eye, 'but he would not have been nearly so tiresome as he was if he had not been genuinely in love. If a man is only playing at love he can be civil and amusing to other people; but,' breaking into an unavoidable laugh, 'was poor David amusing? he had his one solitary everlasting *idée fixe.* My dear soul,' passing her light hand with a stroking motion down Belinda's heaving shoulder, 'what a trial he was to granny and me! And—cheer up!—what a trial he will be again!'

This is all the consolation, if consolation it can be called, that Belinda has to take to bed with her.

CHAPTER XIII.

'Lenore fuhr am Morgenroth
Empor aus schweren Träumen.'

THIS is all the consolation with which she wakes next morning and exchanges the shadowy muddle of her discomfortable visions for the not less discomfortable reality. She had slept—to her own surprise—through the earlier part of the night; but in May-time day and night faint into each other ; and though the light is broad and universal, yet the hour is a small one when she awakes, with that hopeless decidedness, that irrevocable bursting of the chains of slumber, which tells its unhappy victim that all juggling efforts to overtake the flown blessing will be of no avail. She lies on her uneasy bed for as long as she can bear it ; then, since the hour is still far too early to ring for her hot water, and so make public an abnormal condition of mind and body, she rises, and throwing on her dressing-gown, sits down by the open window and watches the strides of the morning, stepping, clean and young and lucent, across the old and dirty earth. Even the ugly Bohemian Railway Station and the stucco houses come in for a portion of his kindness. How much more the little hoary garden plat and the dew-pearled tulips !

It has been an open question since the world began, whether the loveliness of nature assuages or aggravates the

misery of humanity, in its more miserable moods. Belinda
would subscribe to the latter opinion. It seems to her that
she could better bear the look of the day—that it would
not make her so angry—if slant rain were slashing the earth,
or if it were locked in a prison of frost, or wound in a
shroud of snow.

The splendour of the transparent air; the trees, just
lightly wagging their heads in the early wind; even the
short-tailed starlings, cheerfully walking about while the sun
touches up their apparently sombre feathers, and brings out
little rainbow colours in them; each—each has a separate
stab for her. There were starlings at Moritzburg; there
were tulips in the inn garden at Lohmen : can she set her
eyes upon any one common object that does not bring a
memory with it ? She has never been of a very bright or
hopeful temperament with regard to her own future; not
one of those happy young ones to whom the long life ahead
seems swathed in a golden mist. The deep conviction of
her own paucity of powers of attraction, a conviction which
has been with her as long as she can remember anything—
as long as the far-away days of short frocks and coming
down to dessert, when strangers used to pull Sarah's long
curls and laugh at her smart answers—a conviction that for
a bright interval has been shaken, now settles down in its
cold and humbling certainty again in her heart.

'He was not telegraphed for,' she says to herself, in a
tone of surpassing bitterness; 'he had no ill news; but he
was right to go. I am not of the stuff of which the women
that men love are made! Let me try not to forget it
again.'

The clocks one after another, in their different voices,
have just struck eight. Cramped with long sitting in one
position, which she has forgotten to change, she rises, and
is beginning to walk up and down the little room when a

knock comes, a quick, loud, rattling knock, which, in its lively energy, partakes of the nature of the person who has executed it, and who adds to it an urgent calling :

'Belinda ! Belinda ! are you awake ?'

Awake !—is she awake ?   She smiles grimly to herself.

'Yes, I am awake,' she answers in an unwilling voice, that she in vain tries to make sound sleepy.

'Then why do not you open the door ?' cries the voice impatiently, accompanying the question by a long and noisier rattling of the handle.

But Belinda takes no step towards complying. She wishes for no one's company, not even Sarah's—perhaps Sarah's least of all ; for is not she the one person from whom she has been unable to hide her humiliation ?

'What do you want ?' she asks morosely.

'If you do not open the door at once,' replies Sarah, desisting for a moment from her rattling, so that her voice may be the more penetratingly heard, 'I warn you that I shall open your note and read it myself !'

Her note ! In one bound Belinda is across the room, has turned the key, and is palely facing her sister.

'Who was right ?' cries Sarah, strutting in, dishevelled, dressing-gowned, triumphant, and holding in her hand a letter which the other silently snatches. 'I was so certain that he must have written, that I sent Tommy round to his lodgings the first thing this morning ; and sure enough they unearthed this, which they had entirely forgotten, and which we ought to have received yesterday afternoon. Come, it is not a bill this time !'

Belinda has opened the envelope, and is staring strainingly at the paper.

'How stupid !' she says, passing her hand across her eyes. 'Somehow I cannot see it.'

'Is it possible that this is his handwriting ?' cries Sarah, coming to her aid, and examining with surprise the super-scription. 'What a shocking hand he writes!'

'Yes; it is his,' says Belinda, again passing her hand across her eyes; 'but it is very shaky. Something has happened to alter it very much. I think you must read it, please.'

'There does not appear to be any beginning,' replies Sarah, complying with some alacrity. '"I cannot come to meet you this afternoon. Oh, forgive me!" (Then comes a prodigious blot—mixed tears and ink, I expect.) "I have been telegraphed for home." (I told you so; then there is something scratched out; what is it?' looking at the paper aslant and half shutting one eye.) '"A f-r-ight-ful cat"—(what, cat? what is it likely to be?—*catastrophe*—that is it, of course; he has put long legs and loops to all the short letters, but I can quite make it out, in spite of that)— "a frightful catastrophe"—(scored through, you know). "I do not know what I am saying. God bless you!" (Then more blots.)—"D. R." That is all!'

'All!' cries Belinda, stretching out her trembling hand for the note. 'Are you sure that there is nothing over the page?'

'Not a syllable!'

There is a silence. Belinda's eyes are riveted on the few scrawled words—so few—on which all her future is to be built. Among them is there one which will support the weight of a legitimate hope?

'It would have been more to the purpose,' says Sarah, in a tone of wounded common sense, 'if he had given us a hint as to what the catastrophe was, instead of wasting so much ingenuity in making all those unnatural legs and arms to his "*a*'s" and "*e*'s" and "*s*'s."'

'You think that there is one really? that something *has* happened? that he *was* telegraphed for?' asks Belinda, appealing in wistful fever to her cool, shrewd junior.

'Of course he was; of course there has!' replies Sarah decidedly. 'I must say,' with a rather satirical look, 'that you have a high opinion of your admirer; he ought to be flattered by your confidence. No! reassure yourself,' striking the untidy blurred page with her forefinger; 'any one with pretensions to be even an indifferent liar would have been ashamed of this.'

'A catastrophe!' repeats Belinda, as though speaking to herself, and still looking at the note; 'what sort of a catastrophe? I think—I fear—that it must in some way concern his father.'

'Well, anyhow, the poor boy's character is cleared up,' says Sarah gaily, sweeping in her long peignoir to the window, and standing blithely looking out at the tulips and the starlings—as brightly pretty as the former, as robustly cheerful as the latter. 'After all, he has not been driven away by your unladylike warmth, as you had quite made up your mind last night; and as to his father, if it is he, our grief must be chastened by the thought that we have never set eyes upon him. Well, I suppose I must not spend the day in my dressing-gown,' walking to the door.

Neither must Belinda; and yet, for long after her sister has left her, she sits, still poring over the meagre sheet that is her first love-letter. She laughs derisively. Will it be her last, too? At that thought she sets herself to weary calculations. It is, without stopping—he will, of course, stop nowhere between Dresden and London—a thirty-six hour's journey. Probably five or six hours more will be occupied in getting on to Yorkshire. It is a four days' post from England to Dresden. Even if he write to her immediately on arriving—a most unlikely hypothesis—it cannot be much less than a week before she hears. There must be five or six absolutely void black days, that yet will have the same complement of hours in them as the day at Moritzburg or the day at Wesenstein. She lays her hot forehead on the cool wooden chair-back. Oh, if they could but be slept through !

But at this moment the entrance of her maid, with the usual paraphernalia of her toilet, sufficiently reminds her that they cannot. They cannot be slept through! They must be dressed through, talked through, eaten through, made expeditions through, joked through. Worst of all, his departure, its cause, his probable or improbable return, he himself, must be continually discussed and worn thread-bare in her hearing.

This, indeed, is an evil from which she suffers for only two days. After that, he being gone, and never having sought to make himself specially acceptable to any member of the little society save one, he slips from their talk and their thoughts.

She is deeply thankful when their chatter about him ceases, and yet angry with them for so soon forgetting him. And meanwhile the days in summer procession pace stately by, full of sap and growth and laughter. The date of the Churchill departure is now fixed for the 5th of June ; and as that period approaches, a freezing panic fear begins to clutch Belinda more and more tightly in its hold—the fear that her own going may antedate the arrival of his letter ; that he may write to her here, and the letter not be forwarded. The many tales she has heard of lives dismally wrecked upon some such small accident throng her memory.

The house is full of signs of an approaching *déménagement ;* full of packing, disarranging, bustling. It is mostly full also of German officers, who, being aware that their time for enjoying the society and the wit of their love-worthy Sarah is all too quickly passing, are resolved to have nothing to reproach themselves with in the way of not having availed themselves of it while they were able. Some of them are not unwilling to extend their endearments to the elder sister, seeing her no longer monopolised by her surly fellow-countryman; but she has received their compliments so blankly, that, ashamed of their brief infidelity, they have clanked hastily back to their first love, who sees them go and return with the same joyous indifference.

Belinda has been innocent of the least intention to snub them, but how can one receive pretty speeches—any speeches intelligently, when one is continually doing a sum in one's head—36 and 5, 41; 1 day from 4 days; 1 day from 3 days, etc.?

The packing is not of so wholly occupying a nature as to exclude incidental amusements. It does not even forbid a farewell excursion to Tharandt; an excursion planned by Sarah and her rout of Uhlans; with some necessary padding of a lenient chaperon, and compliant girls.

Belinda has believed herself equal to sharing it. Tharandt is rendered agonising by no associations. She has never visited Tharandt in his company, but, at the last moment, a trifle robs her of her fortitude—the sight of her cobwebby Wesenstein gown, extended with unconscious tactless cruelty by her maid on the bed. She throws herself down, ungovernably sobbing, beside it. It seems like the husk of her lost happiness. By and by they are all gone, and the house is left to her and to silence. It is deserted even by the dogs, who have been taken out driving by Mrs. Churchill; Slutty, supinely indifferent to view and air, curled at the carriage-bottom, and Punch standing up on his hind-legs, with his fore-paws on the carriage-side, like an unsteady heraldic lion.

Belinda laughs a little at the thought of him as she returns to the salon, which is beginning to wear a desolate look, reduced to its own lodging-house furniture and shorn of the graces bestowed upon it by the Churchills' Indian rugs and Turkish chair-backs. Its new ugliness, meeting her eye, seems to add to the vexation of her spirit. The sunlight on the street vexes her too. She wanders for a while aimlessly about the room, and then drops as aimlessly into a chair. To an observer it would seem that she were quite without occupation. But it is not so. She is still at work upon that sum. She has just finished it, or rather she has just begun it afresh, when an unexpected interruption drives it, not away—nothing, alas! could do that—but into the background of her mind.

The summer afternoon is at its drowsiest, even the flies buzz inertly along the pane, when the room-door opens and Professor Forth looks in.

'I beg your pardon,' he says formally, 'but I think your page must have been misinformed; he tells me that Sarah is not at home.'

At the sound of his voice, separated by how many seas and continents from her thoughts, Belinda starts to her feet; then, conjuring suddenly up a civil smile, says gently:

'But I am afraid he is not misinformed. I am afraid she *is* out. Did you expect to find her?'

He has entered the room now in his hard and graceless academic black, which somehow looks out of character with the light-coloured room and the blazing day.

'Naturally I expected to find her,' he replies sharply, 'since it is by her own appointment that I am here. After evading on various trivial pretexts every meeting proposed by me for the past week, she herself gave me a distinct and definite rendezvous for this hour and day. *I* am punctual to the moment!' glancing angrily at the Dresden clock.

'I am sadly afraid that she has forgotten all about it,' replies Belinda, bursting into a helpless laugh; but indeed there is no greater fallacy than that one may not laugh heartily, violently, and not hysterically, when one's heart is breaking; 'she has gone out upon an expedition.'

'She is always going out upon expeditions,' retorts he snappishly.

Belinda sighs; her mirth vanished as quickly as it came. She has no energy to take up the cudgels for Sarah, of whose conduct no one can think worse than she does, and of whose meditated villainy she is guiltily aware.

'She is young,' she says lamely.

'I cannot see that that is any valid apology for a systematic neglect of all the more serious duties of life,' he replies fretfully.

He has walked to the window, where he now stands drowned in a bath of golden radiance. Never has he looked less lovable; ill-humour rendering yet more pinched and captious his pinched pedant face; and never has Belinda felt so charitably towards him. 'He is not amiable; Heaven knows that he is not attractive,' she says to herself; 'so much the worse for him. But he is unhappy; what better claim could he have upon my sympathy?'

'Do you want her for anything special?' she asks not unkindly, going up and standing beside him in the rain of sunbeams in her large young beauty; 'anything in which I can help you?'

It is obvious that the idea had never occurred to him that in her he should find either the ability or the willing-ness to aid him.

'You are very good,' he answers stiffly; 'the fact is, I wanted to throw together a few thoughts upon the Idea of Colour among the Athenians,' glancing at a bundle of notes and papers in his hands, 'and I entirely depended upon Sarah to be my secretary. She is perfectly aware,' with a revived and extreme exasperation of tone, 'of the affection in my eyes which precludes the possibility of my writing more than a certain number of hours a day, and which keeps me here in the middle of term, unavoidably absent from my post and Oxbridge.'

'She is very provoking!' assents Belinda soothingly. 'But as far as the writing goes, I write a much better hand than Sarah. She never would learn, when we were children. She was always playing monkey-tricks upon the master all through the lesson. Cannot I be your secretary?' As she speaks, she lifts to his her large serious eyes, full of a compassion that is none the less sincere for being slightly tinged with contempt.

'You are very good!' he repeats ceremoniously. 'I am aware that I have no right to trespass upon your valuable time.'

'There is no one else to trespass upon it,' she answers, stifling a sigh. 'On the contrary, I am obliged to any one who will help me to get through it.' As she speaks she walks towards the writing-table, and quickly and methodically arranging the writing materials, seats herself, and in a few moments is penning her first sentence from his dictation.

She has undertaken the office out of pure good-nature, and at first fulfils it quite mechanically. Gradually, however, as the meaning of the words she is writing penetrates through her ears into her understanding, a slight interest in the subject in hand awakens in her. She asks a question or two. By and by there comes a Greek word.

'May it be written in English letters?' she asks, glancing up. 'No? Well, then I am afraid I must leave it for you to insert.'

'You do not know the Greek character?' he asks, with a slight touch of regret in his tone.

She shakes her head.

'I am afraid I must ask you,' smiling a little, 'not to question me too closely as to what I know.'

'I offered to teach it to Sarah,' he says aggrievedly.

'And she refused, of course.'

'It is not the want of knowledge,' he says, beginning to pace gloomily up and down the room, that is the irremediable evil. It is the total lack of all desire for knowledge—that is what I deplore in Sarah.'

Belinda has paused in her writing, her elbow leant on the table, and idly brushing with the feather of the pen the red curve of her lips.

'I have never known an instance,' continues he, still pursuing his irritated walk, 'of a young person whose character had undergone so radical a change in so comparatively short a period of time.'

'Do you think so?' cries Belinda, surprised. 'She has always been exactly the same as long as I can remember her!'

'When first I made her acquaintance,' he goes on, not heeding the interruption, 'I of course became at once aware of her ignorance—*that* is patent; but she appeared to me not to be lacking in intellectual force, nor in a rather remarkable desire for self-improvement. On the very first evening I met her, she deplored to me the deficiency of her education, and asked me in so many words to aid her in the formation of her mind.'

Belinda drops the pen. It is not a nearly large enough shield to hide the convulsive mirth that this revelation of her sister's hideous hypocrisy has called forth.

'I still cherish the hope,' continues he, fortunately unaware of the character of his auditor's emotion, 'that this may be only a phase; that on her return to her home and her more regular occupations, freer from these senseless distractions,' with an exaggerated emphasis, 'her mind may resume that soberer bias which, from my first impression of her, I cannot but believe to be its natural one.'

Belinda, still unable to speak, contents herself with a

gentle head-shake, as commentary and gloss upon which
there comes, at the same moment, the sound of a scampering step on the stone stairs, of a loudly singing voice, waking to life again the dead dumb house. In a moment the
door flies open, and the person whose mind is expected so
soon to resume its soberer bias stands before them, her hat
a good deal on one side, from the weight of the flowering
may-bough stuck rakishly in it—the may-bough whose strong
and almost pungent perfume comes rushing into the room
with her.

'Are not you delighted to welcome me back so unexpectedly early?' cries she joyously. 'But it was so hot, and
my soldiers were all so cross and low at the prospect of
losing me, and Von Breidenbach had a toothache, and so
—— Mr. Forth!' suddenly catching sight of him. 'Ah!'
with an abrupt change and refrigeration of tone, 'of course
you came about that essay of yours; and, equally of course,
I forgot all about it. Well, I dare say there is no great
hurry! Happily, the Greeks will keep; they will not run
away.'

There is an ominous silence. Then—

'It is unfortunate,' begins the Professor, in a voice
trembling with indignation, while the puckers of anger that
Belinda's mild hand has been smoothing away, again form
their network over his face, 'that, considering the position
in which we stand relatively to each other, our views of life
and its significance should be so diametrically——'

Belinda leaves the room.

CHAPTER XIV.

'How can I ever thank you enough for having paved the way for me?' says Sarah next morning, as the two sisters sit awaiting breakfast. 'I awoke to-day in such a humble, grateful frame of mind. I said to myself, "Thanks to God and my good sister, I am out of my difficulty!"'

'Did you happen to mention that it was your seventeenth?' asks Belinda grimly.

'I said to myself,' continues Sarah, feigning deafness, 'I will put on a clean calico gown, and ask granny to let us have some champagne for dinner, to celebrate my little innocent festival. Really, joking apart, it was almost worth while to be engaged to him, for the pleasure of having it broken off. Cannot you understand that?'

'I have already explained to you several times that I would rather have been burnt alive than be engaged to him at all,' replies Belinda trenchantly.

But the snub, like many kindred predecessors, passes airily over Sarah's yellow head, and leaves no mark upon her satisfied serenity.

'Punch,' she says, taking the two dogs' forepaws in her hands, and looking gravely in their black faces, 'Punch, I am free! Slutty, I am free! Go and tell the cats and the parrot!'

Belinda has sunk back into herself. She is wondering feverishly what is making the letters so late.

'I have not even made an enemy of him,' pursues Sarah, loosing the dogs' paws, and sinking back with a sigh of complacency in her chair. 'I believe that in his heart he was quite as glad to be out of it as I. He was the first of them,' with a slight regretful pout, 'who was glad to be off !'

'I think he was *very* glad !' says Belinda spitefully.

'Say one word more, and I will have him back again,' cries Sarah, roused by this challenge.

But Belinda makes no rejoinder. To her, Sarah and her light loves have become distant and insignificant things. Her strained ears have caught, or she thinks so, the sound of a footstep. Of course it is only Tommy bringing in the breakfast; but he may be bringing her death-warrant or her evangel, too. It is the first day on which, according to her calculation of distances, it would be possible for her to receive a letter from Rivers.

'If you had heard,' says Sarah, smiling rosily to herself, 'the masterly way in which I indicated to him that it was only my consciousness of inadequacy to fill that high post, which made me regretfully retire from it, I think that even you would have admired me.'

'Should I ?' quite inattentively.

'He swallowed it all,' continues Sarah, growing grave. 'Good heavens !' throwing up her eyes, what will not they swallow ?'

The sound has died away again. It could not have been even Tommy.

'I cried a little,' resumes Sarah, with that glow of modest retrospective satisfaction still diffused all over her, extending even to her pink cambric gown. 'Do not ask me how I did it; I could not even engage to do it again were the same situation to return; these strokes of genius do not repeat themselves.'

She stops, her attention diverted into a fresh channel,

for at this moment Gustel throws open the door, and
Tommy enters, his childish arms extended to their widest
stretch to embrace the breakfast tray, upon which, beside
coffee-pot and rolls, lies a heap of letters and papers.
Belinda does not stir, now that the moment so breathlessly
longed for has come; she would fain put it off again, shove
it away a little further.

A paralysis of fear nails her to her chair. She feels an
impulse of anger against Sarah for doing what she herself is
incapable of; for her quick movement towards the tray, her
hasty turning over of the family's correspondence. There is
a second's pause—a pause during which hope still lives:
then in a moment it is dead. Sarah's voice would tell her
that, even if her words did not.

'I am afraid there is nothing very interesting for you,'
she says reluctantly, tossing her three or four letters without
looking at her. Belinda's heart dies; then suddenly there
flares up a tiny flame of hope in it again. Possibly Sarah
may not recognise his handwriting. Probably it is so disguised and disfigured by trouble and emotion as to be
unrecognisable. Was not this the case with her note?
She snatches at the letters and looks dizzily from one to the
other of the superscriptions. Alas, no! they are all in the
handwriting of familiar and habitual correspondents. She
has told herself all night that her expectations were not
highly raised for to-day; that to-day is the first day on which
it would be possible to hear; that, being only possible, it is
not also probable; that her chances are better for to-morrow
or the day after. And yet, now that the disappointment has
come, it seems to her ruinous and final. Her first movement
is to dash the letters down on her lap; then, with that
instinct of self-respect which parts us from the savage and
the beast, remembering that Tommy's round gaze is upon
her, she picks up one, and shakily unfolding it, lets her

misery-shaded eyes fall on the page. Only for a moment, however; a fresh thought makes her drop it and fly to the papers.

In a second she has torn open one of the English journals, the *Standard ;* and seizing the advertisement sheet, greedily turns to the column of births, deaths, and marriages. She runs her eye down the names; she will not allow this horrible swimming to blind her; she will read for herself.

'Abbots, Ackers, Anson, Baker, Callcott, Frith, Forly, Harper, Key—when do the R's come? what a long, long list! Ah! here they are! Raby, Rashleigh, Retford—what a number of R's are dead! Yes, here it is! *Rivers !*' The swimming is gone. She can see it clearly; there is no mistake. 'On the 24th inst., at Denver Hall, Yorkshire, John Appleby Rivers, M.P., aged 54.'

At the same moment, Tommy, his functions ended, shuts the door behind him. For a moment or two Belinda stares dully at the announcement, then silently holds it out to her sister. But Sarah does not see it; her head is buried between the other sheets of the paper, which she has been too impatient even to cut.

'I knew it,' she says, speaking suddenly in a voice that is a little tremulous, a little awed, and yet triumphant. 'I knew it was his father; he is dead; he has committed suicide. Poor David! no wonder he looked odd. There is a para-graph about it.'

'Committed suicide!' repeats Belinda with a gasp, turning as white as the tablecloth, and her great gray eyes dilating, while the image of her poor boy-lover and his whole-hearted devotion to, his innocent enthusiasm about his father, at which she had sometimes smiled, superior yet envious, darts painfully back upon her memory.

Sarah has snatched a table-knife and is rapidly and jaggedly cutting the paper. ' "We regret to announce the

death, under peculiarly painful circumstances, of Mr. John
Appleby Rivers, of Denver Hall, Yorkshire, who for the last
ten years has represented the Borough of Denver in the
Conservative interest in Parliament. The deceased gentleman had retired to rest on the night of the 25th in his usual
health, but on the following morning his valet, on going to
call him at the accustomed hour, found his door locked, and
could obtain no answer to his repeated knocks. The family
becoming alarmed, an entrance was effected through the
window, when the unfortunate gentleman was found extended
lifeless on the floor, with his throat cut from ear to ear.
Medical assistance was at once procured, but in vain, as life
had evidently been extinct for some hours."' Sarah pauses
with a shudder of disgust, even her blooming cheek a little
paled. 'Why *will* people cut their throats,' she says com-
plainingly, 'when there are so many clean ways of dying?'

'Perhaps he did not do it himself,' cries Belinda, catching
breathlessly at this hope. 'Who knows? Perhaps he was
murdered!'

'Wait a bit!' replies Sarah, putting up her hand in prohibition. 'Where was I? Let me go on: "Been extinct
for several hours. The razor with which the deed had been
accomplished lay on the floor beside the corpse!"' Again
she shudders. 'Grisly word! why *will* they use it? Why
do all newspaper-writers love it? "It is surmised that distress
of mind, arising from pecuniary embarrassment, was the
immediate cause of the rash act."' She stops for a few
moments, and there is silence. Belinda has put her hands
over her eyes, before which the ghastly sight is conjured up
in its red horror.

This, then, is what has robbed her of him! This is the
spectacle for which he has exchanged the spring-dressed,
sun-warmed Grosse Garten. This is the errand, falsely and
cruelly supposed by her to be a feigned one, which has torn

him away. She shivers, and the shiver is followed by a warm rush of passionate pity.

'What will he do? How will he bear it? Will he ever get over it?' We ask ourselves and each other this senseless question, as often as an affliction a little severer than common alights upon one that is known to us; although experience, a thousand times repeated, has taught us its folly. But below the horror and the compassion, though both are genuine, there lies in Belinda's mind a thick, deep stratum of inexpressible relief and joy. It is explained then! Suspense is ended; at least for the moment it seems so. There may be a cessation of that weary sum-doing. She may think again of the wood at Wesenstein without writhing. Her past is restored to her. Surely she can live upon it until he comes back to give her a present and a future.

'Pecuniary embarrassments!' says Sarah thoughtfully. 'I do not much like that. However,' with a more cheerful air, 'it is better than having insanity in the family. Poor man! it was a cowardly way of cutting the knot!'

'The 25th,' says Belinda, dropping her hands into her lap, and staring, with eyes still dilated, straight before her; 'that was the day we went to Wesenstein!'

'There is more about him—another little paragraph!' says Sarah, resuming her reading. 'Oh, now we shall find out whom he married. "Mr. Rivers was born on the 1st of May, 18—" (Ah! Ten and ten, twenty, and ten thirty, forty —that would make him just fifty-four)—"and was the eldest son of the late Mr. Rivers, of Denver Hall, at whose death the property was sold, in consequence of pecuniary embarrassments." (Hem! they seem to be addicted to pecuniary embarrassments.) "It was repurchased, five years ago, by Mr. Rivers, who had amassed a large fortune in the iron trade. He married, on the 3rd of June, 18—, the Lady Marion Lovell, third daughter of the late, and sister of the present, Earl of Eastwood" (bravo, David! I knew that he was not undiluted iron), "by whom he has left issue"—(a good deal of issue, I am afraid). "He was an enlightened patron of agriculture, and belonged to several agricultural societies. His death will be widely and deeply deplored."' She lays down the paper. 'That is all.'

'*All!*' repeats Belinda in an awed voice; 'and enough too!'

'What a mercy for David that he was not at home!'

'He will not think so,' replies Belinda sadly.

'He will avoid most of the horrors—coroner's inquest and all!' says Sarah, with a shiver of disgust. 'I wonder what day the funeral was? You could not expect him to write before that. I am afraid that now you must not hope to hear before we leave.'

'Of course not—of course not!' feverishly. 'Poor boy! I do not want him to think of me at all!'

'I expect that you are the one pleasant thing he has to think about,' replies Sarah drily. 'I hope to heavens that the money—' stopping abruptly. 'Will you believe it? There she is! I hear her voice. She has come to tell us. Tommy, Tommy!' flying headlong into the passage, 'we are not at home—we are not at home to *any body.*'

But, as usual, it is too late. Punch, indeed, gallops out in aid, barking irefully. It is not that bark of boisterous compliment which he addresses to most people, but one of a different character—one not unfrequently accompanied by a nip at the heels of the person indicated; a bark which he reserves exclusively for tramps and Miss Watson. Slutty has instantly crawled on her stomach under the settee. To do Tommy justice, he has opened the door as little as he possibly could; but by thrusting her person into the aperture Miss Watson has succeeded in considerably widening it, and now stands in it, talking loudly and

brandishing a newspaper. As soon as she catches sight
of Sarah—

'Have you heard?' she cries eagerly. 'Have you seen
it? Young Rivers' father's death?—suicide? I thought
you might not have seen it.'

'Of course we have,' replies Sarah curtly; 'of course we
have our papers as usual. I am sorry I cannot ask you to
come in this morning; we are so——'

'Do you think he was off his head?' asks the other, interrupting. 'Do you think there is madness in the family?
If so, no doubt they got it from the Lovells; there
is mostly scrofula of one form or another in all those old
families.'

'What a comfort for the new ones!' answers Sarah with
a sneer. 'Well, I am afraid that we are so busy packing——'

'Were not you surprised to hear that he had married
one of the Lovells? I had not an idea that he had married
one of the Lovells. He did not get a penny with her, I
will answer for it; they are as poor as Job. Eastwood is
mortgaged up to the hall-door.'

'Is it? Well, as we have already heard your news,'
taking hold of the door with a determined air—'come in,
Punch, or you will be shut out!'

'What papers have you seen?' asks the other inquisitively. 'I wonder is the account the same in them all.
Would you mind my having a look at yours?'

Sarah shakes her head.

'Impossible! Granny has not seen them!'

'I would lend you mine with all the pleasure in life, only
that I am just going to run round with it to the Freres and
Gayhursts; they take only the *Times;* there are not so
many details in the *Times.*'

A surly silence is the only response.

'Poor fellow! it is too sad, is it not?' continues Miss Watson, her large face beaming with pleasurable excitement. 'I do not know when I have felt so cut up about anything! I shall make a point of writing to him; shall not you?'

* * * * *

'She is going to make a point of writing to him,' says Sarah with a grimace, rejoining her sister a moment or two later, a judiciously placed hint as to the probability of some one being beforehand with her at the Gayhursts and Freres having rid her of her visitor. 'It may be a bad thing to lose a father, but it is very much worse to be consoled for him by Miss Watson. By the bye,' with a change of tone, 'David has your address, has not he—your London address —you gave it him, eh?'

'Yes.'

'Ah,' with a little sigh of satisfaction, 'that is all right then! The sooner we get to England the better, for all reasons.'

Belinda echoes the sentiment. What is there to keep her or her heart here now? In the place of the drag which a while ago she would have put upon the days, she would now use whip and spur to them. If Time were to obey our impulses, in what a strange jerky manner would he proceed! It is beyond the range of possibility that she should receive a letter from him here. It would be the height of filial impiety. How dare she thrust her trivial self between him and the grandeur of his grief? How dare one thought of her cross his mind, ere yet his father is laid in his bloody and dishonoured grave? But by the time that they have reached England, four more days will have elapsed.

Mrs. Churchill has stipulated that the journey shall be accomplished leisurely. Once in England, he and she will at all events be separated by only one day's post, less than a day's journey. In London there are so many posts in the

day. Every two hours does not there come a double
knock? and may not any one of these double knocks
possibly—nay, why be irrationally down-hearted?—probably
bring her salvation? By dint of continued cherishing, her
hopes soar higher still. Why should he write? what is
there to hinder his coming himself? In her heart she hears
his footfall on the stairs; it will fall more softly on the
carpeted London steps than on these bare stone ones.
Perhaps it will be less springy than of yore; grief may have
made it heavier and slower. He will enter in his black
clothes; she has never seen him in black, and tries to
reconstruct him in this sombre habit. He will not smile,
it would not be right that he should; but he will stretch
out his arms to her—Tommy being gone.

At this point her face always falls forward into her hands,
and the carnations overrun their borders. She can no more
look at that picture than she can stare unwinking at the
mid-day sun. But though she struggles earnestly to keep
hope sober and low, it is with an elastic step and a bright
face that she treads the platform of the Dresden railway
station on the day and at the hour of their departure. The
tickets have been taken; their own, that of the luggage,
Punch's. Slutty is small enough to defraud the revenue by
travelling in an ingeniously constructed house of her own,
which has the air of a large dressing-bag, and under which
Belinda, Sarah, and the maid take turns to stagger. And
now Mrs. Churchill and Belinda have already seated themselves and arranged their packages. Sarah still loiters on
the step, half the German army gathered round her. She
has asked them all to come and see her off, and not one but
has answered to the call. Her hands are full of great bouquets
that they have not stretch enough to hold. She is distribut-
ing more addresses than she has time rapidly to pencil.
Apparently, every one of them is to correspond with her.

Belinda has no bouquet, and no one has asked for her direction. Even her last view of the fair city is obstructed by Sarah, who has monopolised the window to lean out and kiss her fingers, crying, 'Auf Wiedersehen!' until the last glimpse of her dark-blue, light-blue, and green admirers is lost to sight. And yet it is with a light heart, that sometimes even dances, that Miss Churchill steams away towards her native shores.

PERIOD II.

'Je ne comprends pas comme on peut tant penser à une
personne : n'aurai-je jamais tout pensé ?'

CHAPTER I.

IT is November; the second November since the Churchill's return from Dresden. A second summer has raced after a second spring; and a second autumn is pursuing both. The full tale of eighteen months is complete. Time has swung by on his mighty wings, which all the centuries are powerless to tire, bearing in his arms diverse gifts. To some he has brought satisfied ambition; to some grinding poverty; to some a surfeit of pleasure; to some a mad-house; and to some a grave. To many only a bundle of little nagging cares and pigmy pleasures, that passed without much heeding.

To the Churchills he has brought—what? To Mrs. Churchill a beautiful new *râtelier ;* to Sarah, six new lovers and one new dog; and to Belinda, a knowledge of the post-man's step, whether distant or near, that she might defy any inhabitant of this or any other street to rival. Before her return home, she had congratulated herself upon the con-venience and number of the London posts. Ere six months are out, she execrates their frequency.

For eighteen months Belinda has been listening, and not once have her ears been filled with the sound that they are ever strained to catch. Not once has Rivers written. Not once has he come in person to explain his silence. He is gone—simply gone out of her life. That is all!

He was free, of course, to come or to go ; as she tells herself, she cannot quarrel with him for that. The why she is at issue with him is that he has taken the taste out of her life with him. For her he has taken the colour out of the sunsets, and the music out of the larks. She looks at the beauty of our mother earth with a grudging, sullen eye. The summers with the glories of their roses, the autumns with the glories of their sheaves, are to her absolutely waste and worthless.

'Even if he came back to me,' she says to herself; 'even if I lived to be ninety, and saw him henceforth every day, every minute, until I die, I could never fill the emptiness of these days ; they will always have been dead, dead loss !'

Now and again she rises up in revolt against the tyranny of the idea that is eating into and corroding her prime. She will cut him out of her life ; will cut off that portion of her life in which he had concern, sheer away, like a precipice.

'I did well before I knew him,' she says to herself, with a sort of indignation. 'He was in the world, and so was I; he smiled as he does now—does he smile now, I wonder? —and I was none the worse for it. He did not blot out the sun ; he did not make it uphill work to eat, to speak, to breathe. Let things be as they were then. Why cannot they be ? They shall be !'

For a moment she is strong and light-hearted ; sings a gay verse of a song ; feels the goodliness of youth. Then a sick qualm comes over her. It is gone, done with ! and the whole earth, the whole of life, is empty, hideous, void !

It is November ; the afternoon is drawing towards its close. Tea has been drunk, and visitors are gone. The hour of dressing draws nigh. This, however, is a fact that neither Mrs. Churchill nor Sarah are willing to admit; Mrs. Churchill because her drive has made her sleepy, and fire and owl-light are drowsy and soothing; Sarah because she is absorbed in the ingenious, if not useful, employment of painting the large white terrier lately added to the establishment, in coloured stripes and spots to represent a clown. Jane is, happily for herself, not a sensitive dog, and submits with stolid good-humour to a process that would penetrate Slutty's heart with agonies of undying shame.

'Belinda is late,' says Mrs. Churchill, drawing herself up into a sitting posture, the first preparatory step towards the unavoidable, dreaded move upstairs.

'I hope she will not come back until Jane is finished,' answers Sarah warmly, hesitating for an instant in the choice of a pigment; while Jane opens her mouth in a large, bored, patient yawn.

'Perhaps she did not find it so tiresome as she expected,' says Mrs. Churchill, reluctantly taking the second step towards departure, and rising to her feet.

'Perhaps not,' replies Sarah absently, drawing back her head the better to judge of the effect of a large splash of gamboge, just applied upon Jane's right cheek.

'What an object you are making of that poor dog!' laughing lazily.

'She likes it!' replies Sarah gravely. 'She thinks it is becoming. Do not tell her it is not. If she is a success, I mean to paint the others as Harlequin and Columbine!'

'I wish Belinda would come,' says Mrs. Churchill, with a little comfortable curiosity in nowise akin to the loving, foolish solicitude that thinks that some unlikely misfortune must have happened to its beloved, if he or she be detained five minutes beyond his or her usual time.

'I hope she will not come until Jane is finished!' repeats Sarah seriously, working away with redoubled ardour.

'I think she must have been amused.'

'H'm!' replies Sarah dubiously. 'If she is, she is the

first person in whom that emotion was ever provoked by an afternoon drum; and Belinda is not easily amused. I think,' with quiet pride, 'that Jane will amuse her. Ah, how provoking! Here she is!'

In effect, as the last words leave her lips the door opens, and her sister enters. If your eyes were shut, or if you were blind, your ear would never have told you that it was a young person's entrance, so measured and unelastic is her step.

'Do not come here! Do not look at Jane!' cries Sarah in an agonised voice, hastily throwing the cloth on which she has been wiping her brushes over Jane's long-suffering back. 'Stay where you are! No! Now you may come!'

'Which am I to do?' asks Belinda; and her voice has as little spring in it as her step.

'Well?' cries Mrs. Churchill in a voice of cheerful expectancy, ready to abridge her dressing-time, to sit down again and be amused.

'Well?' replies Belinda unresponsively.

She has advanced to the fire, and now stands there, a foot on the fender, for the evening is chill; while the cheerful flames, upspringing, play upon the uncheerful beauty of her face, and lend a little of their own dancing to the

> 'Eyes too expressive to be blue,
> Too lovely to be gray,'

that have no dancing of their own in them.

'You are the worst person in the world to send out,' says Mrs. Churchill, disappointed and cross; 'for all the news you bring back, you might as well stay at home.'

A couple of years ago, Belinda would have pleasantly acquiesced in her own lack of observation; would have cheerfully tried to remedy it. Now she only answers, with a sullen look:

'What is there to tell? What is there ever to tell about a drum? There was a mob of women, and a smell of hot sealskins!'

'Not a man, of course?' asks Sarah from the distant corner of the room, whither she has retired with the inchoate Jane to pursue her artistic labours unseen. 'How glad I am I did not go!'

Belinda smiles. When she smiles, you see even more clearly than when she is grave the inexpressible hardening which has happened to her face.

'There were two or three men.'

'The usual refuse that you meet in a second-class literary salon, I suppose,' rejoins Sarah contemptuously. 'Dirty little poets, and greasy little positivists?'

Belinda still smiles a smile that is without gaiety, but is not without satire.

'There was one man there whom you did not think too grimy to bestow a good deal of your notice upon at one period of your history.'

'Who?' asks Sarah, pricking up her ears with awakened yet puzzled interest. 'You would not be likely to meet any of my friends there, I should hope.'

'Guess!'

'Je vous le donne en trois; je vous le donne en dix; je vous le donne en mille!' says Mrs. Churchill, who at the unsealing of her granddaughter's lips has recovered her good-humour. 'Was it—pooh! what a memory I have—Signor Valetta, the singing-master, who went down on his knees in the middle of the lesson?'

'No.'

'I have it! It was the German who wrote "Ich liebe dich!" on the fly-leaf of the grammar!'

'It was not!'

Sarah has paused, brush in hand, her brows furrowed by

her efforts to repass in her mind's eye the crowded phalanx of her suitors.

'They were the nearest approach to literature I ever made,' she says doubtfully; 'except'—a sudden rush of colour and animation into face and eyes—'except—no! it could not have been; it was not—was it—*Professor Forth?*'

'It was Professor Forth.'

'How awkward for you!' cries Mrs. Churchill, interested; 'and of course he is not man of the world enough to carry off the *gêne* of such a meeting!'

In the emotion of the moment, Sarah has unintentionally released Jane, who now trots composedly back to the fire, her incomplete face white on one side and garishly painted on the other—a fact which, even when taken in connection with the distrustful and angry wonder of the other dogs, is powerless to rob her of her stoic calm.

'Did he speak to you? Did you speak to him?' cries Sarah in high excitement, running back to the hearth.

'I talked to him for a good half-hour.'

'He accepted the situation, in short,' says Mrs. Churchill. 'Well, that was more than I should have expected of him.'

'Did he mention me? Of course he mentioned me?' asked Sarah eagerly.

'He inquired after granny; and then he put you in as an afterthought.'

'I dare say that he could not command his voice to ask after me at first?' cries the other, laughing. 'Did his voice tremble at all? I hope it trembled.'

'Not in the very least.'

'You talked to him for half an hour? What did you talk about?'

'We talked about Browning's Poetry.'

'*Browning's Poetry!*' with a disgusted accent. 'What a

bore for you! I thought that of course you would have talked about me!'

'Bore!' repeats Belinda, with a sort of bitter animation. 'I thought it such a blessing. I did not want to talk about you, or myself either, or granny; we are always talking about you and myself and granny. It was such a relief to get away once in a while from people and turn to things!'

'I must say that Browning is a great deal too clever for me,' puts in Mrs. Churchill contentedly. 'I am very fond of poetry; but I like something that I can understand.'

'But did you talk about nothing but Browning's poetry?' inquires Sarah, incredulously lifting her eyebrows. 'Did you talk about it the whole time?'

'We had hardly exhausted the subject in half an hour,' replies Belinda, with a disagreeable sneer. 'And then he read aloud; he was asked to read aloud!'

'And you all sat round worshipping!' exclaims Sarah, breaking into new laughter. 'That is exactly what they did at the house I first met him at. You may not credit it, but I sat round worshipping too!'

'They were rather fulsome!' replies Belinda, her lip curling at the recollection.

'And what did he read? Did he read anything amusing? But of course he did not!'

'He read "The Grammarian's Funeral."'

'"*The Grammarian's Funeral*"!' repeats Mrs. Churchill with a shrug. 'What a name for a poem!'

'"The Grammarian's Funeral"!' echoes Sarah, but with an emotion different from her grandmother's colouring her tone. 'That was the very poem he read the night I first met him. I could not make head or tail of it; but I pretended that I thought it very fine. Belinda, beware! or this family may have a second time cause to rue that that Grammarian ever was buried!'

'How curious, your meeting him!' said Mrs. Churchill, with an amused, leisurely smile. 'How it must have reminded you of Dresden!'

Belinda shudders a little. There is so much need to remind her of Dresden! And yet she herself has been surprised at the extra vividness with which the sight and bodily presence of one of the subordinate actors in the little drama enacted there has brought it back to her. Is her memory growing habitually dull? Oh, if it but were so!

'Is his mother alive still?' asks Sarah, striking hastily in to divert the conversation from the channel into which her grandmother seems disposed to direct it. 'I hope you were not behind hand in civility; and that as he remembered to ask after our old lady, you remembered to ask after his.'

'I did not; I thought she might be dead, but I do not think she is. He mentioned her; he said something about "My mother."'

'Then of course she is not dead!' answers Sarah decisively; 'if she had been he would have said, "My poor mother!" Granny, when you are dead, I mean always to talk of you as "my poor granny!"'

'Do you indeed, my dear!' rather sharply. 'Let me tell you that I have no intention of giving you the opportunity just yet.'

'Did he say anything about coming to call?' asks Sarah, with an interested look.

'Not a word.'

'Did he give you the impression that he was contemplating it?'

'Not in the least.

'Do you think that he will?'

'I should think certainly not; indeed he is going back to Oxbridge to-morrow. I wish I were going to Oxbridge to-morrow! I wish,' restlessly, 'that we lived at Oxbridge.'

'To be near him?' asks Sarah, laughing.

Her sister joins in the laugh, but without heartiness.

'Not exactly; but from what he says—from what every-one says—there must be such a continual stir of intellectual life going on there.'

'Good Heavens!' cries Sarah, shocked; 'what has happened to you? You are growing to talk just as he does; those are the kind of things he used to say to me, and expect me to provide them with suitable answers!'

'It does sound high falutin',' answers Belinda, rather ashamed; 'but it is not, really: it is only that I would give anything to get out of our own little groove into any other.'

'I like our little groove,' says Sarah contentedly; 'by the bye, that reminds me—— Jane, where are you? Jane, how dare you? How can you be so indelicate as to present yourself half dressed to Punch and Slutty? Come here this instant.'

But Jane, though giving a slavish leer and a sycophantic wag of her disfigured tail, makes no movement towards exchanging her warm couch on the deep rug for the uncom-fortable glories of the palette and the brush.

'It may not be a bad little groove for those who like it,' rejoins Belinda discontentedly; 'but it is pleasant to get a glimpse beyond it now and then. I do not know when I have been so little bored as I have been this afternoon.'

CHAPTER II.

SHE says the same thing to herself in the solitude of her own room—that solitude where the least truthful speaks truth. She says it again when she awakes next morning. Is it possible that an avenue to renewed interest in life may be opening before her? Others—Professor Forth, for instance—have lived and live by the intellect; live to all appearance worthily and contentedly. Why may not she too? What—her heart being stone-dead—is there to prevent her?

'If you please, 'm,' says Tommy next day in the afternoon, appearing in the doorway of the little back sitting-room, litter-room, dirt-hole, where a special cause has gathered the three ladies of the Churchill family, 'there is a gentleman from Higgins and Rawson in the hall.'

It is a new Tommy; the old one, having bloomed out into increased size and new vices, has been superseded; a new Tommy with a cherub face, but an education for his profession that as yet leaves much to be desired.

'A *gentleman* from Higgins and Rawson!' repeats Mrs. Churchill indignantly; 'there are no gentlemen at Higgins and Rawson's—it is a haberdasher's shop! Ask him his business.'

The cherub retires, trembling, and his mistress' attention returns to the object from which his entrance had diverted

it ; the object which has called both herself and her grand-
daughters hither. It is the washing of the dogs, a function
periodically celebrated and revelled in by Sarah.

Jane is already washed ; she is a pushing dog, always
putting herself forward, and claiming the chief seats in the
synagogues. Candescently white, cleansed from stain of
indigo and ochre, no longer comic, but gravely beautiful,
she lies in glory, drying on a blanket. It is now the
martyred Slutty who is in the wash-tub, dripping resignedly,
while Sarah's strong white arm is employed in vigorously
scrubbing her fat back, and the soapsuds are falling into her
dreadfully goggling eyes.

Punch is seated in a deep dejection not usual with him
a good distance off, well aware that his fate also is hurrying
to overtake him, but trying to imagine that he may avoid it
by remaining seated in the middle distance, and totally
refusing to reply when addressed.

Belinda sits by, occasionally lending a helping hand when
Slutty struggles, and occasionally turning a page of the volume
of Browning, which, in pursuance of her intention of living
henceforth by the intellect, lies open on her knees.

Tommy has again appeared.

'If you please, 'm, there is a lady with a tambourine——'

'A *lady* with a tambourine !' repeats Mrs. Churchill, in
an awful voice. 'What do you mean, Tommy ? Ladies
do not play tambourines about the streets ! You mean a
woman with a tambourine ! Send her away.'

A second time Tommy retires discomfited, but not for
long. After a short absence he returns.

'If you please, 'm, there is a person in the hall wishes to
speak to you.'

'A person !' echoes Mrs. Churchill commendingly.
'Come, that is better ! A shopman, I suppose ! Did he
say what shop had sent him ?'

'Please, 'm, I do not think he is a gentleman from——I do not think he is from a shop at all. He said his name was Forth, and asked me to give you this card' (presenting one).

As her eyes fall upon it, Mrs. Churchill jumps up with a little shriek.

'Good Heavens!' she cries, aghast, 'it is Professor Forth! What do you mean, Tommy, by calling him a "person," and leaving him in the hall? Show him up to the drawing-room at once!'

'Please, 'm,' replies Tommy, whimpering, 'you said as how I was not to call 'em gentlemen.'

'So he has come!' cries Sarah, in a rather triumphant voice, raising a beaming face from the middle of the steam and suds. 'Do not you think he would like to see the dogs washed?'

'I cannot think what has brought him,' says Mrs. Churchill, in a vexed voice; 'that class of people has no tact. I never could find a word to say to him. Now, pray, Sarah, do not make a fool of him again! It is all very well for you, but you do not reflect what a nuisance he is to Belinda and me!'

'He is no nuisance to me!' replies Belinda coldly; 'I am glad he has come. I wanted to talk to him! I do not think he has come to see Sarah; I think he has come to see me!'

She says it with cool, positive, indifferent composure. With as much coolness, as much indifference, as much composure, she walks up the stairs and into the drawing-room, pursued by her sister's message:

'Tell him that I am coming directly, but that, with me, even Love cedes to Duty, and I must finish washing Slutty.'

Mr. Forth is looking towards the door as Belinda enters;

and an indescribable air of relief steals over his countenance
when he perceives that she is alone.

'I have taken the liberty of calling,' he begins formally;
but she interrupts him.

'I am glad to see you,' she says, with a look direct of cold
sincerity. 'I wanted to talk to you. Will you sit down?'

And yet, now that the opportunity for gratifying that
want has come, she seems for a while to lack the power.

According to his chilly wont, he has chosen the seat
nearest the fire, opposite the window, and she has placed
herself on the other side. As she looks in his face, a cataract
of agonising memories pours storming over her heart. In
the throng and bustle of last night, memory had not been
half so busy. She had thought that she could see him
without pain; with only that dull numbness with which she
sees small and great. But now she finds that for her in
each wrinkle traced by thought about his eyes—in each
pucker of discontent around his lips—there lurks a demon
of recollection.

The little wintry, fog-thickened London drawing-room
has changed to the sunny Dresden salon. It is full again
of Sarah's pungent pleasantries at her lover's cost, and of
Rivers' resounding laughs at them. A hundred worthless
speeches of Rivers', ridiculing the other's foibles, his muf-
fetees, his parsimony, his digestion—speeches trivial and
merry when spoken, now solemn and woful—rush back upon
her mind. Oh, if her heart should turn out not to be stone-
dead after all! But it must!—it must!—it shall!

Her silence has lasted longer than she is aware, and there
is a slight tone of offence—to that, too, a memory is tied—
in her visitor's voice, as he says:

'I hope I have not chosen an inopportune moment for
my visit?'

'Not at all! not at all!' she answers hastily; but the

composure with which she had entered the room, had first addressed him, is gone; a fever has come into her cheek, and a hurry into her words. 'As I told you, I am glad to see you. I want to talk to you. Why have not you gone back to Oxbridge?'

'I am to return by the 4.45 train,' he replies; 'and I thought that I could not better utilise the moments left me than by——'

'Yes, yes, I understand,' she cries, brusquely pushing aside his civilities. 'I want to ask you—I want you to tell me—I suppose that you are a competent judge—is not it quite possible for a person to live entirely by the intellect?'

He looks at her doubtfully. Such a question in the mouth of a Churchill his experience of Sarah has taught him profoundly to distrust.

'I mean,' she says, nervously plucking at the Japanese hand-screen that she has taken up to shade her face—hot, but not with fire heat—'I mean,' panting a little, 'do not you think that that is the best life—the most satisfactory on the whole—the least liable to interruption and disappoint-ment—that is built upon—upon—books, you know—upon the—the mind!'

'You must be aware,' he answers frigidly, 'that the whole tendency of my teaching is to show that the pursuit of knowledge is the only one that really and abundantly rewards the labour bestowed upon it.'

'You think so?' she answers breathlessly, leaning eagerly forward, and fixing her large heart-hungry eyes upon him. 'You think that it would be *enough*—that it would satisfy one—that one would not need anything beyond?'

There is an inexpressible sorrowful yearning in the accent with which she pronounces this last phrase. Oh, if he could but furnish her with this anodyne, how she would fall on her knees and bless him!

'Since there is no limit to the domain of the knowable,' he is beginning, when again she breaks in upon him :

'No, no ! of course not ! I understand ! But how to get at it, that is the question ! I thought—I imagined—I hoped—that perhaps you might help me—might direct me !'

Again he looks at her suspiciously. Is not this the very same request with which the mendacious Sarah had opened her fire upon him ? Is this a thirst for learning of the same character, and that is likely to be quenched with the same surprising ease ?

' Of course,' she goes on hastily, mistaking the source of his hesitation, ' I cannot expect you to waste much time upon me ; but I thought that—that—perhaps, you might be inclined to set me on the way ; to—to—lend me a book or two every now and then.'

'I am not in the habit of lending books,' he answers, still suspiciously ; 'but I should be happy to make an exception in your favour, were I convinced that your desire for self-education were a genuine one.'

'Genuine !' she cries, indignant and astonished. ' Why, what else should it be ? What motive could I have for feigning it ?'

A slight look of embarrassment, mixed with mortification, crosses his face.

'You cannot have forgotten,' he says, 'the interest in literature counterfeited by your sister——'

He stops suddenly ; for, as if the mention of her had conjured up her bodily presence, at the same instant she enters, protected by her grandmother and by a tempest of clean dogs.

' How are you ?' cries she, holding out her hand to him with the same easy, jovial smile as if they had parted yester-day on the best of terms. No confusion born of the recol-lection of their last meeting troubles her good-humour. No doubt as to the present visit being addressed to her ruffles her mind. None such apparently results from the precipitancy with which, upon her entry, her ex-lover begins to seek his hat, and murmur of his train.

'And about the books?' says Belinda, with a hesitating wistfulness when her turn comes to be bidden good-bye to. 'You will not forget about the books?'

It seems to her as if he were carrying off her new, faint, feverish hope with him, and she cannot let it go without a struggle.

'I will think of it,' he answers hurriedly, with a distrustful glance at Sarah; 'I—I will let you know.'

'What about books?' asks Sarah inquisitively, as soon as the door has closed upon him. 'Is he going to lend you books? The old villain! it was with books that he first beguiled my young affections. I believe that he is like Jacob: not having been able to obtain Rachel, he is going to try and put up with Leah! eh, Leah?'

'What an untidy way he has of sitting!' says Mrs. Churchill pettishly, advancing to set right the chair lately occupied by their guest; 'these loose chair-covers are a mistake. I am sure I hope that he will be in no hurry to repeat his visit. One thing is certain; not one of us expressed the slightest wish to see him again!'

'If I did not express it, I felt it,' answers Belinda perversely. 'I wish to see him again.'

Mrs. Churchill's sole response is a silent shrug, a mode lately adopted by her and Sarah of receiving the starts and frets of Belinda's temper—that temper once so smooth and sweet—a mode of expressing that they are to be endured, not argued with.

'How curiously ugly he is!' cries Sarah, chuckling at the recollection. 'I could hardly help laughing when I looked at him. He is like Charles Lamb's Mrs. Conrady: "No one ever saw Mrs. Conrady without pronouncing her to be the plainest woman that he ever met with in the course of his life. The first time that you are indulged with a sight of her face is an era in your existence ever after. You are glad to have seen it—like Stonehenge!"'

Mrs. Churchill laughs lazily. 'What a memory you have, child!'

'I can go on, if you like,' continues Sarah, encouraged by this praise. '"No one can pretend to forget it. No one ever apologised to her for meeting her in the street on such a day and not knowing her; the pretext would be too bare."'

'You have always grossly underrated him,' says Belinda severely; 'there is a side of him, an intellectual side, which you are totally incapable of appreciating!'

'Totally!' assents her sister placidly; 'and so, I hoped, were you!'

'At least I know that it is there!' cries Belinda angrily, beginning to walk restlessly about the room after a fashion that she has adopted during the last year—a fashion that is somewhat trying to her housemates' patience. 'I recognise it; I admit it; I would imitate it if I could!'

'Since when?' asks Sarah drily.

There is something in her apparently harmless question which jars upon Belinda's sick nerves.

'It is very hard,' she breaks out, reddening, 'that one should be thrown back and ridiculed here, when one makes any least effort to improve one's self! What is the use of making any attempt in such an atmosphere as this? What is the use of struggling—of trying——'

She bursts into stormy tears, and leaves the room.

'Her temper is becoming impossible!' exclaims Mrs. Churchill, holding up her pretty, old white hands.

But Sarah only says, 'Poor dear!' in a very lenient voice, and kisses all the dogs.

CHAPTER III.

THE year declines towards its mirk close. Every day a
little more is taken from the light and added to the dark.
London is full and cheerful; with a pleasanter, friendlier,
more leisurely social stir than the overpowering June one.
Two or three good pieces are running at the theatres, and
the shop-windows are warm with furs. Round the
Churchills a crop of small dinners and dances has sprung
up.

The time nears mid-December. Mrs. Churchill's wish
as to the non-repetition of Professor Forth's visit has met
with the usual fate of wishes. He has come again repeatedly;
so repeatedly that the dogs have ceased barking at him,
though they are not so hypocritical as to wag their tails on
his approach; nor, indeed, does he ever, by kind pats or
well-chosen civilities, give them any cause to do so. Even
the obtuse Tommy has learned that he is to be shown, not
into the drawing-room, but into the little back litter-room,
which has been arbitrarily cleared of Sarah's paint-pots,
and the promiscuous rubbish in which her soul delights;
has been furnished with pens, ink, and dictionaries, and
raised and dignified by the name of study. For Belinda's
fervour for learning rages with a feverish heat that might
make a thoughtful looker-on incline to question its solidity
or its continuance.

She is learning Latin Syntax; she is being taught Greek; she has undertaken a course of Universal History; she devotes her spare moments to the Elements of Algebra. Very seldom now does she join her family in the evening. Mostly she remains downstairs, writing Latin Exercises, learning Irregular Greek Verbs; working, working on until late into the night. She would like never to stop; to leave no single chink or cranny by which memory may enter.

And is the charm working? Is the remedy beginning to make its healing virtue felt? This is the question that she never dares ask herself. Sometimes, indeed, it thrusts itself upon her in the sadness of the night. Sometimes the pen drops from her stiffened fingers, or her tired brain relaxes its hold upon the hard-conned page, and she groans out to herself—she alone awake, with her melancholy gas-jet burning above her in the silence of the sleeping house—'Of what use? what use?' Has it given back to life its sweet and wholesome taste? Has it helped her to dominate that terrible irritability which makes no person and no moment safe from some senseless outbreak of her temper? Has it conquered that gloom which renders her the kill-joy of her little circle? There is not one of these questions that she can honestly answer in the affirmative.

But perhaps there has not yet been time enough to test the efficacy of this cure. Its action will doubtless be slow, but all the more lasting and solid for that. She must persevere; it would be madness not to persevere. She passes her hand across her weary, throbbing temples, and catches up the pen again.

The clocks strike two, and she still writes. It is not night now; it is afternoon. Mrs. Churchill and Sarah, furred and feathered, with their bonnets nicely tied on, and their faces alight with placid good-humour, have set off in the brougham on their daily career of calls and shops.

Belinda remains behind in the little dingy back room, with her copy-books. Not once to-day has she tasted the wholesome outside air—wholesome with all its blacks, and fog-charged as it is. She has been alone here the whole day, except for a couple of ten minutes grudgingly snatched for breakfast and luncheon.

She has been alone, but she is so no longer. Professor Forth has just been ushered in to partake her solitude. She meets him with a complaint.

'I expected you yesterday.'

'I was detained by a College meeting, and by other engagements,' he answers. 'I hope,' ceremoniously, 'that you were not inconvenienced by the deferring of my visit?'

'I was,' she answered brusquely. 'As it happened, I wanted you badly. I was completely puzzled by a passage here,' laying her hand upon a school edition of 'Cæsar's Commentaries.' 'I worried over it till I felt quite dazed and woolly.'

As she speaks she draws the volume towards her, and they both stoop their heads over the page; his with its old, sparse, colourless hair, thriftily drawn across the baldening crown; hers with its unregarded riches of nut-brown. The difficulty dissipated, she leans back in her chair.

'It is hopeless to make any real progress,' she says morosely, 'as long as our lessons are so interrupted. How much better it would be if we lived in Oxbridge! How I wish we lived in Oxbridge!'

She is sitting alongside of him, and does not look at him as she expresses this wish. It seems to be addressed with a general vagueness to the air.

He glances at her, sidelong and suspiciously; at the beautiful blooming profile, the discontented mouth, the fine, petulant, small nose, the veiled unglad eyes. He has almost given up suspecting her of late, but her last aspiration has rearoused his distrust. Was not Sarah once fervent and constant in her longings to inhabit a university town ?

'It would make things so much easier,' she continues plaintively, quite unconscious of his disquieting doubts. 'If I were in difficulties I could go straight to you. I had much rather live in Oxbridge than here.'

He is still observing her covertly, and makes no answer.

'It must be a good life !' she says, with the same restless longing as a sick person's for strange food; 'so full of intelligent interests, so absorbing, and must take one so out of one's self !'

As she speaks she clasps both hands at the back of her neck, and stares dreamily up at the ceiling. He has moved his eyes away from her. Perhaps they are satisfied with the result of their investigation. They now look straight before him on Cæsar's open page. Upon his fingers he balances a paper-knife, and an unusual expression has crept about his narrow lips.

'If you are sincere in your desire for a——' he begins rather slowly; but she breaks in upon him hotly.

'Sincere !' she repeats, with an angry intonation; 'I cannot imagine why you preface all your remarks with a doubt of my sincerity ! What could I possibly gain by being insincere ?'

She looks at him full and irately as she speaks, and their eyes meet; the dull old cautious eyes, and the unhappy flashing young ones.

'If my phrase offends you, I will change it !' he answers formally. ' *Since* you are sincere in your desire for a——'

But again he breaks off. There is a ring at the doorbell.

'You have visitors,' he says, in an annoyed voice. 'We shall be interrupted.'

'No, we shall not,' she replies, shaking her head.
'Tommy knows that when you are here I am not at home
to any one.'

It is a sentence susceptible of a flattering interpretation,
that, indeed, would seem to bear no other, but it is uttered
as such indifferent matter-of-fact that he would be indeed
a coxcomb who was elated by it.

'Please go on,' smiling faintly.   'Since I am sincere in
my desire for—what?'

But apparently he has lost the thread of his twice-begun
speech.

'Your servant must have mistaken your directions,' he
says, with a vexed look; 'he is evidently admitting some
one.'

Both listen, and as she listens Belinda's colour changes.

'If we were at Dresden,' she says in a suppressed and
troubled voice, 'and if I did not hope that it were impossible,
I should say that the voice was——'

The door flies open.

'Here I am!' cries Miss Watson, bursting into the room,
in apparently the identical large black and white plaid gown
and grizzled fringe, and in certainly the same burly red face
—perhaps a shade worsened by the battle and breeze—as
of yore.

She is not ushered in, but helplessly followed by the
baffled Tommy, who is raising his puny infant voice in futile
protestations, as his predecessor had so often done before
him.

'I knew by Tommy's manner that you were at home!'
cries she joyfully.   'By the bye, he is a new Tommy!
What have you done with the old one?   I would not give
him my card; I said, "No, I will surprise them!"'

She has succeeded.   Both Mr. Forth and his disciple
have risen to their feet, and now stand regarding their

visitor with a — for the first moments — entirely silent dismay.

'Mr. Forth, too !' cries Miss Watson, snatching his reluctant hand. 'Why, this is Dresden over again ! If we had but Sarah and Rivers here, we might think ourselves back there.'

Neither of Belinda's companions perceives it, but she shudders. Ever since Miss Watson's voice first fell on her shocked ears, she has known that she would have to endure the sound of Rivers' name. In reality not two minutes have elapsed since then, but it seems to her as if for hours she had been dreading it.

'How snug you are !' says the visitor, patronisingly looking round ; 'but why do you sit here? Why do not you sit in the drawing-room? Is not the fire lit there? Oh, I suppose Sarah sits there, and grandmamma? I must go and pay them a little visit just now.'

'They are out.'

'Out !' repeats the other, laughing ; 'Sarah is always out. I wish they would come back ! How soon do you expect them? We should be just our Dresden party, then —all but Rivers !'

Again that shudder, but she sets her teeth. She *must* endure it—*must* steel herself to hear his name—to pronounce it if need be.

'Shocking thing about his father, was it not?' continues Miss Watson, cheerfully pursuing the course of thought suggested by the mention of Rivers. 'Failed for over a million, and cut his throat. They say that he has left his large family—twelve? ten? nine?—how many used young Rivers to tell us there were of them?—upon the parish. But I do not believe it ; one hears of people bankrupt one day, and rolling in their carriages the next.'

Belinda's heart is beating sickeningly, and her hands are

trembling so violently that she has to clench them fast together, to hide their aguish shaking; but she is nerving herself up. Here is an opportunity for obtaining information about him such as may probably not recur for weeks, months, possibly years. Here, too, is an occasion for practising that indifferent naming of him to which she is resolved to attain.

'Does Mr. Rivers roll in his carriage?' she asks, with a strained smile.

The effort to speak is so great that it seems to her as if, when it is overcome, she speaks unnaturally loud; but, as her companions show no surprise, she concludes that it cannot be so really.

'I do not know about rolling in his carriage,' answers Miss Watson, with her loud, ever-ready laugh; 'I know that he can treat himself to stalls at the theatre, which is more than I can. I always go to the dress-circle; one's legs are a little cramped in the front row, but one can see as well as in the best place in the house.'

Belinda has stooped over the table, and is nervously arranging, rearranging, disarranging the exercise-books, grammars, pen-wipers upon it.

'Did you see him at the play?' she asks hurriedly.

'I saw him the other night at the St. James',' returns Miss Watson, inquisitively following with her eyes Belinda's unaccountable fidgetings. 'What are you looking for? have you lost anything? No?—At the St. James. "The Squire" —have you seen it? it is so well put on the stage—Mrs. Kendal quite at her best!'

'I—I think not,' answers Belinda incoherently. 'I mean no; I—I have not seen it. You were saying——'

'What was I saying?' (her eyes still fastened curiously on the girl's purposeless movements)—'you *must* have lost something!—oh! that I had seen young Rivers at the play.

He was in the stalls with a lady—his sister, we will presume —though she was not at all like him,' with a knowing look. 'If *she* was on the parish, it managed to dress her uncommonly well!'

Even Belinda's lips have turned white. She is conscious of it, and rubs them hard with her fingers. He is in London! He can go to the play, can take his pleasure with other women! She has long known in theory that he must have been frequently in London during the past eighteen months; but never before has it come home to her with such cruel practical certitude. Lightning-quick the contrast between their evenings—his and hers—has sprung before her eyes: her melancholy vigils, devoted to distasteful studies in the vain hope of wrenching her thoughts away from him; and *his*, reclining in mirthful ease in a comfortable fauteuil in the lit theatre, beside a beautiful, strange, fond woman. The beauty and the fondness her sick imagination has at once supplied. That she may possibly have been his sister, her bitter soul refuses for one instant to admit.

'I tried to get to him as we were going out,' pursues Miss Watson narratively. 'I saw him on ahead with his lady. He is a most attentive *brother!*' with a laughing accent on the word; 'he was wrapping her up like a mummy! But though I made a great push for it I could not come up with him; there was such a crowd. I never saw a fuller house. I called out to him, and once I thought he had heard, for he looked round and caught my eye; but it could not have been so, for he posted on faster than before!'

At this in happier moments Belinda would have smiled. She cannot smile now.

'Have not you seen anything of him?' asks the other, exploring the girl's wan face with the unflinching inquisitiveness of her eyes; 'has not he been to call—not once? I must tell him that there is a hole in his manners; I shall be sure to fall in with him again before long, and I will send him here. I will tell him that you expect him.'

'You will not,' says Belinda hoarsely, stretching out her hand and turning livid. 'I mean,' helped back to self-possession by the expression of astonished and eager curiosity painted all over her guest's broad face—'I mean that I think I had rather you did not. If he wishes to call, he—he—knows our address.'

CHAPTER IV.

It is next day. Outside, snow is falling; but it is flabby, irresolute, large-flaked snow, that melts as it reaches the slushy street, and makes it slushier still. Mrs. Churchill is standing by the window, eyeing the weather with disgust, and Sarah and the dogs are seated higgledy-piggledly on the hearthrug.

'This is what we are to expect for the next five months!' cries Mrs. Churchill, addressing this exasperated remark partly to the outside mud and mirk, and partly to her grand-daughter.

Neither heeds it. Sarah's whole attention, indeed, is occupied in bribing Punch, by a sweet biscuit brought up from luncheon, to the performance of the most striking in his repertoire of tricks, an affecting representation of death; which, when contrasted with his usual superabundant life, is much admired by strangers, and indeed by his own family.

It is, however, the one of his accomplishments for which he himself has the least partiality. The command to die has to be reiterated many times before he at length rolls reluctantly over on his side; and even then, as he looks up every half a second and jumps up every second, a good deal of the repose of death has to be supplied by the spectator's imagination.

'What a climate!' pursues Mrs. Churchill in angry

ejaculation. 'Good Heavens, Sarah, why do you let Jane make such a dreadful noise?'

She may well ask. Jane, seated on her haunches, is volunteering, in a loud series of forward barks, to die, to beg, to trust, to dance—to do anything of which she is utterly incapable, in order to divert to herself the attention monopolised by Punch.

Slutty, with her usual poor-spiritedness, has crawled away under a chair in sulky annoyance at her brother's social success.

'How anyone that can help it spends the winter in England, is more than I can imagine!' pursues the old lady, shivering back to the fire. 'If we were rid of Belinda we would go abroad.'

'Why should not Belinda go too?—No,' holding up a finger in severe prohibition of Punch's premature resurrection; 'dead! dead! head down! dead!'

'I could not possibly afford it; and besides,' with a shrug, 'she would spoil the whole thing; she is such a wet blanket.'

'Everybody cannot be always on the grin like you and me,' answers Sarah with surly disrespect.

'We would go to the South,' says Mrs. Churchill, perfectly unmoved by her granddaughter's want of reverence, to which, indeed, she is thoroughly accustomed, her bright old eye lightening at the notion of a holiday; 'we would have a week in Paris, and go to the play every night. I must see Judic in this new piece. We would run over to Monaco and try our luck. If only,' her exhilarated tone changing to one of impatient vexation, 'if only Belinda were out of the way!'

Mrs. Churchill is far too much of an old gentlewoman to speak loud, but her utterance is distinct and pure; she does not swallow all the tails of her words, as we English are

accused of doing. It would be impossible for any one entering the room not to hear her; more particularly as Jane has
at length been persuaded to cease favouring the company
with her remarks.

Sarah lifts her head. She had an impression as of the
door softly closing. In a moment a sudden thought has
made her hustle aside the dogs, spring up, and fly out on
the landing. She was right. Sure enough, Belinda is slowly
descending the stairs, with her back to her sister. Even
before she turns her face, which in obedience to her junior's
call she does, Sarah knows somehow by the look of her back
that she has heard. She is in walking-dress, and is evidently
making for the hall-door.

'Are you going out?' asks Sarah, with as guilty a face
and voice as if she herself, and not her grandmother, had
been the author of the ill-natured remarks so unfortunately
overheard.

'Yes.'

'To-day?' shivering.

'Yes.'

'Alone?'

'Yes.'

'Walking?'

'No.'

'In a hansom?'

'Yes.'

'Where are you going?' cries Sarah, with uncomfortable
curiosity following her sister, who has already resumed her
downward progress.

'I am going to the National Gallery to meet Mr.
Forth.'

'To the National Gallery? why cannot he come here?'

'Because, unfortunately, there is hardly so fine a collection
of pictures here as there,' replies Belinda disagreeably. 'He

wishes to show me a particular picture of the early Italian school.'

A cold apprehension steals over Sarah.

'Do not go!' she cries impulsively, catching her sister's hands; 'I am sure his picture is as little worth seeing as himself. Let him wait. Come back to the fire.'

But Belinda resolutely draws her hands away and opens the street door.

'I am glad to be—for at all events a couple of hours—"out of the way,"' she says icily.

As Sarah, discomfited, climbs the stairs again, she winks away something very like a small tear from her jovial blue eye.

*   *   *   *   *

The light is dull. The short afternoon already shows signs of waning. In the National Gallery, strolling about its handsome, all but empty rooms, is the usual sprinkling of odds and ends that represents the daily quota of art-lovers supplied by London from its four millions: two or three *mal-peigné* artisans; three or four ill-dressed women; a child or two. No better meeting-place could be found for any two people who wish to converse undisturbed, but have no reason to avoid their fellow-creatures' eyes. Under this head come the two persons who have so long been standing before a well-known Hobbema (the Giotto, which was the ostensible cause of their meeting, has been already inspected). A passer-by might presume that they were exhaustively criticising each individual beauty, but in point of fact one does not see the picture at all, and the other thinks that she does not. In after days, however, she finds that she must have done, so plainly comes out, printed on her mind, the impress of that long, long straight road going away, away; of those great, tall, wayside poplars, with their perspective of lengthy stems, their high, scant heads raised loftily into the pale sky

—such slight, gray-green heads, each one with a different character about it; of the man walking along the road to the distant red-roofed Dutch village. It has seemed to Belinda as if that man must reach the village before the Professor has finished his slow speech; but he is not yet there, and the Professor has ended. For he has spoken, and not Greek. And now Belinda is speaking. Her eyes are fixed still with a sort of glassiness on the cool and tranquil canvas of the long-dead master; and the poplars seem almost to sway to her breath. Her voice is steady and quiet, though hard.

'I am very glad of what you say as to personal affection having no part in your motives for asking me to marry you. You do not want—love,' she makes a hardly perceptible pause before pronouncing the word, 'and I have none to give; so at all events we start fair.'

He makes a sort of gesture of assent.

'I distrust, and have cause for distrusting, professions of affection,' he answers drily.

A certain flavour of rancour in his tone tells his hearer that he is thinking of her sister, and a trivial passing wonder crosses her mind as to how far Sarah had carried her nefarious simulation of an unlikely passion. Never has it seemed so unlikely as at this moment.

'All that I ask, all that I wish to obtain, is an intelligent, sympathetic companion.'

'*Sympathetic!*' she repeats reflectively. 'I am not sympathetic; I should be deceiving you if I were to let you suppose that I am. No! let us be sure that we understand each other; I have as little sympathy to give as I have—love!'

Again that slight hesitation.

'Possibly!' he answers, with a stiff impatience, looking rather annoyed at her opposition; 'on my side, I think it right to tell you of what you may perhaps be already aware, that the press of my occupations and the condition of my health forbid my indulging in many amusements enjoyed by other persons, but from which I shall be compelled to require you, as well as myself, to abstain.'

'I do not want amusements!' replies Belinda gloomily; 'amusements do not amuse me. I want occupation; can you give me plenty of that?'

His face unbends with a slight smile.

'I think I can promise you that in the life you will share with me, you will find no lack of that. My mother——'

'Your mother!' repeats Belinda brusquely; 'she is still alive then?'

'She is still spared to me,' replies he piously; but a tone in his voice, striking upon her fine ear, tells her that he would not have quarrelled with the will of Heaven, had he not been so successful in keeping awhile 'one parent from the skies.'

'She must be very old,' says Belinda thoughtfully, not reflecting on the unflattering inference to be drawn from this remark.

He assents: 'She is somewhat advanced in years.'

Belinda is silent for a moment or two. Her eyes are still vacantly fastened on the Hobbema; and a vague, absent wish to be walking with that man along that quiet road to that red village is playing about the surface of her pre-occupied mind.

'Is she——' she begins, and then breaks off.

Across her memory have darted various facts communicated by Sarah about her future mother-in-law; facts of a not altogether satisfactory complexion; something about her being out of her mind, and never ceasing asking questions.

'Is she——' it is so difficult to word it civilly; 'doting,' 'imbecile,' 'off her head'—she tries them all, but none sounds polite enough. 'Is she' (she has it at last) 'in full possession of her faculties?'

He hesitates a moment.

'She is somewhat deaf.'

'Is her sight good?'

'I regret to say that it is almost gone.'

'But she keeps her faculties? her mind?' pursues Belinda persistently.

'Her intellect is not what it was!' he answers, so shortly that Belinda feels that it is impossible to pursue her catechism further.

And, indeed, why should she? Has not the tone of his answers sufficiently proved to her that, for once in her life, Sarah had spoken unvarnished truth.

'My mother's bodily health is excellent,' he continues presently; 'I only wish that my own constitution were half as vigorous as hers; but her infirmities are such as to need a great deal of loving care; more,' with a sigh, 'than I am able to spare from my own avocations!'

Belinda is silent, drawing the obvious but not particularly welcome inference that the loving care is henceforth to be given by her.

'I am not naturally fond of old people,' she says slowly. 'I have been very little thrown with them; the only old person whom I know intimately, granny, is a great deal younger in herself than I am. I will be as kind as I can to your mother; but that is not the sort of occupation I meant. I meant,' turning her restless large look away from the restful picture to his face, at which she has hitherto hardly glanced —'I meant something that would fill the mind—some hard study!'

'There is nothing that I am aware of to prevent your pursuing any line of study you may choose to select,' he answers rather pettishly.

'And you think that the taste—the zest for it will certainly come—*certainly?*' pursues she eagerly. 'Did you ever know a case of its failing? I must not deceive you; it has not come to me yet; I take no pleasure in learning; I think that I have as little real aptitude for study as' (Sarah, she is going to say, but stops in time)—'as the veriest dunce. But you think that I shall succeed if I persevere, do not you?' (plying him both with her feverish questions, and with the plaintive importunity of her eyes); 'that perseverance must bring success to any one, however moderately bright. I know, of course'—humbly—'that I am not more than very moderately bright.'

'You have a good average intelligence,' he answers drily; 'it would be flattery to imply that you have more!'

'Of course, of course!' she rejoins, meekly acquiescing in this lover-like expression of partiality; and then there is silence again.

It is broken by Professor Forth. It would not have been broken by Belinda. She is dreamily walking again along Hobbema's straight Dutch road. Would the village be at all like Wesenstein when you reached it?

'I suppose,' he says ceremoniously, 'that there will be no objection to my calling to-morrow morning in —— Street, to announce to your grandmother the step that we propose taking. I am, of course, not aware whether or no she will be likely to oppose it.'

'Not she!' answers Belinda, leaping back from dreamland, and breaking into a hard laugh; 'she will be delighted to be rid of me.'

'And—and your sister?' says he, with that same slight resentful difficulty which he always finds in mentioning Sarah; 'will she, too, be delighted to be rid of you?'

'No—o, I think not!' answers Belinda slowly. 'She would be perfectly justified if she were, for I have done my

best of late to embitter her life; but no, I think not. By
the bye,' looking up and speaking with a quick animation
that contrasts with her late sarcastic indifference, 'I must
stipulate that you will allow her to visit me. You do not
bear malice to her,' she adds naïvely, 'for—for what happened
formerly?'

'I am not likely to bear malice,' he answers with an arid
smile, 'for a course of action for which I at least, as it turns
out, have so much reason to be thankful.'

'That is right,' she answers carelessly, passing by his stiff
politesse; 'then I think that is all. I think there is nothing
more to say, is there?'

She speaks with the same unemotional business air as if
she were concluding the purchase of a piece of land, or of
some yards of cloth. The room is, at the moment, empty
of any one but themselves. It is near closing-time, and the
sparse visitors are trailing off. There is nothing to hinder a
lover-like parting embrace between the two persons who
have just engaged to pass their lives together. But the
possibility of this never once crosses Belinda's mind, not even
when her newly-betrothed steps a pace nearer to her, and
says, in a voice through which rather more of human emotion
than she has ever before heard in it pierces:

'You must allow me to repeat the expression of my
gratification—of my thanks!'

'What for?' she asks, piercing him with the direct look of
her icy eyes. 'It is a mere matter of business that we have
been transacting. You want a secretary, housekeeper, nurse
for your mother; I want a home of my own, and a "guide,
philosopher, and friend,"' laughing harshly. 'I see no room
for thanks on either side!'

To such a speech, what rejoinder is there to make? He
makes none.

'I may as well go home now,' she says, in the same cool,

matter-of-fact tone as before; 'any further arrangements
that there are to make may be made when you come to-
morrow. You ask at what hour? At whatever hour best suits
your convenience; early or late, it is indifferent to me which.
I must ask you to call a hansom for me.'

As they emerge from the building they find that rain is
falling, a sleety rain to which the undecided snow has turned.
It beats in her face as she walks down the steps; she does
not take the trouble to run in order to escape it; she would
as soon be wet as dry. It drives in upon her even in the
hansom, where she has refused to allow the glass to be
lowered. One can get very fairly well soaked in a hansom if
one goes the right way to work. And all along sleety Pall
Mall, all the sleety way home, she is pestered with the sight,
the smell, almost the *feel*, of the wood at Wesenstein!

*   *   *   *   *

'Granny,' says Belinda, entering the drawing-room, walking straight up to Mrs. Churchill and standing before her,
not allowing her attention to be distracted even by the
wagging of three kind tails, distinctly addressed to her.
'You and Sarah may begin to pack your boxes at once;
you may be off to Monaco as soon as you please; I shall be
" out of the way !"'

Mrs. Churchill lifts her eyes, in which is none of their
usual frisky light, and fixes them coldly on her tall young
granddaughter, standing pale and severe before her. She
has always thought Belinda too tall; it strikes her more
forcibly than ever now, as she sees her towering majestically
above her. Belinda is too everything, except amusing.

'Are you hinting at Waterloo Bridge, by way of improv-
ing our spirits?' she asks sarcastically.

Mrs. Churchill is not in her playfullest mood, by which,
almost as much as by her large lawn caps, she is known to an
admiring public. The weather; the fact that several tire-

some and not one pleasant person have been to call; the consciousness of guilt towards Belinda—a consciousness not quite stifled indeed, but diverted into the channel of anger by the smart, and in fact unmeasured rebukes she has had to submit to from Sarah—all, all combine to rob her of her usual suavity. Sarah's rebukes, indeed, would have led to a quarrel could she afford to quarrel with Sarah, but she cannot. Upon her hangs too much of the ease and diversion of her life. But there is no such motive to prevent her quarrelling with Belinda, and she feels that to do so would be a pleasant relief.

'Waterloo Bridge!' repeats Belinda, with a momentary want of comprehension; then, 'Oh, I see! No; there are other modes of being out of the way beside death.'

'Perhaps you mean to announce to us your approaching marriage,' suggests the old lady ironically.

'You have saved me the trouble,' answers the girl curtly, sitting down as she speaks and beginning to unfasten her cloak, whose warmth the hot and scented room begins to make oppressive.

'You are going to be married?' cries the old lady, jumping actively up, and running towards her; *ennui*, ill-humour, and sarcasm together racing away out of her voice, and making place both in it and in her sparkling eyes for a delightful excitement. 'You do not say so! My dear child, you *have* taken us by surprise! I do not know when I have been so pleased!'

'Do not be in too great a hurry!' interrupts Belinda coldly. 'Before you express any more pleasure, you had better hear who it is whom I have promised to marry.'

'I was just going to ask, of course. Who is it? My dear child, I cannot tell you how *intriguée* I am to know,' running swiftly over in her mind the list of Belinda's somewhat shadowy admirers, all of them kept so rigorously at bay that it would have seemed impossible that any one of them could have approached within sight of love-making.

'It is Professor Forth!'

Mrs. Churchill's jaws drop; the dimpling smiles—she still has the remnants of an old dimple or two—vanish from her cheek. For several moments she is totally incapable of speech; and even at the end of them is only able to gasp out the incoherent words:

'Professor Forth! What are you talking about? Nonsense! Impossible!'

'If you disbelieve me,' says Belinda quietly, 'you had better ask him. He is coming to-morrow to inquire whether you can spare me. I told him that I thought you could.'

'Professor Forth!' repeats Mrs. Churchill, gradually but slowly regaining the possession of her senses. 'I cannot think what has happened to the girls; first Sarah, and then you. You must be bewitched!'

'I do not think that he has used any magic,' rejoins Belinda, still with that pallid composure of hers. 'The matter lies in a nut-shell: he wants a wife, and I want a——' 'Husband' she is going to say, but something in the employ of the word in such a connection strikes her as shocking and impossible. She leaves her sentence for ever unfinished.

'Well, *"tous les goûts sont respectables,"* I suppose,' rejoins Mrs. Churchill with a cynical shrug.

'To what are you applying that lying pet maxim of yours, my old friend?' asks Sarah playfully, coming suddenly into the room, rubbing her little cold hands and approaching her grandmother with a conciliatory air.

She feels a vague relief in seeing that Belinda is at home again. Neither answers; Belinda, because she has no wish to rob her grandmother of the pleasure of communicating her piece of intelligence; Mrs. Churchill, because a remnant of hurt dignity ties the tongue which she is longing to unloose.

'To what or whom are you applying it?' repeats Sarah more sharply, glancing suspiciously from one to the other as she speaks.

'To Belinda,' replies the elder woman, unable any longer to refrain herself. 'I do not know how you will like being supplanted, but she has just been informing me, as you once before did, that Professor Forth is to be my grandson.'

'He is not!' cries Sarah loudly and angrily, turning scarlet. 'Belinda,' taking her sister by the shoulder and rudely shaking her, 'why do not you speak? why do not you contradict her? why do you allow her to say such things about you? It is not true! Say that it is not true; it is only a *canard*. You have been saying it only to tease her; say that it is not true!'

'Why should not it be true?' asks Belinda, turning her lovely cold face and her gloomy eyes up towards Sarah.

The latter's hand drops nerveless from her sister's shoulder, and she steps back a pace or two.

'Then it *is* true!' she says, horrified.

'One would hardly imagine from your manner that you yourself had once been engaged to him,' returns Belinda drily; 'and yet I believe that it was so.'

'More shame for me,' cries the other violently; 'but I will do myself the justice to say that I never had the most distant intention of marrying him.'

'There we differ then,' says Belinda, slowly rising, and walking with her cloak over her arm to the door, 'for I have every intention of marrying him; and so, granny,' turning as she reaches it and calmly facing them both, 'as I began by saying, you may pack your trunks for Monaco as soon as you please.'

'How tiresomely she harps upon that string!' cries Mrs.

Churchill peevishly; the more peevishly for the pricks that
her conscience, albeit a tough one, is giving her.

'It is all your doing,' says Sarah morosely, viciously
rattling the fire-irons and boxing the dog's ears; 'you have
driven her to it; sooner or later I knew that you would!'

'Pooh!' replies the other crossly; 'she is not so easily
driven or led either. If it were for her happiness,' with a
little pious parental air, 'I cannot say that I should much
regret her marriage; and if it does really come off—it is a
shocking thing, of course, such an *amant pour rire*, but she
seems bent upon it; and if it does really come off,' the
natural frisky light reilluming her eyes, 'why then, my dear
child, there is in point of fact nothing to keep us from the
South!'

CHAPTER V.

THE morrow has come. Mrs. Churchill has risen refreshed and healthful from pleasing dreams of sunshine and lansquenet. Sarah has tossed between vexed visions and unwonted wakefulness. And Belinda? Belinda makes no complaint of her night. She looks older than when she went to bed, but the cold is pinching, and for the last year and a half she has been perceptibly ageing. The morrow has come, and the Professor. To-day he is not ushered into the little dark back-room, but is led by a full-buttoned pompous Tommy into the drawing-room, where his grandmother-elect sits ready and alone to receive him.

Perhaps they have not a great deal to say to each other. At all events the interval is short before the bell is rung and a message given to request Miss Churchill to come down. She is sitting in her little chilly bedroom, her cheek pressed against the window-pane, and her eyes idly following the dirty sparrows on the leads.

Without a moment's lingering, she obeys. As she enters the room her betrothed advances to meet her.

'I am happy to be able to inform you,' he says in his stiff Donnish voice, 'that your grandmother is good enough to say that she has no obstacle to oppose to our union.'

'I told you that she would not,' replies Belinda calmly; 'I knew that she could spare me.'

The words are simple and simply spoken, with no special stress or significant accent laid upon them; and yet under them the old lady winces.

'It is no case of "sparing,"' she says sharply; 'of course it is a break-up to our little circle; but I have no right to allow personal feeling to influence me. You are old enough to decide for yourself; you are of age; you came of age six months ago. In a case of this kind a third person has no business to interfere; and of course if you are sincerely fond of each other——'

Belinda shivers.

'Fond! it is no question of *fondness!*' she says, breathing quick and short, and in a concentrated low voice; 'you entirely misapprehend. I thought that Mr. Forth had explained to you; it is a *mariage de raison;* we marry one another because we can be useful to each other. Is it not so?' appealing to him with abrupt and uncompromising directness.

'Mrs. Churchill must be as well aware as yourself,' he replies pettishly, 'that I have no reason to wish for exaggerated professions of affection.'

'Well, I will leave you to settle it between yourselves,' cries Mrs. Churchill rather hastily, gathering up her work and making for the door; eluding, as she has made a golden rule of doing through life, any scene that threatened to be disagreeable. 'You will stay to luncheon, of course, Mr. Forth?'

Nodding and smiling, she withdraws; and the dogs, with their usual fine tact, follow her—all but Jane. As soon as she is gone:

'I hope,' says Belinda, fixing her joyless, unbashful eyes full upon him—eyes with enough coldness in them to freeze a volcano—'that there is no misapprehension, that you understand our relative positions as I do.'

'I believe that there is no necessity to go over the same ground again!' he answers snappishly.

His snappishness does not infect her.

'It is better to go over it now while it is yet time, than afterwards, when it would be too late,' she answers earnestly.

He has drawn near his usual magnet, the fire, and is chafing his bloodless hands over it. Perhaps this is the reason why he expresses neither assent nor dissent.

'I want to make it quite clear to you,' she says, still in that same deeply earnest voice, 'so that you may not have cause to reproach me afterwards, or think that I have dealt unjustly with you : I have not one grain of love to give you, nor ever shall have!' letting fall each slow word with a weight of heavy emphasis. 'Many men—most men— would refuse a woman upon such terms. It is open to you still to refuse me.'

The person she is addressing moves uneasily in his chair.

'I imagined,' he says fretfully, 'that we had treated this subject exhaustively yesterday.'

'We cannot treat it too exhaustively,' she answers persistently. 'Though I cannot love you—happily for you, you have no wish that I should—I will do my best by you ; I will be as useful to you as I can. From what I gather of your circumstances I imagine that I can be very useful to you. You are not young ; you have not good health ; you are lonely.'

A certain sound of fidgeting from the chair so chillily drawn close to the hearth betrays that there is something in this catalogue of his infirmities not altogether agreeable to its occupant.

'I am lonely too, in my way,' continues Belinda, with an unconscious accent of self-pity ; 'we can help each other ; you will teach me,' appealing to him with that hopeless, cold gentleness of hers. 'I shall be a dull scholar, and never do

you credit; but you will teach me; we will do our best by
each other.'

As she finishes speaking she draws nearer to him, and
holds out her young soft hand, as if to seal with it this
frosty bargain.   He takes it formally, but does not press it
any more than he had pressed her grandmother's.   Perhaps
he has no inclination.   Perhaps he dares not.

Belinda sits down opposite to him; the light from the
window, such as it is, falling full on her face; her hands
folded in her lap, and her eyes looking straight before her.
There is something so odd and strained in her attitude that
Jane, well-meaning but injudicious, goes up to her and rubs
her long nose and her pink-rimmed eyes against her knees
to cheer her.

'Had your grandmother been able to spare me a few
more minutes,' says Mr. Forth, in a key in which a slight
tinge of umbrage is perceptible, 'I could have wished to
enter with her into some details, upon which, as things now
are, I have been unable to touch.   With regard to the date,
for instance, I should be unwilling to hurry you unduly,
but——'

During the whole of his last sentence she has felt him
watching her narrowly.   Is this the touchstone that he is
applying to her sincerity?   Does he expect her to turn as
dishonestly restive as Sarah had obviously done whenever
any suggestion of a like nature had been made to her?
The idea crosses her mind with a sort of thin fugitive
amusement.

'You need not consult granny,' she answers coldly;
'you had better arrange it so as best to suit your own con-
venience.'

There is such an evident good faith, such an entire
absence of all desire of evasion in her look and tone, that
his scrutiny relaxes.

'It is all one to me,' she says; 'there is nothing to wait for.'

In her tone is such a flat, tame hopelessness that Jane redoubles her rubbing against her knees, and accompanies it with an acute, short bark. If that will not put her in spirits, nothing will.

'I should, of course,' pursues Mr. Forth, 'be anxious to leave you sufficient time for such preparations as you may wish to make.'

'What preparations?' she asks brusquely; 'I need none. You are past the age, I suppose, when marriage festivities would give you much pleasure; and they would be entirely out of place here.'

'It is, however, usual, I believe,' he answers, in an annoyed tone, 'to make some slight sacrifices to conventionality on an occasion of this kind; it is usual——'

'It is usual to love one another!' breaks in she with a bitter laugh. 'What is usual with others does not apply to us; you need not take my preparations into your calculations.'

He is silent, but his face expresses vexation.

'It had better be soon,' continues Belinda coolly; 'I shall be in the way here if it is not. They want to be rid of me; they want to go to the south of France; it had better be soon.'

But even now Professor Forth does not immediately answer. Perhaps this mode of treating the question of an approaching marriage seems to him even more baffling than Sarah's. At last:

'It is extremely fortunate for me,' he says slowly, and without any perceptible exhilaration of tone, 'to find you so ready to meet my views.'

'There is nothing to wait for,' repeats she flatly. It seems as if in this phrase there were a dismal charm for her.

Again there is a pause, during which Belinda's eyes rest upon her betrothed's face with a look of cold expectancy.

'Were I not reassured,' he begins at length, 'by the indifference you express as to the date, I should hesitate to name one so early as the 10th of next month.'

'Could not it be sooner?' asks Belinda curtly.

He looks at her in unfeigned astonishment. In this family is he to experience no medium between disingenuous procrastination and unmaidenly haste?

Belinda sees and interprets his look, but her eyes do not fall; her cheeks do not colour beneath it.

'When a thing has to be done,' she says, with a sort of restlessness for a moment ruffling her hitherto deathly calm, 'it is well that it should be done at once; I hate dawdling!'

'I fear,' he says, in a perplexed and not particularly pleased voice, 'that my engagements will not allow of my suggesting an earlier date. I had thought that the 10th would have left a clear fortnight, before the commencement of term, for whatever journey——'

'*Journey!*' she interrupts almost rudely, breathing quick. 'What journey? do you mean a wedding tour?' with an accent of indescribable shrinking. 'Why should we make one at all? why should not we go straight to Oxbridge?'

'I am sorry,' he answers stiffly, 'to disoblige you; but, quite independently of present arrangements, I have been advised by my medical man to try the effect of a more bracing air, as a corrective to the extreme relaxingness of Oxbridge!'

She is silent for a moment; then:

'Of course,' she says grudgingly, 'if it is a matter of health, I can say nothing; but, as far as I am concerned, I would far rather go straight to Oxbridge.'

*   *   *   *   *

'He is not going to stay to luncheon then?' cries Sarah,

in an exhilarated voice, running into the drawing-room;
after having been hanging perilously far over the upper
banisters unseen, to speed the parting guest. 'Thank God
for that! There are sweetbreads for luncheon, and I should
have been sorry to miss them, as I certainly should, for
nothing would have induced me to sit down with him!'

'I think you will have to get over that little difficulty in
time!' replies Belinda drily.

She had risen to bid her betrothed good-bye, and yet
stands. She is holding her cold right hand, which still
seems to feel the chill impress of his frosty handshake, to
the fire.

'He is gone for good, is not he?' continues Sarah,
hurrying up; 'you have thought better of it? it was only a
joke? As a joke, it was not a bad one; I am not sure,'
with a glance of indignant admiration at her sister, 'that in
that point of view it was not an improvement even upon
mine in the same line; but one may have too much of it.
It *was* a joke, was not it?' with an eager stress.

'On the contrary,' replies Belinda, with as icy a composure as if her lover's bloodless eld were infectious, and
she had caught it; 'the day is fixed!'

In her hasty entrance Sarah had left the door ajar, and
through it her grandmother now enters; having apparently
overheard the last words.

'The day fixed!' repeats she, with her eyes dancing;
'my dear Belinda, you take us by storm! we are in a whirl!
But fixed for when?'

'For the 10th of next month,' replies Belinda curtly,
turning away her dull face from her beaming questioner,
and speaking in a key, if possible, yet more frozen than
before.

'The 10th!' repeats Mrs. Churchill, in a tone into
which she honestly, if not very successfully, tries to infuse a

tinge of regret; 'that *is* soon! You *are* in a hurry to
leave us!'

'There is nothing to wait for,' replies Belinda, mechanically repeating her dreary formula.

'I cannot think how we shall manage about your clothes!'
continues Mrs. Churchill, growing pink with pleasure, and
her old dimple reappearing. 'We shall be shockingly
hurried! we must go about your underclothes and *lingerie*
this afternoon. Mary Smith in Sloane Street is excellent,
is not she, Sarah? but she has already half a dozen wedding
orders.'

'She may be spared a seventh,' replies Belinda, with a
bitter small smile. 'I will have no new clothes!'

'That means, of course, that you are not in earnest,'
says Mrs. Churchill, with a disappointed refrigeration of
tone; 'that the whole thing is a fiction. You might as
well have said so at first!'

A flash of hope has come into Sarah's sunny eyes as she
looks eagerly at her sister; but at the expression of that
sister's face it at once dies down again.

'Do not be afraid,' says Belinda quietly, 'it is no fiction;
but I will have no new clothes: you will have the more
money to spend at Monaco.'

'Monaco! Monaco!' repeats Mrs. Churchill, hiding a
look of conscious guilt under a fretful air; 'you have
Monaco on the brain; it is your *idée fixe!* But as to your
clothes——'

'As to my clothes—simply I will not have any,' replies
Belinda, with a look of imperative decision.

'I should have thought them the one Goshen in your
desert,' says Sarah, with an annoyed laugh; 'them and the
presents.'

'Presents!' echoes Belinda impatiently; 'I will have no
presents!'

'In short,' says Mrs. Churchill sarcastically, 'you and the Professor will crawl in a four-wheeled cab to a registry-office at eight o'clock in the morning.'

'If you substitute a church for a registry-office, you have exactly expressed my intention.'

There is an aghast silence. Sarah and Mrs. Churchill look at one another. Something in their interchange of glances grates upon Belinda.

'You will never understand,' she says, exchanging her icy calm voice for one of excessive irritability, such irritability as of late her family has been too well acquainted with, 'and it is no use explaining to you. I am tired of explaining to you that this is not an ordinary marriage. What is there to make a gala of, and buy new clothes for, in a mere matter of business? I tell you it is a mere matter of business; I keep dinning it into your ears, but you *will not* understand! it is a *mere matter of business!*'

She repeats it over and over again, as if to reassure herself by the strength and number of her own repetitions, and looks round at her two auditors, as if daring them to òppose any contradiction to her assertion. Neither of them does. It is, indeed, some moments before either of them finds anything to say. Then:

'Have you made this quite clear to Professor Forth?' asks Mrs. Churchill drily.

'Quite!' replies Belinda excitedly; 'quite! I made it as clear as the sun in heaven; he quite understands; he fully agrees with me; he is quite of my way of thinking.'

'He must be a very odd bridegroom,' says Mrs. Churchill sarcastically.

'It is a marriage of the mind!' replies Belinda, still more excitedly, looking round with angry suspicion in search of the ridicule which she dimly feels may attach to her last utterance. 'I do not suppose that there is anything very odd in two people hoping to draw a certain amount of rational happiness from such.'

Mrs. Churchill turns away to conceal an ungovernable smile.

'A marriage of the mind!' repeats Sarah, with a disgusted accent; 'well, I have heard of them before, but this is the first time that I ever had the pleasure of meeting one; and I humbly hope it may be the last.'

CHAPTER VI.

THE winter advances; Christmas comes; comes, as it not infrequently now comes to the world's greatest city, in an almost total darkness; a choking yellow darkness. The gas has to be lit at ten o'clock in the morning. Drearily it flares, from the imperceptible dawn until the undiscriminated night. Under its and the fog's pestilent breaths the flowers in the stands wither; the carefully-cherished puny ferns shrink away into death. Through the suffocating obscurity the church bells ring muffled; the cabs crawl cautiously at a foot's pace, and the omnibuses cease to run. None of the Churchill family have been able to get to church; and either by that fact or by the fog their spirits and tempers are sensibly worsened.

Mrs. Churchill likes to go to church on Christmas Day; it is a sort of fetish, the loss of which may entail disadvantage upon her, either in this world or in the next.

'How anything short of absolute necessity can keep any one in England during the winter months, passes my comprehension!' cries she, taking up her old cry, and pettishly clicking together the clasps of the prayer-book, in which she has been reading the lessons for the day.

Sarah, her only companion, makes no reply; not that she is absorbed in any occupation, but because the remark appears to her to be both old and worthless.

'And I am far from feeling sure that we shall ever get away after all,' continues the elder woman, seeing that she may wait in vain for a sympathetic response. 'I feel no sort of confidence in Belinda,' in an exasperated voice; 'she is quite capable of throwing him over at the last moment. What do you think? do not you hear that I am speaking to you? do not you think that she is quite capable of throwing him over at the last moment?'

'It shall not be for want of asking if she does not,' replies Sarah surlily.

'I really do not see that you have any right to put pressure upon her,' rejoins Mrs. Churchill crossly; 'I cannot see that it is any business of yours. Because *you* behaved extremely ill to him, is no reason why you should incite your sister to do the same. In fairness to him, I must insist upon your not attempting to influence her one way or the other!'

'You *may* insist,' replies Sarah undutifully, her soft round face growing dogged and hard; 'but as long as I have one breath left, I shall spend it in trying to hinder her from such a monstrous suicide.'

'*Suicide!*' repeats Mrs. Churchill angrily; 'pooh! you may be very thankful if you ever get any one to make as good a settlement upon you as he has done upon her! *Suicide*, indeed!'

'Why do you not marry him yourself, if you are so pleased with him?' asks Sarah cynically; 'it seems all one to him which of us he marries, so as he gets one of the family; it seems to be the breed, not the individual, that he admires. Marry him yourself, and carry him off to Cannes; I assure you that I will not move a finger to prevent you!'

'He is a man not without distinction in his own line,' pursues Mrs. Churchill, affecting not to have heard her granddaughter's last ironical suggestion; 'though it happens to be a line which you are quite incapable of appreciating. He is not handsome, certainly, but there is a good deal of —of,' hesitating for an encomium—'of character in his face. He has made an excellent settlement upon her; it quite took me by surprise. She is twenty-one, and it is her first *bonâ-fide* offer; I think you will not be acting at all a friend's part in making her quarrel with her bread-and-butter.'

'Whether I am acting the part of a friend or not,' retorts Sarah obstinately, marching towards the door, 'I promise you that I shall carry my remonstrances to the altar-foot; and so would you if you did your duty. You may like to know,' firing a defiant parting-shot from the door-way, 'that I am going straight to her now to resume the subject.'

She is as good as her word. She finds Belinda where she knew that she would find her, in her little back sitting-room, but not employed as she had expected. She had thought to come upon her stooping over her eternal copy-books; but for once they are laid aside. She is sitting on the hearthrug, the gas glaring above her and casting its ugly shadows upon her cheeks, making them look lined and hollow. Strewn about her is a small litter of old writing-desks, old workboxes, childish relics. On her lap lies open a morocco pocket-book, over which, on Sarah's entrance, she hastily puts her hands, as if to conceal it.

'I am setting my house in order,' she says, looking up with a rather guilty smile. 'Did you ever see such a squirrel's nest? Here is the case of court-plaister that you gave me on my eighth birthday. Do you remember how fond we were of giving each other court-plaister? Here is the lady's companion that granny brought me from Bath; I remember crying because she brought you such a much better one. Even as long ago as then,' looking pensively at the little rusty old pair of scissors and the dim bodkin, 'it began.'

'What were you looking at when I came in?' asks
Sarah brusquely, and dropping on her knees beside her
sister.

Belinda starts.   Her first impulse is to clasp her hands
in still closer guardianship over her hid treasure; but her
next corrects it.

'You are quite welcome to see them once more, before
they go into the fire,' she says quietly, though in the yellow
gaslight her cheeks crimson.   'I do not know why I should
hide them; they are relics of an affection almost as warm
and as steady as granny's.   There!' picking up and holding
scornfully between her finger and thumb for Sarah's inspec-
tion one withered flower after another.   'That was once a
gardenia; that was a Cape jessamine; that was a tuberose.
How pretty they look! how sweetly they smell now!   Have
you looked enough at them?   Off with them then!'

As she speaks, and despite Sarah's hand stretched out
with involuntary eagerness to check her, she tosses the little
dry skeletons into the fire, where, with a hardly perceptible
shrivel and crackle, they for ever disappear.

Belinda watches them with a hard, dry eye.

'Are you satisfied?' she says, turning to her sister, and
exhibiting the pocket-book extended empty from cover to
cover.   'There is nothing else in it except my love-letter;
it is humiliating to have but one, is not it?   Would you like
to read it again before it follows those pretty flowers, or may
it go at once?'

'Give it me!' cries Sarah, snatching the little sheet,
which looks older than it really is from obvious hard wear,
continual unfolding, blistering tears.   'I will read it again.
Perhaps, reading it in cold blood like this, the meaning
may strike one differently!'

'If you wish I can spare you the trouble,' says Belinda
bitterly.   'I can say it to you if you wish.'

The fire burns low and dull; and Sarah rises and stands right beneath the gas, so that no lack of light may hinder her examination of the document in her hand. But the rays of a June sun would be in this case of no use.

'I can make nothing of it,' she says dispiritedly, giving it back to its owner; 'but do not—*do not* burn it!'

For a moment Belinda hesitates, considering with quivering eyelids and trembling lip the small and faded paper. Then in a moment it has followed the flowers!

At first it gives a curling writhe, as if it hurt it to be burnt; then one or two sentences come out very clear before flying in black film up the chimney. The one that lasts longest and disappears latest is, 'Oh, forgive me!'

After that there is silence. Sarah has dropped sulkily into an armchair; and Belinda has turned again to her childish treasures, and is beginning to sort and part them. But her hands move mechanically of their own accord, and with that want of purpose which shows that they are not directed by the brain.

When a quarter of an hour has gone dumbly by, Belinda speaks, in that flat and spiritless voice which is now habitual to her:

'I wanted to ask your advice; I want you to give me your opinion. Is it necessary—am I bound in honour to tell Professor Forth?'

She stops with a sudden sobbing catch in her breath.

'If you think that your confidence will be in the least likely to make him break his engagement, tell him by all means!' replies Sarah surlily. 'Not only tell him what there is to tell, but invent a great deal more besides. I promise you that I will aid you with all the powers of my imagination!'

'Must I really tell him?' groans Belinda, with an accent of such acute pain that Sarah's heart smites her.

'Tell him !' she cries compassionately. 'My poor child, what is there to tell ?'

'What indeed !' acquiesces Belinda, in bitter humility. But she looks relieved. 'Even if there were anything to tell,' she goes on a moment later—'but, as you justly say, there is nothing, for one is not answerable to any one for the freaks of one's own imagination—but even if there were, he has no concern with my past, has he ? It is only from the tenth of next month onwards that I am accountable to him for my actions !'

'The tenth of next month !' repeats Sarah fiercely. 'What, is that still the day on which the gallows is to be erected ?'

'If you think that by wording it so offensively, you will induce me to put it off, you are mistaken,' answers Belinda, with an access of miserable, sore ill-humour; 'and you know the sooner I am "out of the way"—I am always in the way now—the sooner you can be off to the South !'

'Save your sneers for granny, who deserves them,' answers Sarah, genuinely hurt. 'I do not.'

'I know you do not !' cries the other remorsefully; 'but you were the nearest thing to me. It seems, nowadays, as if I must put my sting into whatever is nearest to me !'

'That is the right frame of mind in which to be led to the gal—— to the altar, is not it?' retorts Sarah sarcastically; and again they are silent.

'I now wish to Heaven,' resumes Sarah devoutly, at the expiration of a heavy interval, 'that I had married him myself. Intensely as I should have disliked it, he could not have made me as unhappy as he will you. A wineglass holds less than a hogshead; and the pious hope of an early widowhood, which you will be too conscientious to indulge, would have buoyed me up !'

Belinda's only answer is a sickly smile.

'You would have gone on living with granny and the dogs,' pursues Sarah, in earnest narrative; 'she would have grown civiller to you when she found that she had no one else to depend on, and she really is very good company when she chooses; and by and by, some fine day, Rivers might have come back. 'No, no!' resolutely catching and holding down with her small, strong wrists the hands that her sister is hurrying to her tortured face. 'I do not care whether you wince or no! I do not care whether it hurts you or no; you *must* and *shall* hear. *Some day—Rivers— might—have come back again!* He may come back still; but it may be after the 10th of January!'

She pauses dramatically, and fixes her eyes upon the poor quivering features, so barely exposed to her piercing scrutiny. There comes no answer but a moaning sigh.

'I can give you no reason for it,' continues Sarah; 'I know no more about him than you do; but I have a conviction—something tells me, that there has been some mistake, some hitch, some unavoidable delay!'

'An unavoidable delay of eighteen months!' says Belinda, with faltering irony. 'How likely!'

'A letter has been lost.'

'Letters are never lost,' hopelessly.

'Well, have it as you like!' cries Sarah impatiently. 'All the same, my conviction remains that some day he will come back again. How glad you will be to see him! How pleasant it will be for you to introduce him to your husband, Mr. Forth!'

By a great wrench, Belinda succeeds in loosing one hand; but it is a very insufficient shield, and she has failed in liberating the other, so sturdily held in Sarah's small but potent grasp.

'I see him coming into the room with those blazing eyes of his,' goes on Sarah, in a sort of prophetic frenzy—'they were not much like Mr. Forth's eyes, were they?—and you introducing them to each other: "My husband, Mr. Forth! Mr. Rivers!" I envy you that moment!'

But at this Belinda tears herself free.

'This is too much!' she says, in a suffocated voice, and struggling to reach the door. 'Let me go! I *must* go! I can bear no more!'

But Sarah falls on her knees, and catches her sister's gown.

'Do you think it is as bad as the reality will be?' she asks, in a thrilling, clear voice. 'And you will not be able to run away from it! Do you suppose that there will be a single corner in the whole earth in which you can take refuge from it?'

Something in Sarah's tone has, more than her detaining gesture, arrested Belinda's flight. Stock-still she stands, in a wretched irresolution, death-pale.

'It is too late!' she murmurs miserably.

'It is *not* too late!' cries Sarah in wild excitement, clasping her sister's knees; 'it will be too late after the 10th, but it is not too late now. Give it up! Throw him over! What will he care? What harm will it do him? How much the worse is he for having been thrown over by me?'

Belinda still stands, white and trembling, her eyes staring stonily out into vacancy. Before them, though they seem to see nothing, stands that dreadful vision conjured up by her sister; and the sight of it makes every limb shake.

'It is impossible!' she says feebly.

'It is *not* impossible!' asseverates Sarah, in passionate heat. 'Give me a chance, and I will show you whether it is possible or no! Let me tell him. Give me that commission as my Christmas-box; it would be the best I ever had! I will tell him,' laughing rather hysterically, 'that it is a constitutional peculiarity of our family!'

Perhaps it is Sarah's laugh that recalls her sister to a more normal condition of feeling. With a long sigh she comes back to reality.

'Who would tell granny?' she asks, with a sarcastic smile. 'Who would dare break to her that she was not to be robbed of her darling after all?'

'*I* would!' cries Sarah, with delighted eagerness. 'I know few things in the world that would give me a purer pleasure. Let me go now, at once! Strike while the iron is hot!' jumping up, and moving in *her* turn rapidly towards the door. But it is now Belinda who detains *her*.

'Pooh!' she says coldly; 'it was only a flight of fancy on my part. It would be amusing to give her a fright; but she has no real cause for alarm. What change has happened that I should change?' in a lifeless tone. 'Your word-painting was so vivid, that for one moment I thought he had come back; but it seems not. I think,' with a bitter smile, 'that if I waited for him to come back to me, I should wait my life long.'

'I do not ask you to wait your life long,' cries Sarah, re-doubling that energy of persuasion which, as she disappointedly sees, has been hitherto exercised in vain. 'I only ask you to wait *one month!* Surely,' with a scathing sneer, 'the joys that you expect are not so poignant but that you can afford to defer them for four weeks!'

'Why should I defer them?' asks Belinda, with a fierce restlessness in eye and gesture. 'If I had had my will, I should have been married by now. It is this state of transition which is worst of all; one is unhinged; one is off one's balance.'

Sarah has again fallen down on the floor before her sister, and is again suppliantly clasping her knees.

'One month! one month!' she cries beseechingly. 'And before the month is out, you may be down on your knees as

I am, thanking God and me for having saved you from perdition.   One month! one month!'

She has pressed her head against her sister's gown, and through the woollen stuff her tears are soaking—Sarah's rare tears!

There is such a compelling ring in her voice that Belinda's cold, sick heart throbs beneath it.   Again that vision rises before her, but changed and beautified.   Rivers is coming into the room, but between him and her thrusts itself no chill, pedant figure.

As she so stands hesitating, thrilling, in a waking dream, the door of the room does in effect fly open, and some one enters.   Is it Rivers?   Alas, no!

'A merry Christmas to you!' bawls Miss Watson, noisily entering, and throwing her greeting at them like a paving-stone.   'I have just been up to wish granny a merry Christmas, but she does not seem very bright, eh?   Do you think she is breaking at all?   She did not seem up to her usual mark!'

Sarah has sprung to her feet, her habitual *aplomb* gone, and her one impulse to hide, at any price, her tear-stained face from the horny eyes of the intruder.

'Why, *you* do not look very bright either!' cries the latter, looking inquisitively from one to the other of the girls' dismal faces.   'What is it?   Christmas bills?   Colds?   You look as if you had a cold!' concentrating her whole attention upon Sarah, whose face is so little used to being inundated with tears that it resents it, and shows the traces more plainly than does one that is frequently bewept.

'I have,' she answers, snatching eagerly at the excuse, and violently resuming a part of her usual nonchalant self-command; 'a terrific cold.   I have had it for—for *years!* If I were you, I would not come near me, or I shall give it you as soon as look at you!'

'Pooh!' replies Miss Watson doughtily. 'You should take a cold bath all the year round, and wear flannel next your skin. Look at me!'

'Are you the result of taking a cold bath all the year round, and wearing flannel next the skin?' asks Sarah innocently, stealing a covert glance at her own foggy image in the little Chippendale mirror over the mantelpiece, to see how far she is recovered.

But Miss Watson does not hear.

'I am sure I do not know how I ever got here!' continues she, drawing up a chair to the fire, and setting her large feet on the fender; 'there is not a cab to be had. I felt my way all round Berkeley Square by the railings. Five or six times I was as nearly as possible run over!'

'Just heavens, why not *quite?*' murmurs Sarah under her breath.

'I never remember such a Christmas Day; do *you* ever remember such a Christmas Day? I have just been asking granny whether, in all her long experience, *she* ever remembers such a Christmas Day.'

'If you have been appealing to granny's long experience,' rejoins Sarah sarcastically, 'no wonder you did not find her very bright; there is nothing in the world that she hates so much.'

'I told her how ill I thought her looking,' goes on the visitor comfortably, rubbing her knees, advanced in close proximity to the fire. 'She tells me that it is the climate; that it is killing her by inches. She seems to have her heart set upon going to the Riviera; why does not she go?' with another look of acute inquisitiveness darted at her two companions. 'She spoke of there being some tiresome hitch—something in the way; what is it—eh?'

'We cannot bear to go so far away from you,' replies Sarah impudently, but with a nervous laugh and look towards her sister; 'that is it.'

But a curiosity so robust as Miss Watson's is not to be blunted by a jest. That great Toledo blade is not to be turned aside by a light rapier.

'No question of £ *s. d.*, eh?' says she persistently; 'the Riviera grows dearer every year! No? Anything about either of you, then?' trying to get a better idea of Belinda than the rather drooped nape of her white neck and one homespun shoulder afford; 'any little—little *entanglement*, eh?'

'You have hit it!' cries Sarah jeeringly; 'it is useless to try and conceal anything from you: we are endeavouring to arrange a marriage between me and the Archbishop of Canterbury; and, as he cannot conveniently leave his see, we think it as well that I should remain in the neighbourhood.'

It is obvious that nothing is to be made of Sarah; the visitor turns her attention towards the other sister.

'Any more Latin exercises, Belinda?' she asks in a rallying voice; 'has Professor Forth been helping you to do any more Latin exercises? does he often come? do you see much of him? does he ever ask you to go down to Oxbridge, eh?'

To these questions Belinda's answer is so unready that her junior has again to come to her aid.

'Of course,' she answers ironically; 'but he says he will not have us, unless we bring you too.'

'As to that,' replies Miss Watson, her rhinoceros-hide quite unpunctured by the pricks of this angry persiflage, 'I can tell you I have a very good mind to take a run down there. What do you say to our making up a party? we would make him give us luncheon and take us about; they are always delighted to give one luncheon and take one about; and if we can get hold of Rivers, we will make him come too.'

She looks triumphantly round to collect the suffrages of

her companions as to this project; but neither is equal to giving utterance to any opinion upon it.

'Apropos of Rivers,' continues the other, too happy in the sound of her own voice to miss the lacking response, and addressing the observation more especially to Belinda, 'a very odd thing happened to me. I had not gone five yards from your house the other day, before I met him. I asked him at once whether he was on his way to call upon you.'

'And he said what?' asks Sarah, trying to speak lightly, but with a hurry in her voice that she cannot still.

'He said "No."'

'That answer had at least the merit of brevity,' replies Sarah, laughing forcedly and changing her position so as to interpose the slight bulwark of her girlish figure between her sister and their guest.

'I asked him why not. I said, "Do go; they expect you."'

'That did not show a rigorous attention to truth on your part,' rejoins Sarah sharply: 'we did not expect him. But what did he say to that? was his answer marked by the same courteous diffuseness as before?'

'He did not say anything; he walked on very fast and hailed a hansom; but I should not wonder if he did come after all,' consolingly. 'I called out to him, just as he was driving off, to be sure not to forget. Is that the luncheon-bell? Dear me! how the morning has run away! I suppose,' with her loud assured laugh, 'that you will give me a slice of beef and plum-pudding, will not you, eh?'

CHAPTER VII.

AFTER that Christmas morning Sarah spends her eloquence in vain. She may draw what pictures and practise what oratory and cry what tears she chooses. Of what use is it to draw pictures for, or address appeals to, or weep tears over a stone? And as far as any malleability or power of receiving impressions from without goes, Belinda is henceforth a stone. She accepts all her sister's appeals in a sullen, dogged silence. Whether she ever even hears them, Sarah is ignorant. She gives no sign of having done so by any least emotion produced by them. She listens, or seems to listen, with phlegmatic indifference to the sarcasms, vituperations, witticisms, poured from Sarah's cornucopia upon her future husband. They awake in her neither anger nor pain. She makes no effort to check them. Apparently she would as soon hear them as not. But at the end of them, when Sarah, from pure loss of breath—not, Heaven knows, from any lack of goodwill—has paused, things are at precisely the same point as they were when she began.

Beaten and discouraged, she desists at last. Not, indeed, that she ever constrains herself so far as to omit tacking on some abusive adjective to the name of her future brother-in-law whenever she has occasion to mention him. Nor is it until she has exhausted every possible expletive that, as far as she knows, the English language contains, and applied

them not only to him, but to his mother, that she desists at
all. She relieves her feelings by putting all the dogs into
mourning, tying a piece of black crape round each of their
tails ; a proceeding which fills Punch with fury, Slutty with
mauvaise honte, and Jane with pride. Jane has that love for
finery which is implanted in many plain persons.

With a face set like a flint, Belinda marches to her doom.
And neither dogs nor men can retard the approach of the
date of that doom. There are no preparations to delay it.
She has steadfastly adhered to her determination to have no
new clothes.

' A wilful woman will have her way ! ' Mrs. Churchill says,
shaking that head whose eyes seem to grow brighter and her
cheeks pinker and smoother as each day brings her nearer
to the 10th of January and the South of France. 'I suppose
you know your own affairs best ; and I fancy that you
will not have much need for dress at Oxbridge. The
only time that I was there I thought all the women shocking
fagoté !'

She stops and shrugs her shoulders at the recollection ;
but even as she shrugs a smile hovers across her lips. She
is thinking that her French tour will be none the worse for
having her purse made heavier by the weight of Belinda's
trousseau.

' I am *too* annoyed about Belinda,' she says on another
occasion to her younger granddaughter ; ' but you know
how useless argument is ! She is as obstinate as a mule ;
and since she is determined to be no expense to me, I was
thinking,' her eye lightening, ' of getting one or two things
for ourselves. I should not wonder if, after all, I might
manage to let you have that plush cloak trimmed with
fisher-tails that you asked me for at Coralie's the other day.
Come ! what do you say ? ' tapping her cheek with an air
of fond friskiness.

'I say that I will not have it!' replies Sarah doggedly; 'it is blood-money!'

The settlements are drawn up. Belinda's widowhood and her younger children are provided for. Bought are license and ring. The latter Professor Forth brought one day to be tried on; and Belinda, with white, shut lips, pallidly essayed it. There is no bustle of arriving parcels, no wedding presents to be displayed. Miss Churchill has sternly insisted upon an absolute secrecy being observed as regards her engagement. She can bear to be married, but gifts and congratulations upon her marriage she could not bear. So that the comers and goers to the little house in —— Street still come and go, without suspicion that anything out of the ordinary course is brewing beneath its modest roof.

Mrs. Churchill would have preferred that the betrothal should be proclaimed from the housetops. It would give it a body and solidity that just at first she fears it lacks. An engagement known to all the world is much more difficult of rupture than one to which only the three or four persons most nearly concerned are privy.

'Belinda is so odd and crotchety,' she says one afternoon, as she and Sarah are driving home through the Park together; 'why, if she is in earnest, should she object to people being told? Do you think there would be any harm in my just giving a hint of it to the Crawfords, and Dalzells, and Lady Hunt, and—and just our own intimates? They will be so hurt at being left out in the cold; and I am sure that they would give her something handsome. Even if she does not care for personal ornaments, they might give her plate; I do not suppose,' with an amused smile, 'that there is likely to be much plate in the Forth family!'

'And you think,' retorts Sarah, with a fiery eye and a curling lip, ' that the more people you tell about it the more

Belinda will be nailed to keeping it! Do you think that, after all these years, I do not understand you?'

The elder woman looks rather foolish, and does not repeat her suggestion.

And now, indeed, all necessity for it is at an end. There is obviously no need to tie Belinda with the cords of convention and public opinion to her faggot and stake. The 10th of January has come, and she has as yet shown no sign of flinching. To ensure the greater privacy, the marriage is to take place at nine o'clock in the morning. Not a soul is bidden to it. There are no bridesmaids or groomsmen, no train of wedding guests.

Even Mrs. Churchill, on hearing of the earliness of the hour, has, like those wedding guests that Scripture speaks of, begged to be excused. Perhaps it is not only the raw winter morning from which she shrinks. Perhaps she is not particularly anxious to be an ocular witness of that ceremony which she has certainly speeded with her prayers.

'I hope you do not think it unkind of me, my child,' she says, appearing at her dressing-room door in a pretty laced dressing-gown as she hears her granddaughter descending the stairs to the brougham; 'but you know what a London church is, and you know what my neuralgia is. How nice you look!' smilingly surveying the dark, homespun suit, so dark and brown as in the shabby light to look quite black, and the rigidly plain close bonnet which her granddaughter has chosen for her wedding garments.

Belinda smiles too—a smile of which her grandmother is not particularly fond of thinking of afterwards.

'Yes, do not I?' she says—'so like a bride!'

'In point of fact,' continues the old lady rather hurriedly, and not much relishing the tone of this acquiescence in her compliment, 'I shall be far more useful at home; I shall ensure the house being thoroughly well-warmed for you when you come back; you shall find roaring fires in every room!'

'We shall not come back,' replies Belinda quietly.

'Not come back?' (with an accent of extreme surprise). 'You are going abroad then?

'No; but there is nothing to come back for.'

'And whose fault is that, pray?' asks her grandmother with an uncomfortable laugh. 'If I had had my way, there would have been plenty to come back for: a good breakfast; a score of people; speeches!'

'But that was not my way,' replies Belinda, again faintly smiling; 'and, as you say sometimes, *tous les goûts sont respectables.* I am afraid that I shall be late if I delay any longer; good-bye, granny.'

She speaks the two last words quite gently and friendly, and holds out her fair cold cheek to be kissed. Mrs. Churchill is afterwards not much fonder of thinking of the feel of that cheek, than of the look of that smile before spoken off.

'I wish I had not kissed her,' she says to herself fretfully afterwards, as she sits with her still pretty feet resting on the well-warmed fender in the privacy of her dressing-room, when the brougham has rolled away; 'it was almost like kissing a dead person!'

And meanwhile, through the dismal morning streets, dirty with that worst of all dirtiness, dirty snow, and where the lamp-lighters have only just put out the lamps, and would have done better not to put them out at all, Belinda drives, her sister by her side. The angry tears are raining down Sarah's face, encouraged rather than checked by their owner. In her small warm hands (for even on a bitter January morning wrath is warming) lie tightly clasped Belinda's cold ones. The shop-boys are only just beginning to take down the shutters; in the haberdashers' undressed windows, instead of costly fabrics and dainty webs, are to be seen nothing but bare boards and skeleton stands. The blue-armed housemaids are scrubbing the door-steps; through the squares the milk-carts rush.

'I wish you would cry,' says Sarah presently, from among her sobs.

'Why should I?' replies Belinda calmly; 'it is my own doing.'

'This is the worst of it!' cries Sarah passionately; 'if you were doing it for some great cause—to save granny from the workhouse, or me from the scaffold—there would be some sense in it! there is no sense now!'

There is no sense in it! The words keep echoing, dancing—set to a teasing tune—in Belinda's head for the rest of the way. They reach the church-door. The carriage stops.

'We have got to the gallows, it seems!' says Sarah, with a fresh burst of sobs; then, vehemently wringing her sister's hands, she cries desperately: 'Belinda! it is not too late yet! there is still time! it is not too late yet to go back!'

'I have no wish to go back,' replies Belinda firmly, though her voice is low and weak, and her lips are white; 'why should I wish to go back, when it is my own doing?'

So they get out. At the door they are received by a Churchill cousin, who, summoned as Belinda's nearest male relative to give her away, stands awaiting them, cross and shivering.

'Has he come? is he here? I do not see him!' says Sarah, with a last flare-up of hope, peering eagerly into the church, where here and there (only here and there, for they are not nearly all lit) a gas-lamp displays its dreary yellow flicker on the background of thick morning fog. 'Yes; then'—with a sudden collapse into disappointment—'then he has not had a paralytic stroke at the last moment, worse luck !'

They walk up the aisle; a snuffy old pew-opener in a black crape bonnet preceding them; Belinda on her cousin's arm; Sarah, in her ostentatiously paraded grief, bringing up the rear. They have arrived at the altar, the candles upon which are lit, their wavering light falling upon an impatient clergyman and two elderly men; for the bridegroom has brought with him a friend of his own age and calling, whom he has summoned from Oxbridge to support him. The Churchill cousin has never before seen the bridegroom, nor has the bridegroom's friend ever before seen the bride. The opposing parties now stare at each other in unaffected astonishment. All through the service, the young Churchill, who had once himself thrown out feelers in the direction of Belinda, and had them civilly and firmly at once returned to him, is setting himself angrily in imagination by the side of the bridegroom, and wondering what the devil Belinda can have seen in this ugly old curmudgeon to prefer to himself.

All through the service, the bridegroom's supporter is staring in gaping wonder at the beautiful broken-hearted-looking girl, who has mysteriously elected to unite her fate with that of his old friend; ruefully reflecting that she will bring certain death to the constitutionals, and the pipes, and the discussions on the *Enclitic de*, and such-like light subjects, which they have been in the habit of sharing for the best part of the last forty years. All through the service the bridegroom is peevishly glancing over his shoulder to see whence comes the draught of raw air that, despite the black velvet skull-cap with which he has furnished himself, he feels at baleful play about his ears.

Belinda alone looks neither to the right nor to the left. If she were really the statue which her fair, still body so closely resembles, she could not be less conscious than she is of dank nipping air or curious look. She appears to listen with close attention, or is it indeed not attention, but the impassiveness of stone? Only once through all the service does her face come to life ; and then it is stabbed into life, as one has heard in the grisly dissecting-room tale, of him who, thought dead, was brought back to agonising momentary life by a knife-thrust ! The knife-thrust that brings Belinda back to life lies in the words, ' Forsaking all other, keep thee only unto him so long as ye both shall live.'

' Forsaking all other !' She has been spared the trouble of forsaking that other. Has not he been beforehand with her ? Has not he forsaken her ?

Sarah, closely watching her, sees her ashy features contract in such a spasm of mortal pain, that she involuntarily starts forward. Is she going to faint? If she faint, and is carried out of church, may not she be saved even yet ? She is not yet married ! The service is not yet ended ! But the next glance at her face dispels the momentary hope. Belinda is not going to faint; she has gained back her rigidity. She is dead again.

It is over now ; over—even to the signing of names in the vestry. The clergyman offers his congratulations, but he does it hastily and abstractedly. He is thinking whether he will have time for a good warming and breakfasting before setting off for the funeral at Kensal Green, at which he has to assist. The bridegroom's friend and the Churchill cousin also offer theirs ; but those of the first sound incredulous, and those of the latter ironical. Sarah alone keeps utter silence. The brougham stands at the door, the horse fidgety and stung by the cold. A crossing-sweeper and two pinched street children are watching the strange wedding-party's exit. The bridegroom, great-coated and comfortered to the end of his long nose, is bidding adieu to his ally. The bride turns to her sister :

'It is done now !' she says pantingly ; 'there is no going back from it now !'

'None !' replies Sarah dully.

'Say something to me, Sarah ; wish me something good!'

She has flung her arms round her sister in an *épanchement* most unusual with her. Her icy cheek is hard pressed against her sister's hot and tear-reddened one.

'I wish you—I wish you—' cries Sarah, stammering, what between her sobs, the almost ungovernable impulse to invoke upon her sister a speedy widowhood, and the hopelessness of finding any other wish that will not sound a mockery.

'You—you cannot find anything to wish me !' says Belinda tremulously. 'You are right ; there is nothing.'

'I—I wish you,' says Sarah, driven to desperation by this tone, and clinging convulsively to her sister as though ten bridegrooms should not force them apart—'I wish you many happy returns of the day !' breaking into an hysterical laugh. 'That is ambiguous ! I may attach what meaning I choose to it.'

These are the last words Belinda Forth hears, before the brougham whirls her away. The Churchill cousin takes Sarah home in a hansom, and a very unpleasant drive he has, as she cries violently the whole way, in passionate self-reproach at having found nothing kinder to say.

CHAPTER VIII.

BELINDA has been married three days. We are creatures of habit, as every one knows; and it is surprising with what quick pliability we find ourselves cutting off and tucking in whatever angles prevent our fitting into any new niche that it may be our fate to occupy. But this process, though rapid, is usually of somewhat longer accomplishment than three days. At all events, Belinda has not yet got into the habit of being married. There still seems to her something improbable—nay, monstrous—in the fact of herself sitting opposite to Professor Forth at breakfast in their Folkestone lodgings, pouring weak tea for him out of a Britannia metal teapot, and sedulously recollecting how many lumps of sugar he likes, as she has already discovered that he has an objection to repeating the information. Nor is it less monstrous to be warming his overcoat, and cutting his newspapers, and ordering his dinners with that nice attention to digestibility and economy which she finds to be expected of her. They have been enormously long, these three days. It seems to her as if for *months* she has been looking at those hideous ornaments on the drawing-room chimney-piece, and trying to draw the skimp summer curtains that will not draw across the shutterless windows, rattled by the wind. For months she has been listening to the eternal sighing, sobbing, whistling, howling of that same wind, and to the sea banging

on the cold shore.   For months she has been walking with
Professor Forth up and down, up and down the Leas, six
turns this way, six turns that way.   For months she has been
writing his letters till her hand ached, and reading aloud to
him till her voice cracked.   As for the reading and writing,
she cannot have too much of them—the more the better!
There is nothing like occupation—a continuous, settled
occupation—nothing like occupation for keeping out of one's
head those words of Sarah's that ring so foolishly dinning in
her ears, 'There is no sense in it! there is no sense in it!'
She will not listen to them.   Even if they are true, of what
profit to hearken to them now?   And reading and writing
render conversation, too, less necessary.   It is certain that,
however determinately any one may have confined his or her
contemplation of another person's character to the intellectual
side of it, it is impossible to live with that person without
discovering that he or she has another side.   Belinda has
already discovered that her Professor has another.   It is
surprising how much less of his conversation has turned
during the last three days upon the problems of the mind
and the sayings of the mighty dead, than upon the price of
coals and the wickedness of lodging-house servants.   The
first of these topics has led to the proposal that he and his
bride shall henceforth content themselves with *one* fire, to be
fed with (if possible) not more than two coal-boxes per day;
and the second is at present employing his tongue, his eyes,
his thoughts.   They are at breakfast, Belinda seated behind
the Britannia metal teapot, her husband facing her, a dish of
fried bacon before him, which latter object is monopolising
the whole of his attention.

   'It is beyond the range of possibility,' he is saying slowly,
'that you and I can have eaten a pound and a half of
bacon in three days, and I think I noticed that you did not
take any yesterday.'

'Did not I?' replies Belinda indifferently; 'I am sure I forget.'

'And if,' pursues Mr. Forth, his eyes ranging with severe scanning from the bacon-dish to the sugar-basin—'if, as Maria just now told us, those few lumps are all that remain of the pound of sugar purchased by me yesterday, it is obvious that there must be wholesale theft somewhere!'

'It is very dishonest of them,' replies Belinda carelessly, putting up her hand to her hair, which, no longer tended by a maid, feels oddly loose and uncomfortable. 'If you had allowed me to bring Jennings, she would have looked after everything.'

'I discouraged the idea of your bringing a maid,' replies he nettled, 'because I considered, and still consider, that it would have made a most unnecessary addition to our expenses. And as to our provisions,' looking carefully round the room, 'I see that there are several cupboards; there is no reason why they should not be kept——'

'*Bacon* kept in a cupboard in one's only sitting-room!' cries Belinda, breaking into an indignant laugh; 'you cannot be serious!'

'If you are able to suggest any better way of preventing their depredations, I shall be happy to hear it,' he answers tartly.

'If they ate a flitch a day,' replies Belinda hotly, and lifting her disdainful fine nose contumaciously into the air, 'I should say that it was a small evil compared to our living in the atmosphere of a chandler's shop.'

She rises precipitately as she speaks—to *her*, at least, Folkestone has not given an appetite—and walks to the window, where, for the rest of the breakfast hour, she presents a sociable homespun back to the economist at the breakfast-table. It is not the first time during these three days that she has discovered that his standpoint with regard to little social possibilities or impossibilities is different from her own. She had known that she did not love him, but she had not known that he wore carpet slippers in the drawing-room. A tendency towards slippers in the drawing-room, a passion for high tea, accompanied by no change of dress, are not these sufficient to wreck a bride's happiness upon? But worst of all, perhaps because latest of all, has jarred upon her this final instance of how widely asunder are their points of view. It jars upon her still as she stands by the window after breakfast, sullenly drumming on the pane.

In the night snow has fallen, a thin sprinkling meeting even the sea's lip, advancing even to where the dull little gray waves set their chill feet; a shabby sprinkling everywhere: not a good thick cloak of snow, deep and pure, but a scanty rag, through which every footstep shows the hard dark ground. It jars upon her still, as she walks to church alone—it is Sunday morning—trying to persuade herself that she had not felt a movement of gladness on discovering that he had no intention of accompanying her. She walks along the windy cliff to where the church and the red vicarage look out seawards, falling in, as she goes, with a stream of people bound to the same goal. It is a well-fed, comfortable-looking stream flowing prosperously to God's house; smart furry mothers holding the hands of smart furry little children, fathers and tall young daughters, husbands and wives. There is scarcely one, as young as Belinda, who is companionless. But she does not think of this.

Her eyes are turned towards the ocean, that ocean for the most part hugged by a close mist, with only one patch of faintish glory—a pale dazzle of dim gold—on which a small fishing-boat comes sailing, its homely sails transfigured as it goes. She is saying to herself, with a heart sinking so deep that she dare not gauge its profundity :

'Is *this* the man whose *mind* I have married? Is this the man who is to teach me to live by the intellect? Is this the scholar and the sage, whose teaching was to lift me out of the circle of my narrow interests into the sphere of the Universal?' she asks with contemptuous misgivings; '*this*, whose whole soul is occupied by mean parsimonies, and economies of cheese-rinds and candle-ends?'

She has reached the church, but even inside the consecrated door she finds that it is still with her. It comes between her and the Christmas decorations; between her and the bowing congeeing clergy; between her and the prayers. A poor starling has found its way into the building. All through the service it is flying from side to side, above the heads of the congregation, under the arched roof from window to window. Children turn their heads and their eyes, idly curious to look after it. All through the sermon she hears the agonised pecking of its poor beak against the pane, in its efforts to escape. She says to herself that it is in the same plight as she. It, too, entered prison of its own accord. When the service is ended, Belinda loiters behind the rest of the congregation, in order to press half-a-crown into the pew-opener's hand—(what would Professor Forth say to such extravagance?)—and to pour into his ear an eager prayer that he will set all the church doors and windows open, to give her starling a chance of escape. But, alas! what pew-opener can ever let her out?

As she passes homewards, she finds that the day has bettered. The sun has swallowed up the mist, and now shines steadily bright, and even sensibly warm. The little waves are small and mild as summer ones, though the air is still full of penknives. Perhaps it is the increased brightness upon Nature's face; perhaps it is the two quiet hours of her own society, that have braced her to face with a greater courage the lot she has chosen, and the fried bacon that typifies it.

'I *would* do it!' she says to herself sternly, 'and now it is done; now there is nothing for it but to put the best face upon it, and never to own to any one that I would have it undone. There can never again be so bad a piece of my life as this!' (shuddering); 'it is well to have the worst over first, it will be more endurable when we get to Oxbridge. I must try to learn how to look at things from his point of view, to count the grains of rice for a pudding, and save the old tea-leaves!' with a curling lip; 'but *I will not* have the bacon kept in the drawing-room!'

Her resolutions in both respects outlast the day. That to make the best of things has body enough to withstand even the close examination to which her husband subjects the Sunday roast-beef, in order to discover whether it has been robbed of any of its native suet. He has a slow munching way of eating, which fidgets her inexpressibly; but she bears that too. She even resists the temptation to look away from him. Since he is to munch opposite to her till death do them part, would it not be wiser to accustom herself to the sight? Her resolution withstands also stoutly all the little trials attendant on their afternoon constitutional. When they emerge upon the Leas, they see a broad highway of molten copper stretching across the sea to the lowering sun. Belinda asks leave to run down the many steps on the cliff's face to the water's edge, to set her feet in the foam fringe, and watch the long swell heaving ocean's sullen breast; but the Professor will not hear of it. A certain number of brisk turns on the Leas—always the same number—is the kind of walk to which alone he gives his approbation. No stopping to look at the copper sunset, or the fair ships riding past; nothing more likely to arrest the circulation and chill the liver. They meet the same people as they met yesterday and the day before, and as they will meet to-morrow and the day after; the same bath-chairs, the same dogs. The sick, white woman with her attentive burly husband; the deformed child; the frolicsome colley dogs; the frivolous Spitzes; the little blithe Scotch terriers.

Her resolution outlasts even the twilight hour, to her the most trying of the day. If she were to consult her own wishes, there would be no such hour; no space interposed between the fading of the daylight and the lighting of the gas. But it is in Professor Forth's programme that there shall be such an interval when he leans back in his armchair, with his eyes closed, and does not wish to be spoken to; whether in meditation or in sleep she cannot tell. There is nothing for her but to sit opposite to him, with his idleness, but without his repose. The lowered blinds prevent her looking out upon the first sunset-reddened, and by and by moon-silvered sea. She cannot even distinguish the lustres and the vulgar vases on the chimney-piece. She cannot even stir the fire into such a blaze as to enable her strong young eyes to read by it; for to stir the fire makes the coals burn quicker. It is the hour when the happy young build love-arbours out of, and see brave sweethearts in, the red coals. What love-arbour dare *she* build? What sweetheart dare *she* see? Then come the long hours of reading aloud. They are the most bearable of the day. It does her resolution the less credit to hold out through them. However, it does hold out. But will it endure through the next day? If it does, it must indeed be of a stout fibre. For no sooner has the next day risen, than it is clear that there has come one of those rare scourge-days with which God sometimes lashes His world; one of those days whose date is remembered, which is held up as a standard in after years for other fell days to measure themselves by; a day that wrecks ships by fleets; that strikes down centenary oaks by scores; that

whelms trains in its snowdrifts ; that stiffens into frozen death
the sheep on the mountain-side, and the traveller fate-over-
taken in the snow-choked country lane.

Snow often comes stilly ; but to-day it is blowing—blowing
mercilessly: not a bluff west wind, good-humouredly roistering,
but an inhuman north-easter, the furious sleet driven, raging
and sweeping, by its hellish lash.

When Belinda comes down to breakfast, there is not a
soul on the Leas, but the luckless baker's boy butting with
bent head against the razor-edged blast. It is scarcely the
day which one would have chosen to spend in a flimsily-built
seaside summer lodging-house. The Forths' lodgings are no
better and no worse than most others of the class ; with walls
about as puny, with woodwork about as warped, with gaps
between door and carpet about as wide, with curtains as
miserably insufficient as most of their brethren. Though
every door and window is religiously closed, there is the
feeling of being sitting out of doors, only more draughty.
Even in a warm, stoutly-built house one would shiver; but
here ! Well, here the cold is so marrow-piercing, that it
usurps to itself the whole attention of the mind. It is not a
subordinate, governable cold that by an effort of the will one
may forget. It can never be out of the thoughts for one
moment ; from the hour of rising, until that of shuddering
back to bed again.

The Professor, always a chill-blooded creature, sits all day
with his knees within the fender, piled with every article of
his own, and several of Belinda's wardrobe. Throwing
economy to the winds, he has lit the gas, and piled the fire
half-way up the chimney ; though whenever fresh coals are
put on, a great gust of greenish smoke, furiously beaten
back by the blast, comes pouring down the chimney, and
suffocatingly flooding the room.

Belinda, cold as she undoubtedly is, is not near the fire.

She is standing by the window, with a pot of paste and some strips of paper in her numbed hands, pasting up the apertures in the ill-seasoned shrunk window-frames, through which the wind comes icily whistling and piping. Now and again she appeals for directions to the heap of wraps beside the hearth, trying to still her chattering teeth as she does so, to keep out of her tone the intense dispiritedness which has invaded her whole being; not to listen to the ironical demon voice that whispers in her ear:

'This is the honeymoon; that is the bridegroom of your own choosing!'

All day—all day the snow swirls past. All day the sea—dimly seen, sometimes seen not at all, through the white hurricane—booms and thunders on the shore. The snow cleaves to the window-panes, freezes there, darkens yet more the dismal room. Not a soul puts nose out of doors from the dark dawn to the soon-falling night. When at length Belinda has finished her painstaking pasting-up of the windows, she asks in a voice of would-be cheerfulness whether the blast is not sensibly lessened; but receives for answer a melancholy negative. The whirlwind from under the door is such as to laugh to scorn all remedies applied elsewhere. And one cannot paste up the door.

'But one may put sand-bags beneath it,' suggests Belinda, still with that same desperate cheerfulness. 'They may have sand-bags in the house! she will ring and ask!'

But there are no sand-bags, and the landlady, embittered like every one else by the weather, tartly replies that such a thing has never before been asked for in *her* house! However, Belinda is not yet at the end of her resources.

'I think,' she says, 'if you would allow me to fold up all the newspapers in a tight roll, it might keep out some of the wind. Can you spare them all?—*Pall Mall, Spectator, Academy, Times?*'

Having received permission, she begins to turn them over, in order to select those most suitable for her purpose; her careless eye unintentionally alighting on a word here and there. The first two that she catches are her own late and present surnames. 'Forth—Churchill.' It is the announcement of her marriage in the *Daily News.* She drops it as if it had bitten her. The roll of newspapers is about as effective a bulwark against the wind as a child's sand-rampart is against the sea. But since she has at least done her best, Belinda considers that she has earned the right to sit down by the fire, with her fur-coat hoisted to her ears. She offers to read aloud.

'I am obliged to you,' replies the Professor morosely, 'but, in the present condition of my temperature, it would be perfectly impossible for me to concentrate my attention.'

He even looks rather injured when she herself takes up a book. But neither can she concentrate her attention. Her mind strays from the dreary wonder as to whether this enormous day will ever end, to the still more dreary wonder why she should wish it to end, seeing that it will only lead to another like it. There has been no break since breakfast-time, with the exception of the laying and removing of their early dinner, and the altercation about the sand-bags. No one has been near them, not even the postman! Doubtlessly every line is blocked, and all traffic suspended. The dark has long fallen; if that, indeed, can be said to have fallen which has reigned more or less all day. The gas has been turned up higher; the thin curtains drawn, with many futile jerks to the rings that will not run; the fire is new-built, and a sort of air of pseudo-evening-comfort diffuses itself. Belinda's slow pulse begins to beat, and her blood to circulate a little more briskly. It quickens its pace perceptibly, when—oh, blessed sight!—the lodging-house servant enters with a pile of letters in her chappy hand. Thank God, the line is not blocked after all! These are the London morning letters that should have come at 8 A.M. She snatches at them eagerly. They can bring her no great good news, but they make an unspeakably welcome interruption to the uniform dismalness of the long day. They remove the terrible feeling of isolation from all humankind, which hour by hour has been gaining ground upon her. There is a pile for the Professor; and for her a large fat envelope, bulging with enclosures, and directed in Sarah's hand. She draws her chair more closely to the hearth, and folds her soft furs warmlier about her. She will enjoy her letters at luxurious leisure. She unfastens the cover, and the enclosures fall out, six in number; a note from Sarah herself, four letters addressed in well-known and on this occasion warmly-welcomed female handwritings, and one in an unknown male hand. *Is it unknown?*

CHAPTER IX.

'Es ist eine alte Geschichte,
  Doch bleibt sie immer neu ;
  Und wem sie just passiret,
  Dem bricht das Herz entzwei.'

AT first it seems so; but as she looks there rises in her
memory, from which indeed it is never long absent, the
image of another letter, to whose superscription this one,
though less ill-written, has surely a strange likeness.

She continues to look at it; a fear too terrible for words
rising in her heart, and depriving her of the power of opening
it. The fire crackles comfortably. The Professor turns the
page of his letter. It is his third; and she has not yet
opened her first.

'I hope you have good news from home?' he says
politely.

'I—I believe so,' she answers stammering. 'I am not
quite sure yet.'

She must conquer this ridiculous hesitation. Probably,
certainly, she is the victim of hallucination—of an accidental
resemblance. The likeness is no doubt confined to the
address. As soon as she sees the letter itself, she will laugh
at her own foolish fancies. She tears it open, and tremblingly turns to the signature.

There was no hallucination—no accidental resemblance!

She was right. 'David Rivers.' For the first moment she
is drowned in a rush of insensate joy, followed in one
instant by such an anguish of horror as makes her for a
while unconscious of everything around her—everything
but that rending, burning, searing pain.

He has written to her at last! What has he to say to her
now? To congratulate her upon her marriage? He might
have spared her that thrust! She will not read it! She
will burn it unread!—by and by—not now!—when she can
do it unobserved.

Her shaking fingers refold the paper, hide it on her lap
beneath the fur, and take up another letter—Sarah's. She
goes straight through it, nor till reaching the last sentence
does she discover that not one word of its contents has
found entry to her brain. It is no use! That letter must
be read. It burns her knee as it lies on it. It is burning,
burning all through her. It is better to know the worst! But
to read it here under her husband's eyes—*her husband's!*

She casts at him one desperate look, and then, suddenly
rising, flies out of the room. He may call after her—she
thinks that he does so—but she makes no kind of answer.
Up the drafty stairs she flies into her bedroom; turning the
key in the lock, as she shuts the door behind her. The
Professor, relenting, has given her leave to have a fire there;
but the chimney smokes so furiously that it has had to be
long ago let out. The room is piercingly, savagely, trucu-
lently cold; but though she has been thinking of the cold
all day, she is now not aware of it. How can one be cold
with a red-hot iron in one's heart?

In a moment she has turned up the gas and lit the
candles. It is well to have plenty of light by which to read
one's death-warrant. But she cannot spare time to sit down.
A frantic haste to possess the contents of that letter which,
five minutes ago, she had thought herself capable of

burning unread, has laid hold of all her trembling being.

Standing, she reads it; and this is what she reads:

> ' 5, Paradise Row, Milnthorpe,
>   ' Yorkshire.
>   '*January 10th.*'

January 10th ! Why, that was her wedding-day! It is not to congratulate her upon her marriage, then; he could not have known it !

' Thank God ! I may write to you at last, though I do not suppose that it will be much good even now, as I am so mad with joy that I doubt whether I shall be able to make any sense of it. You will have understood—you always understand everything—what has kept me from you hitherto. Of course you heard, as everybody did, of the bankruptcy that preceded and caused my poor father's death. Whatever you may have heard, do not for a moment believe that he was to blame for it. I am such a bad hand at writing, that I can explain to you better when we meet; but I cannot bear you to remain in such an error for a moment longer than I can help. His ruin was caused by a sudden and most unexpected rise in iron, just after he had undertaken an enormous contract to deliver many thousand tons of iron rails in America at a low price. It was a misfortune that might have happened to any one, however long-sighted and cautious. You know what he was to me : I have often thought since of how I must have bored you bragging about him. You may think what that home-coming was to me ! Well, if there had been time for it, I think I should have given in altogether then. Happily for me there was not. If I broke down, where would mother and the young ones be ? No sooner was the funeral over, than we discovered that the smash was so complete that, at all events until the affairs could be wound up—a matter probably of several years—there would be scarcely enough for mother to keep body and soul together. The boys must be educated; three of them quite little chaps. There was nothing for it but to give up whatever hopes one had of one's own! God alone knows whether or not that was a wrench. We took a little house in a dirty back street in Milnthorpe—I am writing in it now; but to-day it looks to me like a palace. I was fortunate enough to obtain a clerkship in a house, one of the partners in which had been an early friend of my father's; a clerkship which, as I was always very bad at quill-driving, and the confinement, to which I had not been used, knocked me up, I soon exchanged for a place in the works. We got on as well as we could: mother has infinite pluck, and the young ones did their best. Sometimes I thought of writing to you. If you had ever answered a note I scrawled to you just before I left Dresden, I think I should have done so; but you did not: of course you were right. For eighteen months I worked without a holiday. Not having been brought up to it, I was at such a disadvantage with the other men. I scraped along from day to day, not daring to look much ahead, until, two posts ago, we received a letter from the lawyer of an old and distant connection of ours, of whom we knew little, and expected less, to say that he was dead, and had left £30,000 by will to be divided amongst us. This of course makes a very fair provision for mother and the children, and leaves my arms free to work for myself. You must decide whether they are to work for you too. Is it any wonder that I cannot write sense? May I come? When may I come? Do not keep me waiting long, or I shall come without leave. Darling! darling! darling! I suppose that I have no right to call you that, but do not be angry; I did not write it! it wrote itself, and I cannot scratch it out, it

looks so pretty written ! After twenty months, one might
be afraid that many women had forgotten one ; but you are
not of those that forget ! Love ! have you forgotten Wesenstein ?   DAVID RIVERS.'

She has read it through, without a break or a pause, to
the signature. There is no more, but yet she still stands
looking at it. For one all-happy moment the present is
dead to her ; only the past wholly lives. *Has she forgotten
Wesenstein ?* She smiles rosily; such a smile as has scarcely
been seen to visit her face since that very Wesenstein day.
'Darling ! darling ! darling !' She counts them. There
are three. He says that they look pretty written. He is
right : they have a pretty look.

A slight noise breaks her trance. It is only the Professor
poking the fire in the sitting-room below; a sound plainly
audible through the thin flooring. But if it had been the
great Trump of Doom, it could not have more effectually
blared and shivered away her visions. There is a growing
wildness in her eyes, as they retrace the sentences of the
just-read letter. It is a good letter. No woman need wish
to have an honester or a fonder one from her own true love.
It has only the one trifling drawback of having come just
three days too late. It is scarcely tactful to have thrust
itself thus untimely between her and the husband of her
choice !

'It is my own choice,' she says ; 'there lies the point of
the joke !' and she laughs aloud. Something in the sound
of her own laugh frightens her. 'Am I going mad ?' she
asks herself.

As she speaks, she staggers to the window, and throws up
the sash; whether—even in this icehouse atmosphere—
gasping for yet more air, or driven by some darker impulse.
For the moment the hurricane has lulled. Outside it is all

white with snow and moonshine : the moon herself not absolutely visible, too low to cut even her accustomed track upon the silvered sea, betrayed only by the sudden pale flash that each loud wave gives in turning over on the strand. Ceaselessly, as it has been snowing all day, the devilish wind has swept the pavement clean and bare. She can see the flagstones' fierce wet shine immediately beneath her. How hard they look ! and at what a distance below her ! One step from that easily accessible sill, and she will be for ever healed of that pain, than which none worse ever made dying man in deadly straits call upon death to set him free. But Death, the gentle genius with the reversed torch laying his soft hand, coolly liberating, on the over-weary heart, is not akin to the grisly, gory, murderous phantom that she in her misery invokes. For that dread step even *her* perfect woe has not yet ripened her. She shivers moaning back from the razor-edged outer air, and shuts the window. She sits down by the table, and spreading out the letter before her, reads it deliberately through again. Not a tear dims her dry eye. They say that the worst of a thunder-storm is past when the rain comes. The worst of a human sorrow is past when the tear-rain comes. But Belinda's grief is far indeed from having reached that better stage. What would she not give for a few tears, or that this hideous keenness of consciousness might melt away blurred into a merciful swoon ! But she is as far from the one relief as the other. If it had been written one day earlier ! If she had yielded to Sarah's passionate persuasions to delay her marriage for one month ! If—if ! There are a hundred ifs ; any one of which might have opened heaven to her ! But not one of them did.

'It is my own choice !' she keeps repeating, half aloud ; and then comes again that terrible impulse to laugh loudly at the ghastly irony of it ! the mirth of it ! *Her own choice*

to be sitting here alone and marrow-chilled—chilled, yet
with a red-hot sword slowly turning and turning in her
heart; afraid even to groan aloud, lest she should be overheard, instead of——

But the reverse of that picture she dare not face. That
is the road that lies straight to madness. Her eye wanders
wildly yet again over the page. Even it, in cruelty, seems
always to fasten on the fondest phrases:

'I am so mad with joy!' 'Is it any wonder that I
cannot write sense?'

As she looks at the words, written in such pure, glad,
good faith, but that seem to stare back at her now in
grinning mockery, a great dry sob rocks her whole body to
and fro. The pity, lavished hitherto on herself alone, now
changes its current, and pours in bitterest flood over him.
'*Mad with joy!*' until when? Until casually taking up the
newspaper, he reads that on the 10th of January James
Forth, Professor of Etruscan in the University of Oxbridge,
took to wife at St. Jude's Church, —— Street, Mayfair,
Belinda, elder daughter of the late John Churchill, Esq., of
Churchill Park, Loamshire. He will not believe it! He
will think that some one has inserted it as a joke. In
humiliating torrent, and with a retentiveness of memory of
which she had not believed herself capable, there rushes
back into her mind the stream of hold-cheap jests and jeers
and quips, in which they had united the forces of their joint
wits, at the expense of him who is now her husband; whom
at this moment she hears shovelling coal on the fire in the
room beneath her. Upon no one's testimony but her own
will Rivers believe it. And what words can she find in
which to tell him? Again that fierce sobbing shakes her
from head to foot; but she masters it. For a few moments
she sits in motionless miserable thinking. Then apparently
an idea strikes her; for she rises, and taking the candle in

her hand drags herself to the looking-glass. For a moment she peers haggardly into it. At all events her face is not disfigured by tears; and the only person to whose scrutiny it will be subjected is no very nice observer of its variations.

Apparently she is satisfied with the result of her consultation, for she moves to the door, and opening and unlocking it, passes downstairs, and re-enters the sitting-room.

Mr. Forth is in exactly the same posture as that in which she had left him, except that, having finished his letters, he has been able again completely to entomb himself—hands and all—in his wraps; out of which only an elderly face— its wrinkles ploughed deeper by cold and crabbedness— now peeps.

'Where have you been? What have you been doing all this time?' he inquires captiously.

'I have been in my room.'

She had dreaded lest there may be something so unusual in the sound of her voice that he may turn round and look at her. But no! he keeps his attitude of peevish crouching over the hearth.

'I hope that the fire was burning well,' he says anxiously. 'If the grate is of the same construction as this one, it will require constant attention.'

'I—I—do not think that it was burning at all,' replies Belinda uncertainly.

Till this moment it has never struck her how many degrees of frost have been adding physical to her mental suffering.

'Not burning. Not lit?'

In a moment he has leapt to the bell and violently rung it; but as Maria's movements in responding to it are marked by no greater celerity than usual, there is time for the whole of the following little dialogue before her arrival.

'Have you been pasting up the windows? If not, I am

at a loss to conceive what can have induced you to spend the best part of an hour in such an atmosphere.'

'I—I—have not pasted them up; I will if you like.'

'You have left the door open.'

'I am very sorry; I will shut it.'

'What are you doing over there? Why do not you come and sit down?'

'I—I—am looking for the *Daily News!*'

'The *Daily News!* What do you want with the *Daily News?* Is it possible that you have already forgotten that you made a roll out of all the newspapers to fill the aperture under the door? not'—ungratefully—'that it has been of any use.'

'I did not take the *Daily News;* I laid it aside.'

She does not explain why she laid it aside.

'What do you want with the *Daily News?*' fretfully, fidgeted by her movements.

She is on her knees before the cupboard to which her husband had planned to confide the custody of his bacon, and from which she has been unable wholly to exclude jam-pots and pickle-jars. She had forgotten that they were there, and the sight of them—unlikely as it would seem that such poor trifles could either add to or take aught from the sum of so great a grief—the sight of them seems to be the last drop that brims her cup. In after life it seems to her as if nothing had brought her so near self-destruction as those pickle-pots! *What does she want with the Daily News?* A desperate impulse seizes her. She will tell him.

'I want it in order to cut out the advertisement of our marriage, to send to——'

She pauses. The name sticks in her throat. With the best will in the world, she *cannot* pronounce it.

'To my mother?' suggests the Professor, filling up the blank conjecturally. 'I have already done so.'

Belinda laughs a laugh like the one that had made her question her own sanity upstairs.

'No, not to your mother; to—to—an—acquaintance of my own!'

She has found the journal now—found it in the very spot to which she herself had—as one does—unconsciously tidied it away. In an instant, as if it were printed in her own red blood, her eye has flashed upon the announcement; picked it out from the long list. Her work-basket, in which lie the scissors with which she must cut it out, lies on the table at her husband's elbow. She stands quietly beside him, snipping, snipping delicately, in the gaslight. There must be no jagged edges; nothing that tells of emotion—nothing that will betray to him to whom it is to be sent that each cut of those fine, sharp scissors was into her own heart.

'I cannot think what is the use of occupying yourself about it to-night!' says her husband, venting the ill-humour engendered by Maria's tardiness in replying to his spells upon the nearest object—as many better men than he have done before him. 'The country post is long gone. Probably all the lines are blocked——'

'I know! I know!' interrupts she harshly; 'but I had rather get it done to-night! to-morrow I—I—may have forgotten!'

* * * * *

She is back in her own room again, having taken the opportunity to slip out unquestioned, afforded by Maria's appearance at last—Maria in that reluctant, grudging humour with which she usually offers services, cheered by no hope of final largess; a hope that the Professor has seen fit, immediately upon his arrival, to extirpate. Belinda is in her room again alone; but alone and undisturbed she knows that she cannot long remain, but that she will be speedily followed by Maria with coal-box and shavings to re-light

the extinct fire. What she has to do, must be done quickly.
She opens her writing-case; takes out envelope and paper;
directs the first, and then writes on the latter, in a large,
painstaking, legible hand, 'From Belinda Forth.' It has
not taken one minute in the doing: Maria's pursuing foot
is not yet heard: happily she will be as slow as she can.
Belinda blots it carefully; then, after steadfastly and with
perfect tearlessness considering her own handiwork for the
space of a moment, she lifts the paper to her dry lips, and
lays a solemn good-bye kiss upon her own name; upon the
'Belinda,' that is, carefully avoiding the 'Forth.' She has
no manner of doubt that he will find it there: and who can
grudge them such a parting embrace?

Then, without any further delay, she folds the paper,
inserts in it the advertisement, closes and stamps the envelope. It is done! accomplished! and now that it is so,
an intense restless craving seizes her, that it should be on its
journey. In any case, it cannot leave Folkestone to-night;
but at least she might do her part. It might be committed
to the post. The thought of it lying here all night; meeting
her again in the morning—God above her! what will that
morning waking be!—is more than she can face. But to
whom can she confide it? To Maria? That high-spirited
person would flatly refuse to brave the elements on such a
night; and neither man nor mouse could blame her. To
that grimy Gibeonite—the boot and shoe boy? He would
infallibly commit it to his breeches-pocket, and dismiss it from
his mind. Why should not she take it herself? There is a
pillar-post not twenty yards from their door. The thought
has no sooner crossed her mind than it is half way towards
accomplishment.

In a moment she has taken hat and additional furs from
the wardrobe; has fastened them on as quickly as her trembling fingers will let her, and has stolen downstairs, creeping

on tiptoe past the sitting-room door; a needless caution, for
the Professor, though not at all deaf, has no longer that
fineness of hearing which is spared to few of us after forty.
Neither does she, as she feared she would, meet Maria and
the coal-box. The hall-door is not locked, and opens easily;
rather too easily indeed, for no sooner is it unlatched than
a force as of ten thousand Titans violently pushing dashes it
back. It is all that she can do, after repeated efforts, and
putting forth her whole strength, to shut it behind her.
When she at length succeeds, it closes with a bang that
—as she is aware by former experience—makes every floor
leap.

Again she laughs out loud. The temporary moonlit lull
is over; the cloud-rack has sponged out moon and sea.
The great hurricane is awake and in wrath again. There
seems to be nothing in all creation but himself and his
terribler snow-sister. The air is so full of the white flurry
—close and fine as flour—that it makes breathing difficult.
Belinda gasps. She has to stand still for a moment, that
her feet may grasp firm hold of the ground, else will the
north-easter, in one of its furious freaks, take her bodily off
them. Then she staggers resolutely on again; a lonely
fighter through the raging winter night. Of every slightest
lull she takes advantage to quicken her pace. Now and
again she turns her back upon the suffocating snow in order
to breathe. But not for one moment does she repent of
having come. She feels no hostility towards, no fear of, the
dreadful elements. Is not she as desperate as they? The
hand-to-hand fight with them does her good. It seems to
lift some of the lead from her brain; to set further away
from her that madness that had loomed so near. But the
twenty yards seem more like twenty miles.

She has reached the pillar-post at last—an opportune
momentary lifting of the storm revealing to her its snow-

whitened red—has found the aperture, and has dropped
into it the letter so carefully, painstakingly kept dry beneath
her cloak.   Yes! it is gone! gone past recall! as past recall
as the wood at Wesenstein; as the friend on whose coffin
we have seen fall the first cruel spadeful of earth.   But
of this she has no time to think.   A fresh frenzy of the
tornado obliges her to cling half-stunned to the pillar;
and the moment that she loses her hold the snow-wind
takes her in its fearful hands and hurls her back along
the Leas.

For one dread moment it seems to her that it is about to
hurl her far away over the cliff into the awful lap of the
bellowing waves that, even now, she can hear in the darkness savagely tearing at the great hewn stones of the quay.
That one instant reveals to her that the life she had thought
herself capable of throwing away is still sweet.

By a great effort her feet recover their hold of the
ground which has fled from beneath them; but not until
she has been swept far past the house to which she is struggling to return.   Battling, blinded, and dizzy; bewildered
by the darkness, and by the hopeless uniformity of the row
of buildings, it is long before, groping for the door that continually eludes her, she at length finds it; at length she
finds herself within its shelter.

Maria does not recognise her at first, so battered and
snow-covered is she; but Belinda pays no heed to her expressions of incredulous astonishment.   It is possible that
she may be so deafened by the elemental roar as not to
hear them.

Without much consciousness of how the intervening stair-
flights were climbed, she finds herself again in her room.
The gas is still turned high up, as she had left it.   Maria
has at length relit the fire; there is plenty of light for her to
see her bridal chamber by.   Plenty of light, too, to see the

blotting-pad on which she had so lately blotted the three
words of her *billet de faire part.*

She takes it up, and holds it to the looking-glass.   How
plainly the three words come out; not a letter, not a stroke
missed!

'*From Belinda Forth.*'   She mutters them over and
over under her breath.   'From Belinda Forth!'   'From
Belinda Forth!'

She is roused by a voice calling from below:

'Belinda! Belinda!'

It is her husband.   Let him call!   The summons is
repeated with more stress and urgency:

'Belinda! Belinda!'

Is not it the voice which will go on calling 'Belinda!'
through life?   Is not it the voice to which she herself has
given the right to call Belinda; to command Belinda; to
chide Belinda; immeasurably worst of all, to *caress* Belinda?
Of what use, then, to break out thus early into senseless,
bootless revolt?   She hastily shakes the powdery snow from
her clothes, drags off her soaked shoes, twists afresh her wet
and streaming hair, and goes decently and orderly down
again; decently and orderly to all appearance, for who can
see the wheels that are whirring in her head, and the flashes
of uneasy light before her eyes?

She finds her bridegroom in his former attitude: it seems
to her as if she could have better borne him and it, if he
had changed his position ever so little.   But no! he is still
mumping, round-backed, over the fire.

'I called repeatedly,' he says, with a not altogether
blamable irritation; 'is it possible that you did not hear
me?'

There is no answer, the wheels in her head are going so
fast.

'Where have you been? what have you been doing?'

'I have been out.'

'*Out!* You must be a madwoman !'

'So I sometimes say to myself,' replies she very distinctly, and looking straight at him as she speaks.

'And may I ask,' continues he sarcastically, 'what induced you to choose this peculiarly tempting evening for a stroll?'

'I went to post my letter.'

'Pshaw !'

She has taken her former seat opposite to him. The north-easter's lash has whipped up a royal red into her cheeks, usually so far too pale.

'There is no accounting for taste,' she says slowly; 'mine has often been blamed. *You*, at least, have no right to complain of it. Shall I read to you?'

As she speaks, she takes up the book laid down overnight, and without further permission launches into the first paragraph she sees. She has been conscious, on coming into the now really warm room out of the frozen stinging air, of an odd sensation in her head. It feels light and swimming, but she reads on. Now and then the type waves up and down before her like the furrows of a ploughed field; but she reads on. The matter of the book and the matter of her thoughts are woven hopelessly together like warp and woof, but she reads on :

'"If it could be demonstrated that any complex organ existed which could not possibly have been formed by numerous successive slight modifications" (*in how many years am I likely to die?*) "my theory would absolutely break down. But I can find out no such case. No doubt many organs exist of which" (*can the worm that never dies sting more sharply than this?*) "we do not know the transitional grades."'

How the print is jigging and bowing; but it will come straight and still again just now. She reads on.

'Pray repeat that last paragraph; I am unable to follow you; you are making nonsense of it!'

But instead of complying, Belinda tumbles the volume noisily down into the fender, and falls off her chair after it. Her wish is fulfilled: she has fainted!

PERIOD III.

'Love goes towards love as schoolboys from their books;
But love from love towards school with heavy looks.'

CHAPTER I.

THE winter, with its terrible stress and fury, is over and past. People sitting in blooming spring gardens or by widely-opened windows, talk comfortably, with lips no longer chapped, of the great snow-storm, and compare notes as to the amount of personal inconvenience and discomfort to which it had exposed them. Anecdotes of the awful night spent in snow-stopped trains have formed the convenient opening for many a dinner talk; the anxiety on the part of each interlocutor to prove that he or she had suffered more than the other, leading to intimacy before soup is well over. Of its ferocity and its devil-work few overt traces now remain, except killed laurel bushes and rare thrushes. Out of how many sweet little throats full of music has it pinched the tender life! But over its wrecks the sea rolls; and in the bottomless sea of mothers' hearts its drowned sailors lie buried. And does the analogy between the material and the spiritual world hold good? Does the sea of oblivion smoothly heave and largely sweep above the soul that went down on that dread night? Does no spar pierce the flood to show where that good ship foundered?

*   *   *   *   *

It would be the opinion of outsiders, who have not visited Oxbridge—if they had formed an opinion at all upon the subject, and were asked for it—that the inhabitants of that

university town dwell in gray and ancient houses, time-
coloured, and with flavours of old learning still hanging
about their massy roof-trees.   In point of fact, their lives
are passed for the most part in flippant spick and span villas
and villakins, each with its half acre of tennis-ground and
double daisies, all so new that scarcely any one has had time
to die there, though numerous people have taken leave to
be born there, and forming in their *ensemble* an ugly, irrelevant, healthy suburb, that would not disgrace a cotton
city of to-day.

It is mid-May, and the hour is one of the afternoon ones ;
an hour at which luncheon is already forgotten, though tea
still smiles not near.   Along the shining river, a mile away,
eight oars, four oars, skiffs are flashing.   Scores of happy
boys are tearing down the path alongside, keeping company
with their boats, exhorting, admonishing, shouting themselves
hoarse.   But their noise, though strong are their young
lungs, does not reach in faintest echoes to the quiet drawing-
room, where the as quiet lady sits, head on lily hand, beside
the window, staring out at her plot of forget-me-nots and the
gold shower of her two laburnum trees.

Warm as the day is, a fire burns on the hearth ; a fire
whose inconvenient heat Belinda is languidly trying to
counteract by the agency of the fan, slowly waving in her
unoccupied hand.   It is too hot even for Slutty, who, shortly
panting in her sleep, lies cast on her fat side in a cool corner.
Upon Slutty's figure, an academic life, and the total absence
of the thinning emotion of envy, and of the bad but emaci-
ating passion of jealousy (an absence caused by the fact of
her being sole dog of the establishment, and having no
longer any cause for suffering from Punch's tinselly accomplishments) has begun to tell.   She could not well look
stouter or less intellectual if she were one of the old Fellows
of St. Bridget's.

When last we saw Belinda, she was lying grovelling among cinders and fire-irons in a fender.   Now she is sitting placid and upright on a window-seat.   Is the change that has taken place in her soul's attitude as much to her advantage as that which has effected itself in her body's?   Who can tell?   She is past the age when a smeared face, puckered lips and bawling cries mean grief; when ruddy cheeks and shouting laughter mean joy.   She does not look particularly happy, perhaps, but which of us is conscious of looking specially radiant as he or she sits alone, with no one to summon to the surface of the skin that latent cheerfulness, of which few have enough to spend it on ourselves alone?   And yet, at this moment, the thoughts passing through her mind are not disagreeable ones; scarcely thoughts indeed, lazy summer impressions rather, of the pleasantness of the tiny sky-coloured meadow that lies, all turquoise, under her eyes, and calls itself her forget-me-not bed; of the round mother-swallow's head, peeping over the nest beneath the eaves. At some further thought or sensation, a slight but definite smile breaks up the severe lines of her young yet melancholy mouth.   At the sound of the opening door, however, in one instant it is dead.

'I find you unoccupied!' says her husband, entering and advancing towards her, with that shuffling gait which plainly tells of slippers (she has not then been able to break him off carpet slippers).

'If I am unoccupied it is for the first time to-day!' she answers coldly.

'Since you are at leisure,' he pursues—his want of surprise at her frigid tone betraying that it is her habitual one—'I have the less scruple in claiming your services.'

'What is it that you want?' she asks, lifting her eyes to his face.   It is pleasant to be looked full at by a handsome woman; but if she has, before looking at you, taken care to put as much frost as they can hold into her fine blue eyes, the pleasure is very sensibly lessened. 'What do you want? We cannot surely be going to have any more Menander to-day; and I have written all your letters—they lie on your study-table, and I have exactly followed your directions as to each.'

'It is precisely upon that subject that I wished to speak to you,' rejoins he, glancing at a paper in his hand. 'You have by no means succeeded in expressing the exact shade of meaning I wished to convey in this letter to Herr Schweizer of Göttingen, with regard to the new "Fragment of Empedocles;" and I am afraid that I must trouble you to re-write it.'

'And I am afraid I must trouble you to excuse me,' replies she quietly, but with asperity; 'my tale of bricks for to-day is really complete.'

There is a moment's silence, during which Belinda turns her head pointedly away towards the laburnum tree and the emerald grass; but the Professor shows no signs of retreating.

'If I were taking you from any other employment, I might hesitate,' he says, with peevish pertinacity; 'but since you are wholly unoccupied——'

'I am unoccupied at this particular moment,' answers she, with an accent of carefully elaborated patience, which, to the meanest observer, would betray the depths of her impatience; 'but in five minutes I shall not be unoccupied; in five minutes I set off to the station to meet Sarah, who, as you are aware, is to arrive by the 4.35 train. You do not, I suppose, wish me to take a hansom?' (with a faint sarcastic smile of a very different quality from that little one lately addressed to the swallow and the flowers), 'and the day is too warm for it to be possible to walk fast.'

At the mention of Miss Churchill, a distinct new crumple

of ill-humour has added itself to the already numerous
wrinkles of Mr. Forth's face.

' I am unable to see that any obligation to meet the train
lies upon you,' he says obstinately ; 'your sister is eminently
well able to take care of herself ! '

Belinda shrugs her shoulders.

' It is a mere matter of habit, of course,' she says in a
key of low resentment. ' If you have been born in a walk
of life in which it is habitual to you to push and elbow for
yourself, of course there is no reason why you should not
enjoy it ; but you must remember that this is not Sarah's
case ; and since you declined to extend your hospitality to
her maid, she is alone.'

At the end of this conciliatory speech she stops, and there
is a pause, which the Professor shortly breaks.

' If you think it necessary,' he says grudgingly, ' I am
willing to send a servant to meet your sister ; but I must
request you to abandon the idea of going yourself, by which
means you will be left free to render me the trifling service
I require of you.'

' You insist upon your pound of flesh, in fact ! ' cries she,
rising suddenly ; her body trembling, and her great eyes
lightening with anger and disappointment. ' Well, you are
more fortunate than your prototype !   You will get it.'

To his death-day, the German savan will never suspect
with what hotly raging and rebellious fingers were penned
those polite, lucid, and erudite lines upon Empedocles'
newly-discovered ' Fragment,' which he shortly received.

It is long before the Professor can satisfy his own fastidious ear and captious mind as to the fitness of the phrases
to be employed.   Many a sheet is angrily torn across by
Belinda ; many a fresh one is sullenly begun before her task
is ended—before her 'guide, philosopher, and friend,' induing,
with her aid—aid given grudgingly and not unasked—his

cap and gown, leaves her side to attend a college meeting.
Not until the banging of the house-door tells her that he
is really gone, does she give herself the indulgence of an
enormous sigh.

Throwing herself back in the leathern chair, in which she
has been sitting at the writing-table, with weary long arms
clasped behind her neck, and dogged eyes staring at the flies
on the ceiling—

'God loveth a cheerful giver!' she says aloud. '*He* is
not much like God!' (to a woman, the man that she loves
and the man that she hates are equally nameless, equally *he*).
'So as he gets his pound of flesh, his tale of bricks, what
does he care?'

As she speaks, acrid tears issue from their hidden ducts,
and brim her eyes; but she shakes them vehemently away.
She will not give to Sarah's penetrating eye the chance of
seeing that she has wept.

'I *will* not be pitied!' she says, rising, and pulling herself
together; 'she *shall not* pity me! no one shall!'

She goes away to her own room, changes her gown for a
fresher one, dresses her hair more becomingly, and practises
looking happy in the glass. Before she has nearly perfected
herself in this accomplishment, she is driven from it by
the sight and sound of a slow fly, rocking top-heavily
under a gigantic dress-basket, which is making for her
gate. Sarah is here, and she will not be at the door to
welcome her. The thought lends wings to her young
heels, and the colour and the smile that she has been
vainly aiming at, to her cheeks and lips. Five minutes
ago she did not think that anything could have caused her
such a throb of pleasure as the dear old sound of that
jovial high laugh, as the sight of that Dresden china face
and of those monstrously irrational shoes are now giving her.
When they lived together, they seldom or never kissed each

other.   Now they cannot hold each other tight enough.
Is it only Sarah that Belinda is kissing?   Is not it dead
youth, dear love, sweet Wesenstein, too, that she is so
straitly embracing?

Over the souls of both sisters—the sad elder and the
radiant younger—the recollection of their last miserable
parting on that hideous January morning has poured!   For
a moment or two neither of them could have uttered a
syllable, had you paid them a thousand pounds a word.
They are brought back to common life by the sound of very
small jingling bells, and by a sensation as of something
tightly wound round their legs.   It is Punch, who, unmindful
of the chain that has bound him all the way down from
London, and delighted to be again in the fresh air and
among friends, is tearing wildly round, offering eager but
unreciprocated greetings to Slutty, who, dodging away from
him, shrewish and snarling, practically refuses to admit him
as an acquaintance at all.

'Why, Punch!' says Belinda, with a rather unsteady laugh,
dropping on her knees, taking the excited little dog under
the arms, and looking kindly in his Ethiop face; '*you* here?
and who invited *you*, pray?'

'I am afraid that nobody invited him,' replies Sarah
demurely; 'but he was so sure that it was an oversight, and
he says Jane is no companion, and he sent so many messages to Slutty, that I thought it was the simplest plan to
bring him; do you mind?' with the old wheedling in her
voice and her saucy eyes.

'Do *I* mind?' repeats Belinda, with a reproachful yet
apprehensive stress upon the pronoun, passing her lips lightly
over the top of his tawny head.   'Punch! is it likely *I*
should mind?'

'Will *he* mind?' inquires Sarah, speaking very low, and
mouthing a good deal, as though labouring under a misgiving

that the person of whom she speaks is in hiding behind the door.

'He is not fond of dogs,' answers Belinda evasively, her face suddenly darkening as if a light had been blown out in it. 'Slutty exists only on sufferance, do not you, Slutty?'

'Whew—w!' says Sarah, pulling a long face, and with a low whistle; 'and shall I, too, exist only on sufferance, pray?'

Belinda is saved from the necessity of answering a question, her reply to which must have been either an incivility or a lie, by the fact that they have now entered the house, and that her sister's roving eyes and attention are claimed by other objects. Preceded by the dogs, Slutty churlishly growling, and Punch animatedly sniffing, they reach the drawing-room.

'Not such a bad room!' says Sarah patronisingly, looking round; 'better than I expected; only it wants pulling about.'

'Mr. Forth does not like rooms pulled about.'

The other breaks into a laugh.

'*Mr. Forth!* Is it possible that after six months he is still *Mr. Forth?*'

'What else should he be?' says Belinda, with stiff embarrassment; 'he has not yet been raised to the peerage. He is not "Lord Forth"!'

'I shall call him "James"!' says Sarah firmly; 'I am sure that he will wish me to call him "James"!'

Mr. Forth's wife laughs grimly.

'It will at least have the charm of novelty for him!'

There is such a bitter dryness in the quasi-playfulness of her tone that Sarah stops suddenly short in her critical survey of the early English chairs, and the Albert Dürer etchings, in which Oxbridge drawing-rooms delight; and focussing her elder with her two insistant eyes, says, taking her the while firmly by both wrists:

'Come now; we are alone; tell me, how does it work? has it answered?'

But Belinda shakes off the small strong hands as Samson shook off the tough withes.

'You must see the rest of the house,' she cries, beginning to talk rapidly and rather loudly, and absolutely ignoring the question addressed to her; 'you must see my room; your own room—yours looks upon the tennis-ground. Have you brought your racquet and your shoes? we must have some tennis!'

Sarah does not press the subject so obviously avoided, but as she follows her sister upstairs she repeatedly shakes her head.

'This is my room,' says Belinda, as they reach the landing, throwing open doors as she speaks. 'This is—*his*' (with a slight hesitation before the pronoun, that shows that only the dread of a repetition of her sister's ridicule has kept her from designating her husband by the formal style and title which she habitually employs towards him); 'and this!' (not opening, but simply indicating a third door), 'this is old Mrs. Forth's.'

'Oh, do take me in! do introduce me!' cries Sarah eagerly; 'it has been the dream of my life to see his mother! You will not mind my saying so, but there is something so humorous in his having a mother.'

'It would be no use,' replies Belinda, not offering to comply with this request; 'she would probably mistake you for her son.'

'Well, we *have* a look of each other,' cries Sarah delightedly; 'but is she as bad as that?' arching her eyebrows till they almost meet, and are lost in her hair.

Belinda nods in acquiescence.

'And does she *never* stop asking questions?'

'Never.'

'And do you always answer them?'

'Poor old woman! why not? if I were not answering hers I should only be answering some one else's.'

There is such a weary, devil-may-carishness in her tone, that again her sister's eyes flash investigatingly upon her; but this time Belinda has been too quick for her, and, avoiding their scrutiny, is doing the honours of a fourth room.

'And this is yours,' she says, a smile such as the one with which she had welcomed her sister sweetening and gentling the now habitual sullenness of her face; 'it smells good, does not it?'

'Why, you have given me all your flowers!' cries Sarah, burying her face in a bowl of freshly picked narcissus. 'I noticed that there was scarcely one in the drawing-room.'

'Mr. Forth dislikes the smell of flowers,' replies Belinda. She says it in a tame level voice; not as making a complaint, but simply as stating a fact.

'He seems to have a good many dislikes,' says Sarah drily.

Belinda lets the remark fall upon silence.

CHAPTER II.

DINNER has been early, and is over. The sisters stand, each cooling a fiery cheek against the woodwork of the drawing-room window, while the latest blackbird is singing his version of 'Glory to Thee, my God, this night,' and the laburnum's lithe bunches hang yellow against almost as yellow a sunset.

'Does he *never* open a window?' asks Sarah, greedily thrusting out her head into the cool greenness of the very respectably grown clematis and jessamine that climb the house-wall.

' *Never!* '

'Then I should make a point of falling off my chair in a faint regularly every day, at dinner, until he did.'

'You would fall off your chair in a faint every day until the Day of Judgment, in that case,' replies Belinda, with stony quiet.

' *But* for the stewpan atmosphere,' continues Sarah, heaving her white chest in a deep and vigorous inhalation, 'it really did not go off so badly; at first there seemed a trifling awkwardness—I think, Punchy, that you would have done as well on the whole to remain at your town house—but my fine tact soon smoothed it over.'

'You did not call him "James," however,' replies Belinda, with a short sarcastic laugh.

'Well, no,' replies Sarah a little blankly, and for once in her life making no attempt at repartee or explanation. 'I did not.' But the next moment—'How soon do we go?' cries she joyously. 'St. Ursula's is the largest college in Oxbridge, is it not? Will all Oxbridge be there to meet the Duke? But I suppose you are all much above setting any store by royalties! It is only the empire of the mind,' pompously, 'to which you attach any value!'

'*Is it?*' replies Belinda expressively.

'Now I am the common British flunkey,' continues Sarah confidentially; 'and so used you to be! I *love* royalties; there is nothing too small for me to hear about them. I should be thoroughly interested to learn how many pairs of stockings the Queen has, and whether she takes sugar in her tea.'

Belinda laughs.

'*Everybody* will be there, then?' resumes Sarah in a voice of the extremest exhilaration, and you will introduce me to *everybody*. What will they think of me? Will they expect me to say anything clever? Will they like me?'

'H—m!' replies Belinda dubiously, scanning affectionately from head to foot the seductive but not altogether academic figure before her; 'I doubt it!'

'After all, they must be human,' says Sarah philosophically. 'When one has pierced the thick crust of their erudition——'

'Perhaps in some cases not so very thick,' interposes Belinda ironically.

'One will find a human heart beating beneath—a heart that may be punctured by my little darts, eh?'

'Possibly!' in a by no means confident tone.

'I shall devote myself chiefly to the undergraduates, I think,' says Sarah thoughtfully. 'Do you know many? do you see much of them?'

Belinda shrugs her handsome shoulders indifferently.

'Poor boys! they come to call; but they are too much afraid of me to open their lips. I have lost none of my power of inspiring terror,' she adds with a bitter smile. 'It is the one of my gifts that I keep in its entirety.'

'We will change all that,' says Sarah piously: 'the reign of fear is over; that of love is begun!'

Belinda has moved to the middle of the room, and is occupied in pulling down the central gas-jet, and lowering the gas, harshly glaring under its globes. Her *pose*—wreathed head thrown back, and long bare arm roundly lifted—brings into evidence the finest curves of her noble figure.

'And do not they admire you either, *par hasard?*' asks Sarah, in a voice of affectionate incredulity.

Belinda shakes her head.

'If they do, they disguise it admirably. Stay!' with a gesture of recollection; 'now I come to think of it, I believe that one young person of an æsthetic tendency was once heard to observe that I was "great and still"; but that is the only civil speech I have reaped in six months, and even that one is perhaps a little ambiguous.'

'*Great and still!*' repeats Sarah, giggling; 'well, at all events they shall not say that of me!'

She is still chuckling, when the opening door admits her brother-in-law. At once her chuckle has an inclination to die, but she bravely resists it.

'I appeal to you,' she says, going boldly up to him. 'Belinda has been taking away your town's character; she says that she is not at all admired here, and that neither shall I be. Is it true? is it possible?'

It is certainly well to be on easy terms with your brother-in-law; but, in a case so exceptional as that of Miss Churchill, it is perhaps hardly wise to address him with an alluring archness that may remind him of former disasters. At all events, in the present case it is not successful.

'I am afraid that I must ask you to excuse me,' he says sourly, turning on his heel. 'I must refer you to some one better qualified to give an opinion on such a point. Belinda, I must request your assistance with my gown.'

There is something in his tone so unequivocally unplayful, that Sarah slinks away snubbed, and for the moment robbed of all her little airs and graces; and Belinda rises with rebellious slowness, flame in her eye and revolt in her nether lip, to render the grudging aid demanded of her. As her reluctant hand holds the gown for her husband to put on, they both find themselves unintentionally standing plump and full before a rather large mirror, inevitably facing their own figures, thus brought into sudden juxtaposition.

Belinda is in gala-dress. In honour of the Duke, and for the first time since her marriage, Oxbridge is to see her neck and shoulders. Upon their smooth sea of cream, unbroken by any trifling necklet—a sea that flows unrippled over the small collar-bones—the gas-lamps throw satin *reflets;* a little chaplet of seasonable cowslips clasps her well-set head, and wrath has borrowed love's red pennon and planted it in her cheeks. She looks a magnificent embodiment of youth and vigour, dwarfing into yet meaner insignificance the parched figure beside her.

Mrs. Forth casts one pregnant look at the two reflections, and then hearing, or feigning to hear, a sound of suppressed mirth behind her, she says, in a clear, incisive voice:

'What are you laughing at, Sarah? Are you admiring us? Are you thinking what a nice-looking pair we are?'

She lays a slight but cruel accent on the noun. *Pair,* indeed! From Fate's strangely jumbled bag were never two such odd ones sorted out before. The Professor has turned sharply away, but not before his wife has had the satisfaction of seeing that her shot has told; but Sarah maintains a scared silence. The fly is late in arriving. Probably it has had many freights to take up and put down on this festal night before the Forths' turn comes. At length, however, and just as Sarah is beginning wistfully to interrogate her Louis Quinze shoes as to their powers of reaching St. Ursula and H.R.H. on foot, it drives up, and they all get in. Possibly Belinda, though she makes no approaches towards a verbal *amende*, may be remorseful for her spurt of malevolence. At all events, she offers no objection to the raising of the window on her side; nor does she, even by a pardonable gasp or two, or an obtruded fanning, resent the insult to the summer night.

The lateness of their fly has retarded them so much, that instead of being first at the rendezvous, as is the Professor's usual habit, they see, on reaching St. Ursula's, the great quadrangle that the proudest churchman built filled with every carriage and bath-chair that Oxbridge's modest mews can boast; filled, too, with capped men and hooded women, hurrying to the goal. They have trodden the low-stepped stone stairs, along whose side lie unwonted banks of green moss that smells of cool, woodland places, planted with young field flowers; have passed the one slender shaft that, upspringing, bears the vaulted roof, and its loveliest stone fans, and have entered the lordly hall, where Elizabeth Tudor once saw Masks, and where one of the sons of her latest successor is listening with a courteous patience, probably superior to hers, to such improvements upon the barbarous Mask and obsolete Allegory as the nineteenth century, rich in the spoils of its eighteen grandfathers, can afford him. In the present instance, the substitute offered is a tale told, not by an idiot, but by an excessively hot young man, striking occasionally sensational chords on the piano, at which he is seated upon the raised daïs, where the

'Fellows" table is wont to stand—a monstrously long tale about a signalman, who, while busied in working his points, sees his infant, through some glaring domestic mismanagement, staggering across the metals at the precise moment when an express train is due. The struggle between his emotions as a parent and as a pointsman is so mercilessly protracted, that the audience, unable to bear the prolonged strain upon their feelings, are relieving themselves by a good deal of *sotto voce*, or not quite *sotto voce* conversation. But the Prince sits immovably polite, not permitting himself even one aside to his *sémillante* hostess, who, all loyal smiles, is posed in glory on a chair in the front rank beside him.

Large as is the assemblage, so nobly proportioned is the great room, that there is no crowd. Every woman has put on her best gown; and every woman has the satisfaction of thinking that every other woman has seen, is seeing, or will fully see it; not, indeed, to do them justice, that this is a consideration much likely to engage the attention of the Oxbridge ladies. Thanks to the height of the carved oak roof, whither the vapours can ascend, below it is cool and fragrant. With the one emphatic exception of the detailer of the signalman's perplexities, scarce one of the living guests has a more heated air than the brave line of judges, bishops, philosophers, premiers—St. Ursula's dead glories—looking down in painted tranquillity from the walls.

'You must introduce me to everybody, and tell me who they are, and what they have done, so that I may say something suitable,' says Sarah, in a flutter of pleasure, looking beamingly round on the, to her, eccentric throng of black-gowned M.A.'s, with their flat college-caps tucked under their arms; of velvet-sleeved proctors, etc.

'For Heaven's sake, do not try!' says Belinda, in serious dissuasion, 'or you will be sure to make a mess of it!'

Sarah shrugs her white shoulders. She is so clamorous

to be presented to every one, that Belinda, after patiently pointing out to her, and, where feasible, making her personally acquainted with the owners of many of the local, all the half-dozen national, and the one or two European reputations that grace the room, at length strikes work.

'You are insatiable!' she says. 'You are as bad as Miss Watson!'

'Unberufen!' cries Sarah, with a shudder that is not all affectation, 'do not mention that accursed name; I could have sworn that I heard her voice just now!'

The room is fuller than it was. About the door, indeed, and the lower part of the hall, circulation is still easy; but who would be content with elbow-room at a lower end, when the sight of a genuine live English royal Duke— no dubious Serene German—is to be fought for at the upper?

'And you say that we are not loyal!' says Belinda, with that irony now so frequently assumed by her, as they, too, push and jostle their forward way. They have to push and jostle for themselves.

Immediately upon their entry, their natural pusher and jostler, the Professor, has quitted them for associates more akin in age and conformable in tastes than the two handsome girls assigned by a sarcastic Providence to his jurisdiction. As they so work slowly forwards, gaining a step a minute, they are conscious of a disturbed heaving of the wave of humanity behind them—as when the ocean is ploughed by some puissant steamer, or monstrous shark. At the same instant a familiar voice, whose accents Sarah had already but too truly caught, breaks in brazen certainty upon their ears :

'I am sure I beg a thousand pardons! but in a crush of this kind it is quite unavoidable. I really must beg you to make way for me! I am naturally anxious to get to the top

of the room, having a personal acquaintance with the Duke,
or what really amounts to the same thing.'

The loud voice grows nearer, the wave-like swell heavier.
She is close behind them now.

Belinda has turned white and sick.   That dreadful voice!
Even here, on this hot May night, in the thick festal crowd,
of what power is it to re-create for her that miserable fog-
stained Christmas morning, on which, in her madness, she
had allowed a few senseless words uttered by that brutal
voice to seal her doom for her.

'Speak to her!' she says, in a choked whisper to her
sister. 'I cannot.'

'Hold your head down!' rejoins the other, hastily putting
into practice her own precept, and burying her nose in the
lilies of the valley on her breast; 'perhaps she will not see
us!'

But when did Miss Watson ever fail to see any one?

One final oaring of her powerful arm has brought her
alongside of them.

'Belinda! Sarah!' she cries loudly, seeing that her mere
presence, although sufficiently obvious, has apparently failed
to attract their attention; 'do not you know me? Emily
Watson? Dresden? Has anything been going on? have
I lost much?—I could not possibly get here before—quite
a sudden thought my coming at all. I heard that the
Sampsons were coming down to see their boy, who is at
King's; so it struck me I would join them and come, too.
I took them quite by surprise—met them at the station.
"Why not see Oxbridge all together?" I said; "halve the
expense, and double the pleasure!"'

She pauses out of breath, and looks eagerly onwards
towards the spot where, beyond his mother's struggling
lieges, the Prince sits, cool and civil, with his suite on their
row of chairs.

'I was so afraid that the Prince might be gone,' pursues she volubly; 'the royalties sometimes go so early, you know. Have you been presented to him? Do you know him? well, enough to present me? No? Well, then I must re-introduce myself: I have no doubt that a word will suffice to recall me to H.R.H.'s recollection. Royal memories are proverbially good, you know. I must get hold of his equerry; I know him quite well—once crossed over in the same steamer from Newhaven to Dieppe with him.'

The last few words are thrown back over her shoulder, as she has already resumed her vigorous fight onwards.

With fascinated eyes they watch her athlete's progress to the front. The human billows part before her. The crowd lies behind her. She has reached smooth water and the Prince.

The signalman's troubles are by this time drawing to their close. His rosy babe has been found lying smiling on the line; the express train having, contrary to its usual habit, passed over the pretty innocent without inflicting a scratch. Most people draw a long breath; but whether at the babe's immunity or their own, who shall decide?

'She is making him shake hands with her!' says Sarah, in a shocked voice, standing on tiptoe, and stretching her neck.

It is too true. In defiance of etiquette and despite the horrified look of the hostess, Miss Watson is warmly grasping her Duke's hand. Against the background of wall and chairs her figure stands out plainly silhouetted—fringe, garish evening-dress, and hot red neck! To their ears come even fragments of her resonant speech: 'Your equerry, sir!' 'Newhaven!' 'Sea-sick!'

'I should like to sit down,' says Belinda, in a spent voice.

This is easier said than done. By slow degrees, however, they succeed in edging out of the crowd; and are lucky enough to find an unoccupied sofa, upon which Belinda seats herself; and whither, presently, various of her acquaintance come and exchange remarks with her upon the success of the entertainment, the excellence of the supper, the affability of the Prince, etc.

In one of the intervals between two of these fragments of conversation she perceives that her charge has left her side; but it requires no very distant excursion of the eye to discover her standing at the supper-table, an ice in her hand, having, by the agency of one of her just-made acquaintance, effected an introduction to a good-looking undergraduate, who in return is presenting to her a second, who in his turn will obviously present to her a third and a fourth.

A little mob of young men is beginning to gather round her. A moment more, and, her ice finished, followed by her *cortège*, Sarah returns to her sister, winking so deftly as to be invisible to the outer world as she comes.

'Belinda,' she says, 'I want to introduce to you Mr. Bellairs, who tells me that he plays tennis remarkably well' (an indistinct disclaimer from the blushing Bellairs); 'and Mr. Stanley, who plays very nicely too; and Mr. De Lisle, who thinks he would play very nicely if he had a little more practice.'

Belinda laughs slightly, amused at the glibness with which her sister has already mastered her new admirer's names.

She has risen to her feet again—Professor Forth's wife—the stern-faced beauty whom in their walks and talks the boys have often with distant awe admired.

'I am sure,' she says, with a sweet cold smile, 'that if you care to try our small ground, I shall be very——'

She is a tall woman, and her eyes are on a level with Bellairs'. She can, therefore, easily look over his shoulder. What sight is it so seen that makes her stop suddenly in mid-speech, with a catch in her breath? The pause is but short. Almost before her auditors have had time to notice the hiatus, it is filled up.

' I shall be very happy to see you any day you choose to come—to-morrow, any day !'

Her words are perfectly collected ; but surely she is far, far paler than she was when she began to speak ; and though her sentences are addressed to the young men, her eyes are wandering oddly beyond them.

'Upon my soul, I believe the woman is off her head !' Stanley says confidentially to Bellairs, as they walk home together in the moonlight. ' Did you notice her eyes when she was talking to us? they made me feel quite jumpy !'

' Off her head !' growls Bellairs, who finds it not impossible to combine a poignant interest in Sarah with a servile moth-and-candle-like homage to the elder and severer beauty; 'so would you be, if you were married to an old mummy !'

CHAPTER III.

AND what was it Mrs. Forth saw over Bellairs' shoulder?
What is the sight that, now that the temporary call upon
her attention is withdrawn, is riveting into such an agony of
search the lovely cold eyes, to which so few things seem
worth looking at? Fortunately for her, a new batch of
undergraduates has hurried up to be presented to Sarah.
Never since the days of Dresden and the German army has
Miss Churchill had her hands so full. Belinda is free to
send her gaze unnoticed round the hall, in a silent, breathless, passionate quest. Quest of what? She does not ask
herself how much the better off she will be if she succeeds
in finding the object of that quest. To find it! to find it!
Come what may of the finding, to find it! Most people
would feel sure that she has been deceived by an accidental
resemblance to Rivers in some stranger; men of his size,
complexion and bearing being, though unhappily in a
minority, yet still numerous among two thousand youths of
the English upper classes. But Belinda would laugh to
scorn the suggestion that at any distance, or in any glimpse
however momentary, she could have mistaken any other for
him.

There exists in her mind no smallest doubt that the face
seen in that one lightning-flash, and then instantly hidden
by twenty other intervening faces, was his—his or his

angel's ! Perhaps he is dead, and that he has come to tell her. A mute sob rises in her throat. Whether in the spirit or the body, she must find him ! At intervals of every few minutes she is interrupted in her search by the greetings and observations of passing acquaintances. She answers them politely and connectedly, but with a brevity that does not encourage a prolongation of their civilities; a brevity that will the sooner leave her free.

The room is thinner than it was, or rather the crowd is distributed more evenly over its whole area. Since the supper-tables sprang into sight—even loyalty giving the *pas* to hunger ; the uncertain hope of a bow from the Duke, to the sober certainty of lobster-salad—the packing about H.R.H. is less dense. The guests are extended along the line of tables. Of Sarah, indeed, scarcely a vestige is to be seen, so closely is she hedged in by a wall of boys. At something she has just said they all laugh rapturously ; those who did not hear it—so firmly assured already in her character as a wit—as well as those who did.

The signalman's biographer has descended from his *estrade*, and is talking as commonplacely to his hostess as if he wotted nothing of parental agonies or points, and as if the rosy babe had been sent to bed with the whipping it deserved. Through the slackening of the press it has surely become easier for one seeking to discover the person sought; and yet for a while she seeks in vain. How many heads there are ! heads bald as Cæsar's ; heads thickly clad as Absolom's ; heads white, heads brown; sandy heads, pepper and salt heads, gold heads; long heads, round heads, knobby heads ! And how they shift and move ! Will they never stay quiet for a moment ? And among them all he is not ! He must have gone—gone without ever conjecturing her nearness !

Again that mute sob rises chokingly. Why should he

not be gone? Why should she wish that he were not gone?
Why should she wish to see him? What has she to say
to him when they meet? But she pushes roughly aside
Reason's cool pleading. *Why* does she wish it? *Why—
why?* There may be no *why*, but she *does* wish it; wishes
it with such a compelling frenzy of wishing, as seems as if it
must produce the fulfilment of that wish. And it does. Its
might prevails. Ah—h—h! For in a moment she has
seen him again. He is nearer now; so near as to be
recognisable past mistake or misgiving, even by eyes less
acquainted than hers with every trick of lip and brow. If
he continues to advance in the direction at present taken by
his steps, it is impossible but that in one minute or less—in
perhaps fifty seconds, perhaps forty—she will come within
the range of his vision. He will be aware of her as she is
aware of him.

'Are you ready to go home?' says a voice at her elbow.

She turns suddenly; eyes alight, and heart madly bound-
ing, to find her husband at her elbow. The revulsion is so
hideous that speech wholly fails her.

'I should be obliged if you would tell me where I am
likely to find your sister,' he continues, taking her silence
for assent, since she is never very prodigal of her words to
him; 'so that I may let her know that we are going.'

But at that she finds voice.

'*Going!*' she says, flashing one look of passionate dissent
at him. 'Why should we go? Impossible!'

'I see no impossibility,' he answers captiously; 'we have
already amply satisfied the claims of civility. The impossibility, as you are perfectly aware, lies in combining such
late hours with early rising in the morning.'

'Then why should you rise early?' answers she, with
tremulous rebellion. 'It is no use talking—I cannot come
away. You forget Sarah; it—it would not be fair upon

Sarah; I have neither the wish nor the right to spoil her enjoyment.'

'I should imagine that nothing would be easier than to find a chaperon in whose charge to leave her,' rejoins he persistently; 'if indeed,' with a slightly venomous look in the direction of his sister-in-law, 'she considers one necessary.'

But Belinda only observes a silence which he divines to be mutinous. He is accustomed in her to sullen compliance, uncheerful acquiescence, loth obedience; but to open revolt he is not accustomed, and, on the spur of the moment, and in so public a place, he is not prepared to deal with it.

'Since you manifest such an avidity in the pursuit of pleasure,' he says resentfully, 'I will indulge you with another half-hour, at the end of which time I must beg that you and your sister will be prepared to accompany me without further remonstrance.'

He does not await the answer, which perhaps he knows he would not receive; but turns on his heel and leaves her —leaves her free to pursue that feverish search which his coming had so rudely interrupted.

It is some moments before she again finds the object of that search; moments long enough for her to tell herself in heart bitterness that she has pushed against her fate in vain. But then, all in a moment, she has found him again. He is further off, indeed, than he was: some trifle must have diverted his steps from the direction then pursued by them; and he is still, in his unconsciousness, slowly widening the distance between them.

Is it possible that he is tending towards the door? that she, unable by word or sign to arrest him, will see him go? Oh, but life is a hard thing! Knowing as she does that at one lightest cry from her he would turn; to be no more able to utter that cry than if a real material gag were choking her utterances! Can it be, then, that her soul's cry has reached his soul's ears? for he does turn suddenly and smiling. Has he seen her, that he smiles? Ah, no! Would he indeed smile if he saw her? She has not given him much cause to smile at the sight of her. Well, he is wise. He has again averted his look. And the half-hour, the inexorable half-hour is passing! How much of it has already gone? Ten minutes, at least, must by this time have passed.

There are only twenty minutes for hope to work upon. Twenty minutes!—and then the close fly, the Early English Villa, Professor Forth, and the Fragments of Menander! To the end of time Professor Forth, and the Fragments of Menander!

Again her thoughts are broken in upon by a voice— Sarah's this time; Sarah having shaken herself free of her disciples; Sarah with a solicitous look and an anxious eye.

'I think it best to tell you,' she says hurriedly, and narrowly watching the effect of her words upon her sister's face; 'I was afraid lest you might hear it suddenly from some one else—some stranger. I suppose you have not seen him yet, but *he* is here!'

'I know it,' answers Belinda shortly, and very low.

'You—you are not going to faint?'

'*Faint!* why should I faint?' with an accent of intense impatience, her eyes still riveted on the now again approaching figure; 'do I ever faint?'

'Would you like to go home?'

'Go home!' echoes Belinda, in an accent of fierce desperation; 'why do you all sing the same song? why are you all determined that I must go home?'

'I thought you would wish it,' replies Sarah anxiously. 'I should if I were in your place. Do not you think it would be better?'

But she speaks to deaf ears. Her eyes, still fastened on her sister's face, see that face's lilies suddenly dyed with a most happy and loveliest flush.

The sun has risen : he has touched the sunless snow on the Jungfrau's crest, and all the world is rosy red. So then he has seen her! There is now no longer any fear of his departing unintentionally ignorant of her neighbourhood.

There is indeed time for one short pang of alarm lest he should do what in her heart she knows if he were wise he would do—and who knows how much of wisdom these two years may have lent him?—turn away, and knowingly avoid her! But apparently he is not wise.

In a moment he has pierced the small portion of crowd that still separates them; pierced it with a goodwill that would not have disgraced Miss Watson. She has one instant of such blissful anticipation—only a thousandfold intensified—as used to be hers in the Lüttichau Strasse, at the sound of Tommy's childish foot pattering up the stone stairs, and her love's firm and eager tread behind it.

The next moment they have met. Their unfamiliar right hands lie in one another; and they say—nothing. Of what use to have mesmerised him hither by her eyes, and the insanity of her voiceless prayers, if she have nothing to say to him now that he has come? But happily, though she and he are speechless, Sarah is not.

'So it is you, is it?' she says in a dry voice. 'Now what eccentric wind has blown you here?'

He does not answer at once. Evidently, as of old, he has forgotten her presence.

'I see that you still have your old trick of not answering me,' pursues she, running quickly on with a flightiness that conceals a good deal of real nervousness; 'but never mind : there "are places where I also am admired," as Goldsmith said. Belinda, do you know that twenty-five young gentlemen of different colleges are going to be so good as to call upon you between the hours of three and seven to-morrow?'

Belinda is struggling to rouse herself out of her intoxication; already so far unintoxicated as to know that it *is* intoxication.

'Are they?' she says, with a weakly laugh; 'I am sure that I am very much obliged to them.'

'And meanwhile what has brought *you* here?' asks Sarah persistently, carrying on her determined talk as a shield to her sister's emotion.

Her speech has the effect of making Rivers, too, put down the wine-cup; of bringing him also back to the bald, sober, morning prose of life.

'I have come to take my degree,' he answers; 'I have been prevented by—by circumstances from taking it before.'

So now she has heard his voice! to have touched his hand; to have met his eye; to have heard his speech! Is not this to have had her wish? Surely now she is content. Surely now she will go home at ease and satisfied. But who was ever satisfied with *one* wish? What wish ever died barren, without engendering a hundred more?

'The half-hour is expired!' says a voice.

The Dresden quartette is complete. Perhaps it is this thought that, rushing simultaneously into three out of the four minds, strikes them momentarily mute. Sarah is, of course, the first to recover herself.

'What a mysterious utterance!' she says, with rather a forced gaiety; '*what* half-hour? any particular half-hour? You remember Mr. Rivers, do not you? Mr. Rivers, you know Mr. Forth, my—my brother-in-law?'

There is a slight unintentional hesitation before pronouncing, and a perhaps intentional slight stress in pronouncing, the last word. Rivers has stepped back a pace or two, isolating himself from the augmented group; but at this summons he again advances, and, except by the two signs of a sheet-white face and set teeth, is not to be distinguished from any other well-mannered young man making a bow. But the Professor would be slow indeed to mark the hue of any undergraduate's, or ex-undergraduate's face, or to note whether his mouth were open or shut.

'The fly is waiting,' he says, returning Rivers' salutation with cursory indifference. 'Belinda, I must beg you to accompany me at once, and not keep it waiting.'

As he speaks, he looks at his wife, as one expecting and braced for fresh rebellion. But he meets with none.

'Come along!' cries Sarah with alacrity; 'we are quite ready, are not we, Belinda? Enough is as good as a feast; and we have supped full of pleasure. Good-bye!' nodding with cool friendliness over her shoulder, and taking her sister's hand.

Belinda offers no resistance; flaccidly she complies, and without one look at Rivers, with only a faint bend of her head in his direction, begins to follow the Professor of Etruscan out of the room. Rivers stands stupidly looking after them. The tart imperativeness of her husband's tone; his employment of her Christian name; her own dull docility—which of these is it that makes him feel as if some one had given him a great blow over the head with a club? Presently he begins, mechanically and purposelessly, to follow them.

The crowd is thick at the entrance and on the stone stairs—the departing crowd. The quadrangle is full of vehicles. Footmen are few in Oxbridge; but such as there are, are shouting their mistresses' carriages: the humbler multitude are pushing, asking, struggling for their flies. Lucky ones are finding them and driving off: unlucky ones are vainly striving to identify horse or driver. Among the latter are the Forths. In coming out, they have been parted

by the press—that is to say, the sisters have lost each other
—the younger loitering in injudicious dalliance with some
of her new sweethearts; the elder plodding on in dull and
woolly oblivion of all but the iron necessity of following that
cap and gown ahead of her.

It is not till the elusive fly is at length found—till her
foot is on the step, and Professor Forth is sharply urging
her in by the elbow from behind, that she becomes aware of
having mislaid her junior.

'Get in—get in !' cries he crossly; 'what are you waiting
for ?'

'But Sarah !' she says, awaking from her unconsciousness
and looking hastily round; 'what has become of Sarah ? we
cannot go without Sarah !'

He makes an irritated gesture.

'No doubt she has joined some other party; no doubt
she will do very well: at all events, in this confusion it is
impossible to attempt to find her !'

'It is much more impossible to go without her !' replies
she firmly, withdrawing her foot from the step; 'I wonder
that you should propose such a thing !'

'She is perfectly well able to take care of herself !'
retorts he, recurring to his old and spiteful formula; 'she
will find her own way home !'

'Then I will find *my* own way home, too !' answers she
indignantly, and resolutely turning her back upon him and
the open fly-door. She is too indignant even to deign to
observe whether he takes her at her word.

The crowd is still issuing, issuing; crossing the moonlit square on foot; nodding good-night out of carriage
windows; away they go ! She retraces her steps to the
stair-foot. It is not pleasant work pushing against a human
tide; and so she finds. It is bewildering to be staring into
every face; peering under all the hoods and mufflers. And

among all the faces, under all the hoods and mufflers, is no Sarah to be found. It is obvious that the Professor is right. She has found her own way home.

The company is melting away so rapidly that, unless she wishes to be shut into the college for the night, she must needs follow her example. Well! there is no great hardship in that! She is in the mood when the abnormal, the unusual, seems more tolerable to her than the accustomed, the everyday. Half an hour of solitude and midnight! Half an hour in which to be Belinda only—not Belinda Forth at all! Half an hour in which to reckon with this night and its work! She has already made half a dozen steps along the stone flags of the quadrangle, when some one comes up behind her. Had she known that he would come up behind her, that she makes no sign of surprise, nor any pause in her walk?

'You are alone?' he says with agitation.

'It seems so,' she answers. It is the same dry voice with which she had so often galled and chilled him at Dresden.

'You have lost your—your party?'

'I have lost Sarah.'

'And your—and Professor Forth?'

'He could not wait, and I could not go without Sarah.'

'And he has left you behind—*alone?*'

She is silent, still speeding along in the moonlight.

'And how do you propose to get home?' he asks, keeping up with and determinately addressing her.

'I am getting home as fast as I can.'

'You mean to walk?'

'It looks like it.'

Her tone is brusque and dogged; but if she hopes by its means to rid herself of her companion she is mistaken.

'In evening dress?'

'Pooh!' she says, with a hard laugh; 'we are not so

fastidious here, *nous autres;* I walk out to dinner every night of my life ! '

' But not alone ? '

Her face darkens. ' No, not alone.'

They have reached the gateway and Wren's domey tower. She has stopped in her resolute walk ; but in the stopping there is as much resolution as there was in the hurrying.

' Here we part,' she says shortly ; ' good-night ! '

' You must allow me to see you home,' he answers firmly.

' I have already told you that it is absolutely unnecessary,' retorts she roughly.

There is an instant's interval before his rejoinder. They are putting out the lights in the hall ; the great building is greedily devouring half the moonlight in the quad, with its raven shadow. It has embraced the fountain in the middle. It is not much of a fountain, but how pleasantly its little voice pierces through the noise of rolling wheels and human shoutings. For how many centuries could she gladly stand here listening to it !

' You *must* allow me ! ' with perfect respect, but obstinately.

' I *must not !* ' Is the night wind heady, like wine ? Her tone changes to one that is almost entreaty. ' I had rather you did not ; I *ask* you not ! '

Her incivilities had left him iron ; to her pleading he is as wax.

' It shall be as you wish,' he says, gravely bowing.

There is nothing now to detain her, and yet she lingers an instant, as though expecting him to say something more. But he adds nothing. She turns out of the gateway and into the street, and walks fast and steadily up it. There are not many towns through which it would be judicious for a young and solitary woman to take her way, bare-headed and in flimsy ball-gown, at midnight; but about Oxbridge, Una without her lion, might have strayed unassailed from sunset to sunrise. Involuntarily she slackens her speed a little, from the almost run with which she had begun her course, though still keeping at a moderately rapid walk. What cause is there for hurry? There is nothing now to hasten from; and Heaven knows there is nothing to hasten to!

She did well to be peremptory; but, after all, he was not very much in earnest; he did not press the point. It is much better that it should be so; but still, as a mere matter-of-fact, he did not. She looks up at the sky, which is spreading out the jewels it has kept hidden through the staring day, spreading them out for

'The fair city with her dreaming spires,'

to look up at and admire; all its bright belts and bears; its gods and goddesses. Then she looks suddenly round. There are still a good many people about, but no undergraduates; for the University mother has gathered her curled darlings to her bosom for the night.

The man, then, who is keeping pace with her, footstep for footstep, twenty yards behind, is no undergraduate. She redoubles her speed again. Pooh! his presence has no reference to her. He is only taking the natural road to his hotel. But she does not look round again until the more bustling streets lie behind her; until she has reached the broad still thoroughfare where a range of gray colleges and a row of sentinel elms hold quiet converse with the stars.

Then, as if the muscles of her neck had been moved by some one else, she not consenting, once again she turns her head. The hotels are long passed. If he is still following, it is she whom he is following. And lo! twenty yards behind her, there he is, stepping through the moonlight!

She gives a low, excited laugh. Well, they have both had their will then : he has not walked home with her ; she has not walked home alone. It is a compromise. Again she looks up to the heavens. What a lovely, lovely vault! What sccd-pcarl of constellations ! What great planet-diamonds !

The clocks have just begun to strike midnight ; the city's innumerous clocks, cathedral, college, church ; the booming bell, the sharp strike, the melodious chime ! How nobly their loud wedded harmony floods the night ! And is there one of the gardens—she has reached the suburb of villas and gardens by this time—that has not contributed the breath of its gillyflowers to make the boon air so sweet ?

She walks on with her strong elastic tread. After all, it is good to be young : to have a fine ear for sound ; a nostril sensitive to fragrance ; and—the consciousness that behind you there is one protecting you where there is nothing to be protected from—guarding you where there is nothing to be guarded against.

She has reached her own gate, and at it halts, her hand upon the latch. Here surely, under the ægis of her own roof-tree—here, where that twinkling night-light shows the exact spot where her husband is addressing himself to his slumbers—she may abate a little of her rigidity.

Seeing her arrived, he too has halted ; nor is it until by a faint motion of her hand she gives him leave to approach, that he ventures to draw near her.

'Thank you !' she says with a smile, to which it is perhaps the moonlight that lends its quivering uncertainty ; 'but it was not necessary. '

He neither disclaims nor accepts her acknowledgments. Gravely he unfastens the iron gate for her ; while above his gold head the laburnum droops her gold curls. The moon has taken their colour out of both, and substituted her own.

Is he then still going to say nothing? But as she passes through, he speaks :

'I—I—am not leaving Oxbridge to-morrow. I shall be in Oxbridge all to-morrow.'

'Shall you?' she says faintly.

'I have not done anything to forfeit your friendship, have I?' he asks, while in the moonlight she sees his right hand tighten its nervous clasp on one of the spiked iron uprights of the gate.

She is quite silent.

'Have I?' he repeats, in a tone as of one who, though patient, will not go without his answer. (Is truth always the best to be spoken? Then let it be spoken!)

'Nothing!'

'Is there then any reason why I should not come and see you to-morrow?'

Silence again ; her look wandering undecidedly over her flower-bed.

'Is there?'

Her eye has caught the Professor's night-light again—that ill-favoured Jack-o'-Lantern that is to dance for ever across the morass of her life.

'None!' she answers firmly ; and with that firm 'None!' she leaves him.

CHAPTER IV.

'He was not far wrong,' says Sarah dispassionately, 'though I am afraid that it was scarcely in a brotherly spirit that he said it; I *am* eminently well able to take care of myself!'

It is next morning, and the girls are beginning the day with a preliminary saunter round the narrow bounds of the little garden, and the newly-mown tennis-ground. They are very small bounds, but within them is room for undried dew; for a blackbird with a voice a hundred times bigger than its body; for a guelder rose, a fine broom-bush, and a short-lived lilac. What more would you have? Beneath one Turkey-red sunshade they stroll in slow contentment along.

'I have no foolish false pride,' continues Sarah complacently. 'When I realised that I was left behind, I saw that the only thing to be done was to make some one give me a lift home. They did not much like it at first, but they were very glad afterwards, when they found that they had "entertained an angel unawares!"'

'And how did they find out that they had?' asks Belinda drily.

'They were delighted with my conversation,' rejoins the other importantly. 'I could not have done it if you had been by,' breaking into a laugh; 'but I talked about the Higher Education of Women!'

Belinda joins in the laugh; nor is there any evidence of her mirth being less spontaneous and bubbling than her sister's. Ahead of them the little dogs are frisking. At least, to speak more correctly, Punch is. What little frisk time and fat have left to Slutty has been stamped out of her by mortification at Punch's reappearance on the scene. When you are no longer in your first youth, there is really not much amusement in having one of your hind-legs continually pulled, mouthed, and facetiously worried from behind.

'And you,' says Sarah, standing on tiptoe to reach a lilac bough, and rub her face luxuriously against it; 'how did *you* get home?'

A red sunshade always diffuses a glow over the face beneath it.

'Oh, I walked,' with an assumption of inattention.

'Alone?'

There is a second's hesitation before the answer comes. Belinda is naturally veracious; but, after all, there is nothing incompatible with literal veracity in answering:

'Yes, alone.'

'Were not you frightened?' asks Sarah.

Her tone is careless; but she has loosed the lilac bough, and her shrewd eyes are—perhaps accidentally—bent upon her sister's.

'Frightened!' repeats Belinda, with an impatience that seems out of proportion to the occasion, eagerly following her junior's example, and thrusting her hot cheeks among the cool and sugared lilac-clusters; 'what a silly question! Why should I be frightened? what was there to be frightened at?'

But to this heated inquiry Sarah makes no answer; a reticence which causes a feverish misgiving to dart across Belinda's mind. But no! her sister's room looks towards the back. Sarah has an eye like a greyhound, an ear like a stag, and a nose like a truffle dog, but even she cannot see and hear through deal boards.

'I must leave you to your own devices this morning,' she says, changing the subject with some precipitation; 'you must amuse yourself as well as you can till luncheon-time.'

Sarah lifts her eyebrows. 'Do you mean to say that you intend to take three hours in ordering dinner?'

'Ordering dinner!' echoes the other ironically; 'ordering dinner indeed! Did you ever happen to hear of Menander?'

'Never.'

'Nor of his Fragments?'

'Never.'

'Nor of his Notes, Philological, Critical, and Archæological?'

'Never.'

'Happy you!' says Belinda drily, beginning to walk towards the house.

'If I were you,' cries Sarah irreverently, calling after her, 'he should be in still smaller "fragments" before I had done with him!'

Belinda laughs.

'Bah!' she says; 'it is all in the day's work. Perhaps it is better to have too much to do, like me, than too little, like you.'

There is such a strong tincture of cheerfulness in the tone with which she speaks, it differs so widely from the dogged submission of yesterday, that Sarah eyes her suspiciously.

'You take a rosy view of life this morning,' she says, with a streak of sarcasm.

Belinda changes colour.

'It is a matter of weather,' she says quickly. 'I am very

much influenced by weather; you know that you always
used to say that I was a Weatherglass!'

But is it a matter of weather? Is it the weather that
sends her humming with irresistible gaiety to her desk and
Menander? Spring-time, it is true, is exhilarating; morning
is exhilarating; life's morning is exhilarating: why, then,
should she not be exhilarated? But is it of these three
innocent stimulants only that she is drinking? There must
be something different from her wont in the very quality of
her step as she enters her husband's study, for he looks up.

'You are late,' he says briefly.

'Only three minutes,' she answers pleasantly; 'and I
will make it up at the other end.'

She seats herself at her escritoire, forcibly and with
difficulty swallowing down the end of the tune that she
has been singing to herself, under her breath, all the way
upstairs. Even the very room—the hated task-work room
—looks different from what it ordinarily does. Usually it is
quite sunless; but this morning a long, slant dart of gold
has squeezed itself in, taking no denial, and on it how the
dust-motes are dancing! Must everything dance to-day?

The Professor, at least, is an exception to the general
rule. He shows no signs of any wish to dance. While
dictating, he is in the habit of walking up and down. She
knows the exact square in the carpet from which he will
start, and that at which he will pause and turn. He has
begun his diurnal course; but there is a moment's interval
before the first words of the first sentence leave his lips.

She pauses, pen in hand, awaiting them; and as she
pauses, following him with her eyes, a feeling of genuine
and potent compassion passes through her heart and brain.

'How dreadful to be old! How hideous to be ugly,
cantankerous, unloved!'

'I think,' she says, under this impulse, speaking in a

gentle, hesitating voice, 'that I owe you an apology for my rude speech about you to Sarah, after dinner yesterday. I dare say,' laughing nervously, 'that you have forgotten it. I am sure it was not worth remembering; but, at all events, it makes me easier in my mind to tell you that I regret it.'

The intention of this speech is excellent; as a mere question of judgment and tact, it is doubtful whether it had not been wiser to have let her stinging jest lie, without resuscitating it even to repent of it.

The expression of his face shows whether or no he has forgotten it.

'I think,' he says aridly, 'that since we are already late, we had better keep to the subject in hand.'

For a moment or two she bows her crimsoned face and bitten lips over her desk, in furious annoyance at having laid herself open to this self-inflicted humiliation. But, ere long, her serenity returns. It is only wounds inflicted by those we love whose sting lasts.

After all, she has done her part; she has made the *amende.* Of what least consequence is it how he has taken it? But her compassion is dead. He may look as old, as pinched, as bloodless as he chooses. No smallest throb of pity stirs her heart again; nor does any other word, unrelating to the subject of her labour, cross her lips.

Through all the fresh bright morning hours, he travels from his one carpet-square to his other carpet-square, elaborating careful, classic phrases as he goes; and she, in docile silence, follows him with her pen.

The sun soars high; the drowsy flies inside the shut window make their futile journeys up and down the pane. The swallows sweep across outside, bells ring, butchers and bakers drive up and drive away; but not one of these distracting objects does she allow to beguile her for one instant of her toil. She will do her task-work conscientiously, thoroughly, wholly, so that hereafter neither he nor she herself may have anything to reproach her with; and then, when it is ended—she allows herself one long breath of prospective enjoyment—why then the sun will still be high; the swallows will still be darting; the lengthy May afternoon, with probabilities too bright to be faced in its green lap, will still be hers.

And, meanwhile, how well the pens write! how clear her own apprehension seems! She has even suggested a verbal emendation or two, which his nice ear has accepted. How quickly the morning is passing! Can it indeed be a quarter to one that the College clocks are striking? After all, there is no great hardship in being amanuensis to a savan afflicted with weak eyes; it is a great matter to be able to be of use to some one!

She looks up, smiling rosily; if not forgetful, forgiving, of her former snub.

'We have done a good day's work!' she says congratulatingly. 'You have been in vein this morning.'

'It is fortunate if it is so,' replies he grudgingly, 'for we have large arrears of work to make up.'

'Have we?' she says, a little blankly, rubbing her cramped right finger and thumb; 'but—but not *to-day?*'

'And why not to-day?' rejoins he firmly. 'I have promised that my "Essay upon the Law of Entail among the Athenians" shall be in the printers' hands by to-morrow, and it is therefore necessary that the proofs should be corrected before post-time to day.'

'Not to-day!' cries she feverishly; 'not to-day!'

The smile and the short-lived roses have together left her face. She looks fagged and harried, but obstinate.

'And why not to-day?' repeats he, regarding her with slow displeasure.

'You forget,' she says,—'you seem to forget that we have a guest.'

'She will, no doubt, provide herself with amusement,' replies he disagreeably; 'she will, no doubt, amuse herself perfectly without your aid.'

'And I?' she says in a low voice, turning very white, and looking at him with concentrated dislike (is it possible that she could ever have pitied him?) 'how am *I* to amuse myself? does it never occur to you that I, too, may wish to be amused?'

'I put no impediment in your way,' he answers frostily; 'you are at liberty—with the exception of the hours during which I am compelled to claim your services—to choose your own pursuits, your own associates!'

'Am I?' she says, hastily catching him up, while the dismissed carnation colour pours in flood back into her cheeks again. 'You give me leave?'

He looks at her with such unfeigned and unadmiring astonishment in his cold eyes, that she turns away in confusion.

'How long will you want me for?' she asks faltering; 'how many hours will the correcting of these proofs take?'

'It is impossible to say, exactly,' replies he, tranquilly leaving the room; satisfied with her acquiescence, and indifferent as to the spirit in which that acquiescence has been given.

The afternoon is three hours old, and Belinda still sits at her desk. The dew is dried, the long sunbeam has stolen away, but though it does not cheer her by its visible presence, she is aware, by the augmented heat of the close room, that the sun is beating hard and hotly on roof and wall. And on these thinly-built houses it *does* beat very hotly. At her side lies a heap of corrected slips, but before her is piled another, scarcely less bulky. She has been at work upon them for an hour and a half, and still she sees no end to her toil. Her head aches with long stooping; she has inked her tired fingers, and her eyes are dull and dogged. Now and again the door-bell ringing makes her give a nervous start. Is it come again—that time of strained continuous listening? those twenty-one months, during which all her life-power seemed to have passed into her ears?

It is the hour when visitors may be with the most probability expected. But is there not also a probability that they may be sent away again? Sometimes, when harder worked or gloomier spirited than usual, she has bidden her servant deny her. Is it not but too possible that, seeing her close slavery of to-day, that servant may take upon herself to conclude that such is her mistress' wish now also.

The idea throws her into a fever. She does not listen. She makes an unaccountable mistake. Again the bell rings. Is it her fancy, or has this ring a different sound from the former ones? Is there in it a mixture of violence and timidity, as of a person who had had to screw up his courage to ring at all in the first instance, and had then over-done it?

She writes on mechanically, dully aware that her husband is rebuking her for the illegibility of her last words. Even if the moral blows he is giving her were physical ones, she would feel them none the more.

The door opens, and the servant enters, with a man's card upon a salver. She scarcely needs to glance at it to tell that it is HIS; but for a moment her pale lips cannot frame the question that has sprung to them: 'Has he been sent away?'

'Is he gone?' she asks, stammering, taking the card, and, with a senseless, involuntary movement, hiding it in her hand.

'I told him that you were engaged, ma'am,' replies the

maid apologetically; 'but he asked me to bring you this card. Shall I say that you are engaged, ma'am?'

The Professor looks up, cross at the interruption, to give a brief 'Yes;' but his wife strikes athwart him.

'Show him in,' she says, with precipitate decision. 'Say that I will be down directly; tell Miss Churchill.'

She takes up her quill again, as the servant leaves the room, but apparently her hand shakes to a degree that is beyond her control; for in a moment a great blot has defaced the printed page.

'Pray be careful!' cries her husband fretfully. 'You have a hair in your pen.'

She throws it down, and takes another. The room in which they are sitting is over the drawing-room. Evidently *he* has been ushered in, and Sarah has joined him; for there is a murmur of voices. What are they saying? What are they likely to be saying?

'You have spelt *allegorical* with one *l!*' says the Professor, in a voice of resentful wonder.

'Have I?' she answers, bewildered and inattentive. 'And how many ought it to have?'

The voices have grown more distinctly audible. They have left the drawing-room; it is obvious that Sarah is taking him out into the garden—the pleasant, little, cool garden, with its blackbird and its broom-bush, and its bees. She draws a hot, long, envious breath at the thought.

'A child of five years old would have been ashamed to perpetrate so gross a blunder!' resumes he, taking the sheet from before her, and indignantly holding it up for reprobation.

She heaves a heavy, furious sigh, and a sombre light comes into her great, gloomy eyes. From the garden is heard a peal of laughter. Sarah is always laughing. It is well to be merry sometimes, but Sarah is too much of a buffoon.

'In errors so palpable, it is difficult not to see intention,' continues he, exasperated by a silence that is so plainly not repentance—a silence which she still observes.

Another burst of laughter from the garden—not Sarah's this time; a man's wholesome, unfeigned mirth. *He*, too, can laugh, can he?

'I should really be disposed to recommend a return to the writing-master,' says Mr. Forth, still ironically regarding the blurred page.

For all answer, she rises to her feet, and throws her pen with violence down upon the floor.

'Your machine has broken down for to-day,' she says, with a pale, rebellious smile. 'Legible or illegible, writing-master or no writing-master, I will write not one word more to day!'

CHAPTER V.

It is Miss Churchill's maxim always to make herself as comfortable, under any given circumstances, as those circumstances will permit; nor has she failed on the present occasion to live up to her own precept. Beneath the garden wall, where the shade spreads coolest, a fur rug, filched from the drawing-room floor, is extended ; cushions, unlawfully thieved from the drawing-room sofa, mollify the hardness of back of the garden-chairs. Upon the unlikely hypothesis of her conversation running short, she has unearthed all the novels she can find. At her feet the dogs alternately sleep, and gnash their teeth—rarely successful—at the flies. In the sun, close by, stands the parrot's gilded cage ; so that, if other resources fail her, she may fall back upon his loquacity. In addition to the dogs, at her feet also lies Rivers, unworthily occupied in tickling the inside of the dozing Slutty's ear with a flower-stalk. This is the tranquil Arcadian picture that salutes Mrs. Forth's eyes as she issues from the house. He has his back turned towards her ! He has not cared enough for her coming, even to place himself so as to watch for it ! How is she to know that it was only a moment ago, in obedience to Sarah's orders, and in dread of the remembered penetration of her eyes, that he had adopted his present position ? How cool they look ! How much at ease ! What a pity to disturb them ! After all she might as well have finished the proofs. As she draws near them, walking so softly over the turf that they are not immediately aware of her, a new burst of laughter fills and grates upon her ears.

'You seem very merry,' she says drily. Sarah exhibits no surprise—as why indeed should she?—at her sister's advent. With her head thrown back comfortably over her chair, she finishes her laugh luxuriously out, but of Rivers' mirth Belinda need no longer complain. There is not much that could be called mirth in the face that—suddenly leaping to his feet—he turns towards her. What a death's-head she must be to work such an instantaneous transformation in him!

'You seem to be very merry,' she repeats.

She is conscious of the resentful dryness of her tone; of the fagged flush upon her cheeks; and the sullenness that she has not quite been able to banish from her eyes; but she is as powerless to correct the one as the others. What has he done to deserve that tone? Beneath it he stands tongue-tied.

'May not I know what your joke was?' she says, struggling not very successfully for a greater amenity of manner; 'why should not it amuse me, too?'

'It—it was nothing much!' he answers deprecatingly; 'I do not know why I laughed; it was only'—looking unhappy and ashamed—'that Miss Churchill was telling me that Punch had once been engaged to the parrot, and that it was broken off because she bit his tail to the bone!'

There is such a contrast between the very mild waggery of this anecdote, and the deep humiliation of the tone in which he narrates it, that Sarah sets off laughing helplessly again; but not a muscle of Belinda's face moves.

'That respectable old jest,' she says, with a slight shrug; 'it has been for many years a family Joe Miller!'

'It was not a Joe Miller to him!' replies Sarah, standing

up in indistinct defence—indistinct through much laughing
—of her pleasantry; 'he may pretend now that he did not
like it—but he did!'

Belinda sits down; but the cloud still lowers on her brow.
To her own heart she says that she does well to be angry.
That here, for the first time face to face with the tragedy of
their two lives, he should be in a condition to be genuinely
amused by so miserable a jest—by any jest! Nor does the
crushing of his merriment please her any better. She, then,
is the wet blanket who stifles his jollity. Times are indeed
changed! If she were to leave them, no doubt the peals of
laughter would at once break out afresh. But for the present
they are effectually stilled. Painfully and sorely conscious
of this, she makes another difficult effort to recover her good
temper.

'I think I am losing my sense of humour,' she says
awkwardly; 'it must be the effect of Oxbridge air. Punch,
will you, too, lose your sense of humour?'

She has lifted the lively little dog up on her knees, and is
half hiding her hot face against his.

'He is losing something else, is not he?' says Rivers,
made bold by her gentler tone diffidently to draw a little
nigher to her, and to raise his eyes in painful questioning to
hers.

As he speaks, he lifts his hand and touches the locket
habitually worn round the neck, and as habitually tried to be
scratched off by Punch; and from which a lock of hair is at
present obviously escaping.

'Why, Punch, do *you* wear locks of hair?' asks the young
man, laughing nervously. 'Whose is it? Slutty's, let us
hope!'

'It is always coming out,' interposes Sarah in a disgusted
voice; 'the fact is,' lazily drawing herself up into a sitting
posture, and looking round explanatorily, 'that people have

a way of giving me locks of their hair—I am sure I do not know why—and as I cannot possibly wear them all, Punch is good enough to wear some of them for me! Punch has worn a great deal of hair in his day, have not you, Punch?'

As she speaks, she calls the dog to her; and becomes absorbed in the contemplation of his jewellery.

'Is it German or English hair, should you think?' asks Rivers, almost under his breath.

There is a smile on his face as he puts this question; but a smile with whose mirth she need not quarrel. In a moment how the Hussars and Uhlans are clanking round her again! How the soft wind is pelting her with cherry flowers! How the old Schloss is towering up against the German sky! She cannot answer him; but those few words seem to have given them back something of their former intimacy.

'Now whose is it?' says Sarah reflectively, having taken out the little lock, and being now contemplatively eyeing it with her head on one side; 'what a memory I have! Belinda, can you help me? whose is this lock of hair of Punch's? Oh, but it must have been since your day; it is not unlike *yours*' (turning to Rivers, and coolly setting the little tendril against his hair to compare them). 'Did you ever give me a lock of your hair?'

He turns with a start. He has been unwisely allowing himself to drift into one of his old speculations, as to whether any woman's ear had ever sat so daintily close to her head as does that of the wife of Professor Forth.

'A lock of my hair!' he cries, jumping up, and falling on his knees before Sarah, with an air of exaggerated playfulness; 'if I have not, I am quite ready to supply the omission; whereabouts will you have it from?' passing his hand over his own crisp curls. 'May I take your scissors, Mrs. Forth?'

It is the first time that he has so addressed her. It is

with untold difficulty that the name crosses his lips, and consequently he enunciates it with unusual distinctness. It is in reality a cudgelling that he is administering to himself for his late lapse, but to her it seems a wanton cruelty.

'May I take your scissors, Mrs. Forth?'

Mrs. Forth's head is, however, bent so low over her work-basket, that apparently she does not hear. Behind the shelter of that convenient receptacle for tapes and needles, her hands are trembling and writhing. At Dresden would he have talked even in joke of giving Sarah a lock of his hair? Why, he never even heard her when she spoke to him! Happily for Belinda, at this point, she is summoned to the house on some trifling errand, which detains her for ten minutes—ten minutes in which she is able to resume some hold upon herself; and it is well that it is so, for the sight which greets her is one not calculated to promote her equanimity. Sarah has abandoned her lazy reclining, and is sitting up, and holding Rivers' hand; not indeed, when one comes to observe closely, in any very lover-like manner, but as one who is examining it with an air of the liveliest interest and curiosity.

'I should be ashamed to own such a hand,' she is saying, with her accustomed candour; 'it is like a workman's hand.'

'But I *am* a workman,' he answers bluntly.

And then he is suddenly aware of Belinda's presence, and snatches it away.

'It really is quite a curiosity in its way,' says Sarah in a pleased voice; 'it is as hard and horny as a day-labourer's. Do show it to Belinda!'

He looks towards her, hesitating and uncertain. She has resumed her former seat, and her work-basket.

'Do!' she says, trying to speak with her newly-summoned tranquillity; and he holds it out to her, palm upwards.

It is a beautiful hand still, shapely and vigorous, but on it are disfiguring evidences of hard, coarse toil. There is nothing particularly affecting in a work-roughened palm : it is a condition to which are subjected the hands of ninety-nine out of every hundred of the human race ; and yet, as she looks at it, she has much ado to prevent the tears from springing to her eyes.

'You know,' he says, 'I told you that I could not stand the confinement of an office life !'

'*We know?*' cries Sarah, pricking up her ears. '*You told us?* What do you mean? When have you ever had the chance of telling us?'

He stops—staggered and white. He had forgotten the presence of an auditor. Nor is Belinda in a plight to help him.

'I mean,' he says floundering, 'that I—I intended to tell you ; and so,' hurriedly resuming his narrative, 'I—I went as an ordinary hand in the iron-works ; and was set to work at the puddling-furnace.'

'The puddling-furnace !' cries Sarah, delighted with the sound; 'and what is a *puddling-furnace*, pray ?' repeating the phrase with emphatic relish.

'A puddling-furnace is a furnace where the pig-iron from the smelting-furnace is worked about at a great heat with iron rakes—*rabbles*, they call them—and I had the honour and pleasure,' with a shy laugh, 'of working one of these rakes, until the iron became malleable.'

Belinda's pretence of work has dropped unheeded on the grass beside her.

'H—m !' says Sarah, still agreeably interested; 'no wonder that your hands are not so pretty as they might be. And was it very hard work ?'

'It was not exactly child's play,' he answers drily; 'but they gave us high wages; they were glad to get hold of a

good strong chap like me.   We had need to be pretty
strong !'

'And did you work at it all day ?'

'We were relieved every six or eight hours.   We could
not have stood it longer on account of the heat; that *was*
pretty bad !'

He pauses a moment, passing his disfigured hand, half
in absence, half in kindness, along Slutty's roomy back;
then adds :

'It is the heat that does it !   As a rule, puddlers do not
live long; it is the heat that does it.'

He says it with complete simplicity, neither expecting
nor wishing for compassion ; as if to spend eight hours a
day in a puddling-furnace were the natural and ordinary
sequel of an education at Eton and Oxbridge.

So this is how he has spent the twenty months, passed by
her in listening for the postman's knock—in this life-shorten-
ing, mind-deadening brute toil !   Well, even so, he has had
the best of it !

There is a silence of some moments' duration, broken
by Sarah, whose sharp ear has caught a sound of footsteps.

'Ha !' she cries with animation, 'here comes my little
flock ; and, as ill-luck will have it, I have forgotten every
one of their names.   Belinda ! quick ! help me !—which is
which ?'

Belinda lifts her downcast eyes : lifts them to see three
young gentlemen, whom apparently the parlour-maid, with
that contempt for undergraduates inherent in the native
Oxbridge mind, has left to announce themselves, timorously
advancing.   They are evidently not very easy in their minds,
and are somewhat obviously each pushing the other to the
front.

Clearly, Professor Forth's house is no habitual lounge

for undergraduates. A movement of irrational relief thrills through Rivers' heart as he realises this.

'They must indeed be fond of you, Sarah, to have faced me!' says Mrs. Forth, with a dry smile. 'How frightened they look! as frightened,' with one quick glance at Rivers, 'as *you* used to be!'

She does not pause to see the effect of her words; but, rising, walks with her long slow step to meet her guests.

'I do not wonder that they are frightened,' says Sarah in a stage aside to the young man. 'Does not she look as if she were going to ask them to what she owes the pleasure of their visit? If I do not fly to the rescue, even now they will turn tail and run!'

But Sarah for once is mistaken. They have no desire to turn tail and run. It is doubtful, indeed, whether, on their homeward way, and over their evening cigars, their limited and artless vocabulary of encomium is more strained to find epithets of approval for Miss Churchill than for her austerer sister. But indeed, to-day, Belinda is not austere.

'Why should she snub them?' she asks herself sadly; 'has not she had enough of snubbing people for all her lifetime?'

And so she is kind to them—too kind, Rivers begins presently to think with a jealous pang, as he sees her pouring out tea for them with her all-lovely hands; endowing them with her heavenly smile; lightening their darkness with her starry eyes. Nor is he, even yet, wise enough in love's lore, or coxcomb enough, to suspect that it is he himself—he sitting by, apparently neglected and overlooked—who has lit the eyes and carved the smile.

Sarah is very kind, too; but they are rather hurt at the hopeless muddle into which she has got their names.

By and by, when well be-tea'd and be-caked, they are embarked upon a game of tennis, and the sound of callings

and laughings, of balls struck and racquets striking, breaks
the Arcadian silence of that hitherto virgin enclosure—
Professor Forth's tennis-ground. It is too small to admit of
more than one set at a time ; and Belinda, as a good hostess,
despite the warm urgencies of the now tamed and happy
strangers, retires in favour of her visitors. It boots little to
inquire whether the sacrifice cost her much.

' Do *you* play ?' cries Sarah nonchalantly, flourishing her
racquet under Rivers' nose. ' No ? Ah ?' with an impudent
smile, 'you are more at home with your *rake !*'

Though it is morally impossible that they could have
understood it, both Bellairs and Stanley are contemptible
enough to laugh at this sally ; a fact which would no doubt
have made Rivers disposed to punch their heads, had he
heard them ; but the jest and its prosperity both fall upon
deaf ears. Sight and hearing are stopped by the anxious
fear :

' Is she displeased with him for refusing to play ? Ought
he to have played ? Will she now expect him to go ? At
parting, will she say any word of further meeting ?'

A lump rises in his throat. Not presuming again to take
up his place on the grass at her feet—though, after all, it is a
privilege that no one grudges even to the dogs—he stands,
uncertain and unhappy, before her. If she so wills it, this
must be the end. Nor does she seem in any hurry to put
him out of his incertitude.

Upon her the day's earlier mood is returning. In what
life-giving whiffs comes the kindly wind ! Did ever homely
coated bird say such sweet things as does the blackbird from
among the cherry-boughs ? and the little vulgar villa-garden
has grown like that of which Keats spake :

> ' Where the daisies are rose-scented,
> And the rose herself has got
> Perfume that on earth is not !

He is here before her, waiting one lightest sign from her to
lie down at her feet and be trampled on. Is it any wonder
that, being a woman, she lets three minutes elapse before
she gives that sign?

At the end of that time, 'Are you at it still?' she asks
abruptly.

It is half an hour since the subject was dropped, and a
dozen others have intervened between; yet he seems to
have no difficulty in understanding at once to what her
speech alludes.

'No,' he answers, with a sigh of relief (for it is evident
that had she wished to be rid of him, she would not have
introduced a new, or resumed an old, topic), taking possession as she speaks of Sarah's forsaken chair; 'I am promoted
to be foreman.'

He pauses for her to comment or congratulate; but she
does neither. She only stitches feverishly on.

'It struck me that the same thing might be done, with
much less expense of labour, by machinery,' he continues,
with the hurry of one who has no assurance that he is not
wearying his listener; 'and in consequence of this—this
invention of mine, which our firm has taken up, I have been
promoted to the rank of foreman.'

He stops so decidedly that she is compelled to make an
observation of some kind.

'And in due time, of course, you will be taken into
partnership, and marry your master's daughter,' she says
with a difficult flippancy.

The blood rushes to his face. He had expected a
kinder commentary. Surely no jest ever so ill became her
whom, in his eyes, all becomes. There is a silence. The
sun's rays are less vertical, and the dogs have awoke.
Punch indeed, under the mistaken idea of being obliging is officiously retrieving the tennis-balls, and being

warmly slapped by the heated players for his good nature.

'Well,' says Belinda, with nervous asperity in her tone, 'is there nothing more? Go on.'

'Others have invented machines of the same kind,' he continues spiritlessly, for her jest has taken the heart out of his narration, 'but they have turned out either complete failures, or only very partial successes; if mine has better luck, our firm holds out hopes of taking out a patent, and giving me a small share of the business.'

'Did not I tell you so?' cries she, laughing rather stridently; 'why, my prophecy is already half-way towards fulfilment.'

Again his face burns, but he deigns her no answer. If she can stoop to so unworthy a merriment, she shall at least enjoy it alone.

'It is evidently all for the best,' he says, trying to catch her callous tone; 'it seems that I have a kind of turn for mechanics. It was news to me that I had a turn for any-thing convertible into money. If—if things had gone smoothly, I might have lain down in my grave without finding out where the bent of my genius lay: and that would have been a thousand pities, would not it?'

He ends with a laugh. Her mirth, which had offended him, has long died; nor has she any answer ready to his question. Her long arms (even arms can look sad) lie listless on her lap, and her great veiled eyes see visions. Vanished from before them are the little square garden and the tennis-players. They see only his future life-path stretching before her; his life growing ever fuller, fuller, fuller of busy, prospering, eager work, with ever less and less room in it for the gap left by her. By and by that gap will close altogether. The sooner the better for him!

But for *her?* Over her there pours a rush of frantic

longing to tear it wide ; to keep it ever, ever yawning. But it will not so yawn always. It will close so that scarce a scar will be left to show where it once was. He is fond of his work already. In how different a spirit he addresses himself to it from that in which, sulky and half-hearted, she turns to her hated toils. A sense of injury and offence against him rises in her heart. He can never have suffered as she has suffered ; his meat has never been ashes, nor his drink tears !

'It is clear that you are Fortune's favourite,' she says in a hard voice ; 'I congratulate you.'

'Thank you,' he answers, deeply wounded ; 'you have hit upon the exact phrase that describes me.'

There is such a sharp pain in his tone, that, though she has been anxiously averting her eyes from him, they must needs seek his in apology.

'Forgive me,' she says with a remorseful watery smile ; 'you know that I was always bitter ; and somehow,' her lip trembling, 'time has not improved me !'

Seeing the sorrowful twitching of that lovely and beloved mouth, he loses his head for a moment.

'It would have been nothing from any one else,' he says, murmuring under his breath ; 'but it came ill from you.'

She offers no denial. Only she drops her eyes ; and a stealing selfish sweetness laps her senses. Not yet, then, is the gap filled.

'Belinda !' cries the voice of Sarah, suddenly striking in, high and mirthful ; of Sarah, returned, hot and boastful, from her finished game. 'Cheer up ! I have some good news for you !'

Belinda gives a great start.

'Have you indeed ?' she says hurriedly ; 'so much the better for me.'

'Mr. Staveley and Mr. Bellairs and Mr.——' (she has

not yet mastered the name of her third young friend, but audaciously mumbles something that is to stand for it), 'and I have concocted a little junket for to-morrow. If it is not your birthday it ought to be! You are going to be taken on the river, and treated to cakes and ale at a pot-house, and towed back by moonlight. Come now, what do you say? are not you grateful?'

Belinda laughs nervously.

'Grateful! of course I am!'

She has risen from her chair and begun to walk about upon the sward. Perhaps by changing her position she may the sooner be free of the heady fumes of this man-dragora that she has been drinking; may the more easily shake off this divine drowsiness, that yet leads to death.

'It strikes me that you are not listening to a word I say,' says Sarah, darting a dry look from one to the other of the culprits.

'Not listening?' repeats Belinda, with a feverish gaiety; 'am I not? Judge for yourself whether I am listening! I am to be taken on the river, and treated to cakes and ale, and towed home by moonlight; come, now!'

'Well, is not it a nice plan? are not you grateful to us?' cries Sarah, again appeased and jubilant.

'It would be delightful!' replies Mrs. Forth, still with that same factitious liveliness. 'I should enjoy it of all things; I am so fond of the water, only——'

She stops abruptly; her rebellious eye wandering to where Rivers—he, too, has risen—stands aloof, out in the cold; obviously uninvited, unincluded in the joyous pro-gramme.

'Only Menander, I suppose,' says Sarah, making a face; 'really, at his age, he ought to be able to shift for himself for one day.'

'It is not Menander,' replies Belinda with embarrassment; 'as it happens, I have a whole holiday to-morrow. Mr. Forth is going to London for the day, to take the chair at an archæological meeting.'

'Only what, then?' looking at her with a point-blank directness that puts her out of countenance.

'Only,' she says, and stops again, irresolute.

Reason is pouring her cold douche over her, and asking: 'Why should he be invited? What sense would there be in it? unreason rather, and madness. Has not she supped enough of hemlock for one while? With how many dreary days and weeks of flat revolt and saltless labour will she already have to expiate this one drunken hour? Let this be the end! let this be the end!'

'Only nothing,' she says, with awkward gaiety.

'I wonder why you hesitated?' asks Sarah inquisitively. 'I cannot fancy ever hesitating when there is any question of amusing one's self. Do not you often go on the water?'

'Never; I am never asked; you never ask me,' turning with a sort of spurious coquetry to the enraptured young men.

'We should be only too delighted,' cries Bellairs; he, by right of his one minute's priority of introduction, having constituted himself spokesman and old acquaintance; 'only we—we—were afraid, we—we—did not venture!'

'You must venture for the future, then,' replies she with a flighty laugh. 'You must take me often! I want to go! I want to enjoy myself!'

Her eye sparkles, and her cheek flames, as she speaks. Is it indeed the expectation of pleasure that has set them both so bravely alight? She throws herself with such a fury of interest into all the details of the excursion, that she has hardly time or attention to spare for bidding good-bye to Rivers, who presently comes up to make his adieux.

'Are you going?' she asks indifferently. 'Good-bye.'

As she speaks, she lays for one instant her hot dry hand in his cold one. She would have bidden even Bellairs good-bye more warmly. None but herself knows the strength of the temptation that assails her to clutch that poor slighted hand before them all ; to lay it on her miserable heart ; to drown it in her tears, smother it with her kisses, and pay it any other tribute of extravagant passionate homage.

Least of all does he suspect it, as he walks away, decently strangling his sick despair till he is out of sight. No sooner is he gone, and the need for defence ended, than she throws away her weapons. Her attention flags so obviously ; her manner relapses so patently from its short summer of animation into its normal frost, that it dawns at length upon the three boys' intelligence that they are running a good chance of outstaying their welcome, and forfeiting the place that they flatter themselves they have won in Mrs. Forth's esteem. They take leave as precipitately as Sarah's many last words, commands, *espiègleries*, jokes, will let them. She accompanies them to the door ; and Belinda, since it is more tolerable to move about than to sit still, accompanies her.

The sisters lean on the low iron gate, and the bland spring evening wraps her arms around them.

Belinda has lifted her gloomy eyes to the laburnum gloriously pendent above her head. Which happy cluster was it that brushed against his hair last night in the starlight ?

'He is not gone yet!' says Sarah, in that voice of shrewd, dry sense which would surprise the admirers of her butterfly phase, could they hear it. 'What is he hanging about for ?'

She has desisted rather suddenly from her occupation of kissing her fingers to her three adorers, who, reluctant to lose one of her last glances, are backing down the road

away from her. Belinda's heart gives a bound. Not quite
the end yet, then! She has done her best! Her conscience is clear! but it is not quite the end yet, then! Can
she be blamed because he still loiters near?

'I suppose the road is public property,' she says doggedly; but her voice shakes.

'You did not ask him to join us to-morrow, did you?'
asks Sarah, with dry rapidity.

'No.'

'Ah!' (drawing a long breath), 'that is right!'

'It would have been the merest civility to have invited
him,' says Mrs. Forth sullenly. A frown less of ill-humour
than of perplexed uneasiness has gathered on Miss Churchill's
satin brow.

'It is no case of *civility* between you and him,' she says
curtly.

The flush on Belinda's fagged face grows hotter.

'I am at a loss to understand what you mean,' she says
angrily.

'I mean,' replies Sarah shrewdly, and enunciating with
the greatest clearness, 'that discretion is the better part of
valour—that is what I mean!'

'Thank you!' cries the other fiercely, and trembling like
a leaf from head to foot. 'Thank you for us both for your
good opinion of us!—*Mr. Rivers!*'

At the last two words she raises her voice into a call;
but it is so unsteady and ill-modulated, and he is so comparatively distant, that one would hardly expect the sound
to carry so far; but apparently it does, for he starts and
looks uncertainly towards her, distrusting his own ears.

Is it likely that she should have called him? she—his
high proud lady—after such a careless cruelty of good-bye
too!

'Mr. Rivers!' she repeats, in a voice that is as unsteady

as before, but louder. There can be no mistake this time. He can no longer distrust his good-luck; and in one second, as if he could not obey her quickly enough, he is hurrying back.

Sarah lifts her arms deliberately from the gate, and rubs them gently to remove the slight numbness produced by contact with the cold iron.

'Blessed are they who let well alone!' she says, gently raising her shoulders, and turning towards the house. 'I have disqualified myself for that benediction; have not I, Slutty?'

So saying, she disappears. Belinda would have liked to ask her to stay, but her pride forbids it. Long before Rivers has reached her, she has repented of her perverse and devil-born impulse. Why has she called him? What has she to say to him when he comes? For the first moment she says nothing.

'You—you called me?' he asks, faltering, surprised at her silence and her strange look.

'Did I?' she says, stammering. 'Yes—of course I did! I—I—you leave Oxbridge to-morrow?'

'Do I?' he answers blankly.

Is this, then, what she has called him back for? To tell him that he must not venture into her presence again?

'You must know your own plans best,' she says, with a forced laugh; 'do not you leave Oxbridge to-morrow?'

'There is no need that I should,' he answers diffidently; 'I have a week's holiday!'

Her rebel pulses leap. A week! A whole week! She lifts her face, on which the sunset is mirrored, and looks towards the west. On what a couch of fiery damask roses, dying into daffodil, the sun is laying himself down! What a treble sweetness the throstle is putting into his song as he addresses himself to his rest!

' A week !' she says aloud.

' Does a week in two years seem to you such a long holi-day?' he asks, rather wounded by what sounds to him the cold wonder of her tone; 'it need not be spent here, if——'

He stops abruptly. *'If you do not wish it,'* would be the sentence's natural ending; but so to conclude it would be to suppose an interest, with which he has no right nor any reason to credit the wife of Professor Forth, in him and his affairs.

She does not ask him how he had meant to finish his phrase. She does not finish it for him. She only stands staring, beneath the level penthouse of her milky hands, at the blinding sunset. What a curve her lifted elbow makes ! From what a marvel of wrist and forearm does the lawny sleeve fall back !

' Is this what you called me for?' he says abruptly; 'to tell me that I am to go to-morrow?'

For a minute she stands irresolute, still looking sunwards; her outward woman a lovely pattern of harmony, grace, and quiet; her inward woman, ugly chaos and dark fight. Shall she say ' Yes'? To say so would be to more than retrieve her late error. Dimly she feels that if she has one ray of sober reason left her, she will say 'Yes.' She heaves a sigh, and lets fall her hands. Her lips have all but framed the fateful word, when :

' Belinda ! Belinda !' comes an old voice, calling impera-tively peevish from the house.

A week ! One poor week ! Only a week ! What can one week matter ? Her manner has suddenly changed.

' It is Mr. Forth !' she says hurriedly. 'I called you back,' reddening like the western cloud-fleeces, and throw-ing a guilty look over her shoulder, 'to ask you whether, if you were not going to leave Oxbridge to-morrow, you—you would join our party on the water ?'

CHAPTER VI.

'Lieb' Liebchen, leg's Händchen auf's Herze mein ;
Ach, hörst du wie's pochet in's Kämmerlein ?
Da hauset ein Zimmermann schlimm und arg,
Der zimmert mir einen Todtensarg.

'Er hämmert und klopfet bei Tag und bei Nacht,
Er hat mich schon längst um den Schlaf gebracht ;
Ach, sputet euch, Meister Zimmermann,
Damit ich balde schlafen kann.'

IN other climes, a sunset of suave sublimity usually means that it will be followed by a sunrise as nobly fair. But in our free isle this is not the case. Even the weather will submit to no tyranny, but follows its own wild and freakish will. You may close your eyes upon a distant steady heaven of molten copper and speckless blue; and open them upon a soaked-blanket sky, half an inch above your head.

During the many wakeful patches that vary the sameness of her night, Belinda has full time to repent of her evening's doings; but not once does it occur to her that the weather may possibly intervene to prohibit the excursion. Among all her half-sincere plans for evading the expedition, the alternative of a wet day has not once suggested itself; and when the morn comes, dim and sad, the poignancy of her disappointment at sight of the dripping bushes and filled flower-cups shows her how much of veracity there was in

her projects of abstinence. *Now* she will have to endure
the pang of renunciation, without having enjoyed the merit
of self-conquest. And yet it is a lovely rain, not harshly
driving, nor rudely strewing the earth with a ravin of torn-off
petals; but gently stealing down from the cloud-roof overhead, softly thrusting itself between the blossom-lips, feeding
the juicy leaves, healthful, wealthful, beneficent, yet execrated by two young eyes that are morosely watching it. It
is execrated by two old ones also. The Professor tentatively
throws out an idea as to the advisability of telegraphing to
the Archæological Society his inability to preside over its
deliberations.

'But you are not sugar or salt!' cries Belinda impatiently,
as she stands, a comforter thrown over her arm, and a mackintosh extended to receive her husband's meagre person;
'you will be in cabs and trains all day.'

'It is not always easy to secure a cab at a moment's
notice on a wet day!' replies he, demurring. 'As I have
often explained to you, it is upon trifles that the laws of
health depend; there may be delay enough to allow of my
getting my feet thoroughly wet—a circumstance amply sufficient to throw a chill upon a liver already predisposed.'

'But will not you be putting the Society to great inconvenience? will not its members be very much disappointed?'
asks she, reddening consciously as she speaks.

What is she saying? What does she care whether they
are disappointed or not? To what depths of disingenuous-
ness has she—truthful as she has been hitherto counted her
life long—already descended? But it may clear—it may
clear!

'I might obviate the difficulty by taking an extra pair of
socks in my pocket to change at the Club,' he says thoughtfully; and then her spirits rise, for he extends his arms, not
to take a parting embrace, but to insert them in the water-

proof-sleeves which she, with wifely alacrity, holds ready to receive them.

He is gone. That one main obstacle to her pleasure is at all events removed. If only it would clear! She is no longer half-sincere with herself. No longer does she feign a desire to extricate herself from the entanglement into which she has plunged, nor a gratitude to Mother Nature for having come to her aid. Without asking *why* she wishes it, she has concentrated all her being upon the one mastering desire to see that cloud-curtain raise its trailing corners, transpierced and put to flight by such a sun as yesterday's.

'It does not look in the least like lifting!' she says, in a tone which she in vain tries to make sound careless, to Sarah, as they enter the drawing-room after breakfast. 'Do you think that there is any chance of its lifting?'

'Not the slightest!' replies Sarah placidly.

With that adaptability to circumstances which makes life to her one long feast, Miss Churchill has arranged herself for a wet day. A small fire—not unwelcome in the rain-chilled atmosphere—brightens the hearth; and to it she has—for to her nothing is sacred—pulled up the Professor's chair: that one of Mudie's novels which, by its large type, wide margins, and plenitude of titled names, seems to promise the least strain upon the intellect, in her hand.

'Who would have thought it yesterday?' says Mrs. Forth, in a tone of mournful irritation, totally unable to follow her philosophic sister's example, and fidgeting uneasily about the room.

'Who indeed?' rejoins Sarah equably.

There is something in the indifferent content of her voice that jars upon Belinda's mood. The dogs have taken their cue from Miss Churchill—Punch has got inside the fender as if it were winter; the cat lies lazily stretched just outside

the parrot's cage; and Polly, exasperated by her air of calm
security, is walking stealthily, head downwards, along the
side of his cage, and when he has got, as he thinks, within
reach of her, is stretching out first a vicious hooked nose,
and then a long crooked gray hand, to make a grab at her
whiskers.

Sarah laughs.

'You were so anxious for it yesterday,' says Belinda, with
an irrationally aggrieved accent.

'Was I?' answers Sarah, yawning. 'I am not the least
anxious for it now; I am thoroughly comfortable, thank
God! Why do not you come near the fire? I have a hundred questions to ask you; we have the house all to ourselves—excuse' (parenthetically) 'my reckoning that among
our advantages—and I have scores of good things to tell
you about Cannes and granny; you used to be fond of
grannyana!'

'I am not cold,' replies Belinda, avoiding compliance by
seating herself where she can at once command the window,
and evade her sister's eyes. 'Tell them me here.'

'Well, you must know,' begins Sarah, prudently ignoring
this ruse, and launching into her narrative, 'that some Poles
had the apartment above ours at the hotel, their salon was
over granny's bedroom, and every night, at about ten o'clock,
they began to dance sarabands, and cancans, and Highland
schottisches, and the Lord knows what in it! You know how
fond granny is of having her old head danced over when she
is courting her beauty sleep.'

She pauses to see whether her hearer is listening; it is
obvious that she is not, as for a moment or two she makes no
comment, and then, becoming aware of the silence, breaks
into a factitious laugh. 'Ha! ha!'

'What are you laughing at?' asks Sarah sharply.

'I had not come to the point yet.'

The other stops, embarrassed.

'It—it was very good even so far as you had gone,' she answers in confusion.

'The end was better still,' replies Miss Churchill shortly, taking up her book again; 'but you shall never hear it!'

'How ill-natured!' cries Mrs. Forth, advancing eagerly towards the hearth, roused into alarm at her own self-betrayal; 'and I—I was so much interested in it. I should like you to begin it all over again.'

But Sarah is inexorable. Presently Belinda desists from her importunities, and not daring to return to the window, also takes up a book, occasionally from behind its shelter throwing a desperate eye on the weather.

It is a hopeless wet day. Once or twice, indeed, there has been a tantalising thinning of, and movement among, the vapours; but it has ended only in a more resolute, inflexible fastening upon the earth. Eleven—that hour of clearing—has come and gone, and brought no clearing with it. After all, she might as well have done her plain duty, and sent him away. In that case she would at least have had the throbs of an approving conscience to keep her up. And what, pray, has she now?

The forenoon is gone; luncheon is over; they are again in the drawing-room. The novel has long ago dropped from Sarah's fingers, and she has slidden into a warm, infantile slumber. The door-bell, loudly jangling, wakes her with a jump.

'It is those hateful boys!' she cries petulantly, starting up. 'Am I never to have any peace from them? and I was in such a beautiful sleep!'

One glance at her sister's face—that sister who has obviously not shared her slumbers; whose watch has been at length rewarded, though by no brightening of the material sky—tells her who is among 'those hateful boys.' Perhaps this fact adds a new tinge of ill-humour to her tone, as she advances, childishly rubbing her drowsy eyes with her knuckles, to meet her admirers.

'You woke me!' she says, pouting. 'I was in such a beautiful sleep!'

This speech is not calculated to reassure three timid young gentlemen, who have already been questioning the wisdom of their own procedure, and doubtfully discussing among themselves the probabilities as to the mood, whether of summer warmth or December ice, that they will find their hostess in. Upon Sarah, at least, they had counted to stand by them. But aid from an unexpected quarter comes to them.

'Never mind her!' says Belinda, with a young and radiant smile of welcome and re-assurance. 'What business has she to be asleep? A wet day? Yes, it is a wet day; but what delicious warm rain! how much good it will do to the country! the farmers are crying out for rain!'

This is the way in which she now regards the lately-execrated downpour. Is *he* not here? and whether in sunny boat on flashing river, gathering fritillaries in the water-meadows, or in little rain-darkened early-English drawing-room, is not it now all one to her?

> 'Vivre ensemble d'abord,
> C'est le bien nécessaire et réel,
> Après on peut choisir au hasard
> Ou la terre ou le ciel!'

'I hope you will forgive our calling so early,' says Bellairs, a little relieved, but still not very comfortable in his spirits; 'we—we wanted to know what you thought about the river.'

'*About the river!*' cries Sarah, still cross and sleepy, casting a sarcastic glance, first at the weather, and then at the young man; 'are we frogs, or young ducks?'

He looks so silly, that Miss Churchill laughs, her good-humour at once restored.

'Now that you are here, you may as well stay,' she says, in a thoroughly wide-awake voice; 'may not they, Belinda? If we depend upon the charms of conversation, I shall be asleep again in ten minutes; why should not we play games?'

'Why not?' responds Belinda readily.

Her cheeks are pink, and her eyes dancing. There is no pastime, however wildly, childishly hilarious, for which she is not in tune.

'Shouting Proverbs!' suggests Sarah joyously. 'Not know Shouting Proverbs?' (with a reproving look at Staveley, who has murmured this objection). 'Why, everybody shouts, and one guesses!' (in lucid explanation). 'It makes a tremendous noise; I do not know that it has any other merit.'

'The neighbours would indict us for a nuisance,' says Belinda gaily, shaking her head. 'Russian Scandal?'

'It does not make noise enough,' says Sarah; 'it is nothing but whispering; we will have no whispering' (rather curtly, and with an almost imperceptible glance towards Rivers, in application of the warning).

'Hare and Hounds is not a bad game in a house,' says Mr. De Lisle, in a small, shy voice. 'We played Hare and Hounds at a house I was staying at the other day; we ran all through every room, from attic to cellar; it was great fun!'

'Your friend evidently did not keep a mother-in-law out of repair upstairs,' replies Sarah, dismissing at once, though with leniency, this not very bright suggestion; '*we* do. What does the company say to Post, eh?'

The company, who are one and all in the mood for riotous jollity in any form, hail the proposal with one-voiced effusion; and it is on the point of being carried into execution, when Miss Churchill suggests an improvement upon it.

'Why not dance? dancing is better than any games! Surely some one can play, or even whistle a tune, or set the musical box tinkling out its one waltz. Room? plenty of room! too much room! Wheel all the furniture out into the passage!'

No sooner said than done. Away trundles the early English suite of rush-bottomed chairs; away the Professor's sacred *fauteuil!* away Belinda's work-table! everything but the piano and the music-stool, to which little De Lisle, having weakly admitted that he can play a little dance music, is at once ruthlessly nailed.

The rain patters, snow-soft outside. The valse strikes up. There is a moment's hesitation. Bellairs and Staveley, generously unwilling to steal a march upon each other, hang back; but Sarah settles the point by frisking up to the one nearest to her—it is all one to her with which she dances; it happens to be Bellairs—and swoops away with him smooth and sure as a swallow darting down upon a moth. Without a word exchanged between them, Belinda finds herself in Rivers' arms. The rain plash-plashes upon the open window's sill. How long it is since she has danced! How madly exhilarating are motion and measure! Is it in heaven or upon earth that that lame waltz is being strummed? After a turn or two he feels her light and buoyant body grow heavy in his embrace.

'Stop!' she says dizzily; 'the room goes round.'

He obeys at once; and fearing lest she may fall, keeps for one moment his arm around her.

'It is so long since I danced,' she says, lifting one white hand to her giddy eyes; 'so long! so long! not since——'

She breaks off.

'Not since your——'

He also breaks off. But she is none the less firmly and irrevocably wed, because of his inability to say 'your marriage.'

' Not since long before then,' rejoins she, hurriedly interrupting, with a nervous dread lest he may complete the phrase ; 'not since—Dresden.'

' But we never danced in—Dresden,' he says, making the same slight pause as she had done before the name of the, to them, sacred city.

' *You* did not, perhaps,' she answers with a charming saucy smile—for under the unwonted joyous excitement her spirits are towering perilously high—'but *I* did. Some Gardereiters came in one evening, and I took a turn with two of them ; it was before your day.'

Distant as is the epoch alluded to, and satisfactorily as he had been persuaded at the time by ocular evidence of the reciprocal indifference of Belinda and the Saxon officers, he cannot avoid a feeling of biting jealousy and offence against those innocent and both in time and space far-off German valseurs.

' At least it is *my* day now,' he says with emphasis ; and she offering no contradiction, away they float into their trance again.

The valse ends ; the patient De Lisle begins to hammer out a galop. They must part ; for Bellairs, emboldened thereto by Sarah's warm approbation, is inviting Belinda, and she dare not refuse. Rivers dances with Miss Churchill. Why need he? Why need he dance at all? Why, above all, need he throw such spirit and animation into his dancing ? He looks as if he were enjoying himself as much as Sarah. Staveley, after having vainly endeavoured to educate Slutty into a partner (Slutty; on unwilling hind-legs, and with tail abjectly tucked in, perhaps in the laudable intention of giving herself a more human air), galops bravely by himself. The galop ends. The musician, bringing out of his treasures things new and old, treats them to a venerable polka.

Once more he and she are together; and in what a different spirit her light feet now move! Bellairs had found her but a disappointing partner; inert, and often begging to be allowed to stop and take breath. In Rivers' arms, her life's tides are running at their highest. It is Staveley's turn tó be Sarah's *danseur*, and Bellairs, emulating his friend's former example, polks alone. But not altogether with his friend's success. For Punch, inspired by a scientific curiosity to investigate the strange phenomena that have appeared on his horizon, unhappily runs between his legs, and brings him to the earth with some clamour. The player stops : the dancers pause.

'We have had enough of this,' says Sarah, drawing her sister into the window for an aside, and speaking with some brusqueness; 'it is not fair upon that poor boy' (indicating De Lisle); 'he is getting cross, though he tries not to show it. As I have not three legs and arms like the Isle of Man, I cannot dance with them all at once, and *you* are not much help! Let us try something else.'

'By all means,' answers Belinda hurriedly, shrinking away from the reproach that her conscience tells her she so richly deserves; 'anything! whatever, you please !'

'The ball is ended,' says Sarah authoritatively, returning to the young men, and clapping her hands to enforce silence; 'but if the company pleases it will be immediately followed by some athletic sports. What does every one say to a game of Blind Man's Buff?'

This second proposal is received with an enthusiasm as much hotter than the former as may be expected from the universal loosening of the bonds of shyness and conventionality which has taken place since that former one was first made.

Sarah at once volunteers to be blindfolded; and in two minutes she is established in the middle of the little room, a Liberty silk handkerchief tied over her jovial eyes, and her hands outstretched in futile blind groping and grabbing.

The rest of the party, in the most approved fashion, pull her gown, tweak her hair, nip her sleeve; but not for long. With one well-directed lunge—so well directed as to rouse an instant loud cry of dishonesty—she has pounced upon Bellairs, who in his turn is blindfolded—is in his turn tweaked and nipped—and in his turn catches Rivers; Rivers catches Belinda.

The fun waxes fast and furious. They have raised every grain of dust latent in the carpet; Punch is cheering them on by volleys of delighted short barks, while Slutty sits wretchedly in a corner with her face to the wall.

Most madly mirthful of all—most intemperately gay, out-Heroding Herod, out-doing Sarah in her wildest mood, with splendid poppy-cheeks and lightening eyes—is Mrs. Forth. She has been old so long—so long! She is making up the arrears of her lost youth.

The clamour is at its loudest. Scarcely less blowsed—bawling scarcely less noisily than were the Primrose family in neighbour Flamborough's kitchen, when annihilated by the entrance of Lady Blarney and Miss Caroline Wilhelmina Amelia Skeggs—is the society gathered on that wet May afternoon in Professor Forth's decent drawing-room.

Belinda, caught for the second time, stands blindfolded in the middle of the room, while shouts of uproarious laughter greet her vain efforts to gain hold of any of the assailants who lustily beset her. All of a sudden, in one instant there is silence. The pushing, and jostling, and nipping have altogether ceased. Without any attempt at resistance some one is in her clasp.

'I have got you!' cries she, in a voice of jubilant

triumph; 'who are you?' and so tears the bandage from her eyes.

It is indeed true that she is grasping Rivers' coat-sleeve in indisputable conquest : but, at the moment that she verifies this fact, the cause of his having fallen so easy a prey, the cause of the instantaneous and entire muteness that has fallen upon the so boisterous little assemblage, breaks in horror upon her stunned eyes.

The door is half open, and through it Professor Forth is looking, with an expression hard to qualify upon his face, at the entertainment got up with such spirit and success in his absence. Not for long, however. In a moment he has softly closed the door again and withdrawn. For several moments they stand staring at each other speechless and aghast.

Belinda's look wanders in consternation from one to other of the faces round her. Disordered hair, red-hot cheeks, panting breath, rampagious eyes ! Bedlam might easily turn out a saner-looking party. In comparison of them Comus' crew were an orderly Philistine band.

The men are bad enough, but Sarah—but herself! Bacchante and romp mixed in just and fine proportions as her sister looks, her stricken conscience tells her that she herself far outdoes her, though she dares not ask the looking-glass for confirmation of this conviction ; but during the past mad hour has not Sarah been tame and mild when compared with her?

'Had not we better be going?' said Bellairs at last, in a lamb's voice, in which no one would recognise the hilarious bellow of five minutes ago.

'I think that there can be no two opinions on that head,' replies Sarah drily. As she speaks she turns to her dazed elder, and lowers her voice. ' Had not you better go and ask him whether he feels inclined to join us?'

Belinda turns in stupid compliance towards the door. As she makes her difficult way through the little passage, blocked with articles of furniture piled one atop of another, her consternation deepens. He must have had to climb like a cat over his own armchair in order to gain ingress into his own drawing-room! It is impossible! It would be adding insult to injury to present herself before him in her present dishevelment. She must needs repair to her own room; must needs, with intense repugnance, snatch a glance at her own disordered image in the toilet-glass. The case is even worse than she had feared. There is even more of the Mœnad than she had apprehended in her reflection. But there is no time to be lost. Each moment that passes, leaving her offence unacknowledged, lends it a deeper dye. A brush snatched up and hastily applied to her revolted hair; two hand-palms, but they are hot too, held for a moment to her blazing cheeks in the vain effort to cool them, and she is off again.

Outside his door she hesitates an instant, listening in scared heart-sinking; but there is no sound audible within, so, plucking up what courage she may, she enters. He is seated at his writing-table, in the leathern chair in which she has passed such countless hours of *ennui* and fatigue, slaving in his service. The thought emboldens her a little, and she advances up the room and stands beside him.

'May I take your place?' she asks in a rather faltering voice. 'I am quite ready.'

It is a whole minute before he answers. There is no plainer mode of showing resentment than by letting sixty seconds elapse between a question addressed to you and your answer. Then:

'I am obliged to you,' he answers woodenly, still writing; 'but I think that, in its present condition, your mind is scarcely capable of serious employment!'

There is something so galling in the implication that her spirit rises.

'Do you think that I am *drunk?*' she asks violently; then, recollecting how gravely in the wrong she has been, she masters herself, and says apologetically: 'I am very sorry; it was very foolish; but—but—I did not expect you home by so early a train.'

He gives a little odious, though perhaps pardonable, laugh.

'That fact was sufficiently obvious.'

'I am very sorry,' she repeats again, with uneasy iteration, shifting wretchedly from one foot to the other, as she stands in her culpritship before him; 'but—but it was so wet, and we could not get out, and—and it was so long since I had danced or played at any games!'

There is a wistful accent audible even to herself in her voice, and she looks at him with a sort of forlorn hope that he may be touched by it. If he is, he masters it admirably.

'Indeed!' he answers cuttingly. 'Well, next time that such an impulse seizes you, I should be obliged by your choosing some other spot than my house to turn into a bear-garden!'

She had thought that her cheeks were already as hot as cheeks could be, but the sudden influx of blood that his words send pulsing into them shows her her mistake. Hitherto, shame at and repentance of her frolic, joined with a sincere desire to make amends for it, have been her predominant emotions; now at once they vanish, and give place to a biting sense of injustice and aversion.

'After all, it was no such great crime,' she says in a hard voice, in which is no trace of the gentle, humble key of her earlier utterance; 'it was silly, perhaps,' with a burning blush, 'but it was an innocent enough wet-day amusement!'

'It is an innocent wet-day amusement against the recurrence of which I shall take measures to secure myself,' he replies resentfully.

There is something, or she fancies so, of menacing in his tone, at which her gorge rises.

'You forget,' she says, in a low but extremely distinct voice, 'that I am young. If you had married a wife of your own age, it would have been different; but you must remember that I am at the beginning of life, and you at the end!' Having delivered herself of this amiable reminder, she walks towards the door, not giving one glance to see how far her shaft has gone home. On reaching her ˙own room she breaks into hysterical sobbing. 'If he had taken it differently, he might have made a friend for life of me!' she cries.

This is, perhaps, putting it a little strongly.

CHAPTER VII.

ONE would have thought that upon the most inveterate pleasure-seekers such a cold-water douche could not have been poured without producing a permanently healing effect; that never again would the members of the little band, so disastrously surprised in mid-romp by the Professor of Etruscan, lift up their humbled heads from the dust, into which that one glance of his narrow eye had abased them. And yet it is but too true—such is the potency of the spring and youthful spirits, when they meet in lusty embrace—that before forty-eight hours are over they are planning another excursion.

A whole long day spent chiefly in her own society, for Belinda has had to expiate by working double tides her short idleness, has convinced Sarah of the wisdom and necessity of catering for her own amusement. By some means, whether of writing, or meeting on neutral ground, she has established a communication with Bellairs and his friends; and in their eager hands, guided by her commanding spirit, the project of a new expedition for the following day—*i.e.*, the day but one after their being put to the rout—speedily takes shape. It is indeed shorn of its former noble proportions, for it is not likely that Mrs. Forth will soon be indulged with another whole holiday; but upon a part—the latter part—of the afternoon she may, without undue sanguineness, reckon as lawfully her own; and now that the evenings are so long, it is of little consequence how late, whether lit by red sun or white moon, they return.

Belinda has no share in the formation of the plan. She knows of it, indeed. Did she not know of it, would she not have broken down under the pitiless labours of the interminable day that intervenes between it and its abortive predecessor? A sort of superstition keeps her from inquiring as to any of its details. To take for granted that it will happen, will, judging by all precedent and analogy, probably prevent it. Much less dares she ask whether Rivers is to be included in it.

'I do not even know of whom your party consists,' she says at last, over-night, to her sister, emboldened by the after-dinner twilight, in which they are strolling round and round the odorous garden plat, and fondly trusting that for once that sister's acuteness may be at fault, and not detect the ill-hidden motive of her words.

'Of whom it consists?' repeats Sarah carelessly, lifting and spreading out one hand, and striking the fingers, one after one, with the index of the other. 'You,' touching the thumb, 'I, Mr. Bellairs, Mr. Staveley, Mr. De Lisle.'

She has reached the little finger, and there pauses.

'Two ladies and three men?' comments Belinda, in tremulous interrogation.

Sarah does not contradict her.

'We should have been six last time,' says Mrs. Forth, after a short silence.

'Yes, six,' assents Sarah.

Belinda's heart beats low. She withdraws her hand from her sister's arm, upon which it has been resting, ostensibly to hold up her gown; but in a moment that gown is again trailing unregarded behind her. Why has she been gazing with such elation at the steady roses and ambers of the west? Promise-breaking as evening skies are, surely no sky could break such a promise as this! If what Sarah implies be true, what does it matter whether that promise be kept or broken?

'You have not asked Mr. Rivers?' she says at last, with abrupt desperation, seeing that her sister volunteers no further information.

'I have certainly not asked him,' replies Sarah gravely, with a slight stress upon the pronoun.

Mrs. Forth does not perceive the significant accentuation; and only gathers that her fears are realised. It is a moment or two before she can speak. Then,

'That was civil!' she says, in a resentful low key; 'but I suppose that in the case of a common workman in an iron foundry——'

'Stay!' interrupts Sarah calmly, 'before you say anything more, for which you might afterwards be sorry. I may as well tell you that he *is* invited. I had, God knows, no hand in it; but Mr. Bellairs invited him, and very officious I think it was of him!'

The morning has come. The sunset has been better than its word. No average fair day is this, upon which it simply does not rain, but one that earth, air, and sky from morn to eve vie in nobly decking; such a day as that one before which old George Herbert poured the nard and spices of his curious sweet verse, which for two hundred years has risen to most hearts and lips on any day of unusual summer splendour. It is certain that this time the weather at least will throw no obstacle in her way. The forenoon, of hot labour to the one sister, of luxurious cool idling to the other, is past and gone. So is luncheon.

The hour for departure draws near. Sarah is already dressed; dressed to the last button of her Paris gloves; to the last bewitching pinch given to the fantastic rural hat, whose pulling to pieces and rebuilding has largely helped in the beguiling of her lonely morning.

Belinda, usually punctual, and to-day, as one would think, with treble motives for punctuality, has not yet appeared. But just as the impatient Sarah is turning over in her mind the advisability of hurrying her by a call, she enters. At sight of her, an exclamation of surprise and remonstrance rises to her sister's lips.

'Not dressed yet?'

For, indeed, about Mrs. Forth there is no appearance of festal preparation; her head is uncovered; she is in her usual working morning gown—a gown to which traditions of ink and folios seem continually to adhere; her steps are languid, and her eyes dead.

'I am not going,' she answers doggedly, throwing herself into a chair. 'I must give it up!'

'Give it up?' repeats the other, with an incredulity born of the recollection of Belinda's passionately eager watching of the sunset over-night; 'why?'

'He cannot spare me,' replies Belinda, in a dull, level tone; 'he says that he is ill.'

'*Ill?* what is the matter with him?'

'I really forgot to inquire whether it was his heart or his liver to-day,' rejoins the other, with a sort of apathetic satire. 'It is always either his heart or his liver; except now and then when it is his spleen!'

'Whichever it is,' says Sarah bluntly—'and I suppose you mean to imply that it is not any of them, really—I do not see what good you can do!'

'I can give him his drops,' replies Belinda, with the same artificial tameness; then, life coming back in poignant pain into her tone: 'While you are on the river, I shall be giving him his drops! Oh!' turning over writhingly in her chair, and half burying her face in the cushion, 'what will not the river be to-day! You will lie under the willows; they will push your boat right under the branches! You have never done it; you do not know what it is to lie under the willows on a day like this!'

She ends with something not far removed from a sob; then, sitting upright again, and resentfully regarding her sister:

'You do not seem very sorry: if one were of a suspicious disposition, one might almost say you looked glad.'

'As usual you are beside the mark,' replies Sarah calmly. 'I was reflecting that in all probability the whole expedition must now fall through, as not even I dare brave Oxbridge public opinion by taking to the water with four young men and without a chaperone.'

'Of course not!' cries Belinda, catching eagerly at this suggestion, and with a feeling as of a burden most unaccountably lightened; 'it would be quite out of the question!'

How comparatively easy it will be to administer Professor Forth's drops, with no simultaneous mental consciousness maddening her of the dazzling water, the sheltering gray-green willow-arch, and of Rivers lying beneath it, laughing as Sarah, alas! knows how to make him laugh, stretched in lazy forgetful enjoyment at her feet. The distinctly disappointed expression painted on Miss Churchill's pink and white lineaments brings her back to a consciousness of her selfishness.

'I could ask Mrs. Baker whether she would take you,' she says slowly, in reluctant suggestion; 'she is fond of the river, and she lives only two houses off. Do you think'— dragging her words somewhat, and hoping, oh, how ardently! for an answer in the negative—'that it would be worth while asking Mrs. Baker to take you?'

'Eminently worth while!' replies Sarah joyfully, the sparkle returning at a hand-gallop to her eyes.

Belinda has already repented of her offer, but shame prevents her now going back from it. She seats herself at the writing-table, and Sarah walks to the window.

'I can see them all at the corner of the road,' she says,

chuckling; 'they dare not come any farther than the corner, and even there I can see that they are in a cold sweat of apprehension.'

Belinda writes on: that most *unkillable* of plants—hope —sending up a little fresh shoot in her heart; after all, fate may be kind. It may have sent Mrs. Baker a previous engagement, a headache—what not? But fate disdains to be dictated to. If it is kind to us, it is out of its own free will, and not at our bidding.

'She will be delighted,' says Sarah, returning in an impossibly short space of time; Sarah, who, to ensure the greater security and speed, has insisted upon being herself the bearer of the note. 'She is very much obliged to you for thinking of her; she is putting on her things now, and will be at the corner as soon as I.'

Miss Churchill is bustling away, perhaps not very anxious to take a prolonged farewell look at her sister's face; but that sister detains her.

'I will go with you as far as the corner,' she says feverishly, catching up a shabby garden-hat, and throwing it on her hot head as she speaks.

Before she has gone six yards she has repented of her impulse. There seems to be in these days not one of her actions of which she does not repent before it is half-way to execution. Why should she, of her own free will, forcing him to a comparison between them, set herself, poor workaday drudge as she is, beside this charming holiday creature —so delicately fine, so infectiously gay? Even now she would go back, but it is too late. The young men have caught sight of her: in a moment they have all met.

Rivers exhales a heavy sigh of relief. He has had bad dreams, and a dragging presage of ill-luck hanging about him; but both dreams and presage are as false as dreams and presages mostly are. Had not they told him that she

would be prevented coming? and is not she here standing
in beautiful bodily presence before him? Is he likely to
observe the age of her hat, or the humility of her gown?
He, never one of those man-milliners who can price, to a
groat, a woman's laces; he, to whom it has always seemed
as if, whatever sheath his bright flower-lady wore, she informed it with her own glory.

'I hope you will enjoy yourselves,' she says, letting her
hand linger for an instant in his, and lifting her melancholy
eyes to his face.

'We!' he says, laughing softly, though his heart mis-
gives him; 'and why not you?'

'I am not going,' she answers quietly, though her eyes
rivet themselves with an intentness of passionate jealousy
on his face, to see whether he looks sorry enough.

He steps back a pace or two, loosing her hand.

'Not going?' he echoes blankly.

His dreams, his presage spoke true after all—worse than
true, indeed! for have not they tricked him with the shadow
of a hope?

'Come along—come along!' cries Sarah blithely, mar-
shalling her pack and whipping up the stragglers; 'we are
late already. Why do not we set off? Mr. Rivers, will you
hold my parasol while I search for my pocket? This is a
new gown, and a horrible misgiving seizes me that it has not
a pocket.'

She addresses him so decidedly that he has no alternative
but to answer her, nor does she again let him go.

Before Belinda can realise that it is so, they are all off,
walking away from her—away to the river and the willows.
Without one word of regret for her absence, without even an
inquiry as to the cause of that absence, he is gone—gone
a-pleasuring!

His face indeed looked blank for a moment, but for how

long, pray? Does it look blank still? Will it look blank
under the willows? If her withdrawal from the party had
been to him what his would have been to her, would he
have gone at all? would not he have framed some excuse
for escape at the last moment? Nor does she, in her unjust
heart-bitterness, reflect that he could have taken no surer
way of compromising the woman he loved! Happily perhaps for her, she is not long able to give herself up undisturbed to reflections of the above kind. She must needs
return without further delay to her treadmill. It is true
that the morning, and the morning's Menander, are over—
ill as is the Professor, he is not too ill for Menander—but
her afternoon taskwork is still unperformed; her daily two
hours' ministrations to her imbecile mother-in-law—two
hours during which that mother-in-law's attendant is released,
and sent out into the fresh air to lay in a stock of ozone and
endurance to support her through the other twenty-two.
The thought of her fellow drudge makes Belinda remorsefully hasten her steps. What business has she, with her selfish
repinings, to defer and shorten that other drudge's holiday?

'Do not hurry back,' she says good-naturedly, as she
relieves guard. 'It is a lovely day; take your time and
enjoy yourself; I am in no hurry.'

Oven-like as is the temperature of old Mrs. Forth's room,
her easy-chair is drawn up close to the blazing fire. The
chill of extremest eld is upon her. Her mind is so completely gone, that she is incapable of recognising or identify-
ing even the persons habitually about her; nor does her
daily interview with her daughter-in-law ever begin with any
other phrase than :

'Who are you, my dear? If you will believe me, I do
not know who you are !'

Her conversation, which never ceases, consists of this
question repeated *ad infinitum;* of inquiries after various

long-dead members of her family, supposed by her to be
alive and sometimes even in the room; and of information
such as that her father has been sitting with her (if he were
alive he would be one hundred and sixty years old!), and that
it is wonderful how he keeps his memory.

Belinda seats herself beside her.

After all, it requires no great call upon the intellect to
repeat at intervals in a slow, loud voice (for, with the other
faculties, hearing too is gone):

'I am Belinda! Belinda Forth—James' wife; your son
James' wife!' varied occasionally by such answers as these,
called forth by appropriate inquiries, 'He is dead!' 'He
died twenty-five years ago!' 'Woking Cemetery!'

But between her mechanical words there is plenty of room
to interpolate thoughts that but little match them.

'They must have reached the river by now. Have they
walked all the way in the same order as that in which they
set off? He and Sarah ahead, and the rest herding behind.
Of course they have. Since both are pleased with the
arrangement, why change it? How murderously hot this
fire is! Is it inside her that it is burning? They are
embarked now. Have they chosen a punt, or a pair-oar?
Perhaps both, since there are six of them. In that case the
party will divide; but how?'

It is easy to tell, by the writhing of her hands, in what
manner she pictures that division effected. Virtually, then,
it will be a *tête-à-tête*. It will be alone together that they will
lie under the willows!

Belinda's attention wanders wide. Twice she has
answered, 'Woking Cemetery!' when she should have
answered 'James' wife'; and is on the point of repeating
the error a third time, when a vague fidgetiness in her
interlocutor's manner—hazily conscious of something gone
wrong—recalls her to herself.

The two hours march by. The nurse has taken her at her word, and is extending a little the border of her liberty.

Presently the Professor enters: enters to pay that punctual daily five minutes' visit, which is the share he contributes towards the tendance of his parent. For a wonder, she knows him, without being told who he is.

'Where is your father, James?' is her first question.

'Gone, my mother.'

'*Gone!*' (with great animation and surprise), 'gone where?'

'To the Better Land, my mother' (very loud).

'Oh, indeed! Well, I only hope that they are taking good care of him : if I know that he is well looked after, that is all I care for!'

Belinda gasps. She has heard it all scores of times before: at first with pitiful wonder; then with a dreary amusement; and lastly with the indifferent apathy of use. To-day there seems to be a new and grisly jocularity about it. This then is life! A youth of passionately craving and foregoing; long pursuing and never overtaking ; of hearts that leap for a moment and ache for a year; of jealousies that poison food and massacre sleep—leading up to an old age of garrulous idiocy !

She is released at last : set free to amuse herself as she pleases. But of what amusement is a mind in such tune as hers capable ? She has taken her hat in her hand, and walks along drawing in great gulps of the exquisite evening air ; while her feet, without her bidding, lead her to the river-side.

Oxbridge is, as every one knows, rich in two rivers, and it is to the lesser of these streams that the boating-party has committed itself. It is this lesser stream, also, which for a short part of its course St. Ursula's green meadow and pleasant walk border.

It is without any acknowledged hope of meeting them that she takes the direction indicated. Is it likely that they

will be so early returning? Is it likely that they, or any one
of them, will be in much haste to abridge such an excursion?
Tasting, as she now does, the delicacy of the air; viewing
the homely loveliness of bushed bank and satin-sliding river,
she can the better and more enviously figure to herself what
its charm has been. But the air and the motion do her
good. Beside her the stream steals along—a soothing,
sluggish companion. No song or rush has it, like the flashing
northern becks; but what green reflections in it! What
long water-weeds, swinging slowly to its slow current! How
the willows—pensive almost as olives in their grave dim
leafage—have printed themselves on its quiet, silent heart.
How riotously green are the fat low meadows that, all winter
long, the floods had drowned!

Here, a May-bush has strewn the white largesse of its
petals on the water, and there another, less overblown, stoops
to look at its own pink face's double. There are two
cuckoos: one loud and near, one soft and distant, answering
each other across the meads. Beneath the bank at her foot,
an undergraduate lies stretched along his boat, with his book.
Three others in a punt are waggishly trying to upset each
other. She sits down on a bench and idly watches them,
till, with shouts of young laughter, they float out of sight.
Another punt, a canoe, a skiff, a boat with ladies in it. Her
heart jumps. Ah, no! not her ladies! a boat freighted with
hawthorn boughs and guelder-rose branches, that tell of a
joyous day's Maying in the country. Endless young gentlemen in flannels, punting, sculling, lying supine. She has
fallen into a dull comparison between their gaiety and her
own gloom, when her attention is aroused by the sound of a
loud voice coming from some bark yet unseen, that is
approaching round the corner. Many of the boys' voices are
loud: what is there then in the timbre of this voice that
makes Belinda, at the instant that it strikes her ear, hastily

rise and pursue her walk? But she might as well have remained seated on the bench.

A punt has come into sight, guided, with an unskilfulness that seems almost intentional, by a young man; colliding frequently with other punts, bumping with many jars against the bank, and with an ample female form reclining complacently—superior to bumps or jars—in its stern.

'Stop! stop!' she cries, gesticulating with her umbrella in a way which alone would have been enough to identify her. 'Belinda! Belinda!'

All the luxurious young gentlemen turn their heads to look. One of the white terriers seated by their masters in boats, sets up his nose and howls.

Reluctant and dyed with shame, Belinda steps to the water's edge.

'George Sampson is taking me out for a row!' cries Miss Watson, in a tone which can leave no member of the University ignorant of the fact related; 'his people have gone back to London. I cannot think what induced them to shorten their visit so much; they came for a week. Why should not you get in and come with us? I am sure you will be delighted' (appealing to her swain) 'if Mrs. Forth will get in and come with us. We are enjoying ourselves immensely!'

The unhappy young man murmurs something that may be taken for assent. The perspiration of anguish pours from his brow, upon which is written a dogged shame and wrath too deep for words.

'No?' pursues the other, in answer to Belinda's emphatic negative of her proposal. 'You are not so fond of the water as Sarah, eh? She takes to it like a young duck. I saw them setting off this afternoon; they looked such a jolly party. I offered to join them, but they evidently did not hear. Why did not *you* go with them? Not *allowed*, eh?'

Without looking, Belinda is hotly aware that a pardonable

smile has stolen over the features of more than one of the listening boys, at the publication of her domestic secrets. There is not one of them who has not dropped his book.

'I will not keep you any longer,' she mutters in hasty farewell.

But Miss Watson has not yet done with her.

'You should have told the Professor that you owed it to your conscience to look after Sarah,' cries she, laughing resonantly. 'Judging by what I saw to-day, you would not have been far out!'

Belinda's cheek, hot with shame a moment ago, grows pale. The impulse to flee leaves her; a contrary impulse, such as draws the palpitating canary to the cage-wires and the cat's claws, roots her to the spot.

'What do you mean?' she asks faltering. 'Was she'— lowering her voice so as not to be heard by any one else, hating herself for descending to such a question, and trying to carry it off with a spurious merriment—'was she—ha! ha! —flirting very nefariously with them all?'

'*With them all!*' repeats the other in loud irony. 'Pooh! that would have been nothing; there is always safety in numbers. The others were nowhere. Rivers had it all his own way!'

This is what Belinda has been angling to hear, and now she has heard it. It is not then the figment of her disordered fancy; it must indeed be obvious to have hit the eyes of so coarse and casual an observer as Miss Watson. Nor does the recollection of how much she had profited by her former prompt action upon information derived from the same source recur to her memory.

'He is a sad dog, is David, is not he?' cries the other jocosely; and then she bumps off again in her punt, bawling, as she floats down the stream, to her oppressed and silent boatman.

CHAPTER VIII.

'Le monde n'est jamais divisé pour moi, qu'en deux régions; celle où elle est, et celle où elle n'est pas.'

A WEEK—a whole week—only a week! There are two opposing ways of looking at this or any other period of time; one of impatient marvelling at its immensity, the other of gasping consternation at its shortness. It is needless to ask which of these two moods is Mrs. Forth's, with regard to Rivers' holiday. Only a week! How many times, during its seven days, does she, with that all-answering phrase, stop conscience's mouth? Of what use for only a week to practise self-government? of what use for only a week to question, with too nice a closeness, her heart as to the cause of its leapings and sinkings? her temper as to the reason of its endless variabilities? her thoughts as to the path they take? or her imagination as to the length of its tether? Only a week! Too short a space to do anything in but enjoy—to enjoy—to enjoy! With eyes resolutely shut to the cost—to the heavy score running up, that at the week's end will have to be paid. Oh, not too short to enjoy in!

It is not all enjoyment. Already, before two days of it are past, it has been marred by irksome labour, by balked expectation, by unreasoning jealousy—a jealousy whose unreason she herself, in her calmer moments, recognises; which in Rivers' presence dies of famine, having less than nothing to live upon, but, once out of the reassurance of his eyes, revives and bulks big again.

Rare indeed is it for one successful excursion not to engender another or several more. The weather holds. The Professor's heart or liver—it is never quite clearly understood which of these organs is affected—has recovered its balance, upset by his wife's Walpurgis day.

Belinda has three consecutive afternoons of freedom— three afternoons of being swiftly pulled down the river, that brave water-way alive with vigorous youthhood—of gaily drinking tea and sucking cider-cup through straws at little river-side ale-houses—of picking the freakish fritillaries in the meadows—of being towed back in dreamy languor at night-fall or star-rise—of loitering homewards with hands full of flag-flowers—of parting at the garden gate.

To that parting there comes, each evening, a deeper deadlier sweetness. It does not lie in words. There is not one word that, did the Professor protrude his velvet-capped head from his bower window, need be withdrawn.

Belinda is living on her capital. At the week's end she will be bankrupt; let her then be merry while she may! Perhaps Sarah acquiesces in her sister's view of the unimportance of any course of action that must be compressed into so short a period of time as a week. Perhaps, being in her way wise, she recognises the futility of interference. Perhaps her hands are too full of her own affairs to have much time or attention to spare for her sister's; for seldom has Miss Churchill been in such amorous straits of her own making as at present.

The course of allurement which had merely warmed up the heavy German soldiers into a pleasant and manageable tenderness, has wrought three inflammable English boys to a white heat. Daily, and in proportion as their inconvenient ardour for Sarah increases, does their friendship for each other—close and warm to begin with—decline, and tend towards the opposite pole of animosity. On the last expedition but one, she dare no longer accept a bunch of fritillaries from one, without instantly crowding her hands with a similar bunch from each of the others. She can now never drink less than three cups of afternoon tea ; as that affords to each an opportunity of handing her one. Even Bellairs, early convinced of the hopelessness of his adoration of Mrs. Forth, is now wholly hers, far more wholly indeed than she at all wishes.

'I am fast getting to hate the sight of them !' she cries, in a tone more nearly approaching tearful vexation than is often to be heard in her joyous voice, as she and her sister patrol in their wonted fashion the garden, on the morning of the week's last day. 'None of them'—by this comprehensive phrase she always designates the noble army of her admirers, past and present—' none of them have ever given me half so much trouble ; why cannot they understand that it is not the *fox* I care for, but the *chase ?*'

'It will be soon over,' replies Belinda slowly.

She says it as a consolation to her sister, but the application that she makes is to herself.

'That is all very fine,' replies Sarah gloomily; 'but there is still to-day. You know that we are to go on the New River this afternoon ; and in a weak moment I promised that ugly Bellairs—but I declare,' with a burst of petulance, 'that they bother me so that I do not know whether I am on my head or my heels—that he should scull me in some little cockle-shell—a dinghey, he calls it—he and I, and nobody by, you know,' with a laugh of annoyance; and I positively *dare not* tell the others. What am I to do ? I suppose,' with something of her old sidling, coaxing manner, 'that *you* would not care to break it to them ?'

Belinda smiles ; a bitter smile of recollection.

'As I was to break to Mr. Forth that you meant to jilt him ? Thank you ! I think not !'

It is true that the last day has come ; and the last excursion. All through the previous night, all morning, Belinda has been dogged by the icy terror—no weaker word suffices —that something may occur to prevent it. She has asked after the Professor's organs, with a solicitude whose treachery makes her blush. The very unbearableness of the idea lends it a horrid probability. In this our life are not the things too bad to be faced, those that oftenest happen ?

The hour comes—the meeting at the corner (never again have the enamoured youths ventured across the threshold of the house they have desecrated !)—the walk to the river. Sarah has vainly tried to hook herself on to her sister ; but —Bellairs having out-manœuvred his fellows, and compelled them to content themselves with the chaperone of a former expedition, civilly invited to complete the party—has dropped resignedly behind with him, her face sufficiently revealing that she is braced for the worst.

The river is reached. In the choosing the boats and arranging the cushions a little diversion is affected, which gives Sarah the opportunity to pluck her sister by the sleeve, and pull her aside.

'It is all up,' she says morosely ; 'he has been telling me as we came along, that if he read my eyes aright, he was far from indifferent to me !'

'And you ? what did *you* say ?'

'What did I say ?' (in a tone of extreme exasperation, and yet unwilling amusement). 'I told him that he had read them awrong; but '—with a rueful glance at the little craft now being made ready for her reception—'you must perceive that the dinghey has become an impossibility ; what is to be done ? There is not room for us all in the other ; quick !'

For a moment Mrs. Forth looks before her in blank perplexity; then, all at once, an idea, habited in a sudden lovely blush, rushes into her mind. Why not? Is not it the last day? But she does not at once clothe it in speech. Instead:

'Cannot you persuade Mrs. Baker to take your place?' she asks.

Sarah shrugs her shoulders impatiently.

'She would not hear of it; she is inclined to scream in a punt!'

There is no help for it, then. What other alternative can she propose? It is no fault of hers; accident, rather—fate —ill-luck! She has done her best. How often during the past week has she told herself that she has done her best!

'I suppose, then, that *I* must sacrifice myself,' she says hurriedly, and not looking at her sister; and then, several voices at once calling upon them, they rejoin the rest of the party.

In a moment, as if some devil were behind her—or what in her present frame of mind would seem to her both more dangerous and more ugly—some amorous undergraduate, Sarah has, to ensure herself against ambush or surprise, skipped into the larger boat.

'My sister's courage has failed her,' says Belinda, standing flushed and downcast-eyed on the bank. 'I am afraid that some one will have to scull me instead.'

No one answers, and she steps—some one giving her a hand—into the dinghey. Some one instantly follows her, and takes up the sculls. It is not till they are well out in the stream, and not immediately even then, that she lifts her eyes. A sort of shame weighs them down.

The manœuvre was none of hers; and yet it is by a manœuvre that she has secured this final *tête-à-tête* with him. She does not even know whether it is in accordance with his wishes that she has acted. He has expressed no pleasure in the arrangement; perhaps—her jealousy awaked in a moment from its always light sleep—he is vexed to have been baulked of Sarah's company. Perhaps, even now, he is silently fighting with his disappointment.

She snatches a fugitive glance at him—a glance that, in an instant, is turned away again; for it has told her what she wished to learn. The cause of his dumbness is one which does not very often make us speechless in this our life. He cannot speak for joy.

She leans back satisfied and smiling. The New River is narrower, less of a great highway than the old one. Here are no imperative Eights, out of whose way all lesser boats must clear, under penalty of being apostrophised by a ferocious 'Look ahead, sir!' and then run down. And yet there is no lack of company here either, on this splendid summer day.

Above, the pale bright sky, holding her forget-me-not-coloured shield; and below, the windings of the slow broad river, and the great expanse of hedgeless meadow-land. The horses, summering there, stand knee-deep in the stream, eating, or pretending to eat, the weeds, one having a wet roll of utter enjoyment in the shallows. Sheets of little ranunculus are all ablow, each stiff, straight stem and small white head erect on the water. Countless geese stalk along the meadow, waddling and cropping the grass. Others, like a white fleet, paddle and dive for water-weeds.

Into the midst of this feathered Armada they see the larger boat, which has shot ahead of them, being lustily pulled to give it a fright; instigated thereto by Sarah, who under the ægis of a female friend, and with Bellairs pulling stroke, and consequently divided from her by nearly the whole length of the boat, has resumed her usual hilarity, and by voice, gesture, and waved parasol, is encouraging her slaves. The geese separate, screeching and oaring away; and one gosling, overtaken by the prow, dives and rises again ten paces away.

Both Rivers and Belinda laugh. There is something healthy and clearing to the moral atmosphere in a joint laugh. Rivers' mirth dies into a long sigh of contentment.

'What a day !' he says, resting on his oars, and staring up at the sky. I *love* the river ; how I missed it at first ! I used to dream about it ! it was one of the things that I dreaded dreaming about !'

She does not ask him what the others were. Possibly she is incurious.

'Perhaps,' he says, bringing his eyes down again from the heaven above him, to the, to him, better heaven of her face, 'perhaps it is worth while to have a holiday only once in two years, to enjoy it as I have done mine !'

As he speaks, a slight frown, not of displeasure at his harmless words, but of reflection and doubt, puckers her forehead.

'Are you sure,' she says slowly, 'that it is quite the first holiday that you have had in two years ?'

He looks surprised.

'Virtually yes. Why ?'

'Nothing !' she answers in confusion ; 'only I happened to hear that you were in London last winter.'

'I was,' he answers calmly, though still surprised. 'Our firm sent me up on business : that was no holiday.'

'And you—you combined business with pleasure ?' she says, laughing awkwardly. 'You—you went to the play ?'

Difficult as it is to look him in the face, while guiltily conscious of the drift of her question, she yet eagerly fastens upon him a glance whose keenness no least tinge of discomfiture can escape. But none such meets her. He has resumed his leisurely rowing, but now stops again.

'Were *you* there?' he cries abruptly. 'Is it possible that I missed you? I looked—I thought—I hoped.'

She shakes her head.

'I was not there! I was not' (with a twinge of self-pity, as she recalls her then mood)—'I was not in a very play-going humour; but I was told by some one who had seen you!'

Surely he will now volunteer the mention of the lady by whom he was accompanied. She has paused on purpose to give him the opportunity, but he does not take it. He leans on his sculls, staring before him in wistful bitter thought.

'You were with a lady,' says Belinda presently, unable any longer to contain herself.

'A lady?' he says, starting. 'Was I?—oh, of course, my sister. Poor girl! she had not been anywhere for so long, that she was naturally keen about it. She was staying with an aunt, who gave us our stalls; otherwise,' with a laugh, 'in the then state of our finances, the shilling gallery would have been nearer our mark !'

So it is explained. How simple it sounds! how obvious! What is there in it, upon which any but a madwoman could have hung distrust or jealousy? And yet it is upon this cock-and-bull story that she elected to shipwreck her life! A sailing-boat, lurching and tacking, and heeling over, after the manner of such, and out of whose way they have to get, rouses them both, and they row on.

The larger boat has pulled into the bank, in order to set the two dogs, in whom Sarah affects to detect symptoms of incipient sea-sickness, on shore, where they instantly begin to give a great deal of trouble.

Punch—a dog of no ballast of mind, entirely losing his head in joy at his enlargement—first frolicsomely nips the sleepy horses' heels, a civility which they return by viciously lashing out at him; then chivvies the geese, a levity which

calls forth from the husband and father an awful chastise-
ment of flapping wings, outstretched neck, and dreadfully
wide-opened mouth.   Slutty, on the other hand, for reasons
best known to herself, has set off galloping in the wrong
direction, with her tail between her legs.   Her recapture
and the recovery and admonishment of Punch take so long,
that the couple in the dinghey have time to get far ahead,
and, rounding a reach of the river, to lose their companions from sight.   On and on they float in their virtual
aloneness, for in nothing do the two men punting, or the
happy young fellow shooting past in his skiff, disturb their
solitude.   They speak ever less and less.   Now and again,
indeed, silence becomes too oppressive, and they speak; but
then speech grows over-pregnant, and they fly back to
silence.

Both are strung up to pleasure's highest pitch, that pitch
for which they will have to pay, and know that they will
have to pay, so extortionately ; for pleasure, like the scor-
pion, is an animal that carries a sting in its tail.   Upon
enjoyment is set its keenest edge.   The lark, lost in light
above them, might be their spokesman, only that to their
song, unlike his, there is ever that minor refrain : 'The last
day ! the last day !'

What a nameless unreckoning elation the warm breeze
lends, and the motion and the very throbbing of the gentle
water against the passing keel !   She pulls up her sleeve,
and dipping in her bared right arm, affects to imitate his
gestures, and to oar the stream with it.

'I am helping you,' she cries, smiling.   'I, too, am
rowing ; do you find any perceptible help ?'

He does not reply.   He rows slowly on in a dream, his
eyes intoxicatedly watching that pendent hand and swaying
lily wrist.   He always thinks her last word or action prettier
and better than all its predecessors.   But surely she can

never outdo this. He might borrow Florizel's words without a changed syllable.

> ' What you do,
> Still betters what is done. When you speak, sweet
> I'd have you do it ever. When you sing,
> I'd have you buy and sell so ; so give alms ;
> Pray so ; and, for the ordering of your affairs
> To sing them too. When you do dance, I wish you
> A wave of the sea, that you might ever do
> Nothing but that : move still still so,
> And own no other function. Each your doing,
> So singular in each particular,
> Crowns what you're doing in the present deeds,
> That all your acts are graces.'

He pulls, still in a dream, beneath the willows. A poplar, shivering perpetually, flutters and trembles against the sky's perfect azure over their heads. Still in a dream, and at her orders, he leaves her lying pensive and cool on her cushions, and scrambles into the field to fetch flowers for her. He comes back with a great nosegay, which he lays in her lap : yellow flags, beckabunga, forget-me-nots bigger and bluer than the petted garden ones, a scrap of catch-fly, a handful of stitchworts, powdery purple grasses, all plucked haphazard, and yet gathered into such a perfect posy as no after-arranging, or sorting, or matching of colours could compass. She tells him so. Was ever man, for so poor a gift, so royally thanked ?

Their companions have passed them again ; the dogs re-embarked, and the whole company singing a gay part-song. No other than ' The Franklin's Dogge.'

> ' B with a Y ; Y with an N ; N with a G ; G with an O ;
> And he called him little Byngo.'

How entrancingly sweet and merry sound the nonsensical old words across the water ! Belinda and Rivers must needs follow them to the rendezvous—the little rural Trout Inn, where they are to have tea. It is brought out to them, in an arbour overlooking the stream, by a stout wench; thick bread and butter, great wedges of plain cake, a tea-set where no two articles are of the same make or pattern.

Sarah, having tided over her Bellairs difficulty, and restored to her happy-go-lucky confidence of being able to keep the rest of her team well in hand, is in delightful spirits. There are too many other visitors at the Trout to make any more glees advisable; but she is good enough to indulge the company with several quiet performances of a juggling nature, which make no noise, and need attract no attention—such as sticking halfpence into her eyes, and disposing them ingeniously about her other features.

Belinda, too, is in wild mirth—as wild as that of the unlucky day of Blind Man's Buff. She is not nearly so clever with the halfpence as her sister; but in point of mere animal spirits she almost exceeds her. When, however, the tea-party and its humours are ended—when, in their former order, they are on their way home again—those factitious spirits drop like a wind at sunset.

The feast is all but over: surely, since the world was, never has any been so poignantly relished. In each moment have not they tasted a hundred years of ordinary tame pleasures? But it is now nigh being done, and pay-day stands at the door. The light is low and level; the geese have gone to bed, gray head and yellow nose tucked beneath gray wing. The horses' shadows stretch, longer than camel-opards, across the meadow. There is scarcely any need to use the oars, wind and current helping them; they are float-ing—oh, how swiftly!—to where the one great dome, and the many spires, momently growing taller, tell where the fair city lies.

The last hour of the last day is running out. When that

dome and those spires are reached, it will have run out. The last hour! How many things there are to be said in a last hour! And yet the only phrase that will rise to either of their lips is, ' It is the last time!' Even to that they do not give utterance : not until they have slidden more than half-way home. Then, at sight of those rapidly nearing spires—those spires that mean the end—a sort of panic seizes Belinda :

' How fast we go!' she says half-breathlessly, looking down as if she would fain stop on the lovely evening water, quickly swishing past with a pleasant low sucking sound ; 'we shall be home in ten minutes !'

' In ten minutes !' he repeats in a tone half-mazed, as of one not realising the sense of the words.

' And it is the last time !' she says very low.

Still the keel quickly cutting the flood, and the water sucking. Why so fast? In pity, why so fast? The very sun—their last sun—seems hurrying more rapidly than his wont to his hot rose and cowslip coloured bed. At first they had had days ahead of them—such riches seem incredible—then hours, now minutes, and but few of them; so few that surely there is not one of them to be wasted! Perhaps it is this thought that sends such a passion of haste into the words with which he answers her :

' Why should it be the last time ?'

She receives the suggestion in dead silence—a silence so dead as to give him time for a cold pang of fear that he has employed these priceless moments in offending his dear lady, and that she will part from him in displeasure. If his hand were laid upon her heart, he would know why she did not speak. In the last drunken week, she has not once had the courage to look her life, that is to be, in the eyes. Who, squandering and rioting in the *now*, dare ever face the *then?* At last she stammers :

'How should not it be the last, since your holiday ends to-morrow?'

'And am I never to have another?'

He is lying on his oars now; but still the boat drifts, drifts. She shakes her head with a little unhopeful smile; though surely no hopeless heart ever leaped and sprang as hers is doing.

'Perhaps in another two years!'

His oars are quite out of the water; he, at least, will have no share in accelerating the end. The drops gently drip from their blades. Twilight is taking her first gray steps across the plains, and the warm dew falls. Two or three of their dwindling store of minutes are gone before Rivers speaks.

'Term will soon be over, then you will go away, I suppose?'

'I think not—probably not,' she answers indifferently, an unacknowledged disappointment at the apparent irrelevance of his remark, at his want of insistance upon his former suggestion, chilling heart and voice.

'You will stay here all through the Long?'

Why is there such a catch in his breath as he asks this question? What is it to him whether she goes or stays?

'Most likely. Mr. Forth will go to Switzerland; I believe he mostly does; but he will not take me.'

'He will leave you here?'

'Yes.'

'Alone?'

'Unless you count my mother-in-law as society,' with a slight satiric laugh.

A pause. A flight of plovers, going bedwards, speck the sky above them.

'Will not you—will not you—be lonely?'

'Not more than usual.'

'Will not most of your friends have gone?'

Again she laughs, and her laugh is of the same unmerry character as before.

'With my goodwill they may all go; I am no great hand at making friends.'

Another pause. The plovers have dwindled to nothing; the other boat is lost to sight, far ahead. What is he going to say that makes him fidget so uneasily with his unused oars?

'It is really no great distance from Yorkshire here.'

Again she laughs; but the irony is gone, driven away by a tremor that is even further from gaiety.

'My geography is not my strong point, but I should have scarcely thought that they were neighbouring counties.'

'Milnthorpe is not more than five hours from here, by a good train.'

'Is not it?'

And then again there is silence. How twilight is taming day's gaudiness! but doing it with so lovesome a mien, that who can regret the gone greens and blues?

'I could,' he begins. How dry his throat is! He would be glad of a draught from the river to moisten it. 'I could —run down—for Sunday—now and then.'

It is out now! For good or for evil, it is said; and in uncontrollable anxiety he leans forward, the better to read in her face how she takes it.

She is as dead silent as she had been at his first suggestion of the possibility of their meeting again; but perhaps he has learnt to interpret that silence better. Must not she needs set some order in that riotous heart of hers before she can speak at all? Surely the earth is mistaken in thinking that night is coming. Is not it the morning that is born?

His hand has lifted a corner of the great night-curtain that has hung, black and impenetrable, before her future life. Dare she let him lift it all?

'Only now and then! Not often!' he says in great agitation. 'If you have not a soul to speak to for four months, you might not mind seeing me now and then—quite now and then!'

Not mind seeing him! At that she cannot choose but smile.

'We knock off work early on Saturday, and there is a fast train that would take me back in good time for Monday morning.'

There is such a desperate urgency of asking in his eyes, that she dare not look at him. What can she answer? Still that unmastered riot in her heart! and how near the landing-place is growing! All the sail-boats with furled sails and lowered masts; all the row-boats gathered home.

'It is rather a mad plan!' she says, with a laugh that has a touch of the hysteric.

'Is it?' he answers blankly. 'I suppose it is.'

There are not more than eight boat-lengths to go. In those eight boat-lengths she must decide one way or the other; for the rest of the party are gathered in hilarious talk about the landing-place—'Little Byngo' and many other worthy part-songs having wrought one and all to the highest pitch of good-fellowship—waiting for them.

'Oxbridge is not my private property,' she says almost inaudibly, and shaking like a poplar leaf, that is never still; 'you have other friends here beside me.'

'I have,' he answers, catching at her suggestion, with a relief proportioned to the consternation with which his eye has been measuring the half-dozen yards left him in which to plead his cause. 'Why should not I come to see them?'

Nor have either he or she the candour to own to themselves or each other what is perfectly well known to both, that in the Long Vacation Oxbridge will be innocent of the presence of any one of those friends. This is their real parting.

CHAPTER IX.

THE week and Rivers are both gone. Belinda's life has returned to its old channel, the channel in which it ran before
the party at St. Ursula's. The weather has ceased to be a
matter of the slightest interest. It is not of the least consequence what weather there is, or whether there is any weather
at all! Done with are all tappings of weather-glasses, watch-
ings of the march of clouds. The door-bell may ring itself
off its wire, without making her attention swerve by one
hair's-breadth from Menander, or interfering at all with the
coherence and patience of her answers to her mother-in-law
as to the date at which they are going to bury that mother-
in-law's husband, whose obsequies appear to have been
unaccountably deferred for twenty-five years. There is no
more talk of water-parties. Sarah herself, too late convinced
of the peril of those excursions, confines herself and her
followers to safe games of tennis in well-overlooked public
places, where they will have no chance of reading her eyes
either right or wrong, or, at all events, of telling her the result
of their readings. Mrs. Forth's life has resumed the tame
course which it was taking on the day of Sarah's arrival;
but how different a spirit now guides it! Whither have
flown the sullen discontent, the dull revolt, the rare mirth
that bit, and the frequent irony that pricked and stung?
Now, if the Professor be cross, she shrugs her shoulders

good-humouredly. He is old! He means nothing by it! It is an infirmity. After all, why should she mind? How does it hurt her? If he keeps her slaving long beyond her canonical hours in his close study, why so much the more does she enjoy afterwards the breath of the garden and the white pinks bursting so quickly into spicy bloom? If he complain of his affection of heart, liver, or spleen, she is equally ready to believe in and sympathise with each and all, to suggest remedies, or apply them.

Never has Sarah been more puzzled, or her sagacity put more at fault, than by her sister's behaviour. For it is not the mood of a day. The consciousness of being observed and of the necessity for self-control might have lent her for a while a spurious cheerfulness; but could it have given her that easy, unforced serenity which lasts undimmed through Sarah's stay—which, indeed, shows every symptom of holding out indefinitely beyond it? It is not from the post, as Miss Churchill at first suspected, that she derives her support.

The postman's arrival obviously causes her not a flutter; nor does she exhibit the slightest tendency towards a surreptitious posting of her own letters—worst sign that can appear in a connubial heaven. It is not, then, upon a clandestine correspondence that she is feeding and blooming, so fair and fine. That an undoubtedly hard-working common hand, or, still more, foreman in an iron foundry, would be likely soon to have another leisure week at his disposal, seems to her improbable. That Belinda can be nourishing any hopes of a visit to Milnthorpe seems to her more improbable still. That, satisfied with the sight of her lost love, she can have settled down contentedly into the perennial jog-trot of an existence without him, seems to her most improbable of all.

She watches her sister narrowly; sees her severe lips

surprised now and then into an apparently causeless smile; catches her singing under her breath, as she waters her drouthy plants; sees her staid walk about the garden occasionally inclined to degenerate into a light-hearted run with the dogs. But she does not surprise her secret. And meanwhile time goes on. The yearly gaieties with which the summer Term at Oxbridge concludes are over and gone. Mrs. Forth, chaperoning her sister, has taken part in them all—balls, *fêtes*, theatre; has seen the masons dance in their aprons, and heard the undergraduates in all the glory of their immemorial screeching. She has taken part in all, and has apparently enjoyed them with a wholesome temperate gaiety; as far removed from the unnatural elation of the Blind Man's Buff, as from the inert gloom of the previous period.

With Term is to end Sarah's visit; and on the day following her departure the Professor is to shoulder his valise for the Bernese Oberland.

The morning on which Mrs. Forth is to lose her sister has come. Sarah is taking her last stroll round the flower-beds, and across the square of sward over which she and Belinda have walked so many miles. Mrs. Forth has just joined her, issuing from the house with the end of a laugh still lingering about her mouth and eyes.

'You seem amused,' says the other, turning to meet her. 'May I be permitted to inquire the cause?'

'It is nothing!' replies Belinda, bubbling over again with mirth. 'It is a shame to laugh at her, only it is so difficult to help it. Mr. Forth has just been reading the Collect for the day to his mother; and at the end she said to him, "You read very nicely, my dear; and, when you are a little older, you will read better still!"'

Sarah joins in the laugh, but not warmly.

'And this,' she says indignantly, 'is the companion with whom you are to be left *tête-à-tête* for four months!'

Belinda bends her charming head in a nod of cheerful acquiescence.

'It is monstrous!' continues Miss Churchill, with a growing energy of ire. 'It is beyond belief! I have a good mind, *now*, at the last moment, to give him a piece of my mind! Where is he?' glancing threateningly towards the windows of the house. 'Let me take him red-handed, in the act of packing his portmanteau!'

There is such a doughty purpose in her voice and her pink porcelain face, that Belinda, seizing her arm in apprehensive detention, cries:

'Do not! It would be no use. Do you remember the proverb about putting the finger *entre l'arbre et l'écorce?* And I—I do not want to go with him.'

At the last words, she has turned her head slightly aside.

'Do you think that he would be a pleasant travelling-companion?' she goes on rapidly, perceiving that her sister does not make any rejoinder, but only looks at her searchingly. 'Do you remember how ashamed we used to be when we haggled over the groschen at Dresden? A tour with him would be one colossal blush.'

'It is a chance of evils, of course,' says Sarah dispassionately. 'Perhaps my early passion blinds me, but, personally, I should prefer him.'

'Should you?'

'Four months!' repeats Miss Churchill, in almost awed reflection. 'How many times, at a rough calculation, in four months will you tell her who you are; and that there is a foolish prejudice in favour of burying people before they have been dead twenty-five years?'

'Perhaps I shall end by joining her in the belief that my father-in-law is still above ground,' replies Belinda; but she says it in a tone of such unassumed equanimity, that again Sarah regards her with astonishment.

'Four months!' she repeats, a third time. 'Do you mean to tell me that you are not *desperate* at such a prospect?'

'Of course I am—desperate!'

But there is not a touch of desperation, or even of milder sadness, in her voice.

'How do you mean to live through it?'

'How do people endure existence on these occasions?'

She has knelt on the springy turf, and is cutting, one after one, a score of young and dewy pinks, to comfort her sister during her dusty up-journey; carefully, and with the grudging hand of a real flower-lover, choosing those that are budless: no easy feat, for there is scarcely one that has not a gray-green successor beneath its perfumed wing.

'Eating, drinking, sleeping, yawning!'

'Are you quite sure that you will have no *other* support?' asks Sarah abruptly, and yet slowly.

For a moment the garden-scissors in Mrs. Forth's hand cease their clipping, and remain suspended and open, like that other pair which snipped her namesake's love-lock, while a dye as opulent as that of the new peony, whose birth the garden-border this morning greeted, stains even the milk-coloured nape of her stooped neck.

'I—I—do not know what you mean,' she says coldly; 'what—what other support should I have?'

'Belinda,' says the other, dropping down on the sward beside her, and griping her shaking hand—scissors, pinks, and all—in her own little eager clasp, 'why should not I come back and keep you company? I may not be a very intellectual companion, but at least I have a firmer hold upon my few facts than has your poor mamma-in-law. Let me come back; we will have Jane down, and Punch shall show her the University'—with a not very assured laugh. 'Let me come!'

But the hands so urgently pressed give no answering pressure. Upon the half-averted face comes no glow of sisterly pleasure or acceptance. A senseless suspicion has flashed across Mrs. Forth's mind, that the present proposition on Sarah's part may be an impromptu *fait à loisir;* that it may have been arranged between her and Rivers; that here may lie the secret of his eagerness to repeat his visit; that —in fact whatever angry gibberish jealousy may whisper to a mind ripe and ready for its reception.

Under pretext of resuming her pink-cutting, she has withdrawn her unwillingly-captured hand; but she is no longer careful: the unblown buds fall as freely as the opened flowers.

'And give up Cowes and Scotland?' she says in a dry voice; 'and what would granny say?'

'It would not be of the slightest consequence what she said,' replies Sarah, smothering bravely a disappointment none the less sharp for being mastered at her sister's reception of her proposal. 'You are aware that my grandmother's words have always been to me as the idle wind; which, I believe, is one main reason of the sincere regard and respect that she cherishes for me. If granny is the only stumbling-block——'

'I could not think of being so selfish!' interrupts Belinda hastily, not allowing her sister to finish her sentence.

'There would be no selfishness if I liked it,' says Sarah persistently; 'and—you may wonder at my taste, but I *should* like it.'

Belinda has risen from her knees, and has turned to a damask rose-bush, to lay it under contribution for her nosegay.

'It is so perfectly unnecessary,' she says, cutting feverishly away; 'you are tilting against windmills. I make no complaint; I think it no hardship to be alone. I am not like you, miserable if I am left five minutes to my own society !'

There is such a strain of impatience through her speech, that Sarah reluctantly desists, nor are many more words exchanged between them. The cab is at the door. The luggage—cursed of cabmen—has been hoisted on the top. Punch is, at Mrs. Forth's petition—a petition certainly not backed up by Slutty—to be left on a visit to her.

The moment of parting has come. Sarah apparently wishes that that parting shall take place without witnesses. She draws her sister back into the drawing-room, and shuts the door.

'Belinda,' she says, when she has somewhat coldly kissed her, looking in her face with a gravity that only once or twice before in the course of their lives has Mrs. Forth seen written on those small gay lineaments. 'Belinda, I wash my hands of you; I would have helped you if I could. I have no reason for saying so—I know nothing, and you will tell me nothing; but I cannot help thinking that you are going to the devil, and that you are taking David Rivers with you !'

Then, without another word, she is gone. Without one last look from the cab window, without a farewell friendly hand-wave; forgetting even to bid good-bye to the dogs, or take their messages to Jane, she is gone. For some minutes Belinda remains standing on the exact spot at which her sister had left her; remains standing, still and stunned. Then she suddenly throws herself into the Professor's armchair, and spreads her hands over her face. She would like not to let a quarter of an inch of it remain uncovered. The light is strong and brutal. She would like to draw the blinds down and shut the shutters. '*Going to the devil, and taking David Rivers with you!*' The blood is singing loudly in her ears. It seems to take the form of these words.

Over and over again.   The moment the sentence is ended,
it begins afresh.   How long she lies there—outwardly a
log, inwardly a shameful fire—she neither knows nor cares.
But after a while a tide of indignation sets in through all
her being, chasing before it the shame, and she sits up.

What disgraceful words for her own sister to apply to her!
and what slightest ground, excuse, palliation even, had she
for so insulting her?   *Going to the devil!*   And pray, what
is it to go to the devil?   Is it to fulfil with nice scrupulosity
every tasteless or even nauseous duty of a most dreary life?
To sing as she walks her tread-mill ?   To smile patiently over
her oakum-picking?   To forego her own hot bright youth,
and clip down its rich proportions to the meagre pattern of
the dry and crabbed age with which it is mismated?   To
be a secretary without pay, a drudge without wage, a *souffre
douleur* without hope of enlargement, a prisoner the term of
whose incarceration lies in the hands of arbitrary death?   If
this be to go to the devil, then she is not only going there,
but has long ago gone.

She laughs sarcastically, and her feverish limbs carry her
up and down the room.   If Sarah had given her time, this
is how she would have answered her—thus and thus.   For
a while she walks to and fro, muttering under her breath,
framing withering sentences of self-exculpation, that must
carry conviction to any mind.   But that mood, too, passes.
As her wrath—spent and exhausted—subsides, another voice,
lower yet more penetrating, takes its place.   *Going to the
devil!*   Is going to the devil to have a husband whose pursuits you abhor, whose infirmities you secretly deride, at
whose accidental touch you shiver?   Is going to the devil to
be speeding with disloyal alacrity that husband's departure,
to be counting the hours to the end of your only sister's visit,
to be living and feeding and flourishing upon a hope that
you dare not look in the face, that you would sooner die

than impart to any soul that breathes? Is this to be going to the devil?

She has again wholly hidden her face with her hands. Again the light seems over-strong and pushing. And plain and distinct, beyond possibility of misapprehension, the answer comes—'Yes! yes! yes!'

*　　　*　　　*　　　*　　　*

A couple of hours later the Professor lifts a head, a good deal reddened and exasperated by long burrowing in the bowels of a portmanteau, to see his pale wife enter his room.

'I came to see whether I could help you,' she says gently, though in a spiritless flat voice.

'The idea has occurred to you somewhat late in the day,' replies he ungraciously. 'It was fortunate for me that I did not depend upon your offers of assistance, volunteered this morning.'

'I was bidding Sarah good-bye,' she answers apologetically, and without any trace of resentment at his tone.

'She has been gone exactly three hours and a half,' replies he drily, glancing at the clock.

She offers no further justification, but kneeling down on the floor, lets her hands, which tremble perceptibly, stray rather purposelessly over the books strewn upon the carpet.

'Pray, mind what you are about!' he cries sharply; 'you are doing more harm than good.'

'They are to go, are not they?' she says, lifting a heavy folio, and looking humbly up at him.

'I am obliged to omit Augustine, Irenæus, and several books of reference, as they would entail very considerable expense upon me in excess of weight,' he replies, peering down through his spectacles at his strewn treasures. 'I the less regret it as, since I am taking no secretary with me——'

How very white her face is ! Has she had some sudden scare ?

'Why are not you taking a secretary ?' she asks in a very low voice. 'Why—why do not you take *me?*'

He shifts the focus of his vision from Irenæus to her face; but apparently the latter object gives him less tranquil pleasure than did the former.

'You have never expressed the slightest desire to accompany me,' he answers chillingly.

She hangs her head, a guilty consciousness staining her pallor red.

'Have not I ? Perhaps I thought that you did not want me.'

There is a deliberate pause before he answers, and her heart goes down, down. He is about to accept her offer ! But his first words reassure her.

'I can see no object that would be gained by such a change of plan,' he replies, in a key that plainly shows his annoyance at the suggestion having been made. '*I* go in search of health ; a quest which you, happily for yourself, have no need to pursue.'

She draws a long breath of relief; but now that the danger of acceptance seems less imminent, her scruples return. Sarah's stinging phrase begins to ring again in her ears.

'You—you forget that I shall be all alone here,' she says, nervously fidgeting with the already packed portion of the portmanteau.

'You will have my mother.'

She shrugs her shoulders.

'She can hardly be reckoned as a companion.'

At her capricious and untimely opposition, his forehead gathers into vexed wrinkles.

'Since it appears that your own society has such terrors

for you, you are at liberty to invite your sister to come and share your solitude.'

Again the guilty head stoops.

'She—she has engagements of her own.'

'So I should have imagined,' replies he with a disagreeable smile ; 'but you can scarcely hold me responsible for them.'

Another pause. She is aimlessly wrapping paper round one of the volumes that are not wanted, that are not to be taken eruditely tripping to the Alps. She will make one more effort. If that fail, no one, not even Sarah, can blame her.

'Does not it strike you that I shall be very dull here, all by myself?' she asks, timorously eyeing him.

'I have always understood, upon your own authority, that you were indifferent to, if not averse from, amusements,' he answers irritably.

'Not now—not now!' she cries feverishly. 'Even if I were so formerly, I am not now ; and even if I were—to be alone for four months !'

'You exaggerate grossly,' returns he sharply. 'There are many residents who do not leave Oxbridge until the end of July, and many who return at the beginning of September.'

'They will do me no good,' she says excitedly. 'How will they help me?'

He shrugs his shoulders silently, as who should say that upon one lost in such mazes of inconsequence and irrationality breath would be wasted.

'Do you remember that I am young?' she says, in a hard low voice, rising from her knees and approaching him.

'It is certainly not your fault if I do not,' replies he peevishly ; 'for you are good enough to remind me of the fact often enough.'

'It is because you always act as if you forgot it,' retorts she, her temper rising under his tone.

'I confess that I fail to see how your juvenility affects the present case,' he says satirically.

'Do you?' she answers with a scorching blush, that seems to burn inside as well as outside her.   'Some men might think that I was too young to be left to my own devices; that I—I might get into mischief!'

He has taken off his spectacles in order to rub their glasses.   He now deliberately replaces them, and regards her attentively through them.

'I presume,' he says deliberately, 'that that last remark is to be regarded as a pleasantry, though I fail to see the point of it.'

'I am so much given to pleasantries,' she says bitterly. 'We are so apt to joke with one another: are not we?'

'It seemed difficult to treat such an observation seriously,' returns he, in a measured voice of displeasure.   'What mischief, may I ask, are you likely to get into, here under the shelter of your own roof, and in the quiet performance of your regular duties?   I cannot but think that the alarm under which you labour is an unnecessary one.'

For all answer, she turns abruptly away.   The infinitely difficult confession which she was half-heartedly struggling to make to him, frozen back by his gibe.

'You have evidently a most flattering confidence in me,' she says, adopting his tone.   'I do not quite know what I have done to deserve it.'

As a reply, the Professor turns thoughtfully back to his folios, weighing the dispensability or indispensability as a travelling companion of each, with an air of having dismissed the subject, and of resolutely waiving further consideration of so senseless a matter.

His wife stands dubiously watching him.

'I do not know why we are sneering at each other,' she says at last, in a disturbed voice. 'I had not any intention of sneering when I came here. I came to ask you in all— good faith' (he does not perceive the slight hesitation which prefaces the last two words) 'to take me with you—will you?'

To so point-blank an appeal he must provide an answer of some kind; though nothing can be clearer than that he would rather have relegated the affair to the limbo of a contemptuous silence.

'I am unable to understand you,' he says, with slow annoyance. 'At the last moment, and when my plans are fully matured, and could only be remodelled at great inconvenience to myself, you suddenly appear with a proposal entirely to disintegrate them. Had you any good reasons to show——' (She has good reasons enough, God wot! but looking at the unlovely and unloving rigour of his face, she feels that to die, to be flayed alive—whatever things in short have been reckoned hardest of endurance since the world was—are but as child's play compared to what the telling them to him would be.) 'Since, then,' he continues, with an air of judicial coldness, and not thinking it worth while to finish his former sentence, 'it is dictated merely by a puerile caprice——'

'It is not caprice,' she stammers urgently, in puissant excitement.

'If it is not caprice, nothing can be easier than to prove it,' rejoins he coolly, and so turns again on his heel.

Behind his back she makes a gesture as of one that throws up a game. Is not he in the right? Has not he a show of reason and justice on his side? Why not acquiesce without further kicking against the pricks? But yet something drives her to a last attempt. Although thrice baffled, although at each new discomfiture her heart has sprung up in joyful relief, she will press her suit once more.

'You know that women never have any reasons to give,' she says with a laugh that has borrowed something from its opposite—a sob, and in a gentler voice than that which she is wont to think soft enough for converse with him; 'but sometimes their instincts lead them right. I—I think that you had better take me with you!'

Envenomed by her pertinacity, he wheels round upon her viciously.

'Perhaps you will be good enough to expose your reasons,' he says, 'premising, that is to say, that they are such as a person of ordinary common sense can permit himself to listen to.'

'I should not be much in your way,' she says humbly, and going so far—for her it is immensely far—as to lay her fair hand on his coat-sleeve. 'Of course my society would be no great gain to you, but I could make myself useful; I could pack and unpack for you; I have learned your ways thoroughly by this time. It would be odd,' with a sad little laugh, 'if I had not; and if you had one of your attacks I could nurse you!'

She has made her plea, and with eyes that feel dry, and breath that comes short, awaits its prosperity or miscarriage. For a while he eyes her with silent suspicion.

'It would be a most unnecessary expense,' he says at last, shortly.

'I should not expect, I should not wish for, any luxuries,' she answers, her pleading growing, perhaps, the more earnest from her consciousness of the intensity of the wish for its ill-success that goes with it. 'I drink no wine, and I do not eat much.'

'Pshaw!' retorts he, with angry ridicule; 'are you simple enough to suppose that the hotel tariffs vary according to the number of mouthfuls you swallow?'

'I have no objection to travelling third-class; I should

never ask for a sitting-room; I am quite capable of roughing it,' she urges tremulously.

'No doubt! no doubt!' he answers tartly; 'all the same, you would more than double the expense.'

'And if I did?' she says firmly—for is not this her last appeal, and is not she bound to make it no pretence, but a real and thoroughly earnest one?—'what need that matter to you? You are well off, and'—lowering her voice a little —'you have no one to come after you.'

Perhaps the plea is an injudiciously chosen one. No man likes to be reminded that he will stand or fall alone; that he is without a stake in the generations to come. At all events, on hearing it, his features assume a look even more acrid than that which they wore before.

'I must request you to consider the subject as closed,' he says with a decision against which there is no appeal. 'I have, for reasons which appear sufficient to myself—and I ask no other arbiter—come to a final decision upon it; pray let us hear no more of it.'

'As you please,' she answers, bowing acquiescently a head whose cheeks have suddenly resumed their carnations, and its eyes their young dance; 'I suppose, as you say, that you know your own affairs best, but I think I have heard that there is such a thing as being "penny wise and pound foolish."'

CHAPTER X.

'How sad and bad and mad it was!
But then, how it was sweet!'

THE Professor has been gone a parson's week. For the same period of time Mrs. Forth has been testing the genuineness of her appetite for solitude; nor finding it fail beneath the experiment. Perhaps it is the extreme clearness of her conscience that upholds her; for do not we all know, either by its possession or its lack, that there is no cheerfuller companion than a clear conscience? nothing that gives such a zest to appetite, or such a point to occupation? And can any one be in fuller possession of this innocent luxury than Belinda? Has not she craved with meek persistency leave to share her husband's travels? and, reluctantly compelled to abandon this hope, has not she provided, with wifely care, for every possible need that may assail him on that sanitary excursion, for whose loneliness none can blame *her?*

Did she forget his Etna? or his eider-down? or his air-cushion? Did she, as many a spouse though otherwise meritorious might easily have done, omit his tin of digestive biscuits? Was there lacking from his kit at his departure one of his heart drops, liver pills, spleen boluses?

What but the consciousness of a duty performed both generously and minutely could enable her to wave her hand at the fly-window with so collected a friendliness; smile such a serene '*Bon voyage*' to the jewel of which that fly is the casket? To assume an inconsolable grief would be absurd, and would take him in even less than herself; but there is no hypocrisy in crying, 'A good journey to you!'

As she returns up the gravelled drive, she stoops to pick up a small stone. How brightly it shines!

'Is it a strayed agate or beryl?'

'Pooh!' (throwing it down again), 'it is only a pebble; it is only the late shower and the present sun that have turned it into a temporary gem.'

But the same rich metamorphosis seems to have taken place in the case of every object upon which her eye alights. Did ever bountiful rose-tree show such a wealth of come flowers and coming buds, as the 'Captain Christy' against the study wall? Was ever little Philistine drawing-room so rich in gold motes lustily astride on the sunbeams? Even the very dogs, the well-known dogs, seem to wear an air of better breeding; manners of higher finish; tails of more watchspring curl than on any previous morning. Even the parrot's profanities—in point of fact, very commonplaces of blasphemy, uttered with an Oxbridge accent—have won a raciness never before theirs.

She wanders from room to room, as it were taking possession. Are not they all her own, her very own now? Even without the explanation to that effect, which in pure wantonness of spirits she has vouchsafed separately to Punch and Slutty, they seem perfectly to understand that they are now at liberty to rumple the chair covers, clatter down the fire-irons, oppress the cats as freely as their soul listeth; that there are no longer any nerves in the house, any dyspepsia, any learning. Nor does the passage of the hours and days bring with it any sensible alteration in this mood, of either hers or theirs.

Daily she sees the piled vehicles rolling past to the station; carrying her fellow-townsmen away to their holiday; stampedes of whole large small families to the seaside (the new Oxbridge swarms and perambulates and crawls with little children, all apparently of the same age to a day); hardy young couples winging bold flights to the North Cape, or more modest Dolomites. She wishes them all a happy time and safe return; but not a twinge of envy goes with one of them.

Home is good enough for her; England far enough; Oxbridge fair enough. Even Sarah's parting words, at first so rankling with poisonous sting, grow gradually powerless to hurt. She begins to think of them at first with indignation, next with indifference, and at last even with a lofty kind of compassionate forgiveness.

'It is the speakers of such calumnious utterances,' she says to herself, without conscious sophistry, 'not those to whom they are addressed, whom they injure.'

She lets her mind run with complacency round the circle of her accurately fulfilled duties. Is there one in a thousand who, considering the nature of those duties, would fulfil them as accurately? Has not she, in addition to the tasks imposed upon her, for fulfilment during his absence by her husband, voluntarily undertaken to make a new catalogue of his library, as a wifely surprise for him upon his return? Does she scamp, by one moment, the time of her visits to his mother? Has not she rather enlarged them by nearly a daily hour? Is not the nurse ready to lick her feet, for her consideration and unselfish sharing of that nurse's burden? Does her patience ever for an instant fail under the old lady's senseless catechisms? Can anything surpass the painstaking discretion with which she conducts the Professor's correspondence, left behind him, in her charge? or the respectful punctuality and amplitude of her own letters to him? Nor is her self-satisfaction less, when she considers her pleasures. Might not every member of the University, every inhabitant of the world, if he saw fit, have leave to pry into each moment of her leisure, as of her occupations?

The happy gardenings—weeding the border, with the dogs yawning their hearts out beside her, in affectionate endurance of a pastime they are so far from participating. Dogs hate gardening; they see no sense in it. Of what use, pray, to dig a hole, when you have no bone to bury in it? The long country walks to the elm-shaded rural villages, and through the late June fields, where man has sown his corn and God has thrown in His poppies; the return home, poppy-laden, to make the house one scarlet bower, though it is embellished for only her own eye.

Never has that eye seemed so open to see. Never has her ear seemed to be laid so close to the heart of the mighty mother, to hear its beatings. Never till this year had she learned all the music that lies even in the trumpeting gnat and the booming evening chafers. Never had she grown into such familiar friendship with the woodland birds. All her life, of course, she has known that the thrush's song is sweet, and the lark's exulting; but not till now—so unobservant are we—has she learned surely the songs of the lesser minnesingers, the minor stars of the great concert. But this summer, by right perhaps of her harmlessness and her solitude, she has stolen into their intimacy. She recognises them lovingly, not only when they sing, but when they converse among themselves. She knows the tomtit's table-talk —like the grating of a tiny saw; the cock chaffinch's—all: she grows discriminatingly cunning in all their little speech.

The dogs enjoy themselves too in their way, though they think that the flowers smell ill; and that the birds' noise is ugly and foolish, not to be named in the same breath with the poignant love-songs of the nightly cats. Slutty, indeed.

has suffered one of those disappointments, from which not dogs any more than men are exempt. For four-and-twenty hours Punch has been lost; and from the more than resignation, evidenced by her during his absence, and the acute depression coincident with his restoration, it is but too clear that she had hoped his disappearance was a permanent one.

June nears her perfumed close. The second Sunday of Mrs. Forth's loneliness has come round. The first was marked by no special incident. Belinda had not expected that it would be. But, indeed, not even to herself does she allow that she anticipates anything for any Sunday. But yet, on this second Sunday she rises with such a feeling of irrepressible blithe excitement, that she must needs casuistically explain it to herself. The air is so good. The smell of the hay comes now into the middle of the town; into street and market-place; how much more hither, where she is in the enjoyment of a sort of suburban pseudo-country. She has ever been fond of Sunday. It is always a favourite day with her; much more so in this Sunday city of innumerable church bells.

She dresses with a resolute abstaining from adding a single adornment, or making any change, however slight, in her usual Sunday toilet. To do so would be to allow that she had some reason for the alteration. Perhaps, with this motive mingles an unconfessed superstition that to presuppose a pleasure by preparation for it, is the surest way to rob yourself of its fruition.

She reads the Lessons for the day to her mother-in-law, with as reverent a distinctness as if the poor old lady could follow them, or were even aware of the nature of the attention. It is a proceeding of whose judiciousness she herself has no great opinion; but it is one of the tasks imposed upon her by her husband, and which she would by no means intermit. When they are ended, having told her the news

of her husband's death, which she receives with her usual
pleased surprise, Belinda goes lightly away to put on her
bonnet for church.

As she walks along, her memory grows suddenly occupied
with the recollection of that other solitary walk to church at
Folkestone; of the griding cold; the ice-bound earth; the
misery of her yet more ice-bound heart; of the wretched
prisoned starling to which she had likened herself. Not
greater is earth's change than that which is wrought within
herself. But for *her* change, what reason is there? Has
the starling then escaped? The question flashes upon her
with an uneasy start, but is instantly silenced again.

The service is one of those brief and modernised ones,
that make us marvel at the patience of our earlier days; yet
to Belinda it seems long. Whether sweetly singing, devoutly
kneeling, or attentively listening, she has no peace from the
buzzing thought—never allowed, never looked in the face—
but always returning, gnat-like : 'When will it be? Where
will it be? How long will it last?' It does not leave her
at the church door, but buzzes and teases all along the sunshiny road. It will buzz and tease until it gets its answer.
Well, let it! For is not that answer now given?

At the turn of the road, close at home, free from the
stream of churchgoers, which has flowed in other directions,
with no more witness than a milkman swinging unconcernedly
along beneath his yoke, there it will be—there it is! Has not
every moment since their parting been but a leading up to
and preparation for this moment? And yet, at the sight of
him she starts, as if it were a surprise, which indeed she still
feigns to herself that it is.

' *You* here?' she says in a voice of airy astonishment,
that would be admirably natural did it not quiver, and were
it not a little overdone. 'Have you fallen from the clouds?'

His answer is not over-ready. He has not yet got over

the stupefaction that the first sight of her after an interval always brings upon him—a stupefaction such as, they say, the sight of the sea, of Niagara, of any overwhelmingly great and noble natural object, produces in him who looks upon it for the first time. How much more beautiful she is than he had remembered her! how pious she looks! how chaste! Probably other women before now have carried large Prayer-books, and 'Ancient and Modern Hymn-books' in their left hand, home from church; but it seems to him to be a wondrous feat of grace and holiness, performed for the first and only time in the world's history. At last:

'Are you surprised?' he asks, still feeling rather dizzy; 'if you remember——'

'I am afraid that you will find all your friends gone down,' she interrupts precipitately.

'Shall I?' he answers, with an indifference that he makes no attempt to conceal; 'probably, no doubt.'

Is it her large Prayer-book that is making her so unapproachable?

'Have you come from Yorkshire?' she asks quickly, not allowing a moment of silence to intervene, with the uneasy idea, probably, of keeping the conversation in the polite and distant society key in which she has elected to pitch it.

'Yes.'

'Did not you find it very dusty travelling?' walking fast, and looking straight before her.

'I came by a night-train.'

'Do you like night-travelling? *I* do not; but then I can't sleep. Perhaps you can sleep?'

'I did not sleep!'

There is a tinge of reproach in the manner in which he pronounces the last words. What has happened to her? Is it to hear these cold platitudes that he has been rushing towards her all through the night, chiding the iron wheels

for being slow—that he has spent his holiday, and foregone
his rest? *Sleep!* With this *to-day*—this *now* ahead of him!
Is it likely that he should sleep?

They have reached her gate, and there paused. She
does not ask him to accompany her in, nor does she make
him any hospitable offer whatever. But that he has neither
expected nor wished—would have declined on the unlikely
hypothesis of her offering it. He has no desire to taste of
Professor Forth's salt. There is something that tells him
that her pause before dismissing him will be only a momentary one; and that if he does not utilise this very present
instant, she will be gone, and he may return to Milnthorpe,
whence he came, at his leisure.

'You will enjoy the country air after your Milnthorpe
smoke,' she says, her hand upon the latch, and with what
he knows to be a valedictory smile.

'What do you do on Sunday afternoons?' he asks precipitately; 'do you do anything?'

'*Do anything!*' she repeats, demurring; 'what do you
mean?'

'Do you go to church again?' very hurriedly, and doub-
ling up his hands in his pockets to hinder their yielding to
their almost ungovernable impulse to stretch themselves out,
and—with her will, or against her will—there detain her.

She casts a furtive glance towards the house—a glance
that makes in him the fear of her flight and the impulse to
check it, yet more nearly beyond his governance.

'No—o,' she says slowly; 'not often.'

'What do you do then? Do you ever take a walk?'

He has his eye upon her. Would it be quite inad-
missible, if she shows symptoms of leaving him unanswered,
to lay one hand quite quietly, so that she should be scarcely
conscious of it, upon her arm? There is a full minute—
sixty seconds well rung—before she answers.

'Sometimes, as it happens, if it does not rain—if I feel inclined.'

'And—and—have you any—any specially favourite walk?'

Again she looks towards the house, behind whose closed doors the dogs are plainly heard, telling her that they know she has come back from church, and asking her why she is dawdling.

'No; none!' she says, lifting the latch. 'Of course,' her words coming with a sort of shamefaced hurry, 'I like the College gardens — everybody must like the College gardens; but,' with a sudden remorse at this concession, 'I very often do not go there, because of the dogs; one may not take the dogs into them.'

She has opened the gate, and is passing through it. He has only half a minute left.

'Which is your favourite? Which do you like best?' he cries desperately after her.

'I have not any favourite. I do not know; I like them all.'

She has taken out her latch-key, and is putting it into the lock.

'That means that you are determined not to tell me,' he says, with a tremor of passionate disappointment in his voice; and so, taking off his hat, turns on his heel. But as he walks slowly down the road, telling his own heart that he has befooled himself—never would he allow that his high lady could befool him—a sort of whisper seems to travel to his ears, 'Some people like St. Bridget's best!'

*   *   *   *   *

Belinda lunches, as usual, alone. The one prime and perhaps sole advantage of solitary feeding is, that you need not eat more than you feel inclined; that if from any cause your appetite has left you, there is no one to make com-

ments on that fact. If, in addition, you have two pet
gluttons on their hind-legs supporting you throughout your
repast on either side, and drawing five sharp nails along
the back of your hand if you do not seem to be attending
to them, not even to the servant need your condition of
unhunger be ever revealed.

Punch and Slutty have never yet understood why, on
that June Sunday, they were feasted so royally on ribs of
roast beef.

From the luncheon-table Belinda passes, according to the
usual routine of her duties, to her mother-in-law's room, for
her daily two hours.   As it turns out, they are more than
two ; for the nurse, relying upon her employer's usual good-
natured laxity, outstays her furlough by fully twenty minutes,
and returns to find young Mrs. Forth, for the first time,
unsmiling and impatient of the delay.   And yet, when released, she seems undecided as to the disposition of her time.

The dogs are staring at her—one sitting, one standing—
as if they knew that their fate was hanging in the balance.
Can any one resist such a litany of goggles as their eyes are
uttering?   It would be a crying shame to disappoint them.
She will forego the trim leisure of the College gardens and
take them to the Fields—a public promenade where dogs
are admitted, and where perambulators push and Sunday
shop-boys jostle.   But she does not call them or tell them
so.   After all, it is a pity to spoil them, and to let them take
it for granted that they are to accompany her wherever she
goes.   On the whole, it is wiser not to hamper herself with
them.   She will make no fixed plan as to the direction of
her walk ; but will simply follow where whim or chance may
lead.   And whim and chance, after a little preliminary
shamming, gone through to impose upon herself, lead her
to St. Bridget's Gardens.

An interlacing of elm-arms overhead ; a thick bed of

periwinkle below; on the left a little classic river, and an unexpected park with smoky deer; on the right the sacred College meadow, where never vulgar foot may fall, save of the haymakers, who have but lately built the grass and flowers into a scented stack. Above, below, around, tranquillity and solitude. For, loveliest of the College walks as is St. Bridget's, it is, strange to say, also the least frequented. Thither the accursed perambulator cannot come; and thither the holiday clerk and milliner come not. It is all, or nearly all, her own. Each Sunday, as the town empties, it will grow more and more her own.

Over the patterned walk, where tree and sun have laid their chequers as a carpet for her feet, she marches leisurely. She has not hurried upon any other Sunday; therefore she will not hurry to-day. No one can or shall be able to say that she has departed one jot from her accustomed habits.

She is making for her usual seat—the one that ordinarily no one disputes with her. But to-day, as it comes into view, she perceives that it is already occupied. The occupant must be a friend too, since, on catching sight of her, he comes hasting—young and most glad—to meet her. Ah—h! it is not a question of the Grosse Garten over again. *To-day* she is not first. Not that there is any parallel between the cases. Not that any one can call *this* a rendezvous. He does not think it necessary to offer any apology for, or explanation of, his appearance, and passes over, with a silent lenity, her little futile and ill-done expression of surprise.

'So we meet here again!'

'Shall we sit down?' he says, pointing to the bench whence he has just risen.

For an instant she hesitates, then—

'Yes, I do not mind,' she says irresolutely. 'I do not know why I should not; I sit here every Sunday.'

Is there in this any slightest departure from use or custom ? He seats himself beside, yet not near her ; for he sees her frightened eye jealously measuring the interval between them; to be sure that it is wide enough. How still it is ! Neither human voice nor metal heard from the city. Every one must be in church. Is this really happening? Perhaps if he speak, if he make her speak, it will grow more real.

'So you are all alone here ?'

'I have the dogs.'

' But besides the dogs, no one? not your sister?'

' Did you think that she would be here? did you expect to find her here?' asks Mrs. Forth quickly, while a storm of colour sweeps across her face.

He has no slightest clue to the origin of that red tempest; he only knows that it has trebled her beauty. Did God ever before create such a wonder of loveliness as she?

'I—I do not know,' he answers inattentively, a sin towards her of which he is seldom guilty; 'I—I do not think I thought about it.'

Wide of the mark, as we usually are in our judgments of those who have either too much or too little interest for us, she attributes his verbal unreadiness to a cause far removed enough from the real one.

'Sarah offered to stay with me,' she says in an ungenial voice, sitting very upright, and looking rigidly before her ; 'but I could not be so selfish as to accept such a sacrifice from her. I could not condemn any one to a life of such unredeemed dulness as mine now is.'

There is an acrimony in her tone that he knows not how to account for; but he does not interrupt her. As long as she will speak, he is ever most gladly silent. Why should the air be disturbed by his coarse and common voice, when it may be enriched by the music of hers?

'It is by no fault of my own that I am left alone here,'

continues she, with some sharpness; 'I wished to go to Switzerland with Mr. Forth. I asked him to take me.'

'And he refused?' with an accent of the profoundest incredulity.

To be asked by this woman for leave to bestow her company upon you, and to refuse her! And how did she ask? With her arms about his neck? With tears and kisses? He writhes.

'It was not convenient,' she answers formally; 'he was unable to make it fit in with his plans.'

The young man's heart burns within him, with a fire of envious indignation too hot to find vent in words. And yet perhaps a little of it may pierce through his next speech.

'He could not make it convenient to take you; and he could not make it convenient to stay with you; and so here you are, alone and dull.'

There is something in his tone—an irony that has the heat of wrath—that rouses again her half-smouldering alarms.

'I am alone,' she answers quickly, 'but I am not dull; I never was less dull in my life; the days are not half long enough for me.'

'And yet you said——' objects he, bewildered by the staring discrepancy of the statements which have followed so close upon each other's heels.

'What does it matter what I said?' interrupts she, with a brusque, nervous laugh. 'If I may not contradict myself, whom may I?'

An elderly couple—two of St. Bridget's rare votaries—have appeared upon the long straight alley dominated by Belinda's bench; an alley named after the short-faced humorist who loved to pace it. Mrs. Forth is glad. She wishes that more couples would come into sight. It is far more sociable.

As they pass, she involuntarily raises her voice in speaking.

She is saying nothing that she minds either them or anyone else hearing. What a comfort it is to have nothing to conceal from the whole world!

As the hours slip by, this happy and confident complacency deepens. But how fast they slip away! She cannot affect to be ignorant of their passage, since from the Cardinal's high tower, rising above the trees, the deep-mouthed bells tell the death of each little quarter. How closely they tread upon each other's heels! How many of them have broken the Sabbath stillness of the mead? She ventures not to ask nor think. But why does she not venture? It is the same as upon other Sundays, for she always stays late. It is with a start that at length—seven solemn strokes having beaten the air—she rises to be gone.

'It is seven o'clock!' she says hurriedly. 'We must go, or we shall be shut in.'

Shut in, in this green enclosure, with the stars for night-lamps, and this woman for fellow-prisoner! How dare she make such a suggestion! It is several minutes before he can fight down the frantic tumult in his heart that her words have raised, enough to say with sufficient composure:

'If you come here *every* Sunday, I suppose that you will be here next Sunday.'

'But *you* will not!' she cries vehemently, stopping—they are walking slowly homewards—and facing him.

'You forbid me?' he says in a low voice. He cannot rid himself of that vision of the star-canopied meadow.

'I forbid you!' she answers excitedly; 'yes—yes—yes! at least,' recollecting herself, 'of course you are your own master; I have no authority over you; but if I might be allowed to advise, I should say,' laughing agitatedly, 'that it would be a most unnecessary expense—like my journey to Switzerland. It is ill manners to remind you—but you know you are poor, until the patent is taken out,' smiling feverishly. 'I must not allow you to make ducks and drakes of your money.'

'The Sunday after?'

Her answer is long a coming; for indeed it is preceded by an eager dialogue within herself, that takes time.

If she prohibit it, so docile is he to her least word or sign, that she knows he will acquiesce; and she will sit upon her bench and hear the quarters chime, and see the tall tower rise, alone. Even when her reply does come, it is a mere evasion.

There is no need to give a direct answer. It is one of those questions which it is better taste to leave unanswered.

'The Sunday after next?' she says with a flighty laugh. 'We may be all dead by then; it is too far off for me to trouble my head about it!'

CHAPTER XI.

'Till Eulenspiegel war vergnügt wenn er Berg aufstieg, weil er sich
darauf freute, wenn es wieder Berg abgehen würde, und traurig wenn
es Berg abging, weil er das Aufsteigen fürchtete—— Was wird mir
Schlimmes begegnen da ich heute im Gemüth so heiter bin : welche
Freude steht mir bevor da mich Traurigkeit so niederdrückt ? '

CAN it be possible that August is here ? Not even early
August — July's hot equivalent — but late August, that has
shaken hands with September. The mornings have a taste
of autumn, though high summer still rules the noons ; and
as Belinda paces along her garden walk, the damp dews
wet her gown, and the swinging gossamers tickle her nose.

Oxbridge is at its emptiest. In a week or so people will
be beginning to return ; but for the present it is a desert.
It is a pity that they should not return to see with what a
kingly red pomp the Virginian creeper is decking the sad-
coloured beauty of their town. Over their worn-gray shoulders
the Colleges are throwing a cope of shaded crimson ; and
from underneath a necklace of rubies, the Renaissance porch
of the great University church looks out.

And alone, among the waxing autumnal splendour, Mrs.
Forth pursues her way. Still she walks to the rural villages ;
still she gardens ; still she makes out her catalogue, and
reads aloud her collects ; and still on Sunday she sits upon
her bench in St. Bridget's walk, every alternate Sunday alone,

every alternate Sunday not alone. Although no further permission than that recorded has been either asked or given, she
has grown to take it as an accepted fact, that, on every second
Sunday, she shall find him there as surely as she finds the green
elm trees and the Cardinal's Tower. Doubtless the ' greenth
and blueth,' as Horace Walpole called them, the repose and
country fresh air, are an almost necessary tonic to him after
the din and labour of his week. If he think them worth the
money spent in railway travelling upon them, surely that is his
affair, and one in which, without officious ill-taste, she cannot
further meddle. There is no slightest mystery about their
meetings. Anyone may know of them. Nor does she ever fail,
in her letters to the Professor, to record among miscellaneous
items of news that she has met Mr. Rivers. Why then should
she abstain from a pleasure so innocent ? We are creatures of
habit ; and she could not well do without her Sundays now.

At the mere suggestion of such an abstinence she shivers
coldly. She has pitched their intercourse in a key with
which no one can quarrel ; has set their intimacy upon a
footing from which it need never swerve. If it were anyone's place to object, it would surely be her husband's ; but
so far is he from so doing, that he has not thought her communication worth even a comment. He has devoted a couple
of closely-written pages to directions where she is to find a
volume of Origen ; but apparently he could not spare speech
or time for a mention of Rivers.

If anything could have lulled her into a greater security
than that which she already enjoys, it would be this fact.
Serene and blooming, with a silent conscience, she walks
entranced through the dreamful days. By a sort of subtlety,
such as Till Eulenspiegel's, she has grown to look forward
to the Sundays on which he does not come, because they
lead up to those on which he does.

To-day is one of these latter Sundays, and she is sitting

down to her solitary luncheon, too happy to eat, when a ring at the front-door makes her start. Can it be Rivers? Unlikely that he, who has long tacitly abstained from even meeting her on her way home from church should present himself at a door which he has always shown such a silent energy of repulsion against entering. Can it be her husband, unexpectedly restored to her? She turns suddenly very cold. Can it be——

There is no use in repeating a question which is already answered.

'Just in time!' cries Miss Watson, thrusting aside the baffled parlour-maid and seeming instantly to fill the whole room with her presence, and her plaid gown and her fringe. 'What a good smell of roast beef! I am as hungry as a hunter.'

Belinda has risen, leaving her untouched plate; the consternation which the sight of Miss Watson does and must always inspire, in this case diluted and modified by relief. At all events, she is not the Professor.

'I can spend a good four or five hours with you!' cries the guest, with loud cheerfulness; beginning to divest herself of bonnet, gloves, and pelerine. 'I am on my way to Wrenbury, to the Sampsons. They do not expect me; I am going to take them by surprise. They have always bragged so much about their place down in Blankshire, that I was determined to find out how much truth there was in it; and the Sunday trains are so awkward that I cannot get on till late in the afternoon. However, it is an ill wind that blows nobody good. I can spend pretty nearly four hours with you.'

Through Belinda's head there darts immediately a calculation. It is now one o'clock. In four hours it will be five o'clock: an hour later, therefore, than that one which usually finds her pacing down St. Bridget's walk. He will have to wait a full hour for her. At this thought a dismay, so disproportionate to the occasion as to frighten even herself, takes hold of her.

'Is not it rather a wild-goose chase?' she asks, forcing herself to speak. 'How do you know that you will find the Sampsons? Are you sure that they are at home?'

'Pooh!' replies Miss Watson carelessly; 'if they are not, the housekeeper will give me a shake-down. One gets to know the ins and outs of a place better when the owners are away.'

Belinda's only answer is a faint shrug of accute dissent.

'I never ate a better piece of beef in my life!' pursues Miss Watson warmly. 'Goes to the servants, I suppose, eh? Else I cannot imagine how you would ever get through such a large joint all alone. Why are you alone? No screw loose, I hope, eh? It seems a little odd your being here all alone, when the town is such a desert. By the by, what is Rivers doing up here?'

If her life here, and her salvation elsewhere, depended upon her remaining motionless, Belinda could not help the start which she can only hope looks slighter than it feels.

'Mr. Rivers?' she repeats stammeringly.

'Yes, Mr. Rivers, if you like to call him so!' with her strident laugh. 'David Rivers; our old friend, David Rivers! Did not you know that he was here? Has not he been to see you?'

Belinda draws a long gasping breath, then answers distinctly:

'No!'

After all it is not a lie—not all a lie! He has not been to see her; and she has made a mental reservation as to her answer applying only to the second clause of her companion's speech.

'H'm!' says Miss Watson, biting her nails; 'that in itself looks odd.'

Since this last remark is not a question, and since she is by no means assured of having even a tolerable mastery over her voice, Mrs. Forth allows it to go by uncommented upon.

'What *can* he be doing up here?' continues the other, still biting her nails, and in a tone of the most poignant inquisitiveness. 'The very deadest time of the long vacation; not a soul to be seen about! Why, you might drive a coach-and-four along the side walk from St. Ursula's to King's! I shall never rest till I have got to the bottom of it!'

Her guest's eyes are riveted upon Mrs. Forth with such an unwinking energy of stare, that she must needs form some halting answer.

'Will not you?' she says, with a sickly smile; 'you had better ask him!'

'I only wish he would give me the chance,' replies the other stoutly; 'but he knows a great deal too well for that. I came face to face with him in Church Street, and before I could get my breath he had slipped away like an eel. If you remember, we used to think him a little deaf at Dresden, but I never heard that he was blind, too! There is always something *louche* in a man obviously avoiding the respectable women of his acquaintance, is not there?'

She repeats the question with such a pertinacity of inquiry, that Belinda is obliged to murmur that, 'Yes, there is.'

When the beef has gone to fulfil that destiny which Miss Watson had prophesied for it—she, at least, has done full justice to it—they move to the drawing-room.

'I am afraid that I must ask you to excuse me,' says Belinda, with formality. 'I always devote the next two hours to my mother-in-law.'

'Pooh! do not mention it,' replies the other cordially; 'it would be very odd if such an old soldier as I did not know how to make herself comfortable. Do not trouble to entertain me. Books? magazines? eh?' turning over the objects on the table; 'there is no fear but that I shall find something to amuse myself with!'

Nor is there. At intervals during the two hours Belinda catches sight of her from the window, bustling round the garden, pinching the few plums on the garden wall, trying to look into the windows of the next houses; hears her opening and shutting doors, pulling out drawers, etc.

For a moment a pang of apprehension crosses Mrs. Forth's mind. Can she ferret out anything? any letter? any paper? But no; a smile of pride and reassurance crosses Belinda's face. What in all her poor archives is there that might not be exposed to the eyes of the whole world? to the gimlet eyes of (if imagination could grasp the idea of such a hideous multiplication) a hundred Miss Watsons?

The two hours are gone. It is a quarter to four; the time at which she usually begins to put on hat and gloves, and saunter, deliberately blissful, towards St. Bridget's. It is clear that it is not the hour at which she will begin to saunter thither to-day. Nothing looks less like departure, more like a prolonged stay, than Miss Watson's bonnetless attitude, plunged recumbent in the Professor's chair.

'I have been having a look round,' she says cheerfully; 'I like to get the bearings of a house. There was one door locked; the Professor's sanctum, eh?'

'He likes me to keep it locked in his absence,' replies the Professor's wife icily, 'as he does not wish his books and papers to be disturbed.'

'You shall show it me by and by,' returns Miss Watson comfortably; 'after all, there is no hurry. I have half a mind to stay till the late train, and have a bit of dinner with you; nothing extra; a cutlet, a grill—whatever you have ordered for yourself.'

'It is a very slow train,' says Belinda precipitately.

'I wonder what train Rivers came down by,' continues
the other thoughtfully; 'of course he has only run down for
the day. I have been thinking it over, and the more I look
at it the more *louche* it looks!'

Belinda has not sat down; in the forlorn hope, perhaps,
that the maintenance of a standing attitude may give a less
established tone to her guest's presence. She now hastens
to the window, and begins to fidget with the blind-cord,
which pulls up and down perfectly, and needs no re
arrangement.

'It is an odd place to choose for an intrigue, too,'
continues the other reflectively. 'I have always been
told that the men are so strictly looked after; but perhaps
it was its very unlikelihood that made him pitch upon
it, eh?'

Possibly Belinda makes some answer, and that it is
drowned in the rattling of the blind, which she is feverishly
jerking up and down. Every drop of blood in her body
seems to have given its fellow rendezvous in her face. *An
intrigue !* Does he indeed come to Oxbridge for an *intrigue?*
An intrigue with whom? *An intrigue !* Is that what other
people beside Miss Watson would call it?

'I shall certainly mention it to his mother, Lady Marion,
when next I meet her,' says Miss Watson resolutely; 'I do
not think it would be acting a friend's part not to do so. I
do not actually know her, but there is a sort of connection
between us; I was at school for six months once at Brussels
with a cousin of hers, and there is no doubt that there is
something uncommonly *louche* about it.'

Judging by the frequency with which during the next
hour she repeats this phrase, it must be a favourite one of
hers. By five o'clock its recurrence has driven Belinda to
the verge of desperation. It seems to her (though that is a
figment of her guilty fancy) that there is a dreadful meaning

and significance in the unblinking look at her with which each repetition of the word is accompanied.

Five o'clock ! He has been waiting for her a whole hour beneath St. Bridget's elms, straining his eyes up the long straight walk. At length :

'I think,' she says, looking overtly at the clock—at which she has long been stealing covert glances of agonized impatience—'that if you wish to catch this train—and you would find the later one extremely tedious—you should be setting off!'

'Should I?' replies the guest indifferently. 'It is of no consequence if I am late; I am a good walker, and I enjoy running it fine; I see no use in kicking one's heels at a station!'

She ties on her bonnet, and adjusts her stone gray fringe with a maddening deliberation; stops in the middle to examine and inquire the history of a piece of *bric-à-brac*, which she had not before noticed; and finally (it is said that no Englishwoman ever knows how to take leave) expends herself in an immense farewell speech, from which the word *louche* is by no means absent. But she is gone at last. Before she is well round the corner—before there is any real security of her not returning, according to her usual custom, to pounce afresh upon her just-freed prey, Belinda has fled to her room; and—her trembling preparations hurriedly made—is speeding, like an arrow shot from a bow, to St. Bridget's. There is no leisureliness about her walk to-day; no feigned indifference, no loitering, no counterfeit indecision, as to her goal. To-day she cannot afford to play her little comedy.

Is not she an hour and a quarter late? Will she find him gone? Will he still be there? Will his patience have held out? In the whole of life, in the whole scheme of nature, there seems to her no other question in the least worth answering.

People look at her oddly, she thinks, as she passes. Hitherto she has not minded how many people she met, or who knew whither, and to what end, her steps were tending. To-day it seems as if they all glance meaningly at her, as who should read her guilty secret in her face. Until to-day she has never thought it either a secret, or guilty. An *intrigue !* That is what they call it ! She is engaged in an *intrigue ;* and by some means they know it.

As she enters St. Bridget's a couple of humble lovers meet her face to face. As they pass her they happen to expand into a grin, provoked, probably, by some ponderous joke of their own making; but she takes it to herself. They know that she is a married woman hastening to an assignation. The very birds seem to chirp, and the boughs to rustle meaningly. Well, let them !

It will be a dreadful memory to face by and by; but for the moment there is no room for any other question but the one—' Will he be there ?'

Before she reaches their trysting bench it is answered. She comes upon him so suddenly, that she has no time to tone down her pace to a decent saunter. He has seen the speed with which she was hasting towards him ; her breathlessness, her pallor, the desperate anxiety of her eyes.

There is no use in shamming to-day. But, indeed, his own condition leaves him no right to criticise hers. Perhaps he is in even worse case than she ; for she can speak, and he cannot.

'You are not gone !' she says with a gasp, such as one might give whose reprieve met him at the scaffold-foot. ' I thought you would be gone !'

For answer, he grips her two hands in his (never before in all his life has he been master, and for how few poor minutes, but of one), and looks at her with a white fixity of passion, to whose relief no words come. Even when they

are both seated on their bench—neither ever quite knows
how they reached it—it is still she who speaks ; nor when
she does so, is it to ask him to release her hands.   Perhaps
in her agitation she is not aware that they are still in his
keeping.

'It was Miss Watson!' she says, with that gasping
staccato utterance, as of one who, after long running, has not
yet recovered his wind.   'She came—she stayed four hours.
She had seen you !'

He nods his head in acquiescence.

'Yes.'

He is plainly incapable of anything beyond a monosyllable.

'She asked why you came here,' says Belinda ; the words
fluttering out on greatly quickened breath, but still with more
coherence.

'Yes ?'

One would say that he was scarcely attending, so distant
and dreamful is his voice.   He is conscious of nothing but
the warmth of those wonderful sweet hands lying in his.   If
he could realise Miss Watson at all, it would probably be
with gratitude ; for it is she virtually who has given them to
him.

'She said,' continues Belinda, trembling exceedingly, and
looking guiltily down on their locked hands, 'that you must
come here for some intrigue.'   She pauses, and then adds in
a whisper, 'She must not say that again.'

He is attending now.   There is a significance both in
her look and in her low words that cannot escape him.

'What do you mean ?' he says thickly.

'I mean,' she says, still scarcely above a whisper, 'that you
must not come here again.'

She looks away from him as she says it, unwilling,
perhaps, to see the immense consternation that her fiat will

have brought into his face; but he observes for so long a dead silence, that she grows uneasy. Has her blow killed him? or is it possible (this latter suggestion is a scarcely less bitter one than the former) that he already acquiesces?

She is just making up her mind to steal a glance at him, when he speaks, and the tone of his voice tells her that her first idea of his case was nearer the mark than her last.

'I am not to come here again?'

'No, I think not; no!'

'I am not to come to Oxbridge again?'

'No.'

'I am not to meet you again?'

'No.'

'Not anywhere?'

She bows her head, unable to speak.

'*Never?*'

She repeats the gesture.

There is such a rising strain of unbelieving agony in his voice, culminating in his last words, that speech has wholly forsaken her.

'We are to live out the rest of our lives without each other?'

Again that acquiescent motion of the head.

'And you can bear it?—of course,' correcting himself, with a bitter humility, 'why should not you? it is not much for you to bear. Well, then, I suppose I must bear it too!'

He has let go her hands, and covered his face with his own. She is free to depart. He has always obeyed her; and he is obeying her now. What is there to keep her? And yet she does not stir. Her aching eyes stare vacantly down the long straight alley. Sweet green walk! Dear solemn tower! Kind chattering birds! Good-bye! for never, never can she bear to look upon any of you again!

She stirs restlessly in her misery; and in an instant he

has dropped his shrouding hands, and is looking at her with a haggard apprehension in his eyes.

'Are you going now?'

'Not at once—not this moment,' she answers faintly; 'there is no hurry. I can stay as long as usual, if you wish.'

If he wishes! He laughs outright in his pain.

There is a long, long silence.

St. Bridget's is even emptier than its wont. Not one visitor besides themselves breaks its entire seclusion. Only the grave tower-clock deals out time's little parcels.

She speaks first.

'I do not want you to be unhappy,' she says, with a sort of sob of compassion for his spoilt youth. 'I should like you to be happy.'

'So should I. Will you show me how?'

'Oh, if I could!' she cries, in a heartwrung accent. 'Oh, if we could but be as we were before——'

She stops.

'Before Wesenstein?' he says.

The word seems to have roused him out of his lethargy of wretchedness. Ere she knows it, he has won back her hands; and before the strangeness of his eyes her own waver.

'We might almost fancy ourselves at Wesenstein, might not we?' he says, with a thrilling feverish smile; 'it was a green, quiet, woody place like this. Do you remember it well? It is odd that we have never talked of it since—is not it? Why should not we talk of it now? You sat on the grass, and I lay at your feet! Do you recollect? Yes' (with a heart-rending inflection), 'I see that you do. You gave me your hand! No! my Ice Queen, you would never have given it me! I took it and kissed it; shall I show you where I kissed it? Just there—and there—and there!' (passionately fastening his lips upon palm and fingers); 'and then—*then* I took you in my arms! Can you believe it?—

and yet I am speaking truth—once I had you in my arms, and *I let you go !—I let you go !* Would to God' (with a terrible burst of agony) 'that I had been struck dead there before I let you go !'

The storm of his passion has carried her away.

'Would to God you had !' she says, frenziedly ; and so unresisting — nay, passionately complying—she gives him that two years and a half ago foregone kiss. One kiss ! That is all. One drunk, oblivious moment, and then the awaking ! She, but now so consentingly embraced, has wrenched herself out of his arms.

'What—has—happened—to—us ?' she says, staggering away from him.

But he awakens slowlier than she.

'You have owed it me, since Wesenstein !' he cries wildly, and with a sort of triumph.

And there is silence. If indeed the loud blood dinning in their ears and hammering their temples can be so called.

'I suppose,' she says, after a while, speaking as if speech were a new weapon, and she ill at handling it, 'that—it—has been—coming to this—all along—only—I did not—see it. I suppose that no one would believe me—but I did not see it ; did you ?'

He makes no answer.

He is still lapped in the Elysium of that long-promised and at last fulfilled embrace.

'Is it possible,' she says, looking piercingly at him, and with a sombre reproach in her voice, 'that you saw all along —you knew—you thought——'

'I thought nothing !' he cries, brought back to his senses by the sternness of her tone. 'Oh, my dear, do you think so ill of me as to suppose that I was willingly leading you on ? I tell you, I thought nothing ! I only knew, that for two hours in every fortnight you allowed me to live ! you let

me into the heaven of your sweet company!—was not that
enough for me? Was I likely to look beyond?'

She has tottered to the bench, and now sits half-crouched
in the corner of it.

'I suppose,' she says, shaking her head hopelessly, 'that,
in point of fact, we have both been living upon our Sundays.'
Then after a pause, with a sort of groan, 'Oh, I thought we
might have been trusted!'

He has not sat down again, but stands before her in
guilty, miserable humility, waiting for his doom.

'I am not very sorry for you,' she says, after a while,
lifting her dull eyes to his face. 'You are mistaken if you
think that I pity you very much. You have your work—
often before now have I been jealous of it, and of the hold
it is gaining over you! This is the best thing that could
have happened to you—a sort of thing that your mother
would rejoice at—the best test after all. No more distractions! No more senseless outlay in railway journeys! it is
almost as good as being taken into partnership!'

She glances up at him at intervals, as she plants her stabs,
to see how much he can bear. He is not yet at the end of
his endurance apparently, for he still stands before her, bent-
headed and ash-white, in motionless patience.

'But will any one tell me,' she says, dropping her arms
hopelessly to her sides, and looking distractedly upwards, as
if to win a response from that sky to which we, in trouble
never answered, ever look, 'what is to become of *me?*'

Her cruelty towards himself he had taken like a man;
but her self-pity is beyond his sufferance.

'I will tell you what will become of you,' he says in a
rapid broken whisper, sitting down again beside her. 'Will
you let me tell you? Are you listening? After all, they
are only a few beggarly hours that we have had to live upon:
I do not know how we have subsisted upon such a pittance

for so long. What is there to prevent us—why should not
we——'

'Stop!' she cries hoarsely, thrusting out her spread hands,
and pushing him away from her. 'I know what you are
going to say! I know it as well as if you had already
said it.'

The terror in her eyes, the shrinking gesture, have set
him almost beside himself.

'You say that you are not at all sorry for me,' he says,
with a sort of hard sob, and I dare say you are right; but I
must ask you to—to—make a little allowance for me! I
am not in my right wits. It was unmanly of me—I had no
right to shock—to outrage you.'

'I am not in the least shocked,' she says with a slow
distinctness; '*that* shows, I suppose, to what a depth I must
have fallen. I stopped you because—because I knew that
if I let you finish your sentence I should—not—have—said
—no—to you : I—should—have—said—yes.'

She pauses, unable to fetch her breath. And yet, despite
the confession in her words of her own defeat and his
victory, something in her air holds him aloof.

'But if—' she goes on presently, fixing him with the
terrible appeal of her eyes, while her face grows sharp and
thin—'if you are—what I have always thought you—if I
know you right, you—will—never—finish it!'

There is a dead dead silence ; she still holding him with
that look, until she knows that in her dreary battle she has
vanquished.

'And now,' she says with a tearless decision, 'go! I did
not tell the truth when I said I was not sorry for you! Oh,
I *am* sorry! I AM! There! go!—what is the use of crying?
I hate to see a man cry! God bless you! God be with
you! Go!'

And he, obedient, goes.

PERIOD IV.

These violent delights have violent ends.

CHAPTER I.

'Unser Sommer ist nur ein grün-angestrichener Winter.'

THE lives of the Professor, of Mrs. Forth, of Sarah—of all those with whom we have had any concern—are poorer by a full year than when we left them. The 'Fragments of Menander' have been given to the world; and as certainly not less than three people have read them, they may be said to have been a success. So much so, at all events, as to encourage the Professor to delve and grub in the entrails of the Fathers for new Fragments. For the present, however, he has to delve and grub alone. For the present, his secretary has broken down; for the present the pack-horse has sunk down beneath its pack. Doubtless it will soon be set on its legs again, and enabled to resume it; but, for the present, its back is unladen, and it is turned out to grass. Months of unlightened, hopeless, joyless labour! Her only wonder in looking back afterwards upon them is that they did not sooner work their inevitable effect. Months of unrelenting application, of chest-contracting bending over manuscript and proof; of entire absence of exercise and relaxation—for of her own will she has forsworn both. Thought is deader, memory fainter—and for what object but to kill both does she now live?—in the exhaustion consequent on overwork. Why and for whom should she spare herself? She will go until she drops. And the Professor, delighted to acquiesce unquestioningly in a metamorphosis so greatly to his advantage, always incurious as to interests that lie out of his own beat, and with the professed invalid's radical incredulity as to the possibility of any one else being either sick or weary, drives his willing horse merrily along, until one fine day she falls down between the shafts. How glad she is when the breakdown comes ! How intensely she prays that it may be the final one ! But it is not so. By whatever door Mrs. Forth is to leave this world, it is certainly not by that of the entire derangement of the nervous system, for which attentive doctors unanimously prescribe immediate change, idleness, pleasure. The Professor is always angry with any one for being ill; but against a sickness which involves undone work, expensive medicine, and a costly move, his indignation is too deep for words. He is scarcely more angry with her, however, for falling sick, than she is with herself for recovering. For as long as possible she has discredited it. Her physic bottles vex him hardly more than do her returning appetite, restored slumber, waxing flesh, and waning fever, herself. She had wished to die; and he, since she has turned out so unhealthy, would not be sorry to be rid of her. And so she lives; lives to put him to the expense of a migration to the English Lakes. He seems unable to shake off the idea that she has done it on purpose.

* * * * *

It has been as usual a wet morning, and to the bounds of the Lowood Hotel on Windermere all its impatient guests have been confined. Now that afternoon has come, it has brought with it a sort of doubtful fairness; more a cessation of storm than anything approaching positive fine weather. Wray's Castle, lifting its gray towers from its woods exactly opposite, has come into sight again. The Langdale Pikes have just shaken the rain-clouds off their notchy crests; but they hang poised above them, ready at once to descend and clip them. They have still fast hold of Wetherlam, though their lucent lightness shows that the sun is just behind them, and will presently drive his brave bright car over their vaporous bodies. It is very clear, from the high-flung windows of a sitting-room on the second floor, and also from the fact of its being a sitting-room at all, firstly that Professor Forth is not in it, and secondly that it is not his. Since his wife's sister and grandmother have thought it necessary to give her the meeting here, he has no objection to her taking advantage of their salon, since he is quite unequal to the expense of providing her with one of her own.

In a horse-hair arm-chair of that peculiar lodging-house build which pinions the arms and forces the head forward, sits Mrs. Churchill, placidly watching an unlading coach. At a certain somewhat early period of old age, given an easy temper and an entire absence of feeling, a person often appears for a few years to stand stationary. Since we last saw her, Mrs. Churchill has stood stationary. Not one more has been added to the number of her few wrinkles, and her old dimple still goes and comes with her agreeable smile. On the sofa, by right of her invalidhood, Belinda is lying, with a crop head of little curls; and out of the window not occupied by Mrs. Churchill, Sarah is hanging most of her body, alternately watching with feverish interest, and looking back over her own shoulder to chronicle the doings of the family who occupy the floor beneath them, and who, happily for her, have a balcony upon which they now and then emerge.

'There are two brothers, and two sisters, and a wife,' cries she animatedly. 'I cannot make out to whom the wife belongs; none of them seem to care much about her!'

'Perhaps she had money,' rejoins Mrs. Churchill. 'Dear

me !' returning to the contemplation of her coach, 'what a
load for those poor horses, and how they are smoking !'

'They are all out on the balcony now,' says Sarah, delighted ; 'come quick, Belinda, and look !'

'I will take your word for it,' replies Belinda lazily.

'It makes one quite wretched to see such cruelty !' says
Mrs. Churchill, in a thoroughly comfortable voice, pursuing
her own subject.

'They have been playing battledore and shuttlecock,'
says Sarah narratively. 'I wish we had a battledore and
shuttlecock.'

'Whom would you expect to play with you ?' asks her
grandmother drily ; 'the Professor, or me ?'

'They have dropped the shuttlecock into the road,'
continues Sarah narratively, and in a tone of breathless
interest. 'There is another man with them now ; he cannot
be a third brother ; they are betting him a shilling that he
will not climb over the balcony and swarm down the iron leg
to fetch it. What a fool he will be if he does ! Surely I
have seen him before somewhere ! I wish he would look
up. Why, granny ! Belinda ! granny !—it is—it must be—
young Bellairs !'

This time both obey her summons ; but whether it be
that their footsteps make more noise than they are aware of,
or for whatever other reason, some of the party below choose
this unfortunate moment to look up ; and in a second they
have all three slunk shamefacedly back again.

'Young Bellairs ! Poor young Bellairs !' cries Sarah,
throwing herself into a chair, and chuckling. 'Young
Bellairs, and the dinghey ! do you remember, Belinda ?'

(It is not very likely that Belinda has forgotten.)

'I wonder is there a dinghey here that I could take him
out in ?' says Miss Churchill thoughtfully. 'Granny, are
you aware that a dinghey only holds two ? but if you insist

upon it, in the interests of propriety, we will squeeze you in as well.'

Mrs. Churchill laughs.

'I need not decide at once, need I?' says she, entering into the joke; 'and as the dinghey is not here, and the carriage is, we may as well be setting off on our drive.'

'He will see me get in!' cries Sarah, skipping to the glass, and adjusting her hat; 'they watch us quite as much as we watch them. Well, let him! I flatter myself that I can get into a carriage with any woman in England!'

They are gone (not, however, before Miss Churchill has once again put in her head to say urgently, 'Mind that you keep a good look-out upon them!'), and Belinda has the sitting-room and all the horse-hair chairs to herself. Perhaps the better to comply with her sister's exhortations, she abandons the sofa, and drawing up her grandmother's chair yet closer to the window, looks dreamily out on the lake, from which the hotel is parted only by the road, a quickset hedge, and a strip of grass. Upon the lower foreground hills opposite—so dark a second ago—what a nation of sunbeams has swooped! and now, as quickly they are gone again, and only the lawn that slopes to the water has become dazzling green as any chrysoprase.

If she had died as she wished, she would not have seen that chrysoprase-green; nor the masterless wavelets sucking in riot in among the stakes of the little pier; nor the small white yacht curtseying and congeeing along over them. Is it worth while to have kept alive, in order to be looking at them here—alone?

What a noise the family below are making? What *can* they be doing? Surely they must be engaged in some pastime more violent than battledore and shuttlecock. They sound as if they were throwing chairs at each other. How plainly she can distinguish Bellairs' voice.

It was at St. Ursula's party that she first heard that voice.
It was in answer to some sentence addressed to her by that
voice, that her own suddenly broke down ; it was while that
voice was still in her ears that she caught sight once again
of him who made her inattentive to all voices ! She moves
uneasily in her chair. She wishes that Bellairs had not
come.

What a sudden spurt of daring glory on the stern necks
of the Langdale Pikes ! She can see their hollow deep clefts,
and their scattered verdure, broken through by green rock-
masses. She discovers a waterfall hanging unmoving on
the mountain flank. How they are giving up their gray
secrets to the sun ! it is cruel to be looking at them all
alone ! to have to look now and for ever at all fair sights
alone! She should be used to the thought by now, surely.
What is it that is giving it such new and pricking life to-day ?
Is it Bellairs' voice ? She will hear it less, perhaps, if she
have some occupation to distract her.

She takes up the advertisement-sheet of the *Times,* lying
near her, on the floor, and throws her eyes over the Births,
Deaths, and Marriages.

For months she has been unable to read the Obituary
without envying every one of the dead people recorded in
it : the old man gently extinguished at eighty ; the deeply-
mourned wife, torn away in her prime ; the strong man
violently perishing in flood or field ; the tiny sister-children
swept away within two days of each other by the hot fever.
There is not one among them all that she does not envy !
They are out of it ! They have done with it ! done with
the tangle, done with the heart-break, done with the strife !
She envies them now. And through them all she still hears
plainly the voice of Bellairs.

Thank Heaven, however, she will not hear it any more
for the present. He has gone out. Surely that is he

sauntering down to the little pier, with a smart girl in a red cotton gown—a red cotton gown that but now incarnadined the balcony beneath Mrs. Forth.

He is unfastening a little boat; he is helping his companion in! Belinda laughs aloud. Some one has been too quick for Sarah! Some one has stepped down into the dinghey before her!

The incident gives a lighter turn to her meditations, and she drops the obituary, and follows with her eyes the little boat and its two occupants, with as eager an attention as her sister might have given it, until it becomes a speck upon the water. She laughs again. There is a sound of wheels. Is it her grandmother and Sarah returning? She longs for them to come back, to have the pleasure of telling them. She leans her charming cropped head out of the window. No! it is a coach changing horses; next a *char-à-banc* disgorging its stiff-legged load; and now, for variety of interest, a steamer is coming churning up to the little pier. Will any one get out of it? Any one to form a new element at the *table-d'hôte* to-night, and be speculated about as one speculates upon the lives and habits of those with whom an hotel life brings one into brief and jostling contact? The steamer is crowded, black with thick-packed heads. But it seems as if no one were minded to alight from her.

Yes, one man has landed; a man now crossing the pier with a knapsack on his back; a pedestrian tourist, obviously. Very likely an Oxbridge man, with a Plato in his wallet, come to woo philosophy in the heart of the hills. If he is so, perhaps she may know him—by sight at all events. She rubs her eyes. What tricks they play one! Do they see ill, or is there a little something in the man's gait that might remind her of—but no! it is the sight of Bellairs, and the memories he has roused, that have put such an insanity into her head. Perhaps sickness has left her vision weak and deceptive. He is drawing nearer—very near, past the strip of grass, through the wicket, across the road. She has been thrusting her head out of window to have a nearer view, and the better to correct her delusion. But suddenly she draws it in again, and with a small, choked cry, falls back in the horse-hair chair. It is not corrected! It is confirmed, and turned into truth and certainty. For a few moments she lies stock-still. Has her face caught from Wetherlam and the Pikes some of their stormy illumination? If she had died, she would not have seen him crossing that pier, treading that path, unlatching that wicket-gate!

It has been hitherto only in her dreams that he has ever walked towards her. She is glad—oh, glad—that she did not die! And what has brought him hither? Is it possible that he has heard of her presence here, and, unable any longer to endure those torments which had so nearly laid her low, has fled hither in madness to rejoin her? But in a second she has exonerated him from the suspicion. She has told him to go, and he had gone; and she knows him well enough to feel sure that, without her bidding—cost him what it might—he would not return. It is, then, an accident! a happy, most happy accident! What pleasant accidents can and may happen! For an accident no one can be blamed. For an accident no one's conscience need smite them. All the consequences of an accident may be taken with an easy mind.

Her eyes stray away towards the high mountains, but once again they are grasped so close in the clouds' moist arms, that not a glimpse of crest or ridge is to be caught. Are not they tired of their centenary—nay, æon-long fight with the vapours? Worsted, worsting, will there never be an end to it? It is like her fight with her own heart. Vapours, sunbeams, waterfalls; to-morrow—to-morrow she will be looking at you not alone. To-morrow! But will he be still here to-morrow? Unless she give him leave to stay (and how dare she give that leave?) may not he be off before day-dawn?

By the noise below her window, she knows that another coach has driven up, and is changing horses. A panic seizes her. What security has she that he may not have halted here for only ten minutes, and be going on by it? She springs to her trembling legs, and returning to the window again, looks out, but this time in hiding behind the curtain. Two or three of the passengers have got down, and are beginning to climb back into their places again. Some luggage is being hauled from the roof. She scans narrowly the crowded travellers, and then draws a long breath. There is not one among them that bears the most fugitive resemblance to him. She is reprieved. He will be here, at all events, till to-morrow. He will dine, almost certainly, at the *table-d'hôte.*

A hot, excited smile breaks over her face. She will have the advantage over him. She will expect to see him; and he will not expect to see her. Will the shock be too much for him? Will he be betrayed by its suddenness into any too evident and overt emotion? But no! He is a man, now; strong and self-contained. How much older he has grown to look! Even her one cursory glance has told her that. A pang of regret for that passionate gone boyhood, which was so absolutely hers, contracts her heart. No! he will show no emotion. Perhaps he will turn a shade paler. As for her, she will not be pale, neither red.

Her thought breaks off abruptly, dispersed and banished by a knock at the door. Ere she can cry 'Come in!' forestalling her permission of admittance, one of the heated and hurried hotel waiters, chronically rushing from Sunday morning to Saturday night, has entered—has deposited a note before her, and has disappeared ere she has time to

put any question as to its source and origin. Not that there
is much need for such, although only twice before in all her
life has she seen that handwriting. A mixed memory of the
two former occasions rushes storming back upon her mind; a
memory of the misery of that early summer morning in
Dresden; of the hell of that Folkstone winter evening. She
has come in for a good deal of misery in her day. She looks
in procrastination at the device on the seal—it is sealed—and
at the address. Surely his handwriting, too, is changed;
more virile, steadier, less emotional. She holds the note between her two palms (how lately he has held it in his !) in a
trembling luxury of delay. It is only the recollection of how
soon, how immediately, how at once, her solitude may be
put an end to by the return of her sister and grandmother,
that at length decides her to open it. What can he have to
say to her? Not much, whatever it is. It will not take her
long to read.

'I have just seen your name in the Visitors' Book;
believe me, it is by a pure accident that I am here; must I
go? If I do not see you at the *table-d'hôte*, I shall understand that I must.

'D. R.'

Long after she has mastered its contents—surely not
difficult of comprehension—she remains staring at the page
with wide dull eyes : a feeling of blankest disappointment at
her heart. And yet, had she expected him, in writing, on a
paper committed to a careless hand—a paper that might
easily go astray, or be lost—to break out into compromising,
culpable endearments? She would be outraged by the
suggestion. But oh ! it is cruel, *cruel* of him to have thrust
the weight of the decision upon her; to have taken their
meeting out of the province of accident into which she had
joyfully recognised it as having fallen !

Since he has forced choice upon her, there is but one
way in which she can choose. He must have known it!
He must have done it on purpose! Honourable of him?
Perhaps! Her mind gives a frigid assent. But oh, cold,
cold, and most cruel! His very face had told her that he
was changed. He has grown wise at last. Well, he shall
never know that she was not as wise as he.

She has crumpled the paper angrily in her hand, and
begun to walk agitatedly up and down the room, pressing and
kneading it with her fevered fingers. Then her mood changes,
and she stops and anxiously smooths out the letter again.
Perhaps she is wronging him. Perhaps in the first stun of
that surprise he has scarcely known what he wrote; has not
perceived the drift of his own words. Perhaps, on a closer
examination, she may find, by the tremulousness of his
characters, that he had not his wits about him. But no.
There is no tremulousness. Strong and decided is each up
and down stroke. The man who penned that note was
obviously in fullest possession of his intellect and mastery
over his nerves. She is still poring over the few matter-of-
fact words, vainly trying to wrench them into a sense that
they cannot bear, when a high, light laugh, which cannot be
ascribed to any one but Miss Churchill, heard on the landing
outside, makes her, in guilty haste, thrust the document into
her pocket. It is only just in time; for there is always a
sort of whirlwind suddenness about Sarah's entries.

'Well!' cries she, in high excitement, 'have you kept a
good look-out, as I told you? Has he discovered that I am
here? Where is he? what has he been doing?'

It is a proof how far Mrs. Forth's thoughts have been
straying from the young gentleman in question, that at first
she looks back at her sister in blank stupidity, not understanding to what or whom she alludes.

'Who?' she says thickly; 'what?—Oh!' (with a forced

laugh; comprehension coming tardily back), 'of course! but I have bad news for you: he went out at once in a *dinghey* —I do not think they call them *dingheys* here—but at all events in a little cockboat—with the girl in red.'

'Did he?' replies Sarah, stimulating the first symptoms of a swoon, and falling in a heap upon the sofa; 'then, granny, cut my stay-laces, and burn every goose-quill you can find in the room under my nose; for there is nothing left me but to faint!'

CHAPTER II.

THE Professor's room, as well as Belinda's own, is at the top of the house. Economy, as is well known, has to be sought in hotels by climbing; and the Professor has pursued her to the leads.

At their first coming, indeed, the numerous flights of stairs to be surmounted ere attaining her sloped roof and her truckle bed, had proved a severe tax upon Mrs. Forth's enfeebled strength; but use and returning health have made them easy. At all events, Belinda does not now think twice about climbing them, even if no absolute necessity prompt the ascent. Is it absolute necessity that, half an hour after Sarah's return, finds her first faintly knocking, and then looking uncertainly into her husband's room?

'Who is there? who is keeping the door open, and creating a draught? Pray shut it at once!' cries a crabbed voice from the interior.

She complies by entering. Owing to the confined space allotted to him, the Professor has to use some nicety of management in the disposition of his property—a disposition which entails the entire going to the wall of his toilette arrangements. Both bed and floor are strewn with folios and MS., which are piled, to the exclusion of basin and ewer, even upon the cramped washhand-stand.

Upon the one chair the occupant of the attic is seated : a

fur-coat wrapped about his thin figure, a skull-cap on his head, his feet aloft upon a hot water bottle, a writing-case upon his meagre knees and an ink-horn in his left hand.

'Pray be careful where you step!' he says sharply, looking up and becoming aware of the tall, fair presence that has enriched his neighbourhood. 'Do not you see that you are treading upon Tertullian?'

She had not seen it; but she at once corrects her error.

'I believe that I expressed a wish not to be intruded upon this afternoon,' he continues, since she does not at once speak or explain her entrance; 'owing to having to support the whole weight of my work single-handed' (with a resentful glance at her idle and obviously convalescent beauty), 'I am very much pressed for time. No doubt you have some good reason to give for infringing my injunctions.'

'I thought that you might be surprised if you did not see me at the *table-d'hôte*,' replies she coldly; 'so I came to tell you that I do not mean to appear at it to-night, and to ask whether you have any objection to my staying away?'

'Is it possible that you are threatened with a return of indisposition?' he asks, with a sudden, quick look of peevish anxiety.

She shakes her head, smiling suddenly and bitterly. It is so apparent that his solicitude is due, not to care for her health, but to apprehension of a new doctor's bill.

'Thanks, no.'

'You appear to be unaccountably out of breath,' he says, in a vexed voice.

'Not more than any one must be, in climbing to this cock-loft,' replies she sullenly.

Perhaps his examination of her face has reassured him as to her soundness, for once more he dips his pen into the ink-horn.

'You have not answered my question,' says she brusquely,

perceiving in him a deliberate intention of henceforth ignoring her.

He makes a gesture of annoyed impatience.

'It scarcely appeared to me to require an answer; I suppose you gave notice this morning to the manager of your intention to be absent?'

'No, I did not.'

'Then of course it is out of the question; according to the rules of the hotel, every meal not expressly countermanded is charged for; and I am really not in a position to countenance such irrational waste.'

At the contempt and churlishness of his tone, her cheek burns.

'It would be no waste if I ordered nothing instead,' she answers, doggedly; 'and I am more than willing to fast.'

'And incur the risk of a relapse?' cries he, in hasty displeasure. 'I must imperatively forbid your exposing yourself to any such hazard!'

'I could have a cup of tea in granny's sitting-room; I am sure that she would not grudge me one.'

'I request that you will do nothing of the kind,' rejoins he, nettled, whether at his interrupted work, or at the accent, which she has taken small pains to render slight, laid by her upon the personal pronoun. 'Your grandmother is, of course, mistress of her own actions; but since it is a well-known fact, that if you once indulge in such senseless luxuries as a private sitting-room, and meals served separately, the rate of charges in your case is instantly and exorbitantly increased, I must beg you at least to conform to the ordinary rules of the house.'

He is so surprised by the entire silence in which she accepts his fiat, that he looks up irritatedly at her, standing in sullen, motionless loveliness beside him; looks up to find her regarding him with a smile hard to qualify.

'It is by your express wish, then, that I dine,' she says, with a low emphasis; 'you *insist* upon my dining.'

'I see no reason for an arbitrary departure from your usual habits,' replies he, with ill-humour; 'you are obviously perfectly restored to your normal state of health ; any one,' with a recurrence of that streak of resentment, 'would be surprised now to learn that you were regarded as an invalid ; there is nothing that gains upon a person more, by indulgence in them, than valetudinarian fancies.'

The singular smile still stays, as it were stereotyped upon her features.

'You speak from experience ?' she says, in a tone of quiet insolence.

The colour mounts to his parched face.

'You are implying,' he says, with deliberate anger, 'as you have frequently and offensively implied before, that I am a *malade imaginaire.*'

She shrugs her shoulders carelessly.

'I do not think—I have never thought—that you are nearly so ill as you imagine yourself to be.'

'Do not you ?' he answers. 'Possibly some day you may be undeceived.'

There is such a pregnant weight of solemn meaning in his look and words, that, for a moment, she glances at him, staggered and half-frightened ; he waving her, in a displeasure too deep for further speech, to the door. But the impression does not last beyond the first flight of stairs.

'Pooh !' she says, reaching the landing, 'he will see us all out !'

*   *   *   *   *

The *table-d'hôte* bell has rung, and, answering its call, the visitors at the Lowood Hotel have poured into the large, light dining-room, and quickly filled up the two long tables, where, as the season advances to its height, elbow-room be-

comes daily scarcer. The established visitors have made their
way to their habitual places, and the new ones been ushered
to theirs. The oldest inhabitant, who always says grace,
has said it, and the landlord is ladling out the soup. Belinda
is in her usual seat, between her husband and her sister.
It is a situation of her own choosing—as far as regards her
sister, at least. The Professor is not a good person to
depend upon for general conversation through a long dinner;
the almost insoluble problem of how to obtain his full
pennyworth—how to eat so much as to ensure that no
extortionate profit shall accrue from him to the proprietors
of the hotel, and yet how to eat so little and so lightly as
not to alarm his coy and skittish digestion—keeping him
for the most part wholly silent. But Sarah is royally
indifferent as to what pecuniary advantage may be derived
from her, and has no more consciousness of digestion than
an emu; so, upon her sprightly comments on their fellow-
diners, Belinda has usually relied to drag her through the
ennui of the long and weary courses.

To-day she lends them but an abstracted ear. Though
she has entered and taken her place without once looking
up, she yet knows at once that for her the full room is
empty. Gradually she allows her eyes to steal round a
glance, in confirmation of that of which she is already sure.
Here are the forms and faces that a week's fellow-eating has
made rather more familiar to her than her own. Here are
the usual *vis-à-vis*, the stockbroking family: jocose red
father, aiming side hits of well-meant pleasantry at herself
and her sister; full-blown, hearty mother; elaborately
elegant daughter. At the far end of the board a few insignificant novelties. That is all! It is true that he may be
placed at the other table, to which her back is turned; but
this, a guilty consciousness prevents her moving her head to
ascertain. Were he there, however, it is certain that he would

be seen by Sarah, who is constantly throwing restless glances
over her shoulder, in pursuit of the object of her own interest.

'Here they come!' she cries, jogging her sister's elbow;
'here they all come!—all but the girl in red! all but
Bellairs! Is it possible that they can be out in the dinghey
still? I shall complain to the manager!'

Belinda smiles faintly. The soup-plates are vanishing.
It is evident that *he* is not coming. Her compromising
concession has been made in vain. It was her part to shun
him; and she has forced him to shun her.

Probably she will never now have an opportunity of
exculpating herself, even to the extent of making her lame
explanation of the way in which it came about.

How these people opposite stare!

She has begun desperately to fan herself; but the Professor at once requests her to stop, as the current of air
produced by her fan makes him sneeze.

'He must have upset her, and drowned her!' says Sarah,
in her sister's ear. 'I hope he has; it would serve her quite
right!—*God bless my soul!*'

This last ejaculation is uttered in a key differing so widely
from the cold-blooded calm of her former aspirations, that
Belinda gives an involuntary start—a start that may or may
not be observed by him who has just quietly entered the
room, and is having a reversed chair at the other table obse-
quiously set on its legs for him.

'Did you know that he was here?' asks Sarah, very low.

But Belinda does not answer. A mad relief—a lunatic
joy is choking her throat.

'Did you?' repeats the other urgently; 'is it possible——'

'Do you think that I sent for him?' says Belinda, in a
suffocating whisper. 'How can I help his being here?'

There is so much of the lion-at-bay in her lightning eyes
that Sarah wisely desists from further questioning.

'It is an odd coincidence that they should both have turned up again on the same day,' she says; her mind reverting to the truant Bellairs.

Happily for Belinda, that culprit now appears on the scene, shortly followed by his companion in guilt; and for the rest of dinner Miss Churchill's conversation becomes an indignant recitative, a running commentary upon their actions.

'I never saw such a brazen pair in my life! how little he thinks that I can see him! Very odd that he has not yet caught my eye! Ah! there, he sees me! "How do you do? how do you do?" Extraordinary! he has not turned a shade paler; he must have gone to the devil altogether. They are *so* much interested : they are asking who we are, and whether we are any relation to the Duke of Marlborough. He is swaggering about us, and promising to introduce us after dinner. If he dares!'

Belinda is well content to allow the stream of soliloquy beside her to flow on unchecked. A silent husband—ever tussling with his economico-sanitary problem; a self-absorbed sister; what better neighbours could she wish for? Even the family opposite, whose notice had before annoyed her, immersed in good cheer, have forgotten her. She can lean back unnoticed, and sun herself in the feeling—not recognised nor formulated enough to constitute a reflection —that though he is lost to her sight, so is she assuredly not to his. He is probably wondering why her hair is cut short.

Does he think it an improvement? Possibly it may appear to him in a high degree disfiguring. It is the first time that the question of the becomingness or unbecomingness of her crop-head has presented itself to Mrs. Forth's mind. She is not one of those happy women whose beauty is *per se*, and to themselves as good, for pleasure and profit, as an estate in the Three per Cents. She has never cared

for it except as it affected him. Is she much disfigured?
She lifts one hand and passes it over her shining tendrils,
as if to obtain an answer by touch. In so doing, and in
consequence of the small space allotted to each diner,
her lifted elbow comes into momentary contact with her
husband's sleeve.

'I beg your pardon!' she says, starting.

No galvanic shock sent with uncomfortable sense of dislo-
cation along bone and joint could have brought her down
more suddenly from that vision-world through which, happy
and crop-headed, she has, during three courses, been walking.

'You eat nothing!' says the Professor, glancing up-
braidingly at her empty plate, and contrasting resentfully in
his mind his own heroic efforts with her supine and culpable
abstinence; 'it is a mere farce—a throwing away of money
—to set good food before you!'

'It would be a worse throwing away of it, if I were to
gorge myself when I was not hungry,' replies she surlily;
and with that their conjugal dialogue ends.

The dinner, too, has ended by and by. The oldest
inhabitant has given vent to his second grace; and there is
a rustling and streaming through the passage into the hall,
and out upon grass-plat and pier.

Usually the Churchill party do not participate in this
latter outward movement. To watch the humours of the
company from the privacy of their sitting-room window has,
on previous evenings, seemed to them better than mingling
with them. But to-night Belinda lingers. She *must* speak
to him. In justice to herself, to him, to her husband even,
she must speak to him. It would be impossible to leave him
in that misapprehension about her, under which he must
necessarily now be lying.

'Are you going out?' asks Sarah, with a sharp look in
her sister's agitated face. 'So will I. She has actually had

the bad taste to whip him off to their balcony again. After all, they were not in the least anxious to be introduced to us. Pr—r!' (shivering), 'it is cold; I will go and fetch my little French hood; if *that* will not bring him down, nothing will!'

She runs off, and Belinda, with as composed an air as she can muster, strolls towards the pier, and, leaning her arms upon the rail, looks down into the troubled lake water. It is a chill and unsummerlike night; raw-aired and boisterous. The clouds hug the hills and smother the struggling moon. Many people, feeling the nipping breeze, have hastened indoors again. Others come out, fortified by Newmarket coats or fur capes. How *can* they find it cold? To her it seems to be torrid. Her eyes are fixed upon the angry little waves, sucking, and fighting, and dashing themselves against jetty and shore; and the steps of the promenading, cigarette-smoking, chatting idlers, pass to and fro behind her. They do not all pass her. Two feet pause hesitatingly beside her.

'Did you get my note?'

His face may be older than it was, and his handwriting steadier, but at all events his voice trembles quite as much as ever it did. What sense is there in being glad at that? And yet she *is* glad.

'Yes,' she answers whisperingly, neither looking up, nor expressing any surprise at his presence, nor at his omitting all the forms of conventional greeting; 'but you must not draw any inference from my being here.'

She pauses; but, except that she hears his quick breathing beside her, he may be gone : in so entire a silence does he await her explanation.

'My—my—Mr. Forth insisted upon my dining,' she says, growing burning red at what she feels must appear the wretched inadequacy of this explanation. 'It—it—is a very prosaic reason,' breaking into a nervous laugh, 'but he did not wish my dinner to be wasted!'

Still silence. Has he nothing to say? not even one poor word of pleasure? Probably he is nerving himself up to exact an answer to that question of his, which she has virtually never answered. Probably he is going—oh, barbarous!—to throw the decision again upon her. But perhaps he has learned, within the last hour, to let sleeping dogs lie. At all events, when his speech comes, it is not the one she had dreaded to hear.

'You have been ill?'

'You judge by my hair, I suppose,' replies she, laughing again; 'otherwise, as Mr. Forth says, it would certainly never occur to any one that I was an invalid.'

It is the second time within two minutes that she has quoted her husband. Does she feel a sort of chaperonage in his very name? At that name a slight shudder passes over Rivers' frame.

'But you have been ill?'

'Nothing interesting,' she says, with a cynical shrug; 'no brain fever, or charming hectic. I simply—a very common complaint in Oxbridge, you know—broke down from overwork. I always tell every one I broke down from overwork; it sounds so well.'

In his ears, possibly, it does not sound so well.

'*Overwork!*' he repeats, shocked. 'Has your—who has been overworking you?'

'Nobody; I myself!' replies she, quoting Desdemona, and with about as much truth in her speech as there was in that of the Moor's wife. How loud and restless is the waves' wash beneath them! 'And you?' she says softly; 'how has it been with you? At all events,' with a melancholy smile, 'however hard you may have been working, *you* have not broken down!'

'No,' he answers, with a sort of humility, as if he were ashamed of having to make the admission; 'I have not broken down.'

'It would take a great deal to break *you* down,' she says, glancing at him with a sort of reproach for his health and vigour; 'and yet, in point of fact, men die more easily than women; you die when you do not want to die, and we cannot die when we wish: that is about the state of the case in this best of all possible worlds.'

She has raised herself from her bent posture, and has lifted that face, whose character seems to be changed and gentled by her babyish hair, to the sky. What strange clouds, like giant curls and columns of sacrificial smoke from the altar of some dark God! and the bright gibbous moon shouldering her way through a sullen pile before she can reach a clear sky space, and make the dark mere chastely splendid. How few people are left upon the pier! By what right is she left? They have closed the windows of her grandmother's sitting-room. She can see the silhouette of Mrs. Churchill's cap upon the blind. Why is not her own silhouette there too? Alas! in five minutes it must be!

'Do you wish to die?' he says, in a shaken, low voice.

(Can this wonder desire that the world should be made dark by her extinction?)

'Yes,' she answers dreamily. 'No—yes—on condition that I might come back if I found it even worse than this; and *you?*' looking at him with a moonlit wavering smile— 'but no; you would not leave your "rabble," and your patent. By the by, how is the patent? is it taken out yet?'

'The *patent!*' he cries, breaking into a sudden, unsteady, tender laugh; 'is it possible that you remember about the patent?'

'Do I remember it?' returns she, in a kind of scorn; 'then, if *I* had taken out a patent, you would not have remembered it?'

'It is an old story now,' he answers, still with that tremulous, unglad laugh; 'it was taken out some months ago. Our firm has adopted it with success; others have followed their example, and——'

'And you are on the highroad to fortune,' interrupts she, with a quivering lip; 'to the gilt coach and the Lord Mayor's gown. I have always told you that you would end by being Lord Mayor! Yes,' dragging out the slow syllables one after another, 'on the highroad to fortune.'

'On the highroad to fortune!' repeats he after her, with something not unlike a sob in his voice; 'so you used to tell me at Oxbridge; is it such a good joke that it is worth repeating?'

There is not a soul remaining on the pier beside themselves. Even Mrs. Churchill's shadow has disappeared from the blind. It is clear that she has had the fire lit, and has drawn up her chair to it. Has no one, then, a glance for the black and silver water? for these great cloud-bulks, and this victorious maiden moon? Not a soul! It is all their own, his and hers! all the night's cold steely splendour! all the wind's wintry song, and the waves' loud lap! Surely their voices are no sadder than his—his, with that sob in it! How easily she could sob too! Perhaps her spirits are weakened by recent sickness.

'There is no pleasing you!' she says, half hysterically; 'what would you have?'

'What would I have?' cries a high, matter-of-fact voice, striking suddenly in; 'why I would have a warming-pan, and a fur coat, and some mulled claret: that is what I would have. Oh, it is you, is it?' with a very slight and cursory recognition of Mrs. Forth's companion. 'Belinda, are you quite out of your senses?'

There is something in Miss Churchill's tone, and in the decision of the way in which she has put her arm under her sister's, and is leading her away, that it would require a clearer conscience than Belinda's to resist.

'I—I—was waiting for you,' she stammers.

'And David was helping you? Well'—shrugging her shoulders, and relapsing into a lighter tone—'I was detained; he waylaid me on the landing; I never knew that little *capote* fail. He has been telling me about them; she plays the banjo: that seems the great feature! I will play the banjo too!'

CHAPTER III.

ALTHOUGH there may be something in Professor Forth's remark that no one, not let into the secret, could now conjecture his wife's invalidhood, yet, by right of that invalidhood, she has hitherto been excluded from the longer excursions made by her grandmother and sister in the neighbourhood, as being too severe a tax upon her not yet completely restored powers. But on the morning succeeding her lake-side colloquy, Mrs. Forth is, it appears, expected to resume the habits of health.

'I must request your kind chaperonage,' says Miss Churchill, running to meet her sister, as that sister enters Mrs. Churchill's sitting-room after breakfast, and lifting a cheek as fresh and sweet as soap and water, health and jollity, can make it to hers. 'Granny has struck work, as she has frequently done before: she has always in her heart hated the picturesque, and to-day I have induced her to own it; eh, granny? As for me, for reasons best known to myself, I am going to spend a long and happy day at Coniston; and I see no earthly reason why you should not accompany me.'

By the extreme positiveness of her tone, and determination of her eye, it may be inferred that Sarah looks for a demurrer to this proposition. If such comes, it comes in silence.

'You had much better say "yes,"' pursues Miss Churchill warmly; 'if you do not, and if you continue to look as robust as you do now, you will certainly be tied by the leg again to Menander before you can draw breath!'

Belinda laughs, a little unnaturally.

'That shows how little you know about it; Menander has been three months before the public.'

'Well, no doubt he has left plenty of little brothers behind him,' rejoins Sarah lightly; 'what do you say?'

'Do you think it is safe to venture?' replies Belinda, walking to the window, and pointing in faint objection to the blind vapours that feel about the mountain-crests; 'do not you think that the weather looks rather uncertain?'

'Does it ever look anything else?' retorts Sarah drily. 'Come, quick! "yes" or "no"?'

'I will ask Mr. Forth if he can spare me,' says Belinda reluctantly, leaving the room with lagging steps.

'Tell him that he shall be put to no expense; that you shall not even pay the turnpikes,' cries Sarah saucily after her.

She returns presently with still more lagging steps.

'Well?'

'He has no objection,' answers Mrs. Forth slackly, sitting down, and letting her arms drop depressedly beside her.

'You tried to make him forbid you, and he would not,' cries Sarah sharply, and with a pungent laugh.

'You are really too clever,' replies Belinda, reddening, and with a petulance which shows that this shaft has gone home; 'you have got your own way; you always get your own way. I am going with you; let us hear no more about it.'

The carriage is at the door, and a few such idlers as mostly watch the arrival and departure of each coming and

going vehicle, hang about it. Sarah is already seated, and
is exchanging such chastened and diluted gallantries as the
publicity of the situation will admit, with some one hanging
over the balcony overhead. Belinda has purposely loitered
over her dressing, in the hope that some opportune mountain storm may even yet intervene to hinder the execution
of the, to her, so distasteful project.

But in vain. The perverse and hostile sky is, all too
obviously, clearing. As she issues from the hall, she glances
furtively to right and left. Yes, he is here! His voice,
which but for Sarah's manœuvring might have been all day
in her happy ears, is addressing her.

'You are going out?'

(Do they all hear, as plainly as she does, the blank
disappointment and discomfiture of his tone?)

'Yes,' she answers, lifting for an instant her eyes with an
instinct of ungovernable plaintiveness to his; 'for the day!
on a pleasure-trip! Wish me joy!'

She has taken her seat, and, just as they are setting off,
she leans forward, and addressing the driver, repeats in a
peculiarly clear and distinct voice that direction which has
already been given him, 'To Coniston!'

'You are determined that there shall be no mistake as
to our destination, I see,' says Sarah sarcastically.

Belinda's chest heaves.

'I thought that you might like Mr. Bellairs to know,' she
answers ironically. 'By the by, who is to keep watch and
ward over him in your absence?'

'I have received private information that they all mean
to come to Coniston too,' replies Sarah tranquilly. 'I
thought I would be beforehand with them!—a poor project,
but mine own!'

Away they go from the wind-freshened lake, whose waves
are running riot in the sun; while, as they pass along,

the clouds roll up and up from fell and scaw and nab, leaving only a lawny kerchief here and there about their necks; as though loth all at once to desert them. And by and by kerchief and veil are swept away too, and the hills are free.

Through loveliest pasture-fields, crowded with great blue-bells and vetches, and meadow-sweet that smells of almonds; by meadows where women are tossing the late hay, beside the laughing Rotha; under Loughrigg and over chattering Brathay's gray stone bridge they go. Up and up they climb; between the weather-painted walls, with their lavish ferns and their crannied flowers; till at the top of the long ascent they pause to breathe the horses, and look back.

Fair mountain-wonders, now again conversing with the clouds; and yet lit on your bare flanks by the sun: Red Screes, Fairfield, Wansfell Pike, with your pointed head! to which of you shall we give crown and sceptre, as Queen-hill, in this your morning glory? For a while they both look in silence. Then:

'It seems a pity that we are not in the least enjoying ourselves,' says Sarah regretfully.

Belinda's heart gives a passionate assent, though her lips are closed. Is not life full of such pities? of exquisite spread feasts, and gagged mouths that are not allowed to taste them? With what an agony of pleasure would she be looking at these curly mists and shining shoulders; at these heavenly becks, rain-swollen in their noisy mirth, dashing in happy bounds down the hillsides, if only—if only! And this is such an easy, probable 'if,' too!

'If you could but think it, you know,' continues Miss Churchill, turning in calm reasoning to her sister, 'I am really much better company than David; and it is no great stretch of imagination to say that you are not much duller than Bellairs, eh?'

But Belinda is still staring in sullen grudging misery at the wasted loveliness before her.

'Shall we try to pretend, at all events, that we like it?' says Sarah persuasively. 'It would be more to our credit; I think *I* could, if you could.'

But Mrs. Forth is unable to promise even thus much.

'You cannot do it?' says Sarah leniently; 'well, I am the last person who has any right to blame you. Personally, I have never cared for a landscape without figures in the foreground!'

But as time goes on, this seems to be the species of landscape to which Miss Churchill is to-day to be condemned. Although Coniston has been long ago reached, luncheon eaten, and several coaches and *char-à-bancs* driven up and unloaded, yet is there no sign of the appearance of any one of the ornamental foreground figures for which she had confidently looked.

'Beaten by a banjo!' says she tragically; 'if it had not been for the banjo I should have *walked* away from her. I will never go anywhere without a banjo again!'

Belinda laughs grimly. 'I would not!'

'I suppose there must be some tiresome sight to be seen here,' says Sarah, yawning; 'it would never do if they found out that we had not seen it: not the lake—no! I could not bear that; it would remind me of the dinghey! What did the waiter tell us? copper-mines and a waterfall? Come, do look a little livelier, and brace your mind to copper-mines and a waterfall!'

They set out dispiritedly, but before they have gone five yards:

'I will leave word which way we have gone,' cries Sarah, brightening, 'in case any one asks for us.'

'A most unnecessary precaution!' replies Belinda morosely.

A walk undertaken in such a spirit is not likely to be productive of any very acute enjoyment.

'We are to turn to the right when we reach the Black Bull!' says Sarah gloomily; 'I wonder what would happen if we turned to the left?'

But they have not the energy even to make this experiment. They have passed village and white-washed church, and asking their way of the civil villagers, presently find themselves climbing a mountain road, with a little gay river frisking over its worn boulder stones on their right, and a green fell on their left. Ere long the road leaves the bright beck, and climbs higher than it; and trees interpose a leafy shield between them and their noisy friend. But it calls to them from beneath, 'I am here; you will find me soon again.' And so they do. For by and by the road swerves to the right, and they are once more free from the envious sycamores and mountain ashes, with their red rosaries, and are standing on a roughstone mortarless bridge with parapet broken down, and beneath them the stream plunges in a little storm of foam. Is this the waterfall? They do not know; they do not much care. It is a little waterfall, even if it be not the one in search of which they have been sent.

'My cup is full!' says Sarah, sitting resolutely down. 'I am hot; I have not a leg to stand upon; my pretty project has *avorté*; if Niagara were round the corner I would not go to look at it. Oh, why did I leave my granny? dear granny! how she would have hated this!'

'Even more than you do?' asks Belinda cynically.

Mrs. Forth is still standing, her eyes riveted on the little cascade, and her heart repeating over and over to itself that bitter morning plaint: 'How pleasant! if only—if only— what?'

'Belinda!' says her sister, after a while, in a voice of cautious triumph, 'do you see anything moving between the

trees? yes? I thought so! A more direct answer to prayer
I have seldom heard of!' Then, with an abrupt change of
tone to one of sharp and real annoyance: 'If he has not
brought that eternal David with him!'

     *   *   *   *   *

'Are you going to see the copper-mines?' says Miss
Churchill demurely, a couple of minutes later, addressing
the new arrivals; 'so were we. But we have broken down;
perhaps you will tell us about them this evening!'

'We never heard that there were any,' replies Bellairs,
with an unvarnished boyish bluntness. 'We came to look
for you; we understood that you had left word.'

For once in her life Sarah looks a shade foolish.

Belinda, still standing, has remained looking, as if in ab-
sorption, at the waterfall. It is not much of one, after all.
Its noise does not deafen you; its spray does not drench
you; it is but a few feet that it plunges. But how snowy-
clean is its foam! How agilely it springs down! How
pleasant its voice! Like the voice of Undine calling to her
false Huldbrand! What wondrous green ferns lip its waters!

'You said "To Coniston!"' This is the murmur that
comes to Belinda's ear. Is it the brook that utters it? She
turns her head sharply away; but not before he has seen
that the rowan-berries are scarcely redder than she.

And then (neither inviting, nor being invited) they
saunter away together, as if they would fain follow the
stream to its springs in the mountain-lap. At least, they
may lend it their company for a little while. Almost in
silence they linger along, and gravely watch its lovely antics,
as, in little cataracts and water-breaks and jumps, it sings
and dances along in its jubilant old age (for how many
centuries has it sung and capered?) that is so like youth!

'I wish I could think that I should swear as well!' said
Mrs. Forth, with an excited laugh, sitting down on a

gray stone beside the road that leads up to the copper-mines.

The sun has gone for awhile, and the fells look serious and careworn. They are old, too, like the brook ; but they scarcely carry their years so well. He has thrown himself at her feet, that favourite symbolic attitude of his—body and soul, past, present, and future—is not he always there ? In their ears is the booming of the mountain bees, and the rivulet's warble. There is no longer an '*if*'!

'How long are you going to stay at Lowood ?' she asks abruptly.

She had not meant to put the question, and bitterly regrets it when it is pronounced; but it forces itself out in spite of her.

'I shall go when you tell me.'

Her forehead contracts with a furrow of angry pain.

'You have no right to throw the decision upon me,' she answers indignantly ; 'it is ungenerous. Why, are not you perfectly well able to judge for yourself ?'

'Because——' he answers, looking full at her, and speaking steadily, though very low, 'because I broke down once ; what security have I that I should not break down again ?'

Her eyes drop, and now the rowan-berries claim no kinship with her cheeks.

'That was *my* fault !' she answers faintly, turning dead-white.

'No !' he says slowly, yet with agitation, 'it was not ! Perhaps your being late that day may have accelerated it ; but it would have come anyhow,' with rising passion. 'It would have come anyhow ; how could it help coming ? When I am with you,' speaking with a sort of despair, 'how can it ever help coming ?'

Her hot fingers pick the cool mountain daisies.

'You must do as you think best!' she murmurs, half in tears.

How solemnly the hills are listening! The higher ones, indeed, are out of sight; so forwardly have grim Coniston Old Man's younger brothers thrust themselves before him.

From the bridge come sounds of rapturous manly merriment, which tell how far ahead of the banjo and its owner Sarah's tongue is triumphantly carrying her.

Rivers has raised himself into a sitting posture, and in his hand he is bruising and crushing a bit of the dwarf bracken that grows beside them.

'You—you would give me another chance, then?' he says indistinctly; 'you—you would let me try again?'

Is there any slightest doubt as to what her answer should be? and yet she hesitates.

'I—I—have so few friends,' she answers, as if apologetically and sobbing; 'as I have always told you, I do not know how to make friends! my life is so empty, and now that I am obviously perfectly recovered,' with a sort of exasperation, 'will no doubt be so long! You must do as you think best!'

He looks at her in a dumb agony for fully a hundred heart-beats. Does she know what she is asking of him? In her divine high innocence she does not understand. It is for him to understand for her! Her head is bent, and upon her white hands and whiter daisies one slow tear splashes. Until that tear it was possible to him! Until that tear!

'I must do as I think best?' he cries in passionate excitement, wholly carried away; 'is that what you tell me? Then I think best to stay! The case is changed—it is not what it was then: I was taken by surprise. I was off my guard!—forewarned, forearmed, you know! Yes, it is quite safe now!'

'But is it?' she says, shuddering, too late terrified by the wildness of his look and the mad triumph of his eyes; 'is it?'

*　　　*　　　*　　　*　　　*

Is it indeed? There has been a week in which to answer this question.

'It is putting one into such a disagreeable position!' says Mrs. Churchill pettishly.

The hour is the immediately after breakfast one; and she is sitting at the table, an open writing-case before her, papers and a hotel bill spread around. Her usual equable brow is ruffled. The manager of the hotel has just left the room.

'Being apparently all of the same party, it is so difficult to explain that we are not responsible for his eccentricities,' continues Mrs. Churchill in a tone of growing annoyance.

'Heaven has so obviously framed you for each other, that they cannot disabuse themselves of the idea that you are husband and wife,' says Sarah in an amused voice from the window. 'I saw incredulity in the manager's eye when you were laboriously explaining that he was your grand-son-in-law; he wondered why, if you must tell a lie, you should tell such a bad one!'

'I fancy that there is not the most paltry item of his bill over which he does not haggle,' says Mrs. Churchill indignantly. 'It is too petty! it makes one quite hot! I am sure that they would gladly pay him to go away! Of course it will end in his driving *us* off! Oh, Belinda, my dear, are you there? I am sure I beg your pardon; but what is said cannot be unsaid, and you really come into the room in such a creep-mouse way that one does not know whether you are in it or not!'

'It is not of the least consequence,' replies Belinda, though her face burns. 'I will certainly try to make more noise next time; and for the present perhaps I am best away.'

As she speaks she walks to the door, opens it, and closes it gently behind her; then deliberately mounts the stairs to her husband's attic. His occupation seems to be of somewhat the same nature as her grandmother's. At least, before him too, papers and a bill are spread.

'I was on the point of summoning you to my aid,' he says, looking up as she enters; 'I wished to consult you as to several of these items,' indicating them with his long thin forefinger, 'of which personally I have no knowledge whatever. A couple of stamps on the 15th, a bottle of Apollinaris water on the 18th, envelopes on the 19th. May I ask whether these entries are correct, or whether they are due to carelessness on the part of the manager? in which case I shall of course at once take him to task for such culpable oversight.'

'I have no doubt that it is all right,' still with that burning in her face; 'what can it matter?'

'In my opinion it matters extremely,' replies he sharply; 'your memory can, at all events,' again referring to the bill, 'go back so far as yesterday? you can at least inform me whether or not you ordered a bottle of seltzer-water yesterday?'

'Yes,' replies she, defiantly shrugging her shoulders— 'two, three, half a dozen!'

He looks at her with a not altogether ill-founded exasperation.

'You are obviously resolved, for some unexplained reason, to thwart my purpose,' he says slowly; 'but it is of the less consequence, since I have made up my mind at once to leave this place, where the scale of expenditure into which I am led—probably owing to a mistaken notion of my connection with your grandmother—is indubitably higher than I was taught to expect.'

She has been looking straight before her, with a dogged *insouciance ;* but at the mention of his purpose of departure, that look vanishes, and her cheeks blanch.

'You mean to leave this place?' she says, in a low voice; 'and yet,' with irony, 'wherever you go you will have to pay for the postage stamps I buy and the Apollinaris water I drink.'

'It is not merely a question of expense,' rejoins he, colouring faintly at her tone; 'I have daily more reason to be convinced that the air of this place does not suit me; I have slept worse, and my palpitations have been sensibly severer since my arrival. I am aware that you always assume a look of incredulity when I allude to my maladies.'

'Do I?' she answers, with a preoccupied air, as if she were not thinking of what she was saying. 'I beg your pardon; I did not mean it.'

'I have written to engage rooms for to-morrow at the Lodore Hotel at the head of Derwentwater; a coach starts from here at eleven o'clock in the forenoon, and——'

'Do you mean to say that we are to go—to leave this place—*to-morrow?*' she interrupts, with a sort of gasp.

Her eyes are dilated, and there is a roughness in her voice which she herself hears. He makes a sign of assent.

'It is *impossible!*' she says, speaking low and rapidly; 'you have never asked my opinion; you have never consulted me. How can the air of one of these lakes differ from that of another? it is fancy—all fancy! As you said to me the other day, there is nothing that gains upon one so much by indulgence in them as valetudinarian fancies!'

He turns his eyes slowly from the bill, on which they have been, until now, riveted in painstaking search for errors, the discovery of which may diminish the total, and fixes them piercingly upon her.

'You seem to be unaccountably reluctant to quit this

place,' he says, very slowly; 'why are you so much attached to it?'

There is that in his tone, or she thinks so, which is unlike anything she has ever heard in it before—that which at once strikes her murmurings dumb.   But a passing frenzy seizes her, bidding her answer him, for once truly; tell him, in so many words, face to face, *why;* to throw the game up— have done with it!   It is true that the longing for that lunatic relief is but short; a brief insanity that leaves her trembling and terror-struck—not at him, but at herself.

He has long removed his scrutiny from her face, and has been, for many minutes, re-immersed in his dissection of the bill, before she speaks; and when she does, it is clear that he has no further insubordination to fear from her.

'The coach starts at eleven?' she says, in a very low voice. 'I will be ready!'

So saying, she rises, and drags herself to the door.

'If you see a waiter, will you be good enough to tell him that I wish to speak to the manager?' says her husband, looking up; 'they are apt to disregard my bell, and there are several of these items which I shall indisputably contest.'

Having docilely fulfilled this commission, Mrs. Forth once more returns to her grandmother's sitting-room, and looks in.

'Is granny here?'

'She is not,' replies Sarah, from her usual watch-tower, the window.   'To tell you the truth, I have been giving her a little piece of my mind, as to her incivility to you; she knew as well as I did that you were in the room.   I have been making her so angry,' breaking into a laugh, 'by telling her that she is certainly growing a little deaf!'

Since the coast is clear, Belinda has entered, and sunk inertly into a chair.

'It *is* a little annoying for her, one must own,' resumes

Sarah, with an air of impartiality, 'to be suspected of collusion with the economies of our friend upstairs; it would not be a bad thing if we could manage to establish the fact that there is no connection beyond a tender family affection between us and him!'

'You cannot be more anxious to prove it than he is,' replies Belinda; but, as she speaks, no hot red wave of shame flows this time over her face; stronger emotions than that which had called it forth have too successfully driven the blood back to her heart; 'but in any case you will not be troubled with him long!'

'Is he going to die?' cries Sarah, with extreme animation, leaving her post of observation, and hastening to her sister's side.

'He threatens that if he stays here he will!'

'I wonder is there anything really the matter with him?' says Sarah, in a tone of acute curiosity. 'There is something very interesting about his diseases; I always regret not having utilised my former opportunities to learn more about them. I suppose there *must* be something odd about his heart, or the doctors he consulted would not have given him drops for it.'

'And would not they have given him pills for his liver, or draughts for his spleen either?' asks Mrs. Forth bitterly. 'Is not it a little improbable that *all* his organs have been hopelessly deranged for the last sixty years? No, no!' with a shrug, 'you need not be alarmed; he will see us all out!'

'Then why are we not to be troubled with him long?' inquires Miss Churchill, puzzled.

'He imagines that this place disagrees with him,' replies Belinda, in a dull, flat voice; 'and so we are to leave to-morrow for Derwentwater; to-morrow morning, by the coach that starts at eleven.

'And you have consented?' (very sharply, and with an accent of excessive astonishment).

Her sister's answer to this simple question seems not at once forthcoming. And when it does come, it is by no means a direct one.

'Sarah,' she says slowly, and turning even whiter than she already is—though, indeed, that is scarcely needful—'do you remember once telling me that you were afraid I was going to the devil, and that I was taking'—a pause and a sort of gasp—'David Rivers with me?'

'Yes, I remember!' replies the other drily.

'Then why'—Mrs. Forth's voice has sunk to a whisper—'then why have you never told me so lately?'

Miss Churchill's eyebrows rise.

'My dear soul,' she says bluntly, 'you did not receive my first exhortation in such a spirit as to make me very anxious to hazard a second.'

Belinda's head has sunk forward upon her chest.

'You were not very far wrong then!' she says faintly, 'but you would be still nearer the truth now!'

There is a silence. Sarah has begun to march unquietly up and down the room, with her hands behind her. Perhaps the confession just made her does not partake much of the nature of a surprise. For there is less of astonishment than of genuine concern in her face.

'And you are going?' she says abruptly; 'but who is to prevent his following you?'

Belinda's lip trembles.

'He will not, if I tell him not.'

Her eyes wander wistfully away through the window to mountain and mere. The high peaks are still withdrawn into the mystery of their morning vapours, but all the lovely lake is at play with the sun. To-morrow, to-morrow, he was to have rowed her on that lake!

Suddenly her attitude of subdued wretchedness changes to one of more violent pain.

'What am I thinking of?' she cries, starting up; 'I had forgotten! I shall not see him again; he has been obliged to go to Milnthorpe to-day on business; and by the time he gets back to-morrow, we shall be gone! we shall be *gone!*'

'He will be after you by the next coach!' replies Sarah, with cynical good sense.

Belinda utters a low groan.

'I must write to him!'

'Do not!' cries Sarah dissuasively; '*never* write! Whatever else you give up, adhere to that one golden rule! In the length and breadth of Europe,' says Miss Churchill, with a modest pride, 'there is not a square inch of my handwriting to be obtained!'

Once again Belinda moans.

'If I do not write, he will certainly find out where we have gone to; unless'—her eyes still taking that miserable farewell journey to the lake—'unless I leave word that we do not wish it known.'

'That would scarcely do,' rejoins Sarah drily; 'it would be hardly advisable to take the waiters into our confidence.'

A pause. Miss Churchill still pursuing her restless walk, and undistracted even by the strains of the banjo clearly heard from below, and the sound of a male, as well as a female voice, obviously accompanying it.

'I suppose,' she says by and by, sighing impatiently, 'that the end of it is, it will devolve upon me: our *rôles* are reversed. All my life I have been asking you to undertake disagreeable commissions for me, and now I must do you the same kind office. I suppose that *I* must tell him!'

'*You?*' cries Belinda, wheeling suddenly round, a

passionate dissent from this proposal in voice and eyes, and with a new rush of her lately dormant old and senseless jealousy; 'why *you?*'

'Would you prefer granny?' asks Sarah quietly. 'Some one must tell him; you can hardly suppose that I very greedily covet the office!'

At the cool rationality of her sister's words Belinda's rebel blood slowly subsides again, and her head sinks once more upon her breast. How thin these floors are! One can hear each word of the idiotic melody warbled by Bellairs and the girl in red; but Miss Churchill never flinches. Belinda is the first to speak, though it is not at once easy to comprehend the drift of her words, so unsure and muffled is her voice.

'You will tell him as kindly as you can?'

'Do you think it will kill him?' replies Sarah, with a touch of sarcasm; 'if you remember, you thought that his father's death would kill him, but it did not! Pooh! They take more killing than that!'

CHAPTER IV.

'Often, however, was there a question present to me : should some one now at the turning of that corner blow thee suddenly out of Space into the other world, or no-world, by pistol-shot, how were it ?'

THE wrench is accomplished. The coach that starts at eleven o'clock has started. Within the close precincts of its interior it has carried away, among other persons, the cautiously-enveloped figure of Professor Forth ; and among its mackintoshed and umbrellad outside passengers it reckons his wife.

'I never was so glad of anything in my life,' says Mrs. Churchill, walking briskly back to the fire from the rain-blurred window, whence she has been waving adieux of accented tenderness to her descendants.

'Not even when you first hailed him as grandson ?' asks Sarah caustically.

Mrs. Churchill reddens.

'Poor soul !' says the girl, with an accent of heartfelt compassion, following with her eyes the departing vehicle.

'I never can understand why you should pity her !' retorts the elder woman, with irritation ; 'there is no greater mistake than to measure every one by one's own foot-rule.'

'I suppose that without offence to any one, I may pity her for getting extremely wet,' replies Sarah surlily.

And certainly, on this account, Mrs. Forth, by the time of
her arrival at the Lodore Hotel, does deserve as much
compassion as she can get. Stiff and drenched, she has
climbed down from her perch. Pouring as is the day, the
coach has been crowded. Belinda's ribs on each side feel
indented with the continued nudging of her companions'
elbows; and there has been such a cordial interchange of
drips between all the umbrellas, that it would have been a
sensibly drier course to have taken no umbrellas at all.
Upon the tarpaulin that covers the luggage, lakes of water
have collected, which, at each fresh jolt of the coach,
discharge themselves refreshingly upon the passengers'
knees. As far as any glimpse of mountain that the blanket-
clouds have allowed them to obtain is concerned, they might
as well have been in Holland. Dunmail Raise, Skiddaw,
Saddleback—what have they been but various names for
the one huge white pelt? It is a grand day for the becks
—the foaming, jumping, brimful becks, and they are the
only cheerful things she has seen; they, and the long
lythrums growing lushly beside them.

'You have no one to blame but yourself,' says Professor
Forth, emerging, dry and warm, from the steaming interior,
and severely regarding his half-drowned wife; 'had you
taken my advice——'

'I blame no one,' she interrupts, apathetically; 'there
is no great harm in being wet; it is very easy to get dry
again!'

'You have every appearance of having taken a chill,'
scrutinising her shivering figure with an angry solicitude
that might appear the outcome of an anxious affection; 'it
would be extremely vexatious if, thanks to a mere caprice
on your part, you were to be so soon again laid up. I
must insist upon your at once drinking a glass of hot
brandy-and-water as a preventive!'

'I have taken no chill,' she answers faintly, but she obeys with a dull acquiescence.

There is no draught he could offer her, from Socrates' hemlock upwards or downwards, that she would not think it less trouble to take than to refuse. The rain pours on and on, all through the *table-d'hôte*, all through the long, long evening. There is a public drawing-room to which, after dinner, the other guests betake themselves, shawl-wrapped, grumbling, and uttering aspirations for a fire. Belinda has not the heart to accompany them. She climbs the stairs to her bedroom in the roof, although at eight o'clock it is scarcely possible to go to bed. No sense, indeed, of the prematureness of the hour prevents her flying to the blessed keeping of sleep; but the knowledge that whatever moments are filched from consciousness now will be asked back with usury in the gray morning hours— those grim gray hours that only the tiny minority of the quite happy and the completely innocent dare face.

Her window is open, and looks to the back; to the wooded hill rising so immediately behind the house that it seems as if, with outstretched hand, one might touch it. The rain swishes past: now and then, when the freakish gust takes it, swishes in. She sits down on her bed and listens to it. For two hours she will listen to its swishing; and then, perhaps, she may dare give herself—tired body and sick heart—to slumber. With the rain mixes the never-ceasing noise of the waterfall. On a sultry summer night no doubt it is sweet and lulling, falling coolly beneath the stars; but it seems to treble, to centuple the dreariness of this inclement drenching evening, cold as winter, and without winter's palliatives of thick curtains and blazing logs. It gets upon her nerves at last. It seems as if she must stop it for one instant or die. If its wet din would fill her brain, indeed, as it fills her ears, crowding out other presences, she would thank it, and bless it on her knees; but, on the contrary, its clamour seems to make thought sharper, memory intenser, fancy wilder. With what a dreadful liveliness does she rehearse—set to the murderous monotony of its tune—the scene of Rivers' back-coming to-morrow! It grows at last so hideously real that she asks herself in bewilderment. 'Has she really seen—is she really seeing it?'

She passes her hand across her forehead and rubs her eyes. In what room of the hotel—in which often-trodden spot by wave-lipped mere will the blow fell him? How will he take it? Will it kill him? She laughs aloud. 'Pooh! as Sarah says, "they take more killing than that!" And how much killing will she herself take?' This Sarah has never told her. How much of this slow death? A great, great deal! Was ever any one so full of obstinate life as she? Other women—women who prayed to live, women with little children's chubby arms about their necks, with passionate, fond husbands, wetting their faint hands with good-bye tears—would have died of such an illness such as hers. She, childless, hated and hating, has survived. A sense of impotent, dark rebellion fills her soul. Of what use to save her alive? What sense in it? To save her alive in order to show her just one small glimpse of what life might have been, and then to hurl her back into what life is! What life might have been! Oh, the terrible vividness of that vision!

She has fallen sideways upon her bed, which, as well as her whole body, is shaken with the force of her silent sobs. They must be silent, for the walls are thin, and her husband's attic is next door.

'If we had once belonged to each other,' she says, with a violent agony of emphasis, 'even if afterwards I had seen him struck dead at my feet, still, I should have known what is the very best thing that life holds ; I could have said, " I have lived !" but now I shall lie down in my grave, knowing that there has always been something immeasurably better than anything I know, just beyond me !'

After that she lies quite still, a sort of numb calm succeeding the hurricane, and outside the rain swirls always, and the waterfall tumbles. There must be more of soothing properties in their joint sound than she gives them credit for, since by and by their sullen music grows dim in her ears, and she sleeps.

She awakes in the early morning, forlorn and cold, to find that she has lain all night fully dressed, outside her bed. She is down in good time, and stands outside the hall-door, waiting for breakfast to be announced. The rain has ceased. The wind has torn and hurled the clouds apart, and let the sun look through ; and also swept clear little intensely blue islands in the sky. The shadows are flying, speedy as dreams, along Skiddaw's flanks, and Derwentwater lies—all billowy and disturbed—at the foot of her girdling fells. On the bit of marshy grass that intervenes between Belinda and the lake, several horses are grazing, and two rolling. One cannot roll quite over, which seems to annoy him.

' I hope that you are recovered from the effects of your yesterday's imprudence,' says a voice at her elbow.

She starts.

' There were not any to recover from,' she answers, with a shrug.

' In that case,' says her husband stiffly, ' and since you have every appearance of being in other respects perfectly restored to health, I think I am justified in proposing that you should return to your normal habits, which have been for so long, and at such great inconvenience to myself, interrupted.'

Belinda smiles slightly. She is well aware that it is only the presence of her grandmother and Sarah that has, up to this time, prevented the pack-saddle from being replaced upon her back. It is being now, at the earliest opportunity, strapped on again. Well, what matter?

'I perfectly agree with you,' she answers hastily. 'I have not the shadow of an excuse for any further idleness. After such a holiday,' catching her breath in a sigh, 'a little work will do me good.'

But people's ideas as to what a little work is, differ.

'I need scarcely tell you,' says the Professor, when, after the *table-d'hôte* breakfast, he and she have mounted to his bedroom, which, as at Lowood, is also his study—'indeed, it has once or twice struck me with surprise that the idea of a spontaneous offer of assistance should not have occurred to you—that my correspondence is very seriously in arrears; moderate application, however, will to-day reduce it in a great degree to order. I have briefly indicated, upon each letter, the tenour of the answer I wish drawn up.'

As he speaks, he places before her a large pile of docketed letters. If any dismay at its height and breadth enters her soul, she swallows it down in silence. The sun comes forth in summer strength, but though the room is not a tenth part as large as the Professor's Oxbridge study, the window is as rigorously closed as ever it was there. The garret, like her own, looks to the back, and in it there is no escape from the waterfall's loud pouring. She is still teased by that maniac notion that she must make it stop or die. Unused, for the past couple of months, to close air, to confinement, to toil, her head soon begins to ache, sometimes swims, burns always, but she makes no complaint.

The clock strikes one; she hears cheerful voices, and steps trooping down the passage outside to luncheon. The Professor is no great advocate of luncheon, even when he can eat it at some one else's expense; at a hotel he simply ignores the possibility of its existence. But she cannot complain. He is willing to share with her such hospitality as he extends to himself. Biscuits bought at a shop in Ambleside, so that there may be no danger of their figuring in the hotel bill, and weak brandy-and-water—the brandy also his own. She declines the brandy, would fain decline the biscuits too; to eat in such an air, and with such a heavy head, seems impossible, but she dreads being scolded for her sickliness if she refuse.

Two o'clock strikes! Three! Half-past three! Four! Even now her pile seems scarce perceptibly diminished. Two or three times she has been thrown back by having to draw up a fresh draft, her muddled brain and wandering thoughts having led her to mistake the sense of his directions. Hopeless tears fill her eyes as she tears across each sheet and begins another. As the clock strikes four the pen drops from her numbed fingers.

'I think you must excuse me,' she says faintly. 'I—I —do not feel very well!'

'Not well?' returns he sharply; 'then your indisposition is, of course, attributable to the chill you contracted yesterday!'

'The chill?' replies she, laughing hysterically, and pressing her hot hands to her throbbing forehead. 'The *chill?* Oh, how delightful it would be to have a chill! No, no! it is only the old story! It is only that I have broken down again!'

'Impossible!' he cries angrily; 'in that case, your health can never have been really re-established!'

'I suppose not,' assents she dully. 'Well, may I go?'

'Why do you ask?' retorts he waspishly, and regarding with a dissatisfied air her uncompleted task. 'Do I ever put any check upon your actions? I merely reserve to myself the right of requesting that you will not incur the risk of contracting another chill.'

She is very willing to buy her liberty at the price of this most unnecessary promise. At what price would not she buy air, the liberty to gasp, the privilege—beyond all value —of being alone? Without much thought she has taken, on leaving the hotel, the Borrowdale road, walks along it for some distance confused and woolly-headed, conscious only of the relief of having temporarily escaped from suffo-cation—from the waterfall—from *him !* But by and by the loveliness around her wakes her again—wakes her to new and keener sufferings. She is aware of the road that winds in gentle companionship with the windings of the Derwent; she is aware of the marvellous coloured water, tinted a strange fair green by the stones in its bed, and clear as the crystal stream in the Apocalypse.

Above, the great crags rear their steepy heads; the Castle Crag that, at one point, seems to block the valley, guarding hid treasures behind it, and saying austerely, 'You shall not pass me!' the Gate Crag, that looks down, be-nignant though awful, on the prattle of the river curling round its feet, looks down with its solemn purple-gray rock-shelves and sheer slopes of slate.

As she nears a village, she turns off a road to the left, and begins to climb the hill. She proposes to herself no goal. She does not know where she is, or whither she is going. She only knows that each step takes her farther from the waterfall, and from *him.* Climbing, climbing, climbing, through a wood, up a mountain path, until at length, panting, she attains the hill-crest, and turning, looks back upon all the beauty and majesty of Borrowdale. But even here she only halts to cast one breathless glance at the great hills, thrown about as if in Titan play, and looking over each other's shoulders, silent, wondrously-coloured, august !

She is not far away enough, even yet. With knees that tremble and give beneath her—for she has been but little used to such a walk—a walk undertaken, too, almost fasting —she descends the hill on the other side; and at its foot finds a most lonely tarn, here, in the heart of the fells.

A little ale-house, lonely too, sits near it, backed by three or four storm-wrecked Scotch firs; and around, the fells lift their harsh faces, scored by the channels of their winter weepings. She asks the stout housewife at the little inn for a drink of milk; but she does not inquire where she is, nor in which direction Lodore lies. She would far rather not know. She has lost her way, and will be late for the *table-d'hôte!* Well? He will be imagining that she has contracted some new and expensive chill! *Well?* She may go astray upon the mountains, and perish like the sheep in winter! WELL? The milk has a little revived her flagging powers; and she walks on again. Whither? She neither knows nor cares. She only knows that she is among friends —among the stern, yet summer-softened hills that lend her the sympathy of their silence; among the crisp and frolic mountain airs, and the beds of bog-myrtle that smells of bay leaves; while—friendliest of all—blithe comforter and comrade—a mountain beck tinkles, a hand-breadth off, beside her. But there is a limit even to the sustaining powers of a cup of milk; and by and by she sinks down, faint and spent, by that flower-lipped brook, upon the dainty bed of ferns and sundews with which it is set round.

Why should she ever move hence again? What inducement is there to her ever again to lift up her tired limbs and leave the mute society of these bald limestone crags and steeps of shingle and flint? Whither could she go to better herself? In what direction on earth's broad face does any good for her lie? Why should not she lie down and die here? *Die!* But is it such an easy thing to die? Has not she already tried hard and failed? Oh, if she could but gently depart here now! Surely no one could ever wish for a sweeter, fragranter death-bed!

She stretches herself back upon the bog-myrtle and sun-dews, and closes her eyes, trying to fancy that it is over, and that she *is* dead. Oh, if she might but be gently spunged out of being! It seems such a small thing to ask, and yet she might as well bid the mountains bow down and the sun make obeisance to her. She asks for no other life instead. Has her experience of this one been so pleasant that she is greedy for more? If there be another world, what security is there that it is a better one? May not it resemble this? the same long hopes that go gradually, sickeningly out; the same poniard-stabs of recollection thrusting one through in the hour of the uncoloured dawn; the same tiny, weakling joys!

She has raised herself from her recumbent attitude, and her head is bowed forwards upon her knees, which her long arms embrace. Neither by death nor by life is there any escape for her! But there is a mode of outlet for her nearer at hand than she wots of. It is noiseless walking upon the fine mountain herbage; there the heaviest foot falls mutely—so noiseless that until he who has been approaching her stoops and most gently touches her on the shoulder, she is unaware that any one is nigh. She springs up staggeringly, with a loud cry.

' *You!*'

'Yes, *I!*'

It seems as if she had spent all her breath on that one monosyllable, since, for a while, nothing more comes; then, at last, a gasping whisper:

' Did not—Sarah—tell you?'

'Yes; she told me.'

Her breath comes hard and laboured. How is it

possible to interpose any words between such heart-beats?
At last:

'You—have—always bragged about your obedience to
me,' she says slowly; 'you have always boasted of doing
what I told you—is *this* doing what I told you?'

He offers no exculpation. He only stands doggedly
before her, white and burning-eyed, but not trembling.

'This—it—is,' she says, with that same slow intensity—
'this—it—is—to throw yourself upon a man's generosity!'

His lips twitch, but his eyes are still dogged.

'I will go at your bidding; I will go at no one else's!'

She looks distractedly round at her silent friends—the
scarped slopes, where the lady-birch finds difficult footing,
but yet keeps her place, and hangs her delicate tresses: in
her sore need she consults the beck, but the hills are
speechless; and though the beck talks fast, she cannot
distinguish the meaning of its words.

'I will go if you tell me; and I will stay if you tell
me!'

Her look still wanders wildly; and her ear detects the
sound of a little oozing runlet, lost hitherto in the noise of
its elder brother; a runlet filtering through the red moss on
the hillside.

'Which shall it be? go or stay?'

His voice, that hitherto her lightest word has awed into
silence, presses, imperatively asking, upon her hearing.
(Which shall it be? *Which? which?*) Oh, if some one
would but answer for her! If mountain or runlet would
but take the responsibility of that one all-weighty word off
her? *Go?* Leave her to drag her tired limbs back into
that bondage which seems already to have endured for
centuries? and for a limit to whose mean and sordid
sufferings eye and heart consult the long future in vain.

'*I am waiting! which shall it be?*'

Hideous future! Hideous past! Hideous present! She has given it a fair trial. No one can say that she has not given it a fair trial.

' *Which?* '

And she has broken down; mind and body her tyrant has broken her down. He will break her down again if she give him the chance. Why should she? It has been his turn hitherto! Let it be hers now!

' Which? ' His voice is no longer dogged; heart-rendingly urgent only. ' Which? ' He has taken her hand, and has laid its palm upon his burning eyes. ' *Which shall it be? go or stay?* '

Her look, staring yet unseeing, is fixed upon the little zigzag green paths on the fell, worn by the small feet of the mountain sheep. Not a bird's voice breaks the silence of the hills.

' It—shall—be—*stay!*' she says, almost inaudibly.

Before his eyes the sun dances, and the steady hills go round. Yet, mixed with a joy so awful and utter that his whole strong frame reels beneath its weight, there comes too a pain keen to agony. He has prevailed. His high goddess has fallen from her pedestal, and it is he that has dragged her down! Her divine fair head lies in the dust, and it is he that has laid it there!

' Do you know what you are saying? ' he cries, in suffocating excitement. ' Sometimes I think that you say things of which you do not understand the meaning! Do you understand what "*stay*" means? It does not mean "Stay to-day, and go to-morrow;" it means "Stay *always*, ALWAYS, ALWAYS!" it is *all or nothing* for which I am asking. Do you understand? Which? '

She draws a long heavy breath, as one recovering from a deep swoon

' *All!* ' she answers, whispering; and so breaks into an

exceeding bitter cry of anguish and revolt: '*I will not die
without having lived !*'

Then, indeed, the pain goes, swallowed up and stifled in
the enormity of his gladness.   He knows that hereafter it
will return, but now he is only, *only* glad !   Great God !
how glad !   He has thrown himself down before her, and is
kissing her tired feet, and clasping her knees.   But when
he seeks to gather her into his arms, she pushes him
convulsively away.

'No ! no !' she says wildly ; 'not now !'

'What !' he cries, with a hideous revulsion of feeling ;
' you have been fooling me, then ! you are not in earnest !'

'*Not in earnest !*' she says, with a heart-broken smile ;
'do you think that I am *joking?*   Cannot you understand
that I have fallen low enough for *one* day ?'

Her voice dies away, and her head sinks on her breast.
His high Queen !   Already she looks discrowned and dis-
sceptred.   By and by she lifts her haggard face and speaks.

'We must be going home,' she says dully.

He complies in silence, and they set out.   Before they
have gone far, one of those swift changes, so common in
mountain weather, has sent a sharp storm driving in their
faces.   She is unprovided with umbrella or mackintosh,
and the large drops soon saturate her light gown.   He puts
his arm in anxious protection round her.   Her first impulse
is to shrink away from him; but, bethinking herself, she
tamely submits.

'Shall I stick at such a trifle—*I,* that stick at nothing ?'

CHAPTER V.

'This wrong world.'

It is evening. Professor Forth's chillness has for once vanquished his parsimony; and in the grate of his attic room, a small, carefully nursed, never-poked fire burns sparingly cheerful. But he cowers over it, and stretches his hand to its frugal blaze alone. One would have thought that such a walk as that undertaken by Mrs. Forth would have been enough to satisfy the energies of any reasonable woman; and yet she is again out of doors. She is not walking, indeed; she is standing upon the rustic bridge that leads to wood and waterfall; standing there in the soft dusk—not alone.

They have passed the windows of the garishly-lit public drawing-room, where lamps and jets of gas are making a gaudy glare; a heterogeneous assemblage of people, forced into unnatural sociability, irksomely driving through an evening in common. Some are working; some are playing whist; some are yawning; one is feebly singing; and all are in the fullest blaze of the gas and the paraffin. How much better to be outside in the moist, sweet dark! His arms are about her, she no longer resisting; and her tired head is resting on his shoulder.

Henceforth she will always have that shoulder on which to lay down her head. What matter, wading through what waters she has reached its refuge? A throb of mad, reckless joy thrills through all her uneasy body. Since she is to pay the price—and such a price!—let her at least have some joy to show for it! Oh, if it were but all right!—all on the straight!—what could heaven do better than this? Ay! but the might of that 'if'!

'And you *must* go?' she says sighingly; 'you think it is quite unavoidable; you *must?*'

'I must!' he answers, in a tone as grudging as hers; 'there is no help for it; there are '—hesitating—'there are arrangements to be made—that I must make personally—that could not be done by writing; and I must also go to Milnthorpe, to see about my work.'

She has raised her head.

'It—this—will not make any difference to your work?' she asks rapidly, and in a tone of acute alarm; 'it—it will not injure your prospects?'

'Of course not; of course not!' he answers, in a tone of feverish reassurance; 'why should it? what connection is there between a man's private life and his business relations? What concern is it of theirs whether or not I—I——'

'You run away with your neighbour's wife,' she says, in a low, hard voice, finishing his sentence; 'why do not you speak out? if a thing is not too bad to do, it is not too bad to say!'

But through the dark he divines the agony of the blush that accompanies her words; and again that sword-like pain, which had marred the first moments of his triumphant bliss, once more traverses his heart. There is not a breath of air. What has become of yesterday's hustling north wind? By the starlight they can dimly see that the clouds no longer fold the mountain-heads. They have dropped to their waists, and airily girdle them.

She is resting her feverish hands on the wooden railing,

wet with the recent showers, and looking down on the half-
seen shining rocks, and the water flashing white in the semi-
darkness.   How pleasant is its continuous rush and low
roar ; and yet there is something oppressive in it ; something
that makes one out of breath !

'You will not be long away?' she says, with a passionate
wistfulness ; 'you will not leave me long alone? you will
come back as soon as you can?'

'Need you tell me that?'

There is almost derision in his tone.   He has drawn her
back to her former resting-place, and is most soothingly and
half-timidly caressing her hair.   Not yet can he realise that
it is the glorious proud head which has always seemed
farther above him than the stars, that is lying in prone
abandonment on his shoulder.

'You will not despise me more than you can help?' she
whispers, with a sob ; dark as it is, hiding her face on his
breast.   'Of course you *must* despise me ; but you will try
and hide it as well as you can, will not you?'

Are his wits wandering?   Can this be his divine and
lofty lady, preferring this miserable prayer?   Can this be he,
blasphemously listening to it?

'How *am* I to get through these days?' she moans,
clinging to him ; 'oh, come quickly back ! come quick !
quick !   How am I to look him in the face without telling
him what I am planning against him? if he says one kind
word to me, it will be the death of me !   Happily for me,
he never does !'

For all answer, he only strains her more desperately to
his heart.   What words can he find with which to console
her?   Surely that silent embrace, strongly enveloping her
with its love and its pity, is best.

'I shall be always fancying that you are growing tired of
me,' she says, still whispering, and her speech broken by

dry sobs; 'promise not to grow tired of me! promise! Remember that I shall have nothing—*nothing* but you in the whole wide world; and that when you are gone from me, *everything* will be gone! But what is the use of making you promise?' with a despairing change of key; 'how can you help it? If you grow tired of me, you will grow tired; and there will be an end of it!'

She has pulled herself out of his arms; and now stands apart from him, as if in prophetic renunciation. He puts up his hand to his head as if his brain were turning.

'When you say such things,' he cries incoherently, 'you make me feel as if my senses were gone! *I* grow tired of *you! I! I!* Oh, my love, my lady, my Queen!' falling down at her feet, and kissing the hem of her gown, as if no humility of posture could adequately express the abasement of his soul before her; 'if you knew how I am eating my heart out with the thought that *you* may grow tired of *me!* that you may find out I am not worthy of the sacrifice you are making for me!—that *I*, only *I!*—oh my poor love! my poor love!—may not be enough for you!'

He stops, choked, pressing his head against her trembling knees; and his scalding tears filter through her gown. The intensity of his emotion calms her a little. At all events, he is not tired of her *yet!* She stoops, and lays her hand almost protectingly upon his head.

'Yes!' she says; 'you will be enough!' But in the dusk her face looks livid, and she ends her sentence with a sob.

The next morning he goes—goes, leaving her to live through, as best she may, the days that must intervene before his return. How—by what process as yet unconjectured by her—is she to live through them? They will pass, of course. No day has yet dawned upon sad humanity that did not pass; even Damiens' death-day passed. But how? The weather, at all events, will not come to her help. It has changed from capricious showers back to such headstrong, hopeless rain as accompanied their drive from Lowood. There will be no seeking escape in mountain walks; no tiring down thought by tired muscles.

'How *am* I to live through them?' she says, as she stands alone, at the window of her husband's room, staring vacantly through the smeared pane, which baffles sight, and waiting for him to be ready to begin work.

He has entered the room without her perceiving it. Has she spoken her last words aloud? She hardly knows.

'What are you looking at?' he asks.

She gives a great start.

'I—I—am looking at the rain!'

I hope that you will content yourself with looking at it,' retorts he drily. 'I must exact a promise from you that you will not, by exposing yourself to it, incur the danger of that relapse with which you were obviously threatened yesterday.'

'I promise,' she answers docilely.

Since she is going to be guilty of this one enormous treason against him, she may at least pay him the mint, and anise, and cummin of any tiny obedience that comes in her way.

'But I shall have no temptation,' she adds feverishly. 'I want to work to-day: I am up to a great deal of work. You need not be afraid of overworking me to-day!'

(It is an uncalled-for caution! He has never been at all afraid of overworking her.) And yet, indeed, it is from him, and not from her, that the first suggestion of an interval from labour comes. The afternoon is four hours old, and the faint smell of the brandy-and-water that temperately irrigated the Professor's luncheon is beginning to die out of the close room, when:

'Your writing has become unsteady,' he says, looking

critically over her shoulder; 'I presume that your hand is growing tired. Perhaps we had better desist until to-morrow.'

'No! no!' she cries vehemently; 'why should we? I am not at all tired! it was only carelessness. I will take more pains.'

'You are unable any longer to concentrate your attention,' he says, pursuing his examination; 'you have omitted two most important words.'

'Have I?' she answers remorsefully; 'but indeed I am not tired! I had much rather go on; there—there is no time like the present!'

'To-morrow,' he begins; but she interrupts him.

'*To-morrow!*' she repeats feverishly; 'who knows what may happen to-morrow? We may both be dead to-morrow!'

The Professor dislikes the mention of death.

'Psha!' he says crossly; 'what is the use of indulging in puerile suppositions?'

But she has her will. Until the hour of dinner she toils on. She has not, indeed, attained her end—that state of numb woolliness to which yesterday a less portion of labour had brought her. To-day, overwork has had the contrary effect of sharpening to its highest capability every power of thought, memory, and imagination.

She goes down to the *table-d'hôte* alone. The Professor, labouring under some real or fancied accession to his ailments, has (having, however, previously taken care to notify in good time his intention) restricted himself to the delight of a basin of gruel over his own fire. Belinda is placed at dinner beside a couple who had been fellow-inmates with her of the Lowood Hotel, and who, like her had come on hither. She had been on terms of friendly civility with them, and they now express pleasure at having again met her, and try to draw her into conversation. But she repulses all their efforts with a surly brevity. They shall not have to say afterwards that she let them talk to her.

And now the day—*one* day—is ended, and it is night. Oh, these nights! Dreadful are they—dream-haunted, nightmare-ridden! and yet neither dream nor nightmare are comparable for horror to their waking moments. And through them all, the waterfall pours, pours, in its maddening monotony. Sometimes she feels as if she *must* tell some one; *must* rush out to some of the sleeping strangers and tell them! Perhaps it would not sound so bad if it were told! After all, such things happen every day. Her loss will be no loss to her husband; an economy rather!

She laughs bitterly. He will be glad to be rid of her. Has not everybody with whom she has lived hitherto been glad to be rid of her? Could her grandmother contain her joy at having shaken her off? Professor Forth, too, will be glad to be rid of her. By and by, *he* will be glad to be rid of her! Oh, the despair of that thought! She will see him growing tired of her! Loyal gentleman as he is, he will try his best to hide it; but he will not hide it from her! She will be jealous of the very air for touching his face; every day she will ask herself, 'Is he *quite* the same? Is he *quite* as glad to see me as he used to be? Does he call me his darling quite as often as he did?' She will see his love slowly sliding—sliding away from her. What will she have to bind him to her? Not honour, for she will have cast off honour; not real love, for real love goes only with respect, and she will have said good-bye to respect; she will have shaken hands with shame. The cold sweat of agony stands on her brow. Whether or not there be a hell elsewhere, she has found hers here.

The last day has come; the last of the three that are to intervene between his going and the morning when she is to meet him at Keswick railway station, bidding, for his sake, farewell to husband, friends, and good repute.

Two nights such as the one I have described; two days which, though inferior in agony, seem yet to have been crammed as full of mental suffering as they can hold, have brought her to the verge of a nervous fever. At the lightest noise it seems as if she must scream out loud. She is, as usual, at her toil in her husband's room. She has changed her position, so that she may not see him as she writes; so bitter is the remorse with which the sight of his withered face and shrunk figure fills her. Poor old man! What has he done to her, that she should deal him this murderous blow?—for a murderous blow it is to his honour, if not to his heart. By what right is she stabbing him in the dark? Because he is old, sickly, and peevish? Was not he all three—did not she know him to be all three— when she married him? How little he suspects her! Exacting and undemonstrative he may be, but how perfect is his confidence in her!

'You look feverish,' he says.

There is, or she fancies it, a tone of kindness, almost compassion, in his voice; and in a moment she has fallen on her knees. It is not too late, even yet! She will tell him all.

'What the duece are you about?' cries he acrimoniously. It is very seldom that he employs even so small an oath as the one recorded; and his present indulgence in it is a measure of his irritation. 'You have let fall a great blot of ink upon Gregory Nazianzen!'

For a moment she still kneels there, stunned; then, slowly recovering her senses, and healed completely of her impulse towards confession:

'I beg your pardon,' she says, stammering; 'I—I had dropped something. I—I—was going to look for it!'

The hours passed by. They seem at once to crawl and

to rush. With no one but her husband does Belinda exchange a word. She has sufficiently snubbed into silence, and rejected with eager rudeness, the efforts of the civil visitors; who, attracted by her beauty, and compassionating her apparent loneliness (the Professor has adhered to his *régime* of solitude and gruel), have tried to include her in their talk. She has harshly rebuffed a little child, who, encouraged by former notice, has run up to make friends with her. None of them shall be able to say afterwards that she forced her company upon them—that company which they will then look upon as pollution.

The dinner hour is near, and she is standing outside the hotel door, drawing long gasping breaths. Is it a little easier to live out of doors than in? It has been another wet day; the sun has been neither seen nor heard of; but now, so near the hour of his daily dying, he asserts himself. From beneath a lead-heavy pile of rain-clouds he is thrusting his head; but his radiance is tempered to a weird, moony splendour. About the hills' necks are thrown cobwebby kerchiefs of vapour; and to all these he lends a nameless pale opulence. In the sky he builds up an aërial city, augustly fair as that one seen in trance at Patmos; and on the waters his sovran feet have trodden a straight path of quivering diamond. Across this royal path a little boat has the presumption to take its course; and at once is harmonised into a solemn unity with the transfigured water and the mountain pinnacles—pinnacles as of the great City of God.

Belinda looks at it all with a wild, dry eye, and a choked throat. Oh, beautiful, cruel, terrible world! Would not it be easier to endure if it were ugly and unsightly? if there were not this horrible contrast between its fair shows and its hideous realities? The sight is of such strange loveliness that at every window of the hotel heads are thrust out to admire it. A little group of people have followed Mrs. Forth's example, and issued out into the road. The lady with whom she had been on friendly terms at Lowood is standing near, and addresses her.

'Why will you never speak to us now?' she asks, in a wondering voice; 'I am afraid,' laughing a little, 'that you must think that there is something wrong about us; that we have run away, perhaps, and are not married! Mamma met some people like that at Spa last year; it was so awkward, for she had made quite friends with them!'

She stops abruptly, for the woman she addresses has turned ghastly, unaccountably pale. The evening is one of extraordinary stillness. On the satiny water the heavens lie exactly copied, cloud for cloud, clear sky-field for clear sky-field! That strange pallid effulgence—lessened indeed, fainting away by slow degrees into obscurity—is yet still there; an effulgence not of the gold and carmines and purples that one usually associates with sunset; but of a paler, whiter, lunar quality.

Again those sobs rise in her throat. Oh, lovely, ironical world! when will you cease jeering us in our misery? And now it is night. She has gone to bid her husband good-night. Often, on previous occasions, she has omitted this ceremony as nugatory; but now a morbid impulse to be at all events lacking in no little dues of courtesy towards him, possesses her.

She finds him sitting stooped over his hearth, with his empty gruel-basin beside him, and his fleshless hands absorbing the last warmth of the expiring fire.

'I have come to say good-night.'

'Have you? Good-night.'

Now that the ceremony is concluded, it is clear that he expects her to retire; but still she lingers, and again that longing to fall on her knees and tell him all sweeps over her. Poor old man! How old and feeble and lonely he looks!

'You are not ill?' she says, unsteadily.

'According to you, I am never ill,' replies he drily; 'I enjoy the most robust health; if I were to tell you that I were ill, you would discredit the assertion!'

'Oh, but I should not,' she cries remorsefully; 'I quite believe that you often, often suffer. Is there—is there —nothing I can do for you?'

'You can shut the door,' replies he, with a snarl; 'a thing that, since the beginning of my acquaintance with you, I have never known you do! and since it is already past my usual hour for retiring to bed, I will ask you to shut it upon the *outside!*'

CHAPTER VI.

'Look up ! There is a small bright cloud
   Alone amid the skies ;
So high, so pure, and so apart,
   A woman's honour lies.'

AND now the night has to be faced. With what dread has she watched the slow declension of the summer evening; but no dread comes up to the reality, to the miserable endless hours of hand-to-hand fighting with the terrible battalions of thought and remorses, that come up, ever fresh and fresh, against her; that, while all around her are softly sleeping, take her by the throat in the blackness, and will not let her go. To no dream or nightmare, indeed, does she give the opportunity to torment her, for she makes no attempt to sleep. Fully dressed, widely, burningly awake, she sits all night writing, writing, writing endless letters of farewell to him, who, parted from her only by a flimsy lath-and-plaster partition, lies tossing in the light and uneasy doses of old age. How many does she write? They must be a score, at least; prayers for forgiveness, cries of remorse; and no sooner are they written than she tears them all. Prayers for forgiveness of a wrong that is unforgivable! Cries of remorse for a sin that her action shows she has not really repented of! Why insult him by such? The dawn has come by the time that she has at length written the three lines which, without reading over—if

she read them over, she knows that she would tear them too
—she feverishly folds and places in an envelope. In them
there is neither petition nor repentance.

'I am going to leave you for always. You cannot think
that I have been a worse wife to you than I think myself.
'BELINDA.'

To have toiled all night for such an outcome! She
walks to the window, feeling stiff and chilled. The morning is bringing all night's secrets to light. Again the wooded
hill rises a hand-breadth off; the little patch of sky that it
allows her to see is putting on day's blue livery.

Well, then, it has come! There is no going back now!
no more shilly-shallying! There is nothing for it but to
make the best of it! She has turned from the window, and
accidentally faced herself in the glass. What a spectacle!
What heavy smouches under the eyes! What baked white
lips! But in her face, is there something else too? Something
new and unqualifiable? Is it already beginning to assume
that pitiful, brazen look, that women such as she wear?
Well, if it is, what wonder? If it is, there is no help for it!

The time is so short—so short now! Surely for that
short time she can manage to keep thought at bay? She
moves noiselessly about, busying herself with this and that.
She takes off her wedding ring, and making it and the few
paltry trinkets that her husband has ever given her into a
small packet, directs and places them beside the letter; then
she tries to ruffle her bed, and give it a lately occupied air:
no easy task, for a bed that has not been slept in *will not*
look like one that has. Then she undresses; and by and
by, when her hot water is brought, makes her toilet afresh,
having first placed letter and parcel in a conspicuous situation upon the chest of drawers which serves as dressing-
table, and goes downstairs.

How near the time is now! She refers, for the hundredth time, to the paper of directions left with her by Rivers. At such an hour she is to set off. It is within five minutes of that hour. She has ordered over night a carriage to convey her. It is true that an omnibus plies between hotel and station, but from its publicity she shrinks with unconquerable aversion. It will be full of people. They will be talking and laughing. They will talk to her; perhaps —quite as likely as not—they will ask her where she is going!

So she has ordered an open fly for herself. It shall be no expense to Professor Forth. She can easily return him by post the money for it. Yes; but *whose* money? A scorching blush burns cheek and brow, and she covers her miserable face with her hands.

It is three minutes past the appointed hour, and the carriage is not yet here. Perhaps there has been some mistake! Perhaps it was never ordered! But no sooner has this sickly hope—that is scarcely a hope either—flared up in her mind, than it is extinguished again. For an open fly comes rolling briskly up to the door. Perhaps it may not be hers. Other people order flies too. Perhaps it may be for some one else. But this delusion also dies.

'The carriage is ready, ma'am,' says a waiter, approaching her.

'Are you sure that it is mine?' she asks huskily. 'Are you sure that it is not meant for some one else—that there is no mistake?'

'No mistake at all, ma'am!'

There is nothing for it but to get in. As she takes her seat:

'Will you dine at the *table-d'hôte* to-day, ma'am?' asks the waiter innocently.

In an instant all the truant blood has poured back into

her show-white face.   Does he suspect her?   Has he asked
her on purpose?

'No!' she answers almost inaudibly—'no, not to-day.'

And now she is off!   The die is cast!   Nothing has
happened to prevent her.   To the last moment she has
dimly believed that something would happen to prevent her.
But no! nothing has!   No fire has fallen from heaven to
consume her!   No accident has occurred to hinder her!
By what small accidents—happening at the last moment—
have other people been saved!   No accident comes to save
her!   Neither God nor man cares what becomes of *her!*

The morning is lovely, with morning's fresh look of new-
ness, as if the ancient hills had but just been turned out of
their Maker's workshop.   Lapis-blue is the lake, as a
summer lake should be ; and with its little islands laughing
in summer forest-green upon its radiant lap.   Over one
mountain shoulder, indeed, a few slight cloud-shadows,
thrown light as guazy scarves, still lie.   But on his brother's
granite knees there is strong resolute sunshine, and in their
ravines shadows cut hard and black.

Oh, cruel world!   Again you are jeering her with your
beauty!   Her eyes roll wildly round, and thought after
thought courses with mad rapidity through her head.   Little
irrelevant incidents out of far-away childhood, fragments of
forgotten books, texts of Scripture.   'I will look unto the
hills from whence cometh my help!'   That is what teases
her most.   And yet what applicability is there in it to her?
Does any help come from the hills to her?   Beneath the
trees that lip the lake, and through whose leafage come ever
glimpses of its dazzling gaiety, the sweet road winds.   Along
it some of the inmates of the hotel are leisurely walking, and,
as she passes, look up to nod and smile at her.

Would they nod and smile at her did they know whither
and on what errand she is bent?   What right has she to

leave them under such a delusion? She must undeceive them. So distraught is her brain that she leans out of the carriage to accomplish this lunatic purpose, but they are already left behind. How fast the driver drives!

Why does he drive so fast? She calls out to him to go slower; and then, with a new and contradictory longing that it should be over, should be irrevocable, bids him drive faster again. And still, numberless as sand-grains, quicker than lightning, the thoughts rush through her head. It is a sentence out of 'Sartor Resartus' now that is beating and hammering in her brain; a 'Sartor Resartus' casually left behind by some stray guest at the hotel, and as casually opened by her yesterday. 'Love not Pleasure; Love God: This is the Everlasting Yea!' Why should it buzz in *her* ears? What has it to say to *her?* How short the drive is! The roofs of Keswick are already in sight. That was a short drive, too—the drive to church on her marriage morning. With what dreadful vividness does it now return in each detail of its pinched and icy misery upon her memory; she sitting there in dead despairing obstinacy, and Sarah sobbing beside her, telling her that it was not too late! Sarah was right. It was not too late then. If Sarah were here now, would she still tell her that it is not too late? Oh, why is not she here then? At every step of the road her agony heightens, and a cold sweat stands on her forehead. It is not too late! *It is not too late!* This is written in letters of fire all over the mountains; all over the lapis lake and sapphire sky. *It is not too late!* How plainly she can read the words! They are taking the character of a command! *It is not too late!* Dare she disobey such a mandate?

'Stop!' she cries, standing up suddenly, like one possessed. But her emotion is so overpowering, and her throat so dry, that no sound issues from it. The horse

still trots rapidly on. '*Stop !*' she repeats, but once again
her disobedient organs play her false, and the horse trots on.
'STOP !' she cries frantically, a third time ; and now, at last,
the coachman hears, and pulls up. 'Go back !' she says
hoarsely, and almost unintelligibly ; 'go back to the hotel !'
then, becoming aware, though sight is dim and head giddy,
of the unbounded astonishment depicted on his face—'I—
I—have forgotten something !'

'We shall lose the train, ma'am,' he answers, civilly
demurring ; ' we have not too much time as it is.'

'Go back !' she repeats, huskily ; and then, indeed,
wondering, he obeys.

She sinks back, and covers her face with her hands.
What has she done ? She forbids herself to ask or think.
But has she done it in vain ? If, during her absence, her
letter has been discovered, she will have returned in vain.
Even if it has not been already discovered, every minute
that passes lessens its chance of escape. At this very
moment it may be being found, and she will have turned
back in vain.

'How slow you drive !' she cries harshly ; 'drive quicker !
quicker !'

How could she ever have thought the distance short ?
It is immeasurably, unbelievably long ! The hotel is in
sight ! A few people are standing about the door. Have
they heard ? Are they talking about it ? The fly has
stopped. Is she in time ? It seems as if there were an
ominous silence about the idlers hanging round. Have
they heard ? She dare not look the waiter, who comes to
help her out, in the face. She staggers past him into the
hall ; then, by a tremendous effort, steadying herself, she
rushes upstairs. Is she in time ? Flight after flight she
mounts, with that question surging in her ears. She has
reached her room—has burst into it. Is she in time ? One

glance gives her the answer. Yes, she is! Undisturbed, exactly as she had left them upon the top of the chest of drawers, lie letter and packet. She *is* in time! Oh, the relief of that thought! And yet, so complicatedly contradictory are we, that, at the sight so madly desired, a distinct pang of disappointment crosses her heart. Had the letter been discovered, there would have been the one and only refuge left her, and no one could *then* have blamed her for availing herself of it. She starts, shuddering at herself. Is she already repenting of her repentance? What security has she that she may not again go back from it? Within her there is none; if there *is* a security for her, it must be one outside her. She has taken the letter into her hand, and stands for a few moments motionless; a desperate determination gaining strength in her heart, and painting itself on her haggard yet resolute face. Since the letter has not yet been delivered to him, she herself will deliver it. She will tell him under what circumstances it was written. *This* shall be her expiation.

Without giving herself time for hesitation, she moves quickly out of the room, and knocks at her husband's door. There is no answer, and she knocks again. Still no reply. Perhaps, though it is not likely, he may be out. So she enters. No, he is in his usual seat, by his improvised writing-table. He could not have heard. His attitude is not quite his usual one, for he is apparently unoccupied, leaning back in his chair, and with his head bent a little forwards on his chest. He must be thinking, and will probably chide her for disturbing him. Well, it cannot be helped. Heaven knows he has cause enough to chide her!

'Can I speak to you?'

Her voice sounds strangely resonant in this silent room. There is no answer, nor does her husband show, by any movement or slightest change of position, that he is aware of her vicinity. It is very odd. She has spoken loudly and distinctly, and he is not deaf. He must be asleep; and yet, he is not apt to fall asleep in the morning! A chill terror is creeping over her, but she tries to shake it off. Her nerves are unstrung. Why should not he be asleep? How apt old people are to slide into a doze.

Conquering the nameless, senseless dread of approaching him that has come over her, she walks firmly up to him, and laying her hand on his arm, stoops and looks into his face. The next instant a sharp shriek rings through the hotel, and when frightened visitors and chamber-maids, hurrying from all quarters, reach the room, they find Mrs. Forth lying stretched on the floor beside her husband, as inanimate as he. Only that in time they bring *her* round again. As for him, he has for ever vindicated his character from the imputation of being a *malade imaginaire*, and the Professorship of Etruscan in the University of Oxbridge is vacant!

FINIS.

Also of interest

THE LOVE CHILD
by Edith Olivier
New Introduction by Hermione Lee

At thirty-two, her mother dead, Agatha Bodenham finds herself quite alone. She summons back to life the only friend she ever knew, Clarissa, the dream companion of her childhood. At first Clarissa comes by night, and then by day, gathering substance in the warmth of Agatha's obsessive love until it seems that others too can see her. See, but not touch, for Agatha has made her love child for herself. No man may approach this creature of perfect beauty, and if he does, she who summoned her can spirit her away...

Edith Olivier (1879?-1948) was one of the youngest of a clergyman's family of ten children. Despite early ambitions to become an actress, she led a conventional life within twenty miles of her childhood home, the Rectory at Wilton, Wiltshire. But she wrote five highly original novels as well as works of non-fiction, and her 'circle' included Rex Whistler (who illustrated her books), David Cecil, Siegfried Sassoon and Osbert Sitwell. *The Love Child* (1927) was her first novel, acknowledged as a minor masterpiece: a perfectly imagined fable and a moving and perceptive portrayal of unfulfilled maternal love.

"This is wonderful..." — *Cecil Beaton*

"*The Love Child* seems to me to stand in a category of its own creating...the image it leaves is that of a tranquil star" — *Anne Douglas Sedgwick*

"Flawless — the best 'first' book I have ever read...perfect" — *Sir Henry Newbolt*

"A masterpiece of its kind" — *Lord David Cecil*

THE SHUTTER OF SNOW

by Emily Holmes Coleman
New Introduction by Carmen Callil and Mary Siepmann

After the birth of her child Marthe Gail spends two months
in an insane asylum with the fixed idea that she is God.
Marthe, something between Ophelia, Emily Dickinson
and Lucille Ball, transports us into that strange country of
terror and ecstasy we call madness. In this twilit country
the doctors, nurses, the other inmates and the mad vision of
her insane mind are revealed with piercing insight and
with immense verbal facility.

Emily Coleman (1899-1974) was born in California and, like
Marthe, went mad after the birth of her son in 1924. Witty,
eccentric and ebullient, she lived in Paris in the 1920s as
one of the *transition* writers, close friend of Peggy
Guggenheim and Djuna Barnes (who said Emily would be
marvellous company slightly stunned). In the 1930s she
lived in London (in the French, the Wheatsheaf, the
Fitzroy), where her friends numbered Dylan Thomas, T.S.
Eliot, Humphrey Jennings and George Barker. Emily
Coleman wrote poetry throughout her life — and this one
beautiful, poignant novel (first published in 1930), which
though constantly misunderstood, has always had a
passionate body of admirers — Edwin Muir, David
Gascoyne and Antonia White to name a few.

"A very striking triumph of imagination and technique...
The book is not only quite unique; it is also a work of
genuine literary inspiration" — *Edwin Muir*

"A work which has stirred me deeply...compelling" —
Harold Nicolson

"An extraordinary, visionary book, written out of those
edges where madness and poetry meet" — *Fay Weldon*

PLAGUED BY THE NIGHTINGALE

by Kay Boyle
New preface by the author

When the American girl Bridget marries the Frenchman
Nicolas, she goes to live with his wealthy family in their
Breton village. This close-knit family love each other to the
exclusion of the outside world. But it is a love that festers,
for the family is tainted with an inherited bone disease and
Bridget discovers, as she faces the Old World with the
courage of the New, that plague can also infect the soul...

Kay Boyle was born in Minnesota in 1902. The first of her
three marriages was to a Frenchman and she moved to
Paris in the 1920s where, as one of that legendary group of
American expatriates and contributor to *transition*, she
knew Joyce, Pound, Hemingway, the Fitzgeralds, Djuna
Barnes and Gertrude Stein: a world she recorded in *Being
Geniuses Together*. After a spell living in the bizarre
commune run by Isadora Duncan's brother, she returned
to America in 1941 where she still lives. A distinguished
novelist, poet and short-story writer, she was acclaimed by
Katherine Anne Porter for her "fighting spirit, freshness of
feeling." *Plagued by the Nightingale* was first published in
1931. In subtle, rich and varied prose Kay Boyle echoes
Henry James in a novel at once lyrical, delicate and
shocking.

"A series of brilliant, light-laden pictures, lucid, delightful;
highly original" — *Observer*

"In delicate, satirical vignettes Miss Boyle has enshrined a
French middle-class family...The lines of the picture have
an incisiveness and a bloom which suggest silverpoint"—
Guardian

Other *VIRAGO MODERN CLASSICS*

ELIZABETH von ARNIM
Fräulein Schmidt & Mr Anstruther
Vera

EMILY EDEN
The Semi-Attached Couple &
    The Semi-Detached House

MILES FRANKLIN
My Brilliant Career
My Career Goes Bung

GEORGE GISSING
The Odd Women

ELLEN GLASGOW
The Sheltered Life
Virginia

SARAH GRAND
The Beth Book

RADCLYFFE HALL
The Well of Loneliness
The Unlit Lamp

WINIFRED HOLTBY
Anderby Wold
The Crowded Street
The Land of Green Ginger
Mandoa, Mandoa!

MARGARET KENNEDY
The Constant Nymph
The Ladies of Lyndon
Together and Apart

ROSAMOND LEHMANN
The Ballad and the Source
The Gipsy's Baby
Invitation to the Waltz
A Note in Music
A Sea-Grape Tree
The Weather in the Streets

F. M. MAYOR
The Third Miss Symons

GEORGE MEREDITH
Diana of the Crossways

EDITH OLIVIER
The Love Child

CHARLOTTE PERKINS
    GILMAN
The Yellow Wallpaper

DOROTHY RICHARDSON
Pilgrimage (4 volumes)

HENRY HANDEL
    RICHARDSON
The Getting of Wisdom
Maurice Guest

BERNARD SHAW
An Unsocial Socialist

MAY SINCLAIR
Life and Death of Harriett Frean
Mary Olivier
The Three Sisters

F. TENNYSON JESSE
A Pin to See The Peepshow
The Lacquer Lady
Moonraker

VIOLET TREFUSIS
Hunt the Slipper

MARY WEBB
The Golden Arrow
Gone to Earth
The House in Dormer Forest
Precious Bane
Seven for a Secret

H. G. WELLS
Ann Veronica

Other *VIRAGO MODERN CLASSICS*